DEJA VU

JAYNE GRANT

To order additional copies of this book, contact:
Bookwhip
1-855-339-3589
https://www.bookwhip.com

CHAPTER 1

T he Sunday afternoon church service was not over yet. Dora, a single mother in her late thirties, sat next to her thirteen-year-old daughter, Lauren. Dora was more than fidgety on the hard church pew. It was unclear whether she was uncomfortable because her mind was racing in so many different directions or because of the new Italian leather shoes she was wearing, were too tight and which she was going to be paying for on her credit card for two more months. As the patrons of the church stood up to sing from the hymnbook, Dora took this as her cue to grab hold of her daughter's hand and sidestep down the aisle and out the back side door of the church. Lauren wondered about the reason for their sudden departure but kept silent through their unexplained jaunt out of the church.

Once in the parking lot, Lauren thought of asking her mother the reason and whether she was okay; but the male doormen of the church stepped out the closed doors, eyeing their every move like they perhaps had stolen something. Dora saw their unnerving glare while sitting in the car, thinking in her mind the only thing that they could have walked away with was the hymnbook. She didn't wake up at night thinking about how badly she wanted to sing the hymn from page 210. Lauren noticed the actions of these men and, seeing the look on her mother's face, decided she better keep quiet until they turned out of the parking lot.

"What is it, Mom? Why did we have to run out of church like that?"

"I just thought of something that I needed to do, just a feeling. You know, like when you're doing something, and you think you should be doing something else. That's how I feel now." Dora turned the wheels of the car to head out of the parking lot and then stepped on the gas, she looked at her daughter and not at the view of the road in front of her.

"Mom!"

Dora looked closer at her daughter. After seeing the fear on her panicked daughter's face, in a fraction of a second, she blinked her eyes and looked out the front windshield, swallowing the fear that for an instant froze her body. Taking her foot up from the brake, she took her clenched hands from the steering wheel and swallowed deeply before opening the driver's door.

Before even noticing that the front of her blue '90 Impala was bashed in, she noticed the dent in the trunk of the black Mercedes in front of her. Swallowing once again, she was having trouble finding the right words and making them come off her tongue, probably because she could find no sensible reason for her stupid actions. Swearwords that she had tried so hard for years to shield from her daughter's ears were being blasted in the calm spring air by a middle-aged man with brown hair, with the sun streaking through it and showing red highlights. He was wearing dark glasses, and his body was medium in build though strength was certainly felt at this moment in his pacing back and forth in anger, like the rage of a heavyweight in the boxing ring. "Goddamn! What in the hell were you doing or thinking? Jesus Christ, woman!" He stopped his swearing upon seeing Dora's daughter standing submissively to the side of her mother's car. He hurled his body to the side of his own car, and just a moment before it looked like he was about to kick in the door, he turned his body and hit the open air to the back of him instead. In unnerving and seemingly endless passing seconds, he calmed his body and walked softly to Dora who was standing rigidly at the side of her own car.

"I don't suppose you have insurance, enough to cover the damage to my car anyway? Being as your car is as old as it is, your damage couldn't possibly be that much. I'll probably have to wait an hour for you to find your coverage anyhow."

Dora had never followed the women's movement that closely, but she felt like punching him with the fist of Helen Gurley Brown.

Trying her very hardest to keep from exploding back to his arrogance, she, instead, raced to the other side of her car and opened the glove compartment; and in less than one minute's time, she handed him a packet containing all of her insurance information. At this moment, she was glad that she paid the extra $100 on her coverage for full liability. In taking the packet from her hand, he closed his grief- stricken eyes. It now physically appeared that he was embarrassed but too manly to ever admit it.

Having trouble pulling air into her lungs, as though an astronaut whose oxygen had been cut off, she took a deep breath, fighting to inhale all she could to fill her lungs. "Look, I'm sorry. I know that this seems redundant to say, but I really am a good driver. I just . . ." The mystery man jumped into the conversation, walking closer to her and lowering his glasses. Seeing his eyes, Dora did not know if she was blinded by the rays from the sun through the tree-shaded street or what caused her to feel this way. It felt like she was pushed off her feet and had to steady herself from falling backward. He saw this while tilting his head back, and he slowly moved to the side before recapturing his maddened stare.

Instantly, a shadow ran through Dora's mind, mixing light to dark; and she saw something that had happened on a sunny street. The image of a man appeared before her, then a blast so loud she awakened to her senses in a cold sweat. Opening her eyes, she saw this man standing before her and their damaged cars.

"Look, lady, I don't have much time. And I can't leave you a number where I'll be because right now, I'm at a lot of different places. Give me your number, and I'll get in contact with you about the repairs although I don't know if you really can afford to pay for the damages anyway."

Dora responded back to him slowly like she was trying to figure out what happened before awakening from a dream. He saw this and wondered whether she was okay, okay on both mental and physical levels. Hearing her daughter's voice from the side of the car threw Dora back into reality. She opened her wallet, feeling embarrassed that she didn't have a business card of her own. She grabbed the first card she had in her wallet. Ironically, it was the business card of the car dealer she went to for tune-ups. Against her better judgement, she wrote both her home number and her address on the back of this card. Being a very private person, she hardly ever divulged her phone number to anyone and found herself surprised that she had written it down for this unnamed stranger.

After taking the card from her, he put it in his inside lapel and silently proceeded to his car. "Wait! Wait!" He turned his head, listening to her;

but still, he did not stop his movement of getting in his car. "What is your name? Don't leave. I need to know."

Placing his dark glasses back on and opening the door of his car, he got in, then lowered the driver's window. "You just talked to me. You couldn't forget the sound of my voice that quickly, could you?" The sound of him pushing the gas pedal down was electrified as he sped away. Only after he was out of view did the traffic on the street resume.

"Lauren, get in the car. You could get hurt standing there on the street." Lauren instantly got in the car as did Dora. Dora didn't remember turning the engine off. She tried to think and shook her head and turned the key while praying in her mind that it would start. Even with the damage to the front end of her car, the engine started smoothly. She waited her turn to merge in the traffic and go home. At this moment, she couldn't even remember what had jarred her mind so much that she had to leave the church.

Back in traffic, she could sense that her daughter wanted to talk to her. Lauren was scared of saying anything while her mother was driving, wanting her mother to stay in full control of the car so as not to get in any more accidents. Lauren was still puzzled as to what possessed her mom to catapult out of the church like that. Once Dora turned onto the residential street she needed to go down to get to their rented house, Lauren thought it was okay for her to talk. "Mom, what happened back there? Not just with that man, but what made you grab me and run out of the church?"

Dora's mind raced trying to think of a reason, any reason, and how to construct something believable; but she knew full well that her daughter knew when she was lying. "Hmm, let's wait until we get in the house, and then I'll tell you." She then bit her lip and nodded her head. She didn't look, but she could feel her daughter looking at her, and she felt this look as though someone was throwing knives at her.

Dora parked the '90 Impala in the driveway of their rented home, a house on top with a large abandoned garage underneath. It was dark brown, the color of wood logs, with an outside staircase to the left side. It seemed like it would always be on the cold side because of all the tall pine trees behind it. There was no backyard, and the hill behind the house sloped up steeply.

On the walk from the car and up the stairs into the house, not a word was spoken. Once inside, Lauren went straight to the bathroom, leaving a feeling of relief in Dora. She walked to the all-white kitchen in the left front of the small home. Pouring water in the teapot and then placing it on the stove, Dora rationalized that it was best just to tell her daughter she forgot, especially right now because she herself could honestly not remember what had made her leave the church in such a hurry. Any thoughts of what to say were swept away with the returning picture of this mystery man's face. An image of a past memory was trying to surface in her mind, but it was being blocked from surfacing by some sort of force.

Dora fought in her mind, trying to keep a balance on things and trying to resist wanting to grab the bottle of scotch from the cabinet above the refrigerator. *No, I know full well that will only make this matter worse.* The whistle from the teapot and her daughter's voice calling her both seemed to shake her focus back on what was in front of her. Lauren ran her fingers through her brown hair to the side of her face with a questioning look at her mom. Dora had already poured hot water in a cup and placed a tea bag to the side. Another empty cup sat next to the one she just filled. "Lauren, would you like a cup of tea?"

Lauren took her fingers from her hair, flinging her locks behind her. "Sure, Mom." Dora placed both cups on the kitchen table, then fully opened the window, and looked out. This house was in the middle at the end of a court, so the only view was of the street, but just the sunlight coming in seemed to help.

Lauren stirred sugar in the cup of tea, and the sound of the occasional clanking of the spoon against the side of the cup was soothing, rhythmic instead of annoying. Dora took a sip, placing the cup back down on the table, and found the strength to look her daughter in the eye, then tilted her head to the side. "Mom, you don't have to make an excuse for whatever it was that you say you forgot. It's okay, but who was this . . . that man? You looked at him like you remembered him from somewhere or sometime, but with hesitation like you didn't want him to see you, or you didn't want to see him. But then in another moment, it seemed like you wanted to be in a Harlequin romance with him or something. Who is he?"

Her mother looked straight at her though not really seeing her, like she was trying to figure out the theory of a maze, and then took her hand to her mouth, bending her fingers down and moving them across her chin. "That's just it. I don't know."

"Does it, or he, have something to do with what you told me happened in Chicago years ago when you had to go through all the sessions with the psychiatrist?"

A shiver encircled Dora's body from her toes to her face, and it more than showed. She moved her head forward while curling her fingers, then realized she was showing pain. She tried to relax her body while looking blankly out the window. She prayed silently for an icebreaker—something, anything like the ring of the phone or a knock on the door—but nothing happened. Exhausted at trying to find anything to do or say, she took another sip of her tea.

"Mom, I'll leave you alone about this if you want. It's just kind of scary." Lauren got up from the table with the teacup in her hand and walked around the table, taking the cup to the sink. Lauren passed the door to the house and locked it, something that Dora saw, but she couldn't let on that she was glad Lauren had done it. She just had to show peace over her body while feeling her insides tremble. She heard Lauren turn on the television, and then the sound of a videotape was heard playing inside the machine.

Well, Lauren is getting her mind off this, but I know I can't. She's right—I am going to have to find the card of that doctor and call him. That'll be an easy trip. I live in Los Altos, California, and this doctor is in Chicago. Well, tomorrow's Monday, but I have to work. And during lunch, I have to take my taxes in to be done. Nice peaceful day. Oh, and the car repairs . . . when will I hear from him? God, he has my phone number, and now he knows where I live. Why did I give that to him? I felt like I was somehow forced to do it. It was like he had unquestionable power over my mind and my conscience, a memory that I cannot remember, and I am still looking for why. It's like it is just blocked somehow.

Raising her eyebrows, she shook her head, got up from the chair, and closed the drapes of the front window of the house. Next, she sat on the love seat next to her daughter, laughing at the movie *Ghostbusters*. The evening ended with the two of them going out to downtown Los Altos and having a fried-chicken dinner in a restaurant that they frequented once a week on a steady basis.

After dinner, they returned home while it was still light out and made sure that the door and windows were fully locked before relaxing for the evening. That night was spent much like every Sunday night, watching television shows and laying out clothes for the always-dreaded Monday morning. Although Lauren was very mature for her age, Dora still went in her room and kissed her good night. Tonight, the only difference was that she also checked the window of Lauren's bedroom, making sure it was locked. It was closed, but it wasn't locked. Her daughter lifted the corner of her eye watching this action. As her mother left, she closed her eyes and made her head more comfortable on the pillow.

Coming out of the bathroom in her nightgown and bathrobe, Dora started to untie it, then contracted her body to a tightened stance, left it tied, and placed another knot in it. The shades were down over the two rectangular windows, one to the left side of the bed and the other on the wall against the tall pine trees in the back of the house. Dora knew full well that she was going to imagine everything from the noises that the trees would make in the wind tonight. Resisting both a sleeping pill and a glass of scotch, she tried just calming her body by deep breathing and humming to herself.

In bed, with the soft light of the lamp still on, she folded the comforter all the way over her neck and stopped it just before her face. Smiling like a child expecting Christmas the next morning, she closed her eyes, hoping for a full night's sleep. Just getting to the first stage of sleep, she was awakened feverishly by the image of this mystery man in the car that she hit. She knew him, but from where? And why was part of her memory blocked? It took a long time for me to get over whatever it was that plagued my body years ago so that I had to move halfway across the country to forget. Everything is and has gone good, so why am I thinking about this now? She did not answer herself but knew full well that the identity of this man had or was the answer.

The noise of a tree branch hitting the sidewall of her bedroom made her feel like she swallowed her heart. Come on, I'm the adult here. I know full well that was just the sound of the trees and the unusually strong wind. Sleep. Sleep. Her mind raced in circles around locked memories trying to resurface, but the real question was, did she want these memories to be known?

In struggling with her mind during the course of the night, she did fall asleep. She heard the sound of the clock radio wake her. The DJ was talking about something, but she really didn't want to focus on what it was, hoping in any way to stay asleep. Reality overtook her body as she next found herself in the shower.

Everything was quiet while the two had a bowl of raisin bran. Before Lauren rinsed the bowls in the sink, she reminded her mom that she only had half a day of school because of some construction they would be doing in some of the classrooms. Many times, Lauren had taken the bus home and been alone in the house for a few hours in the afternoon before her mom made it home from work; but with the recent course of events, she found this instance different. "Lauren, why don't you go over to one of your girlfriends' houses after school is over today? I'll pick you up there on my way home from work."

Slowly, like the anticipation of waiting for a leaf to fall, Lauren asked why, then changed the expression on her face and said, "Never mind. You know, I could go to a matinee with Scott." Dora instantly turned her face upon hearing a boy's name and then remembered that this was a time in her daughter's life when hormones started racing.

Tapping her finger on the counter, Dora said, "No, why don't you go over to Brittney's house instead? I know her mom is home in the afternoon." She watched Lauren nod her head to this comment with a devilish smile. To make sure of her daughter's whereabouts, she opened the phone index and dialed Brittney's phone number. Confirming that Lauren would be there that afternoon, she felt better. With keys in hand, Dora held the door open for Lauren to go out before double-locking it with the key.

Downstairs, Lauren walked with books in hand to get in the passenger's side door of the car. Her mom stopped and asked Lauren to step back from the car while she looked around the car and lifted the hood, looking inside. "Mom, what are you doing?" Dora stepped back before answering, thinking that she had seen detectives do this on TV before they found a bomb in the car. She has no idea what she was looking for or what it would even look like.

"I don't know. Just a feeling, I guess." "So, Columbo, did you find anything?"

Running her fingers through her short hair to the side of her ear, she was surprised that her daughter knew of the television show *Columbo*. A cable rerun was the only way. "No, Magnum, I didn't." Both smirked while getting into the car and driving away.

Unlocking the door of the realtor's office she worked for, she threw the keys in the center pullout drawer of the desk and turned on the telephone answering machine while starting the coffee. She heard nine messages from different people wanting the same house on Summerhill Drive. Who would have thought ten years ago that the bidding for this house would turn up in the million-dollar range? The success of Silicon Valley. Just the rent on a decent apartment was ridiculous. The pastor of the church owned the house over the garage that she rented. He lived in the house next door to it. He was more than going to ask why she cut out of church early the previous day. The only excuse she could conjure up in her mind without having to lie to a religious man was that she just wasn't feeling well.

She heard her boss's car stop at the side of the office and could see his approaching shadow through the half-open blinds on the window. The coffee was still brewing, so she took a cup and placed it underneath the brewing pot and filled up her boss's cup, then replaced the pot on the burner. She held a folded napkin between the cup and her hand as not to burn herself. The cup's fingered handle was to the front for him to grab. She was surprised to see Mr. Mann come in the office with two bouquets of flowers.

He did not stop or speak to her but took the coffee cup from her and placed one of the bouquets on her desk. She smiled, thinking maybe she was being thanked for doing a good job. He took the other bouquet and placed it to the side of his desk inside his office. Then he walked forward to Dora and motioned to the bouquet on the side of her desk. "Good morning. Could you place that one over there to the side of the waiting room couch on that table? These flowers are the same color as the flowers in the front yard of that house I showed yesterday. They are for the clients—possible buyers." Hearing this from Mr. Mann, she realized her cheap, powerful boss hadn't changed a bit. Next, she handed him the messages from the nine people bidding on this house. His smile got ever wider looking at each figure. "You know, I didn't have time to have breakfast this morning. Can you walk down to the doughnut shop on the other side of the parking lot and get me a maple bar?" Dora reached for money in the inside drawer of the desk and went to do this without saying a word.

Once back with his maple bar in a brown paper bag, she found two different couples in the waiting room about the sale of the earlier-mentioned house. In the course of the next three hours, the house was sold for cash at $1.8 million—an average suburban tract house with one fireplace, three bedrooms, three baths, a two-car garage, and a hot tub in the backyard. She thought to herself, If only I had invested in real estate when I first moved here to the Silicon Valley—but how many other people wished the same thing?

Pulling the latest faxes out of the machine, she gently tapped them on the top of her desk, getting them in perfect order to give to Mr. Mann. Turning her head to view the time on the wall clock, she saw that he'd soon be leaving for lunch and that one of the assistant realtors, Mr. Crane, should be in the office for work soon. Just as she finished turning around from looking at the clock, the front door closed; and Mr. Crane walked in, asking her for the latest listings. "The current copies are right here in my hand. And the Jensen house, the one on Summerhill, just sold."

"Is there anything new on whether the county is going to change the zoning on the corner piece to the side of the hospital?"

"No, no word yet. I guess the right people haven't offered a bribe yet." Mr. Crane turned his head, giving Dora a puzzled look. "Well, isn't that the way it works?"

"Yes, but you don't say anything about that until after the second martini in the clubhouse and the plans have been approved."

"Okay. Back to work. In five minutes, I'll be headed out the door for lunch. Do you want me to turn the answering machine on?"

"No, I have a few calls I'm expecting."

Trying to start her car in the parking lot, the engine wouldn't turn over. Yeah, okay, I know I need to get you fixed. But that's another thing I have to do—go to the insurance company about a claim. But how am I going to make one when I still don't know the identity of this mystery man, and how am I going to tell the insurance man about that?

Ten minutes later, her car was parked in the lot at Sears; and she went to the second floor, waiting her turn to give the papers to a tax agent. Once a male agent went through her papers and started the work on his computer, he reminded her of the fact that she sure cut it close—close to the deadline when taxes had to be done. He then told her that she would have to come back that evening for the papers. Thinking "Oh no, I can't," in her mind, she looked at him with soft, puppy dog eyes, not saying anything but looking forlorn.

"Okay, go downstairs, get something to eat, and be back here in a half hour. I'll just take a shorter lunch." Saying nothing, she just left, hoping he wouldn't have a change of heart.

Now on to the other things that she needed to get done before getting back to work on time. Once out of the cleaners, she carefully hung up the bagged clothes on the hanger in the backseat. Breathing out a sigh with her body leaning against the side of her car, she decided it was against her diet, but the ice cream store was right in front of her, and she did need some lunch before going back after the tax papers and returning to work. In less than a minute, she walked back out of the ice cream store with a cup of caffe latte-flavored, frozen yogurt in hand.

With the driver's door open to her car, she stood there eating the yogurt, debating in her mind whether to try and finish it down really fast or to get in the car and try to eat it while driving back to pick up her taxes. Remembering yesterday's crash, she then sat down on the bench in front of the store. Only after throwing the Styrofoam cup and plastic spoon in the garbage can did she take the keys out of her pocket and proceed to the car to leave. Looking twice in her rearview mirror and over her shoulder before backing out, she made sure that the angered driver who wanted her parking place earlier was no longer there.

She successfully made it back to Sears and found her finished taxes sitting to the side of the tall cash register to be picked up and paid for. After charging the $85 fee on her store credit card, she raced back to her car in the parking lot. She looked at her watch and saw that she had ten minutes left to get back to work, hopefully before Mr. Mann did.

She stopped at a red light in the left-turn lane to turn into the parking lot of where she worked. The light had changed three times for traffic to go in the other direction, but it still had not changed for her to go yet. There were no other cars waiting in either direction. She was the only car at that light, but still, it hadn't changed. Dodging in her mind whether she had the courage to make it through a red light, she thought, Come on, who am I going to hurt? I'm the only one here. She knew that with her luck, though, a police officer was probably hiding in a neighboring parking lot with pen in hand. She noticed her boss driving down the road in the opposite direction towards her, and then the light changed to green for her to go.

Fighting her first inclination to floor it, to make it in the parking lot before her boss saw her, she carefully turned in the lot slowly and then parked in her usual place against the fence on the side of the building. Once out of her car, walking to the door of the office, she saw her boss still at the light, talking to someone in the car to the side of him; so maybe he hadn't even noticed her. With keys in hand, she opened the door, remembering Mr. Crane was still there; so she didn't have to lock the office. The coffeepot was nearly empty, something that Mr. Mann knew she would never let happen, and the radio was not on one of her stations. With coffee filter in hand, she turned the knob of the radio, and soft rock then filled the area of her work desk. She poured an open coffee pouch inside the filter and pressed the Start switch before it even clicked into place. In her rush to sit in the chair behind her desk, she almost fell to the floor trying to sit and turn at the same time. She caught herself, tapping her feet to the floor, and twisted her ankle in the process. Hearing the phone ring, she answered it on the first ring, feeling relief that she would not have to answer any of Mr. Mann's questions when he came in the office door.

The door was opened and shut without even time to notice, but Mr. Mann did give her an inquisitive stare while looking at the last drip fall from the coffeepot. Sensing his suspicion, she looked up briefly only to acknowledge him, then put the party on the phone on hold. "There is still a couple wanting to make a higher bid on the Summerhill home. What do I tell them? I thought the deal was closed. Do you want to handle this? It's on line five."

Mr. Mann was already walking into his office. Knowing his greed, she knew his thought patterns. Starting to think again of the events of the previous day, she moved her head from side to side and quickly raised the volume on the radio, hoping a reminiscent song from her youth on this older rock station would get her thought pattern on something else, preferably work. The sound from the fax machine, signaling something coming in, diverted her attention from the radio, which was running a commercial. She smiled and walked to the fax machine, taking the paper and reading it while walking back to her desk—a sold-out condominium complex in San Jose on the border of Santa Clara was releasing another complex tomorrow, but they were already accepting bids today. She made copies of this fax and placed a copy at the door of each agent.

She took the mail from the mailman and spent the next two hours going through the mail, placing it in order of importance and separating it into different piles for each agent, then placing them in their file boxes. The rest of the workday proceeded in the normal pattern. After Mr. Mann walked out, the last agent to leave, she grabbed her coat and purse, juggling each in separate hands while she took her office keys from her teeth and locked the office door.

Thankful her car started on the first turn instead of driving up the street after the light to make a U-turn (she couldn't make a left out of the parking lot because of the raised cement divider in the road), she took a right on the side of the parking lot and went south about five miles out of her way to get on the freeway in the north direction. The very next exit was the one that she needed to get to her house. The wheels turned in her mind over the fact that she hadn't bought anything for dinner, so dinner would be a can of soup or instant Chinese noodle mix. Her daughter seemed to be aware of her emotions right now after the events of the previous day, so Dora believed she would not get any flack about it. It was a good thing that she had thought of her daughter's feelings because she had forgotten that she had to pick Lauren up at her friend's house.

Driving there, she hoped that Lauren would be looking out the window waiting for her arrival; then she huffed, knowing that this would not be the case. She dreaded the idea of making small talk and gossip with the mother, but she was nice enough to look after Lauren in this instance, so Dora reasoned that she was just getting her just deserts. To her surprise, when she got to the side of the house, the girls were in the driveway, and a teenage boy whom both girls had their eyes on was showing off his new electric scooter. Not wanting to be the bad guy, Dora just honked her horn, looking at Lauren. The friend's mother waved out the window, and Lauren gave Dora an almost-evil glare. While Brittney made a tactical smile at the boy, Lauren got in the car without saying anything. When they were driving away and out of sight of the house, Lauren asked her mother why she had come after her so early. Dora huffed, raised her eyes to the top of her head, made a brief look at her daughter, and then solemnly replied, "I thought that you missed me."

Lauren dropped her body into a locked transitional state until she got out of the parked car in the driveway of their home. The pastor of the church, their landlord, walked over to Dora, seeing them exit the car. Lauren saw this, then proceeded up the stairs and into the house. Dora changed her sardonic look to a smile, viewing the approaching pastor while she got her story straight in her mind about the reason for her sudden departure from church yesterday.

Pastor Graham stopped in front of Dora. She coyly smirked, then quickly explained about her abrupt departure from the Sunday service, mentioning a sudden upset stomach and fear of throwing up. The pastor's face turned from a questioning smile to distaste, and Dora was thankful for the quick appeasement. The pastor turned away, then stopped, remembering her words; and he turned his face from hers, relaxing and looking at the pebbles on the ground. "There is a basketball game this afternoon, in about twenty minutes, for the youths. Being that you are still probably not feeling that well yet, how about if your daughter joins us?" Dora smiled at him, yet she knew he would not notice and gave him a thank-you in an uplifted tone.

Only seconds after closing the door, Dora felt the weight of the look she received from her daughter. She remained complacent in her stature and movements. In sitting down at the kitchen table, she opened the newspaper to finish reading what she wasn't able to finish that morning and gave a sideways stare to her daughter. It was like she was almost foaming at the mouth in anger. Dora knew her normally quiet, sweet daughter was now a teenager—seven years of this to look forward to.

With a face raging with emotion, Lauren walked, almost stomping, to the table, stopping just before hitting the chair with her hardened body. "Why did you have to do that?"

Swallowing before speaking, trying her utmost to keep an even, calm temperament, Dora calmly told her that she had no idea that she had done anything to offend her.

Lauren showed that she tried to control her rage by placidly lifting her foot up and down; then she screamed about how she was so rudely embarrassed.

Dora huffed, dropped her shoulders, then straightened her posture in the chair. "Look, all I did was pick you up. Maybe we should get walkie-talkies and use some kind of secret code so that I know what to do. I am your mother, and if you don't—"

"That's just it. You are my mother. Where is my father?"

Dora opened her mouth and stopped breathing, then drew in a deep breath in silence. She had only a vague memory of Lauren's father, her husband. Closing her eyes, she saw stills running together, trying to form a memory without a plot or a reason. It was something she couldn't reach for or put together no matter how hard she tried. She gave Lauren no answer.

CHAPTER 2

She was married. She was told this man lurked in the recesses of her thoughts, and he was there. The answer lay in what happened in a hospital in Chicago. There was something about a hospital in a period of time that was overshadowed in her conscious mind. She could see it. It was like a sudden blow to the head, and everything had just snapped in her life. There was no question that her life had somehow changed, and now there was a jolting reemergence of the truth wanting to be spilled out, but there was also an overwhelming fear that kept it buried. Her daughter's age was just one factor in her desire to know about her father, but why now? There was so much comfort in disregarding or omitting the vacuous truth.

Dora's mind was snapped from this consuming thought by Lauren slamming the door and leaving, saying that she was going to the church basketball game. She had a lot of frustration about everything right now, and maybe the time away would give Dora a chance to figure out something to tell her about the truth and why she shielded it from her. The sound of stomping down the stairs left her with a feeling of relief but also despair. There was nowhere to turn and no one to turn to. She got up from the chair, then instantly caught herself, and reached for the counter for balance. The world had turned dark—as dark as the asphalt on a busy street in the dead of night, a torrid blast, a wide-open mouth trying to scream, but with no sound coming out. Everything swayed, and light enveloped the room; and she opened her eyes and grabbed her head, feeling the uncomfortable feeling after a twisting roller-coaster ride. My god, I'm lost, tormented with mind games of whirling, painful emotions. What happened?

No drink and no food was going to calm her. She sat in the deep bamboo chair from Cost Plus, then tried to look out the half-open curtain but saw nothing. She pointed the remote to the TV and snapped it on. Sports announcers were talking about the outcome of the previous game. She instantly changed the station but found nothing except commercials or shopping channels. In making one more sweep around the dial before deciding to turn it off, she stopped on what she thought was probably a UHF channel. No one was recognizable on the TV screen, but the sound of their voices was comforting. Only moments into the program, she realized what she was watching; and common sense told her to turn it off, but she remained captive to it. It was a paid program advertising a psychic network. The psychics were listening to people and giving them help in dealing with their problems and changing their lives. In only five minutes, she became totally engrossed in it.

The screen showed five different psychics all talking on the phones to various callers, all with separate problems. They all had different problems, yet they were all united in some way with problems that mostly a forlorn housewife would have—feelings of loss and wanting recognition for their actions, gratitude, and mostly love or relief from a swarm of pent-up emotions. Feeling overwhelmed by everything she heard, Dora was transfixed by the callers and the show of emotions and concern from each individual psychic. She had already picked her favorite, the one in booth 3. Maybe someone would listen to me. Maybe they could help me remember or tell me that it was best to forget. Maybe someone would listen without judging—without judging me. She took her hands to her face, pressing them together and covering her nose, then slid them down over her mouth. She breathed out rhythmically and picked up the receiver and began to dial the phone number listed on the screen. However, she abruptly stopped and hung up the phone upon seeing pictures of credit cards flash across the screen. That's all I need. I'm having a hard time staying within my budget right now. She put the phone back down and picked up the remote to the TV; yet she still had trouble turning it off, feeling compassion, almost like the feeling of holding a puppy, from these women on the screen. She scratched her hand, briefly looked away, and then turned the set off. If only I had someone—someone now.

She took off her wristwatch and then threw it through the doorway of her bedroom. It landed on the bed. Well, isn't that what she was aiming for? If she had missed the size of that target, it would have been pretty bad. Then she found herself walking to the kitchen. The first thing she did was check the time on the wall. The logical thing to do now would be to start dinner, but how much time do you need to boil water for a cup of noodles? I'm already in the doghouse with Lauren, and when she comes home hungry from the ball game and finds out that is what's for dinner, oh boy! She leaned into it, then opened the side door of the freezer. She was filled with happiness seeing a quart of Dreyer's rocky road ice cream. Well, maybe that will make up for dinner. She then began to set the table; that was hard—two forks and two napkins! She then put the last two cans of soda on the table, a Diet Coke and a Squirt. Boy, this really is slim pickings. Thank God tomorrow is payday. I know I'll get the Coke, so I might as well put it in front of my place.

Airing a gasp of disgust at both her present situation and the current events that she wanted an answer to but then thought it better to forget, she left the table and stopped scouring the reality of the empty kitchen cabinets and moved her attention to her floor pillow against the wall to the side of the stereo. She hadn't done it in a while and reached to the sky, then back down to her knees to try and loosen up for some basic yoga moves to bring relief to her troubled mental state of being.

She squatted on the pillow, and to her amazement, she found comfort in just being in the correct position on the mat. Let's see, this will be an absolute perfect state of being. Number one thing, relax to the correct state of being. She held her arms out vertical to her chest and expanded her lungs, slowing the rhythm of her heartbeat. An even composure and balance achieving Zen. Sanctify all pure and good, and embrace my soul. She had brought down her racing heart rate and found relaxation. Her mind gazed at a clear field, the wheat grass gently swayed in the light breeze, and the only sound beneath the silent sky was the whisper of a nearby stream. Tranquil meditation, serenity, relaxed eye movement, and quietness—all that could remain was a deep, silent slumber.

The scene in her mind drifted from the quiet whispering fields to a dark overhead ceiling beam. She was trapped in an office. Unable to move her strapped hand from the deep dark leather chair, she cried out in panic. Who was in that room with her? Was it real, or was she dreaming? Sweat dropped from her forehead. Somebody else was there—one other person. Shoes—she saw tight brown leather men's shoes. In desperation, she tried looking up to the vision that engulfed her mind. This appearance, who is it? Stay, stay. A dark tone of a pant leg, the bent knees, one leg crossed over another, a writing pad, a yellow pad on a clipboard, a belt buckle with a monogram engraved on it. It was a hospital. Was it the crest of the hospital or of a name of a prominent doctor? A doctor—was it a doctor? Look up, look up to the face. The face—who is it? What is plaguing my mind and harboring at my emotions, leaving me gasping in fear? Is this man, this doctor, trying to help me? Or what is he doing? Hear, listen, anything. What is being said? Is there any sound? Is it reality? It is so vivid—it has to be. How could I be imagining this? It is part of my past. His belt buckle—what symbol is it? It is a symbol—the vision of the buckle enlarged, yet it was somewhat blurry. It was a crest. There was no writing. A snake, a wrapped snake. She moved her coiled body in the chair, trying to look upright but wanting to shrink and disappear, to be out of there, out of the inquisition. That's what is was. They, he, wanted to know something from her.

A sudden sound punctured the room and the feeling she was caught in. She trembled and bent forward, then opened her eyes, and saw her teenage daughter storm into the room in a sweat, yelling the question, "What was for dinner?" Now I'm caught in trying to make an excuse for dinner and convincing myself, at the same time, that all that I just envisioned was just a dream. She got up and went to the stove to start boiling the water and made no answer or affirmation to her daughter who just shut the door to the bathroom and turned on the shower.

Lauren came in from her bedroom wearing her cat pajamas. Dora took note of this but made no verbal response. She was glad that Lauren was wearing her pajamas because she knew she wasn't going to get any flack that evening about her going out and meeting with the "group," which she knew included young hormonal teenage boys wanting something to talk and brag about at the gym lockers. Lauren took the small salad plate off the top of the cup of noodles and stirred it. Dora was surprised when she didn't hear any sarcastic comments about the cheap dinner, then wondered why Lauren wasn't complaining. Could she have broken a window or damaged something playing ball? Then she remembered the way Lauren had stormed into the house on her return, and she caught herself trying to hide a laugh when she realized that the calm demeanor and change in her daughter's behavior was only because Lauren knew that payday was tomorrow and wanted money for something. It seemed only reasonable to Dora that she should say something complimenting her daughter on her good behavior, but that would just leave the door open for her to ask for an allowance or the famous borrowing of "just a little bit of money" that she felt she had coming to her anyway. Well, two could play at this game.

Dora smiled at her daughter and pushed the can of Squirt closer to her, then proceeded to pop the top of the can of Diet Coke and took a swallow. Before any words could be exchanged, Dora turned the channel of the tabletop radio to her daughter's favorite rock 'n' roll station and hummed along with the music. There was no response from Lauren. Dora wondered if she had gotten herself out of the eventual situation or whether she had just dug the hole deeper. Both of them finished the meager meal, even down to drinking the last drop of broth. Dora took the cups, then placed them in the garbage container under the kitchen sink. Just as Lauren opened her mouth to make a comment, Dora turned around with a half gallon of rocky road ice cream in her hand.

Lauren raised her eyebrows, liking what she saw, then grabbed the bowls and the spoons and set them back down on the table. The two of them proceeded to enjoy the ice cream in silence. The bowls were cleared from the table; then Dora turned to her daughter and looked her directly in the eye. She knew she had Lauren's attention and then asked her if she had any homework. She got an evil glare from her daughter as she walked away and went back to her bedroom. Dora rinsed out the dishes and then turned the radio station back to the usual morning news/talk program that she listened to in the mornings.

Dora plunked down in the deep, pillowed love seat and wondered what she should do to keep her mind from catapulting to what could be an awakened reality. It most definitely had something to do with this man. When would he call, what would he do, did he remember her? Could the whole event have been staged just to get the needed information from her? She quickly shook her head and thought of how she was writing an Agatha Christie novel in her mind. Come on, I've just had chocolate. Chocolate and sex are both supposed to have the same effect on the mind, aren't they? I've never felt lonely for male company until now. Well, I am a healthy, single, relatively attractive, young, middle-aged woman. That's another question. Why haven't I wanted or felt like this before? My past is from Chicago. I even remember all the brats that I went to high school with. I went steady with Chris. He was going to be a doctor. He had already made plans to go to the University of Illinois College of Medicine. She took her hands to her mouth, partially covering it with her upper fingers, and the sound of her breathing was intensified.

Come on, I just need something new in my life. After I get my paycheck tomorrow, when I deposit it, I'll just keep a little bit more cash and get myself something—a new music CD. I haven't bought one of those . . . my god, I haven't bought a music CD since two years ago when I went to that Kenny Loggins's concert. My god, I am getting old. I still remember when the Rolling Stones were considered controversial. Old friends—I ought to call an old friend, but I don't remember any. It is like my life is planned out following an allotted course, a preplanned, programmed course. Come on, turn on the television, and get lost in it. Stop trying to psychoanalyze yourself. That's dangerous. Things are working. Just let them be.

A car very slowly turned around in front of the house. Then the man stopped, got out, looked at their house, then got back in, and drove away. The sound was noted by each of them. "MOM!"

"Don't 'MOM' me!" Dora double-locked the door, then looked Lauren up and down. "I was wondering who this stranger was. I was scared and then wondered if it was the gentleman that I ran into at church the other day. I was scared! And it turns out to be probably one of your friends!"

"What makes you say that?"

"What makes me say that? Oh, let's see. You've been alone in your room with no outbursts to me about anything, and when we had dinner, you were wearing your pajamas. Now you're dressed and with your shoes on, no less."

"I was . . . I was just cold, so I got dressed."

"You were cold at the end of August? I better take you to the doctor. You must have some kind of flu—a strain so bad that it even causes your feet to be drastically cold, so cold that you have to cover them up with your shoes while you're still inside a house in sunny California."

Lauren made a further attempt to express her silent anger, then slammed the door to her room. Dora tracked instantly to the bedroom door that was just slammed. "You do not do that in my house, young lady! There are rules."

The door wasn't opened, and her daughter talked loudly, but just not loud enough to be yelling her response. "There are rules? You act like a nutcase averting your fears and your lust at the same time, and then you call me nuts. Oh, don't think that I don't see."

"Well, maybe . . . maybe you're going to have to go somewhere else to live then, somewhere like a private boarding school."

Lauren opened the door and looked her mom in the eye, then stepped back so as not to get too close. "You don't have the money for that."

Dora tilted her head back, breathing, thinking of how she was being defeated. "Well, I'll just make the time to talk to your counselor. I remember at the start of school, in the packet of papers that you brought home for me to read and sign, there was something in there about an after-school program for teens that they had, a program for teens who were having problems."

The door was then slammed in Dora's face. She felt lost, more than lost, like what is the use. It . . . this wasn't her daughter talking. It was her trying to rationalize the change in her mother's life. She didn't have a neighbor that she could go talk to either, and she was going through adolescence. That alone in today's society was a feat in itself. Her daughter was good, though. She didn't have to worry about her doing drugs, but maybe the peer pressure just hadn't started yet. More church—I have to get us in something. We—I have to have something right now, something.

Well, Lauren's in her room, Dora thought to herself. She walked over to the television and turned it off and retired to her bedroom for the evening. Rest, sleep would be a godsend right now. Fighting her heightened sense of security, she opened the side bedroom window; and a light, gentle breeze instantly filled the room. She got under the covers, then sat back up before turning off the lamp. She threw the blanket and bedspread off the bed. Only the white cotton sheet covered her. She turned off the light and blinked twice before slowly closing her eyes, wanting reassurance that the night would bring good dreams or no dreams at all. The idea of hearing the blasting alarm on the clock radio in the morning was actually welcoming.

She lay flat on her back, unmoving, for about a minute, then rolled to one side, and instantly turned to the other side. No comfort was found in either position. She grabbed the pillow from the other side of the bed, then raised her head up, and put that pillow underneath the one that was already there, searching for any way to find comfort. Well, there is good news to look forward to—tomorrow is payday. Right now, Hamburger Helper is a welcome thought.

Dora opened her eyes to the blaring radio alarm before she even realized she had been asleep. Next, she found herself groggily going to the shower and laying out her clothes for the day. She and Lauren finished their breakfast cereal earlier than usual. The morning news on the radio seemed to be just endless commercials. She turned it off, then tapped her fingers on the table, capturing Lauren's attention. The feeling in the room was uneasy. Dora grabbed her things for work and told Lauren to get her books for school. She would give her a ride this morning.

Dora parked her car in the parking lot in front of the school and went to the office. They walked side by side until Lauren got wind of her friends; then she quickly drifted from her mother. Alone, Dora went to the office, made her introduction, and explained to the secretary there that she wanted to make an appointment to see a counselor and what her problem was. The secretary punched the information into the computer, then gave Dora a slip of paper with the time of the appointment. Dora thanked her and placed the slip in her purse without even looking at it as she had just noted the time on the wall clock and thought of how she was going to have to hurry to work. The thing to do would be to get a programmable coffeepot, but Mr. Mann was too observant of every small thing and change in the office as well as every penny spent.

Arriving in the parking lot, she was surprised that there were no cars from the neighboring business in the lot. She got the well-sought- after space under the elm tree. Seeing the office still dark inside and the absence of her boss's car, she quickly remembered to turn off the alarm before using the key to open the office. Two newspapers were inside, and Dora bent over and picked them up, taking the rubber bands off them while walking around the side of her desk to get the coffeemaker ready. Successfully placing the coffee in the filter and back in the machine before spilling any, she thanked the Lord for this small miracle. She started to throw the papers on Mr. Mann's desk, then decided to neatly place them on top of the desk instead, knowing that he was such a stickler about everything.

Mr. Mann came in, expressing . . . well, really, expressing no look other than that of an astute businessman. He walked into his office without saying hi or so much as even a head nod. Dora did not relish this day and poured coffee into his cup, pausing by his door before proceeding into his office. She placed the cup in his open hand. He nodded and smiled at her in thanks. She could tell by his motions and facial tone that he was looking for something to open up about something, but she just wasn't in the mood. She made quick steps back to her desk, hoping, just hoping, for the sound of the telephone to give her an alibi.

A young yuppie couple walked into the office and explained that they were looking for a house to buy in the Mountain View area. Dora smiled at them and told them to take a seat. It would be just a minute. Instead of paging Mr. Mann on the telephone, she went into his office and told him the news, wanting to see the smile that this would bring to his face. In doing this and seeing his expression at the news, one couldn't have been paid for a smile like that.

Mr. Crane came into the office and asked for the latest reports. She smiled at him and made small talk while she handed him the papers. The day progressed in the usual fashion, with one exception. When the paychecks were delivered after lunch by the regular carrier, she proceeded to put hers directly in her purse, then stopped to take her checkbook out from her purse, and placed it inside, only to take the check from the envelope to look at it first. She was blown away by what she saw. She had received a pay raise, and she hadn't even pleaded for one—a raise of $1.25 an hour. A quick calculation in her mind gave her the figure of a $50-a-week raise. She smiled a joyous smile. Remembering the restrictions of the office atmosphere, she quickly filled out a deposit slip and returned to her office persona.

Dora paid more attention to everything for the rest of the workday, wanting to make a quick exit from work at the end of the day. After work, her first stop was the bank. She took that extra $50 in cash to add to her spending money for the week. She drove through the coffee kiosk and ordered a tall decaf latte. She enjoyed every sip of it while walking through the grocery store. The natural thing to do would have been to buy something extra from her usual shopping cart of groceries, but she didn't know whether she wanted to keep her raise a secret from her daughter and just keep the extra money to have on hand. She savored the coffee down to the last drop, and with the plastic stirrer, she even retrieved the very last speck of foam.

She placed the groceries in the trunk of the car, being careful to place the ice cream, frozen vegetables, and Marie Callender's frozen chicken dinners in the very back part of the trunk, hoping that would keep them cooler. Then she went into the massive music- and-computer store, drifting by and smiling at the salesmen trying to sell the computers and appliances at the front of the store, and went to the back part of the store on the right side and started going by and looking at the various CDs. At the endcaps, she even stopped to listen at the headphones to the most recent top 10 music CDs on sale. She squinted hearing the first two but quickly remembered that she was probably being watched, which she was. She really only liked one of them but didn't feel that she liked it well enough to buy. Walking down the aisles, she came to the conclusion that she just ought to buy something that she really liked and would enjoy, regardless of the age of the recording. She came to rest in front of Alice Cooper's CDs, remembering how she would always sing along to the music when they were on the radio. His looks were extreme. But then, she thought, well, it was his trademark.

The clerk looked at her and the CD twice before ringing up the sale. She made note of this but said nothing. When she was in her car, the first thing she did was play the music after starting the engine. She was very familiar with most of the music but was then surprised at two of the songs in particular. She had heard them before and thought how beautiful they were, but she had no idea that Alice had recorded them. She was more than happy about her decision. When she stopped in her driveway, she had to replay and listen to the song "You and Me" again. Upstairs, with her shoes off in the apartment and feeling a light breeze through the windows, she relaxed her body, then realized that she had forgotten to unpack the groceries from the car. Well, maybe they can just wait there until Lauren comes home. And I'll tell her if she wants her allowance, she is just going to have to unpack the car first. She started to laugh at what she just thought, then suddenly remembered the ice cream. Oh, sh . . . jeez, I'll just put my slippers on and do it. Downstairs, with the trunk open and keys in her pocket, she reached deep in the back of the trunk to get the frozen foods out first. In a sudden jolt, she felt fear from someone watching her. Fearful, she raised her head and turned it, looking up. In doing so, she hit her head on top of the raised trunk lid. She put her hand to her head and fell forward in the trunk in pain. The pain only aggravated her fear as she just took the frozen food and meat in her hands and made it up the stairs swiftly. She locked the door and put the frozen foods in the freezer, then returned to the door, and looked out the window at her car. She saw nothing and didn't even notice the howl of the wind.

There was something or someone there, though. She then felt stupid and thought she was just psyching herself into a science fiction novel. What am I looking at? I'm worried about the boxes of cereal locked in the trunk. I think they'll make it. If Lauren tells me she's bored, which I know she will, she can have the eventful job of bringing in the groceries. I know that will make her happy.

CHAPTER 3

Lauren arrived home in a peaceful mood. They talked to each other of nothing of any importance. Her daughter seemed to have, for that moment, returned to her usual quiet state. Dora thought that her recent outburst was maybe just nerves from her anxious reaction to everything that had been happening. At dinner that night, they had a Hamburger Helper enchilada-flavored casserole and a green salad, with fresh pears for dessert. The number one thing about dinner that Dora enjoyed was a can of Coors Light. Beer was great with Mexican food, and just the satisfaction of having one was pure enjoyment. Sitting down, relaxing, and quietly contemplating things, she remembered the remaining groceries in the trunk of the car and mentioned this to Lauren while throwing her the keys, which she caught in her hand. She heard her daughter go down the stairs; then instead of listening to a CD, she reached for one of the three unfinished novels that she had started and put back under the table to finish on a rainy day. No rain was evident, but with the heat of the end of summer, she had the relaxed feeling of being inside a warm room.

The groceries were even put away in the correct cabinets and drawers by her daughter who hadn't even made any comments. The phone rang, and Dora was surprised that Lauren didn't make her usual run for it. It was like she knew the call wasn't for her. It was the counselor from the high school calling, which surprised Dora. The counselor told her that she had tried to reach her earlier that day to discuss the drop in Lauren's grades, but there must have been something wrong with her phone line because there wasn't even a ring. Dora frowned at hearing this news, then thanked her for calling.

She told her of the problems. Lauren's grades were seriously slipping, and her teachers feared that she wouldn't graduate with the rest of her class. They sensed a problem but didn't know what it was. Her behavior had changed from a quiet, good student to one of unconcern, and a rebellious nature was emerging. Lauren was in her bedroom, and Dora was cautious about her voice level, not wanting to get an angry reaction from her daughter. It was explained to her that counseling would have to be done for both Lauren and her too. This news surprised Dora, having the feeling of not wanting to have to succumb to a school setting again, the feeling of being constricted by a teacher. She had already done her time and didn't want any more.

She hung up the phone, showing a look almost of remorse for what she had done. She would have to ask Mr. Mann to get off early from work. This was something she felt should be owed to her, being that year, she had taken only one sick day; but she still felt a cringe go down her spine at even the thought of having to ask him for this time off.

She knew that she had to be on the most even ground with her daughter, especially tomorrow, so she raised her voice just to a high- enough level for Lauren to hear her in her room. She handed Lauren a twenty-dollar bill. Lauren looked quite surprised by it, then quickly placed it in her pocket. Dora gave the explanation that she still owed Lauren her allowance from Sunday and thanked her, knowing it was hard dealing with her mother's erratic behavior. Lauren kissed her on the cheek, then ran into her room with the cell phone.

Instead of looking relieved by what she had just done, Dora made a sorrowful expression. I just bribed my own family. I can't believe it. She put down the novel, closed it, and put it back under the table. Then she turned the television set on. Flicking through the channels with the remote, she saw three different movies on. Let's see. It's *Jurassic Park*, *The Terminator*, or *George of the Jungle*. She turned the set to a channel and started laughing. Brendan Fraser, looks like you win.

Mr. Mann did give her the early leave but gave her "the look" when she headed out the door for her daughter's school to meet the counselor. In the school office, her daughter started to greet her, then pulled back.

Dora expected that reaction. They met briefly with a tall thin woman in her fifties. She looked quite well-read and knowledgeable. Dora was glad to see that. Inside her office, the stated problem was spoken by this woman, Mrs. Fisk; and Dora was surprised when Lauren was excused from the office and told that she could wait either in the library or in the gym. Mrs. Fisk then explained that she already had a counseling session with Lauren earlier that day. Mrs. Fisk proceeded to ask Dora about her problem and listened to her to give an answer as she read an open manila folder on her desktop. Dora wondered what this file said about her. "Mrs. Fisk, do you seem to think that there is a problem with me? I mean, I just assumed that this problem was from a change in my daughter's behavior because of, well, adolescence. Why are you questioning me?"

Mrs. Fisk closed the file and looked directly into Dora's eyes. "What makes you think that you have a problem? Tell me about it. You have quite a history."

"History? History? I have a history? Look, I called you for help. I am a working single parent just trying to make it through life and raise my daughter in a world that I think is changing too fast for its own good." Hesitation was expressed by Mrs. Fisk, and Dora was unclear whether it was because she did not hear the answer she wanted to hear from her or because she was leaving the door open for her to ask her a question.

Mrs. Fisk took a business card from the side of her desk and handed it to her. Dora hesitated, then took it, looking to her for an answer. "That card has the number of social services that you need to call to get some help for yourself regarding the matter that you are going through."

Dora sat back in the chair and started to look in her eyes, then raised her eyes to the ceiling instead. She looked at the card, then slowly stood up. "Don't worry. I'll call, so you don't have to write me up or call the police. I didn't rob a bank or anything." She paused, then looked at Mrs. Fisk. "Oh please, don't write me up for that. I was just being facetious." No expression showed on Mrs. Fisk's face, and Dora just left the office. She did not feel like searching through the campus to look for her daughter. She did not even know what her feelings towards Lauren were right then, but she surely knew she was not going to talk to her about anything more than the weather, then wondered if her daughter would report that to Mrs. Fisk. What am I doing, or what did I do? I can't recall my past, but that was so long ago. And in going back through the course of that time, I don't know what Lauren could possibly remember about that anyway. She was so young. Or is someone from our past, my past, communicating with her now? Oh, here I go again. I'll just wait in the car for her. I'm sure Mrs. Fisk has already informed her of my whereabouts. Everyone knows about my life, my entire life right now, except me. Dora took her middle finger and index finger to her mouth and repeated, in her head.

In the car, she sat quietly, making no show of emotions whatsoever. In a silent huff, needing something to do, she turned the key backwards in the ignition to get power without starting the motor and put a CD in the car stereo. Okay, Alice, take me away. Track 7 had just ended when the passenger door opened, and Dora heard the noise of her daughter getting in the car. After she heard the seat belt snap shut, she started the car engine. On the way home, she made a detour and pulled in the drive-thru of Burger King. She ordered two hamburgers, two French fries, and one cola for Lauren. She knew full well that when she got home, she was going to have a beer. Now more than ever, she needed one. A beer wasn't the answer, but it seemed like it helped in her present situation, wondering when that actually started.

At home, she placed the burgers on the table, then opened all the windows. There wasn't much of a view other than the sides of tall pines, but it was some small relief that she didn't have to look her daughter in the eye. Not a word was spoken through dinner, and there was no arguing over cleanup—it was just thrown away. Dora expected Lauren to retreat to her bedroom as she usually did, but instead, she grabbed her purse and headed out the door and down the stairs. Dora had no idea where she was going or with whom, but the way she felt right now, she didn't even want to know. If Lauren did run away, the social services really would be after her. She made a call to Brittney's mom, and sure enough, that was where Lauren was going.

Whom do I call? Who knows about me? She huffed. The government? The government! Who first? Birth certificate—Chicago. I'm from Chicago. Nice small place. I'm sure anyone on the street could tell me, easy. My social security card. When did I get it and from where? Call a private investigator, but that's opening a can of worms. There are some things in my past that aren't meant to be known. Now I'm defending the unknown. Tomorrow, I'd better go to the library and find any information I can on how to find information. I'm remembering things that were buried. That man must have been the trigger. I was scared of him . . . I know or knew him. He was the trigger. How come I don't have any family? My only memory of family is that my parents are dead, or was that what I was told? Regressive memory? I have to go back.

She sprung up from the chair and reached for her purse, then took out a paper from the file cabinet in the closet. She read the number, then dialed it. On the third ring, the line on the other side was answered. "Yes, my number . . ." She then recited her number from her card and the number on the paper. "I have enough miles? When is your next flight to Chicago from either San Jose or San Francisco? . . . That sounds good. San Jose." She grabbed the pen and wrote the numbers down. "I'll have to pick the tickets up. I don't have a printer here. An extra charge for that? . . . Okay." She gave her the card number and then hung up the phone. So much for the library, I'm going directly to the source. I'll just ask the pastor's wife to take care of Lauren while I'm away. The excuse? Someone died. I've never talked of family. My aunt . . . my aunt who helped my mother raise me. She took me to church on Sundays and the whole bit. A name . . . I need a name. Alice. Alice Cooper. That would be too much. Last name. She looked out the window. Night. Alice Knight.

After being with the pastor and his family for a few days, she'll sure appreciate it here. What do I say to her, though? She might know my history better than me. I'll tell her it's for medical reasons. She won't tell the pastor's family. She wouldn't want to say her mother is a nut—going blind to Chicago, knowing nothing, but looking for something. Maybe I am nuts. It's just something I have to do. I feel drawn to it.

Mr. Mann heard the news of her aunt's death and could not understand why she had to fly there to her funeral when they had been apart for so long. Dora had lived in the Silicon Valley for almost twenty years now. She had just gotten a raise, and she knew she was pushing it. He had already called a temp agency for her replacement during her absence. The lowered cost of pay for this temp was a plus in his estimation. Mr. Crane, with his usual niceties, wished her a good trip and left her his condolences for the loss of her friend.

The look that Dora got from her daughter when giving her the news of her upcoming trip to Chicago and the fact that she would be staying with the pastor's family . . . well, that look could have cracked a mirror with the intensity of her stare. Dora went on the Internet looking for the weather in Chicago so she would know what to pack. The first thing she placed in her suitcase was a Windbreaker, but being that it was the end of September, there could still be the humidity of the hot summers. Cool cotton tops and skirts were also packed in subdued colors since she knew that most of the trips back there were going to be to hospitals, medical clinics, or state-county buildings, not to Wrigley Field or to the audience of the *Oprah Winfrey Show.*

Not wanting to bother the pastor any further for a ride to the airport and to avoid the high cost of parking her car in the long-term parking, she took a taxi to the bus station, then boarded a bus to the airport. She enjoyed sightseeing from the side window without having to worry about the torment of driving on the freeway. Approaching the entrance of the airport and driving by the hangars for the private planes, she scoured the area with intensity. Larry Ellison had a plane there. She thought she had read that somewhere. He is a megagiant and married. She looked down, then back up again, still engrossed in the expectation of seeing him. She saw a scooter pull in an open hangar, and that was it. They were hurriedly departing the bus and unpacking and tagging the luggage. It was easy to spot her light brown plastic suitcase in the midst of the Samsonite and designer signature brands.

Already waiting in the check-in line, she waited at the boarding terminal. Thoughts and visions of the man in the Mercedes bombarded her mind. She missed the first announcement for her plane's boarding call, being engulfed in thought. On the second call, the tip of her shoe got run over by a wheeled cart. She felt no pain from this, just surprise, and fell forward to a run to the boarding gate. Walking down the aisle of the plane, she feared whom she was going to be sitting next to—a "before" picture of a Jenny Craig commercial, unbathed and unshaven.

To her surprise, no one else sat in this three-seat row, the very back row of seats on the left side of the plane. The window seat was vacant, but the stewardess explained to her that she would have to sit in the aisle seat until the plane had taken off and the sign had displayed that it was safe to take her seat belt off.

CHAPTER 4

Airborne for half an hour, the seat belt sign had still not gone off although the food cart with sodas and peanuts had already gone down the aisle. She passed on both. She had brought a bottle of water, but it was in the overhead compartment. Just contemplating what she would find there in Chicago made her stomach turn cartwheels. The thought of putting food or anything, even water, in her stomach right now was revolting.

The "unfasten seat belt" sign was finally displayed, indicating that it was all right to move about the plane. They were midway through the flight. She looked at her wristwatch. Let's see. We departed at 9a.m. and are scheduled to arrive there at 3:00 p.m. It's a six-hour flight, and we're halfway through, so three more hours to go. Maybe I will eat something, but airline food? Maybe not. Dora got up and took the bottle of water from the overhead compartment. When the flight attendant did come down the row with the food cart, she asked her what the meal was, but it was almost as though she didn't listen to the response and just asked for a couple of bags of peanuts instead. The flight attendant had to go to the center food station to retrieve them. Well, peanuts and bottled water. I don't think I can get too sick on that.

She did doze off, and when she woke up in the upright-seated position, she wondered how she ever slept. A man from two rows ahead of her and to her right turned around and looked at her. She saw this; and then when he saw her look at him, he gave a brief smile, then turned his head back, looking at the seat ahead of him. She wondered if she could have been snoring in her sleep and was embarrassed by the thought of that happening. She viewed the time on her watch. In twenty minutes, they would be landing. Everything was on target. An overhead announcement was made saying just that—the skies were clear, the flight went smoothly, and conditions were good at the Chicago O'Hare International Airport. The "fasten seat belt" sign flashed as the announcement was made. She wondered then what would be the first thing to do once she was off the plane—check the phone book for a hospital there that specialized in psychological research. They just encountered some turbulence in the sky, and this gave her a queasy feeling. She hoped the road ahead to her findings wasn't going to produce this same uneasy feeling.

Walking out of the hallway into the busy airport, she was already lost and scoured the face of every passing person as though they held the answers she sought and needed. Looking at the directory signs in the airport, she found the route she needed to take to get her luggage. On the way there, she passed and then backtracked into a ladies' room. Washing her hands at the sink in the restroom, she saw a lady turn her view sideways to her with a questioning yet almost-sinister facial tone. Grabbing a towel and approaching this woman while wiping her hands, she studied the woman's face, trying desperately for some memory to surface to tell her who this was. Coming eye to eye with her, she was almost absorbed in fear. The woman stepped back and then changed her expression to a look of concern. "Is there anything wrong, dear? Can I help you? Are you lost?"

Dora composed herself and relaxed so she could really see this woman. Then she realized this woman was no danger to her—she was a nun. She wasn't wearing the white cornette hat, but she was a nun. Dora raised then dropped her stance. "No, I'm sorry. I . . . it's just that, well, I'm new in this place. And I don't know my whereabouts. I guess I do look rather lost."

"Oh, dear, you're not lost. My, you do look like something is bothering you, though. Come down to the clergy tonight. We'll get reacquainted. It is so good to see you again. It's been such a long time. Oh, I do have to go now. The bus is probably waiting for me. They always say that I hold them up. Good-bye, Jane." The nun went out the door of the restroom, and Dora tried to perceive what she just heard. To get out of the way, she sat in the chair by the mirrored wall and counters where the women checked their makeup before exiting the restroom. She knew me . . . but as someone else . . . she called me Jane?

She could hold the answer! Dora ran out of the restroom, and once outside the door in the hallway, she searched to the east and then to the west. On the west, you would be heading for departing flights. Straight ahead of her was just a boarding gate, so east it was. She could see an escalator heading down to departures and to the baggage claim and taxi area. Running to the escalator, she saw the top of this woman's head heading down to the next floor. Dora tried to push her way forward on the escalator, but it was packed too tightly with people, and she wasn't going to be the valiant hero in the movies who ran atop the side to catch the culprit on the bottom floor.

At the bottom of the escalator, people were already exiting to the left and right, knowing where they needed to go. Dora stopped at the bottom and panicked in fear, trying to catch this woman and not get knocked over by people scattering through the congested area. She was trapped in a maze and had to move. She caught sight of this woman leaving through the glass door of the airport to her right. She started to run in that direction, but blocking the clear path in front of her was an older woman who had stopped and was bending down to tie her child's shoe. Dora couldn't just jump over them. The woman tying her son's shoe saw Dora and apologized, but she had to tie his shoe, or he would trip. Dora looked down and smiled, trying to shield the anger running through her veins.

The path was clear again, and she just made it to the doors but now had gained the interest of the police and the valets. They approached her as she watched the woman board a bus. The door closed in front of her, and the bus drove away. The police officer approached her from the left side and asked about her frenzied behavior. Dora loosened her posture, huffed, and then breathed in a deep breath before responding, "I missed my bus." She pointed at the bus that the nun had just left on.

The police officer pulled back, then laughed. "There'll be another bus going to the same destination, the Grant Park area, in fifteen minutes." She turned to go back in the airport and claim her baggage while thanking the officer.

She found the correct baggage carousel to get her luggage and found that in the time it had taken her to claim it, someone, probably an attendant, had already removed it from the turnaround bay. Of course, a tip was required, and she handed him a five and then took her bag. Depressed by the loss of an answer, she thought the best thing to do at that moment would be just to look in a phone book. She found a row of pay phones and sat down at one and took hold of the large phone directory. She found it was extremely hard to hold it and look at it with the weight of the hard plastic case that surrounded it. Just when she found the hospital section in the yellow pages, she misbalanced the weight of the book, and it closed and fell to the floor. Reaching down to pick it up, she dropped her purse, and her change from it rolled on the floor. In quick response so as not to lose her purse (since it was all she had right now), she grabbed the money and the wallet, then catapulted her purse to her side, giving passersby a dirty look. No one came to help her. She gathered herself back together, then found the page in the phone book again.

Dora fell back against the wall behind the row of chairs, first in disbelief and then with the thought, Well, everything else was going that way, what should I have expected? There were nine hospitals in Chicago as well as doctor's office complexes and clinics. What was the name of the hospital on *ER*? George Clooney isn't on that show anymore. Hmm, maybe he has the answer. Oh, that would be a dream. Back, back to reality. Grant Hospital. That nun's bus was going to Grant Park. Maybe a clue—I hope. Anything at this point. I only have about three more hours of daylight left anyway. To the bus! Boy, things must be bad—I'm happy about boarding a bus going to . . . what? She raised her eyebrows and replied, "The unknown," then gave a brief laugh while walking outside to the bus stop.

She did her best to convince the driver to let her take her two suitcases on board, but he explained to her that she couldn't have any carry-on luggage that big on board. His bus did not have the storage room for her baggage. She then explained about the nun she saw previously. He then told her back that maybe that "nun" didn't have any luggage. She could wait for another hour for a bus that did take luggage and went to all the upper-class hotels, or there was always a taxi. Lowering her head in defeat while giving him a stare, she turned with bags in hand and found a cab, giving him only the direction of "a good hotel downtown close to Grant Park if possible." He gave her no verbal response; he only pressed the gas pedal and proceeded to take the highway to get to the downtown area of Chicago.

Dora thought to herself that she should have brought a map with her. She would probably have to pay three times a map's worth at any tourist shop. Feeling relaxed about having the whole backseat to herself and not having to worry about where things were for an instant, she forced herself to look out the windows both forward and to the sides to observe all the things they were passing. It could be anything at all right now—something else to jar open her memory. That man at the church parking lot whom she had never heard from again, he was out there, and she would hear from him again; and the nun, she had to meet up with her again too. Two clues to the puzzle—her memory had been awakened but not opened.

The cab stopped at the downtown Marriot in the medical district. She got out of the cab, standing in front of a valet waiting for her suitcases to be handed to him from the trunk of the cab. She looked at him, but it was like she saw right through him and was looking to the height of this hotel. Seeing its luxury, she then hoped it would take her AAA card to get a discount.

She straightened herself, seeking perfect posture and form in the correct walk, looking for female flirtations to get the best she could get on anything right now. At the front lobby registration counter, the attendant left her bags and gave her a receipt for them. She tipped him, and then he left, tipping his hat to her in thanks. She turned and saw a mirror and side table against the side behind the waiting area. She went there looking in the mirror to check her makeup and hair. Opening her purse, she took out her comb, brushing the hair around her face. Then she applied more lipstick. Satisfied with her appearance, she got in-line and was waited on sooner than she expected.

The clerk nodded his head, then looked at her for the opening conversation. She explained to him that she had just gotten in and needed a room for that night. She did not know how long her stay would be and wondered if she could get a less-expensive room. In just saying the words "less expensive," he looked down to the computer and huffed. She pushed forward her AAA card and smiled at him. "It's just me. I only need a bed and a bathroom."

He looked at her and said, "We are not the YMCA. All our rooms are very nice and of more-than-acceptable level. You have no reservation, and with three conferences going on right now, we are very booked up. We just got a cancellation for a room with a delightful view, a king-size bed—the best." He stood back and looked downward to her, then stepped forward looking directly to her eye view. In a deep, steady voice, he asked her if she wanted it. It was $189 a night. She involuntarily grimaced when she heard the price. She was only looking to pay half of that. Thinking quickly of the time and the need for a room in a city of strangers, she blankly replied to him that she would take it and handed him her VISA card. Taking the receipt and the key card, she shook her head no to the bellboy and found the elevator and went up to the sixth floor.

The room was nice. The large bed seemed elevated though it wasn't. The decorations gave the appearance of gold with red-gold toss pillows and a beautiful gold bedspread. The windows that looked out to the view were covered by floor-length gold drapes. She walked over to the sliding window and opened it partway. That was all you could do, open it partway—probably a restriction for the hotel's safety so no one would try and jump out the window. She saw what she thought was part of Lake Michigan. It was too bad about the cost of the room because she did love it. Then she remembered the reason she was here.

Over on the table by the window and bar area of the room, she saw papers atop the table. There . . . there it was . . . what she was looking for—not only a map of downtown Chicago, but also a map of the medical hospitals and buildings. She sat down in one of the two padded chairs at the table, and a large smile covered her face. Sorry, Oprah, but I'm busy. We'll have to do the show another time. Thanks for being so understanding. She turned her head back and forth. Oh god, I am tired. Well, there is a coffeemaker and coffee behind me. She got up and set the pot to Brew. Her stomach growled in hunger, and she looked around the room thinking maybe there would be some fruit. No such luck. She took a pen from the top of the table and started looking at the map and comparing the locations to hers at the Marriott to chart out a path for where to search. Grant Park, it looked like, was right next to the hotel. She would just ask one of the bag boys in the morning if he knew of a church, a nunnery, or a convent in that area—then another tip. She thought it would be better to ask the man at the outside newsstand. He was probably bombarded with questions about various locations in the city all day long.

Noticing the darkened room, she walked to the partially opened window and shivered. She closed the window and thought of how odd that shiver was, just a shiver down her back; yet her back remained rigid, her torso unmoved. Again, she heard and felt the growl of her stomach. She took the change purse out of her bag and grabbed hold of the key, leaving the room to find a vending machine somewhere on that floor. Five minutes later, she returned to the room with a Milky Way candy bar in hand. She threw the key card on top of the dresser next to her purse, then ripped the wrapper off the candy bar.

She hesitated, standing in front of the table by the coffeemaker on the bar. She contemplated whether to take a bite from the candy bar or to pour herself a cup of coffee first. She was scared that biting into the bar in a hurry would cause some of the candy bar to break off and fall to the carpeted floor. Not wanting to lose so much as even a speck, she got the coffee first, thinking she didn't want to lose any of it especially since it cost her $2.50 for that one candy bar. She could have bought a famous Chicago hot dog for that price. It was just the idea of staying in the comfort of the room. She took a filled cup to the table in one hand with two packets of coffee creamer in the other hand. She looked at the coffee, creamer, and the Milky Way bar on the table and smiled in delight. She didn't spill a drop of coffee and had a makeshift meal in front of her.

She pulled out the chair and sat down very carefully, not wanting to spill any coffee, especially since the maps were there on the table. It didn't look like there would be that much distance between some of the facilities, but closeness and proximity were two different things. She remembered how hard it was to go anywhere in San Francisco because of the changes in the road direction—many one-way streets and steep hills.

Done with the candy bar and the last sip of coffee, she looked happy but then searched the wrapper for any remaining morsel. There wasn't anything in the wrapper but air. Well, I do feel better. At least I have an idea of where I'll be going tomorrow. Tomorrow, early checkout. Where will I put my luggage and belongings? I have to shield myself from this feeling of paranoia that I am surrounding myself with. She glanced at her wristwatch to again check the time, 8:30 p.m.

I am tired. It's just that if I go to bed now, will I be able to sleep through to morning? She jumped up from the chair at the table and went to the telephone on the nightstand to the side of the bed. Quickly checking the print on the face of the telephone, she found the number to call for the front desk. The tone of voice of the man who answered the phone was the same as that of the man who checked her in when she registered. She told him her name, and he sighed when he heard it. She then knew whom she was dealing with and remained in a formal, even business tone through the conversation. He told her that she was in luck—the party that canceled the reservations on that room had it for the following night also, and he hadn't filled the room yet. He would be checking on her credit card, though, and would call her back before morning if it did not go through. She hung up, thankful that this was one credit card that she did not have a balance on. It would go through.

She showered and put on her white satin pajamas in the bathroom. Walking out to the bedroom, she returned to the bathroom and looked around it and then back to the side of the bed. It's like I'm looking for something, anything not feeling right. I can't go and check on Lauren before I go to sleep. This is the only night that I have been away from her that I can remember, other than when she stays at her friend's house, and then we were only about five miles away from each other. Leave it alone. If I call the pastor's house to talk to her, she'll just yell at me for something. There's sure been quite a change in her and her behavior . . . in just the matter of a few days. I don't know—it's something more than just teenage rebellion taking place. She talked with her counselor of my past, and that nun today talked to me like she knew me and called me Jane. Am I? She fell back, then took the covers off the bed and got under them.

Thinking in her mind that the only thing she wanted at that moment was sleep, she lulled her body into a deep slumber. Unmoved, unchallenged, rest was what her body needed. Well into the early-morning hours of slumber, she started dreaming. She envisioned a man. He was still a handsome, debonair, masculine, alluring character but was just younger, in his late twenties.

The thing that was so captivating about the vision was he still carried the essence of being aloof, yet he was smiling and pushing a baby carriage. He reached down to the cradle of the carriage and picked up, ever so gently, a baby wrapped in a pink blanket. There were ruffles on the cap she had on her head. Gunshots were fired. He dropped the baby back into the carriage; the baby screamed a loud, piercing cry. He ran, ran out of view. She saw her hands push the carriage away from the scene.

She bolted straight up in the bed, fighting opening her eyes to what was the unknown. She was lost in terror of the living dream and felt a heavy weight on her chest. She opened her eyes to the darkened room—gasping for air, feeling the blood pound through her body, weak and almost feeling crushed. She opened her mouth to a silent, slow breath, fighting an evil spirit that was taking over her resting brain. She turned her body to rest sitting at the side of the bed and pulled her hands in front of her face. She opened her fingers and then pulled her fingers together, locking them in a tight grip, then stretching them out again and tightening them again. Her entire body shivered, then contracted in fear. What is happening? What is real, and what is this overwhelming nightmare that plagues my soul, my very being? Am I imagining this? But how? Such strength in power and fear toying with me. I've got to find help. Someone knew me . . . the me that I was . . . the nun.

She reached for the lamp, then decided against having to focus her vision in the light. Instead, she felt her way to the window and opened the drapes just a fraction, just enough for some light to streak in the room. In straight/forward steps, she went to the small refrigerator and took out a small single shot-size bottle of vodka. She twisted off the lid, then looked at it before taking a quick swallow. She blinked fast after the swallow, then placed the bottle back down on the counter, choosing not to take any more of the half-full bottle that remained. Walking back to the bed and getting under the covers, she said to herself, I'm going crazy. Am I doing this to myself? Deep slumber . . . all I want now is deep slumber without any dreams.

Resting, still on the bed, she held her hands and fingers together over her chest, breathed out, and bit her lower lip. She turned to the side of the room with the open drape, then huffed when she saw it, not wanting to get back up and close it. She turned to the other side, then back to rest on her back. George Clooney, where are you when I need you? I sure wouldn't be thinking about what I just dreamed of if you were here. Sleep, sleep, I have to sleep because I have so much to do tomorrow.

Dora tossed and turned until sleep finally overtook her body, falling asleep absorbed in fear. Early in the morning, the telephone rang. She reached for it with eyes closed, first dropping it off the cradle, then taking it to her ear and whispering "Hello" in the receiver. It was a recording—her wake-up call as requested. It took three times before she was able to set the phone back in its cradle the right way for it to rest there. Rest, rest, all I need is more rest. She lay back down and proceeded to close her eyes in the dark room. I'm in Chicago. I can't sleep. Jolting out of bed, she tripped and caught her shin on the end of the bed. Grimacing in pain, she brought her leg up, bending the knee, then took her hand to where she had hit it. No time for pain. Shower, dress, put on my makeup, go through the map of the city to see where I am going to go first, make the coffee, try and find something to eat, and read the newspaper at the door. I think I can do all of that in about a half hour—easy. She laughed as she went to the bathroom to shower.

CHAPTER 5

Dressed in a beige pantsuit, she wrapped a brown designer scarf around her neck, checked it in the mirror, then thought she better not to wear it, not wanting to draw attention to herself. She opened the paper while taking a sip of coffee. The Cubs are in the World Series. I don't think I'll find the answer in the batter's cage. On to looking at the map. She pulled up from the table after writing notes of addresses on the hotel notepad. She opened the phone book and turned the pages to Convent, hoping that would lead her to the location so she could find that nun.

After pointing her finger to the inside left page of the directory under the heading Convent, she started to fall back, then caught herself, looking more closely at the page. She breathed out, then took another sip of coffee. I expected that there would be only one convent and that it would be easy to find this woman whom I only met briefly at the busy airport—one convent. She made a laughing huff. This city is bigger than I thought. There are six convents, and with my luck, they are all probably at different places in the city. How big is the circumference of this city anyway? I don't suppose the man at the newsstand would know where she is . . . the man at the front desk asks like he knows everything.

Downstairs, she asked the valet who continued to offer to help her how to get to the nearest hospital. He told her there was a nurse and a first aid station at the hotel. She broke into a stupid tourist act, exuding her femininity. She was there to see a friend who was dying in the hospital. She was told on the phone that the hospital was close to the hotel. He then explained to her that there was more than one hospital that was close to the hotel. She could take the number 2 bus (the bus stop for that was across the street), and that would take her to one of them anyway. If that wasn't the right one, she could get back on board that bus and catch the number 16 bus at the east stop. Then across that street, she could wait for the rail and take it to the second exit to the right, get off there, walk down three lights, and then she would be kitty-corner to it; but she had to know what entrance to the hospital because there were five entrances, and two of them went to towers that didn't connect with the rest of the hospital. The medical staff could use the connecting elevators, but not the public.

She broke him from his dialogue and scratched the back of her neck. She thought to herself she wished she'd brought a tape recorder to record those directions. She tipped him, then crossed the street to board the bus that had just stopped there. The first hospital was mostly a birthing facility. She asked at the information booth in the hospital for information on other hospitals or medical facilities that specialized in psychological services. The pleasant man there informed her of a hospital to the southeast of where she was. It would take her about forty-five minutes to get there. After riding three separate buses, she finally did arrive. There was less information available at this hospital. The staff there were very busy, and it showed in their actions. Visitors were just objects that got in their way. Visitors were unnoticed and not welcome.

She thought the best way to handle herself there would be just to blend in and make observations on anything and everything. After three walks around the bottom floor of the hospital, she had acclimated herself to the facilities and felt more at ease blending in. If she just had a white lab coat, she'd have access to more of what she was looking for.

She found the cafeteria on the third floor and bought a cup of tea. She sat down at the end of a table with doctors and nurses seated at the middle. Making it look like she was just relaxing, she paid the closest attention to every word from their mouths. These doctors and medical staff followed the proper rule they were bound to—not one of them talked of a patient or the care in the facility. Most of the conversations were of different sporting events they'd watched on television, the latest book read, or meals their wives had cooked. Dora was surprised thinking that more entertaining talk was to be expected from doctors. She couldn't hold back her hunger any longer. She took her change purse from her bag and went to the vending machines. She returned to the table with a Twinkie in hand. She unwrapped it and took a bite, then looked at it and thought, Well, I'm getting my daily ration of beef fat. It tasted so good, though.

Finished eating and bored from the lack of information, she got up to leave, then stopped as she saw the table clear of the medical staff there. She watched them leave, then looked back down to the table to get her belongings. One of the lab techs there had left his white lab coat. Going against the urge to call him back to get it, she remained there, calm and unmoved. She made a casual observance of the nearby patrons and saw that none of them were paying attention to her. She took the jacket off the chair and hung it over her arm and walked out with her belongings. Once out the door of the cafeteria, she went to a stall in the ladies' bathroom and put the jacket on, folding over the flap with the name on it but still making the identification label visible.

While roaming the halls of the hospital unnoticed, she found the chart room and operating rooms were in the basement although patients scheduled for surgery were brought to the second floor before their operation and then brought back to the other side of the second floor for recovery. The chart room was in the basement, and the x-ray lab was on the first floor. Patients' rooms were on the fourth and fifth floors, and various doctors' offices and the janitors' rooms were on the third floor.

Walking down the halls of the basement, she took a chart off the empty nurses' station. She had it in her hand, clutched to her side, when someone shouted from behind her. She sped up her pace. The shouting got louder, and footsteps chased her, intensifying in sound the closer they got. A hand grabbed hold of her shoulder. She trembled in fear and stopped. "McKlinskey, why did you run from me?"

She had been noticed but as someone else. She couldn't turn around and face this person, or he'd catch her. She turned her head to the side and took a Kleenex to her face, faking a cough. "We need that x-ray in the surgery room, stat. What's the holdup?" Dora acted out another cough; then in a deep, hoarse voice, making it seem like McKlinskey had a cold, she told him it would be right there. Then she again quickened her pace and turned the corner to another hallway.

In the hallway, only accessible to medical staff, there was an EKG machine. It blocked a solid steel door that was opened, and it looked like a locksmith and a uniformed male medical staff—who was watching him, most likely for security—were standing in front of the opened door. She stopped and waited behind the cart, staying as quiet as possible. They had recognized her presence. She listened hard to their dialogue. Their voices were not that loud, and the overhead pages could still be heard, drowning out whatever they were saying at the moment.

The locksmith was installing a code box on top of the key lock for added security to get into this room. She heard them say that with this new code box, the keyhole would still be there underneath it, but it would not be functioning. He took a bolt out of the keyhole. Now there was a magnetic field that would close the door at the code box. Another nurse walked down the hallway. Dora's nerves froze rigid, not knowing what to do. She just stayed there in silence and was relieved when the nurse walked straightforward past her and the chart room. Older charts were stored in this room, and the present working charts of the patients in the hospital were stored in an open room down the hall and to the right. There were two attendants in this room. The locksmith said that they were almost finished. All he had to do now was just set the code. He took a paper from his working case and adjusted his glasses to read the number, making absolutely sure of the number before setting the code box to that number. The new code he read out loud while he set the combination to the lock-100766. After setting the code, he tried it twice, making sure that it functioned properly.

She repeated the number code over and over in her mind, then realized it was her own birthday, October 7, 1966. That was easy to remember. What was the likelihood of that happening? It was just the matter of when she would be able to get in there, and if there was a chart on her in there, what name would it be under? The nun had called her Jane. Was that her name, or was there a coincidence of her just thinking she was someone else?

She started making her way down the hallway from the way she had come in after she saw the two men leave from the chart room's door. She was caught by a nurse. "What are you doing here? Where is that file that the doctor needs?" Dora was scared about being found out but then was instantly relieved at being thought of as a worker there. The nurse must be asking for the same file that the doctor had wanted. Where was this man whose lab coat she took, and why hadn't he gotten the file? "What is that file on the side that you are holding? Is that it that you're walking around so blindly with?" The nurse ripped the file from her side, then held it open to read the name on it. It was the needed file. The nurse turned and walked away, saying that she would deliver it herself, and she would be reporting her for her slowness.

Too many things are just coming together suspiciously. Am I dreaming or being set up? She leaned back against the wall of the hallway and scratched the side of her head. I'm no longer flying blind, but what am I flying in? Or where am I going? Now to get in that room, I wish I had a German shepherd that I could send out to see if the coast was clear. Go get them, Lassie. No, I want Rin Tin Tin. No, he made too much noise. He had that rattling collar. Oh, I don't have time for this, my so-called humor. I have to make introspection of my life.

Observing the clear coast of the hallway, she ran to the door and started to punch the code, then grabbed hold of the box at just the precise instant. She turned away and walked slowly down the hallway in the other direction to the elevator and took it to the third floor. She went to the side waiting area by the library and sat in a close empty chair against the wall of the waiting area. She thought this hospital surely has video surveillance and being that the code was just set, she doubted that anyone even had it yet unless the code was given to them before the door was even set to change. A meeting—that would have been discussed in a hospital meeting. She returned to the cafeteria and went to the wall on the right side of the dining area by the partial glass door of one of the administration rooms. She remembered she had seen papers posted on the wall. She thought, What if I was seen reading these papers? She was just reading information and being in the cafeteria on her lunchtime, so what would the problem be?

With her hands in her pocket in a relaxed state, she read the first page of the posted clipboard of papers. It was a message to the doctors regarding the changes in the operating times. She flipped up that page, scoured over the next page that made no sense to her, and kept going through the papers until she was at the fifth page. There was, in fact, a memo about the change in the door to the chart room. The new code would be placed in the locked desk drawer of each nursing station on each floor in the separate wards of the hospital on that day. The information would be available by two o'clock that afternoon.

I have one hour until that information is released. It's a good thing I stopped myself from going in there earlier. I'm not feeling good. She stood up, then felt her body falling. She instantly caught herself and stood rigid so as not to draw attention to herself. I'd better go back to the nurses' locker room and get my things and get out of this lab coat although I'm keeping it. I'll just fold it inside my bag.

She followed a group of nurses inside the locker room, the same as she had done when she first entered it. She panicked when she saw that her belongings weren't there. She turned and looked at the women in the room as though they were all thieves. Where did my bag go?

They looked at her but said nothing, only resumed their dressing and placing items in their lockers. She went through the entire locker area, even opening the various shower stalls. Come on. She held back tears from her eyes. What do I do? Another part of my identity missing. Forlorn, the only thing she could think to do was leave the room and go back through the hospital, searching if she could find it anywhere, maybe at the lost and found. She passed by a female janitor pushing her cart. She had to lean against the cart to make way for the group of doctors coming down the hall in the other direction.

She looked at the items on the cart; various cleaning supplies, a mop, and a broom were rising from the cart. The female janitor stopped the cart at a room to the side of her, then opened the door, and went into the room with the broom. Dora crossed the hall to where the cart was just parked. Her bag was there on the side of the cart. The janitor must have found it. Could she just take it? It was hers, but would the janitor or any watcher think it to be thievery? Oh, I'm just so tired of this.

She knocked on the door of the room that the female janitor was cleaning and proceeded to tell her she couldn't find her bag and the last place she had it was in the nurses' locker room on that floor. The reason that she didn't place it in her locker was the fact that her necklace that had her locker key was broken, and she thought it would be safe just to place it there at the side of the lockers, being that she only had a half shift that day. She then moved her arm that held the lab coat, so it was noticeable.

The janitor showed reluctance in returning it to her. "Look, I'll even give you my name, and you can see if it matches the name on the driver's license inside the beige Halston wallet inside the bag." The janitor showed further reluctance, then opened the bag, saw the beige Halston wallet inside, handed her the bag, and told her to be more careful. She couldn't guarantee that if she ever left it there again that she would even find it. Somebody else could take it. She should have known that she could have left it in the nurses' booth in the ward that she worked at if that happened.

Dora nodded her head and thanked her, making a quick escape down the hallway of the hospital and thought of what happened and how she felt she just ought to leave for the day. Mr. Mann would just have to understand that the funeral took longer than expected. The funeral home was delayed. What was the holdup? She would have to call home tonight at least to find out how Lauren was doing and if her actions had changed any from the rebellious teenager she had become. She had changed from the mild-mannered little girl that she was all too quickly.

At the entrance to the hospital, she went outside and felt the noted Chicago wind. It was September, but the humidity and the brisk wind were fierce. What are the winters like here? These people who live here are brave. Now to remember the maze of buses that I took to get here, there was the number 2 bus, or was it number 12? There was a 2 in it. I want to go to the southeast. Well, first, I have to cross the street. Crossing the street, she heard a tall Negro woman tell her young son who looked about seven that they were going to have to go to the social security office between Washington and Madison off Jefferson. Now she knew where it was; it was just getting there, and she was still at a loss for directions not being able to establish her bearings yet. North was behind her, and south was in front of her, or was it the other way around? Next thing on the list of things to buy—a compass. This is sure a busy city partial to presidents for names of the streets, the Eisenhower Freeway, the J. F. Kennedy Expressway—a city of art and culture and a rich history. There is nothing that this place doesn't have to offer, maybe even what I am searching for.

Waiting at the bus stop, she decided to see a part of this beautiful zooming, fast metropolis. This city is dazzling—the professionals, the loop, the wondrous shopping with designer shops and every department store as well as specialty stores. She wished she had the money to buy even one suit there, but then she brought herself back to the reason for her venture there. After being on the third bus to get back to the hotel, she saw the sign for Grant Park. This wasn't so much a park as it was an area on the shore of Lake Michigan. A wide arrangement of buildings was there—the most acclaimed was the Art Institute of Chicago. She got off the stop nearest the institute.

Inside, the art was impeccable. The most noted piece there was *American Gothic*. She had seen pictures of this painting many times but never knew that was where it was located. It was as captivating as the *Mona Lisa*. The American farmer was patterned after the painter's dentist, and the woman standing slightly behind him was modeled after the painter's sister. The artist was Grant Wood. The background was a Puritan building. He was territorial—the look he gave. In her look, she wanted more. It proved that labels can be misleading—that was the impression. In other works there, she found a lot of impressionist paintings. The one that caught her eye the most was *City Landscape* by Joan Mitchell. Looking at it, you used imagery to place things. There were lots of Picasso paintings—the most memorable of his was the painting of his wife holding his child. They separated and got divorced. Beside this particular painting was a painting of him. Another, the most potent of the paintings there, more than caught her eye. She remembered having a poster of that painting in her room, Hopper's *Nighthawks*. The picture was of the few patrons sitting in the diner in the night. There was no door in it; it was like they were trapped there. None of them showed emotion. They were humanly on their own.

There was so much more there—paintings, figurines, statues. Never had she remembered such a trip worth taking. Looking at her watch, though, she thought it was time to leave. Outside of the building, twilight was in the air although there was no decline or slowing down in this bustling city. The lights that adorned the skyscrapers were a sight to behold—a whole new city. Her appetite was the only thing that stopped her from viewing the skyscrapers. She was mesmerized by their beauty. She went to the Prairie Restaurant, which wasn't too far from where she was or from her hotel.

Apprehensive about being alone, she tried to reassure herself and to not appear like a tourist. She could have just gotten off work and stopped there for a meal before going home. The interior of the restaurant was inspired by the architect Frank Lloyd Wright. The food flavors were of the Midwestern states—a thoroughly American restaurant. First, she relaxed with a glass of merlot; then she ordered and enjoyed so much the grilled buffalo with sweet potato risotto and sweet corn chowder. The food was superb.

Finished eating, she sat back and relaxed in the chair, then took a look around the room to see the eyes encircling her during the course of dinner since she was alone. A few women glanced her way, but they were not directly staring at that moment. They were just looking around the room in the normal course of their dinner. The waiter came back to her table and asked her if she wanted a nightcap. She replied no, then ordered a decaf coffee. Savoring just relaxing there, she knew full well that when she left there, she would have to call home, then plan out her next course of action or more like course of attack.

The waiter came to her, and another man followed right behind him on his way to his table, she presumed. She just reached to the other empty chair and took her bag to get her wallet to pay the bill. The waiter left the coffee and a plate of plastic half-and-half containers on the table, then placed the bill at the side of it and left. The other man stood still beside the table. She took a sip of coffee, then looked up to a good-looking hesitating younger middle-aged man. He cast a deep, unrecognized, but somehow familiar shadow over her in the dimly lit room. She looked up at him and held back her anger, bewitched by his presence. She changed the look of skepticism on her face and smiled as he did. There was an attraction here—a magnetic force that seemed to draw them together.

Since she didn't hear him speak, the floor was open for her to do so. She was constrained as to what to say. He pulled towards her, but it almost seemed as though he was drawing back. Was he trying to make a flirtation or was just asking for something as simple as directions? In a very soft voice, she looked at him, trying to catch his eye. His eyes were moving across the room, looking at each and every face there. She cleared her throat, hoping the noise would make him look down again. "Uh, can I help you?"

He made quick recognition of her, then looked back up as if he was looking for someone else. In a man's deep voice, he responded, then raised his voice in midsentence, "I'm sorry. You just looked like someone else that I knew, and I thought you were . . ."

"You thought I was someone else? I've been getting that a lot in this city."

He looked like he was fighting a force to leave, but he stayed. "Did you . . . used to live here, in Chicago?"

She pulled back from the magnetizing force, questioning a deceptive motive, and mouthed a quiet yes.

"What was your name?"

"What was my name? My name is Dora Stevens. What is the reason for your questions?"

He started to drop his raised guard but would not let himself yield to doing this. He was very well trained in how to deal with situations like this, but he revealed the truth instead of making up a lie. "I thought you were Jane Miller. My mistake, and I am sorry for the interruption. Let me make this up to you, my intrusion that is." He flagged the waiter who came there immediately. He then took the bill from the table, looked at it, and gave the waiter a one-hundred-dollar bill that he took from his lapel. He lowered his head to her at the table. "Dinner is on me. My apologies." He then walked away, gaining speed with each step. She was amazed by what he had just done. She got up from the table and started to walk in his direction, but after three steps, he was already out of view.

Sitting back down in the chair, she saw all the eyes in the restaurant looking at her. Well, naturally, after what just happened. She thought she'd better just go. No more dillydallying. I have to get answers and fast. The corpse is decomposing—the funeral has to happen and quickly.

Outside the restaurant, the sounds of the elevated railway system pounded in her head. The city was smoky. It always was. The beauty and history of the city ceased to be appealing. I need answers and fast. I want to leave tomorrow. With or without the answers, I have to leave tomorrow. She stopped walking and held herself tight, fighting off the blustery wind that came off the Great Lakes. She stood there fighting off the wind for countless seconds or minutes. In her mind, everything seemed like an eternity now.

She stopped at the front desk and told them that she would be checking out the next day. Since her flight was not going to leave until the evening, she asked if her luggage could be held there at the desk.

They could do what they said, but only for that day. She shook her head in agreement, then went upstairs to her room. Inside, before even taking off her jacket, she dropped her bag on the way to the telephone and called home to the pastor's house to talk to her daughter. She was pleasant through the small talk with the pastor's wife, tapping her clenched fingers quickly over the tabletop, nodding her head, and wanting only to talk to her daughter and get it over with.

Lauren answered her call and told her how busy she was, and she loved her. She then told her about two new music CDs that she wanted. Dora told her she loved her, and she'd be home soon, avoiding giving her an answer to the music CDs. She then asked if she could talk to the pastor's wife again. "Is she behaving?"

"Yes, she's quite polite, and the very first thing that she does when she gets here is open her schoolbooks and study. There is no phone or playtime until her homework is done."

Dora was pleased by hearing this and wondered how she could ever make that happen. She was thankful that it was happening now anyway. "Well, tell her that I'm going to try and be home tomorrow night or early the next morning. Thanks again very much for the help." She said good-bye and hung up. Standing up, she sighed deeply.

I want so much just to go to sleep. That bed looks so welcoming. I just want to sleep, not dream of my past, and no nightmares—I want answers. Oh, this whole quest—am I doing anything? She walked over to the table and opened the telephone book, trying to balance it on her lap and focus her sight on the small print. If I don't get the answer I need at the hospital, I can't just open the door to every convent and ask for a nun whom I saw at the airport, or was she just a planted decoy? Is there any pill so you don't dream? Coffee, you don't sleep.

Here it is—Medical. She placed her finger down the page, reading each listing. On the next page were ads describing various clinics, etc. On the bottom of the left page was a block advertisement—Institute for Psychoanalysis, Clinical Services for Adults and Children, South Michigan Avenue. She took a pen and paper and wrote down the address and phone number of the clinic, then placed it in her bag. Maybe I'll get somewhere after all. Tomorrow, the hospital, the clinic, the nunnery. She sat back and showed no emotion, blankness looking to the emptiness and silence in front of her. I'm chasing nightmares.

Transfixed in deep thought and still mesmerized by the mystery man in the restaurant, she felt he definitely knew something about her and her past. It was almost as if he was afraid, but with his magnanimity, how could he be scared? He captivated her to a degree that she wanted more—more of him or more of what he could give her. What could he give her alone in that room—lonely, lost, looking for answers or compassion? She thought more deeply that it wasn't something he could give her, but something that he reminded her of not something but of someone.

My mind is playing with me, and I'm not even on drugs. She talked out loud to herself in almost a whisper. The haunting resources of my mind. She rocked her body forward, leaning into an imaginary shield in front of her—trying to break it, needing answers, lost in flight, but still catapulted by something that felt more like a force than a feeling. I'm lost—she clasped her hands together tightly—Dora Stevens, Jane Miller.

I guess the only thing for me to do is rest, sleep or try to. She went to the bathroom to get ready for bed; and instead of coming out of the bathroom in her nightclothes, she came out wearing only her underwear, feeling the sultry heat of the night. Under the covers, she pulled the blankets off the bed, so only the white sheet was draped over her body. She felt the need of a man. What man do I want? I know him. I just don't know who he is. Unfortunately, I know he's not George Clooney. I like the guy, don't I? Well, I'm not thinking about the other one now, am I?

In talking to herself in the dark quietness of the warm room, she lulled herself to sleep. She stood looking at the edge of a shoreline; a light layer of clouds covered the sky to block the sun's piercing glow, but the warmth was felt. The peacefulness of Saturday afternoon in the park drifted through the sky. Peace, joy, and serenity filled the climate. The sky was filled with carefree laughter, a solemn celebration of life. Love lifted her heart; looking to her side view, she saw her husband, dark hair waving back from his face, light eyes that seemed to sparkle. He was pushing a baby carriage, their child. Suddenly, the sky became still. Gunfire penetrated the air; shaking uncontrollable fear embraced captivity. The carriage rolled from his direction. He reached inside his coat and took a handgun out and searched for the target, then fell to the side as a bullet lunged into his chest.

She saw her hand reach for the handle of the baby carriage and ran away. A police siren volleyed through the air but couldn't overshadow the screaming and the repeated echoing sound of the bullet. She was sweating, moving around, entwining her body in the bedsheet, rolling and trying to break free from the nightmare that pulsated through her skin with a numbing force. She fought to break free and rolled off the bed entwined in the sheet, hitting the carpeted floor. She opened her eyes wide in panic and desperation, and fright froze in her face the feeling of the living nightmare she had just experienced. The velocity of the heavy dream played with her conscience.

Unwinding the bedsheet from her body, she rolled to the foot of the bed and leaned towards the mattress, deeply gasping for breath. I lived a dream in that nightmare, but was it real? Is that what happened? They did something to me so that I wouldn't remember that. It's surfacing now because . . . I experienced a vestige of what happened. What happened has come to be. They can't find out. I was this other person. She pulled the sheet off the bed and wrapped her body in it, then went to the table by the refrigerator. She pulled out a bottle of water and pulled off the cap, then let the cap drop to the floor. The sound of it hitting the carpet was more than haunting, but she shivered with the occurrence, then collapsed in the chair. Then she took a swig of the water, then opened and closed her eyes.

Who do I call about what happened, about Jane? Should I ask, or should I run from her? I do feel that there is an evil force pulling at me. She let loose from her locked state and shook her head, huffing out to herself in a light laugh. I'm paranoid about something I know nothing about. Would I or should I call the police or the FBI to find out? Witness protection agency—that's how I got a new identity. They did something to my brain. She clasped her hands together and placed them in front of her lips, looking like she was praying; but she only breathed deeply into her fingers, still absorbed in a clenched fear.

My husband—did he die, or is he still alive? He was a—she stopped and ran her hands across each side of her head while breathing out ever so slowly—a gangster, but a good gangster. Oh yeah, a good gangster. Well, there are good and bad police officers. Were those real memories that volleyed through my mind? I mean, how could I have known?

I have to go somewhere tomorrow. Since I am here, I have to get at the truth. What archives do I go to? Back to the hospital? I have the lab coat and the combination code to the door. I've got to hide myself. That man in the restaurant—he must have been part of the group, the gang that my husband was in. He probably told his boss that he saw me, and now they're going to be looking for me. But maybe they'd protect me. There has to be a gang against them. I mean, someone shot my husband. My husband—I don't even call him by his name, Chris. She froze, then blinked her eyes, and moved her body. I don't want to go back to my life, but I have to hide. I'm not safe.

How did they get me to forget everything or just that part of my life? I was programmed or drugged, that's it. Today, medicine is the cure-all. I was drugged, but it stopped. Was I conditioned through therapy? Psychiatry? That had to have been it. Well, I've got the synopsis; now I just need the details and the right path to follow in the next course of events. The only thing to do now is get some much-needed sleep. Okay, George, you are the only thing I want to dream about or I could dream about going back to work. She made a sour face after making that comment. She folded the sheet back over the bed, wrapped herself loosely in it, and then replied, George, I'd much rather think about you, but—she looked at the time on the clock on the nightstand—seven hours of me I don't think you could handle. She laughed, then closed her eyes, praying for sleep.

In only moments, she could hear the sound of raindrops pulsating against the window. She breathed out softly and smiled. She loved the sound of the rain, something relaxing. This was more than what she needed right now, and she thanked the Lord for it. She sat up straight in bed, then reached forward for the blankets, and went back to sleep, thinking about George. Then his image was shadowed by Chris's smiling face. Sleep, I just have to have sleep. It came more quickly than she even knew.

Six o'clock in the morning, the sun could not even cast its shadow on the city yet. Rain clouds blocked every corner of the sky they could enter. The mood was gloomy. Though rain was not in the air, the cold moisture of the rain was evident. No light came through the partially opened drapes to the side of her bed. She was lost in the deep slumber that usually occurs in the early-morning hours. A vibrating pounding on the door to the room caused her to rise. She opened her eyes, gazed about, then closed them again, not wanting to come out of the realm of sleep.

She rolled out of bed, focused, and refocused her eyes, not being able to see in the darkness of the room. She reached for the lamp on the nightstand twice before laying her hand over the knob to turn it on. Then once on, she had to shield her eyes from the bright light, retreating from it. At this hour, you have to be kidding. Who or what? Her first inclination was to pull open the door to find the source of this intrusion; then she remembered the paradox from the day before. She looked out the peephole in the door ever so quietly. No one was there, or were they? They could be down the hall just out of view and able to still see who answered the door. She retreated back to the bed and covered herself in the blanket, scared and not knowing what to do.

She hadn't received her wake-up call yet, but it was too early. No bellman should be there to get her bag since she hadn't even checked out yet. It couldn't have been room service. She didn't order anything, and she wouldn't anyway. She lifted her body back up in the bed, sat up, and rested her hand on her forehead. My god, they know I'm here. Reaching for any possible clue to lead her to a different conclusion for the early-morning intrusion to her day, she silently trembled in fear ever so deeply.

Turning the showerhead to a warm stream, she thought that maybe somebody just could have been knocking on the wrong door, trying to get into their own room; but at that hour, it would have been highly unlikely. A prank—it could have been just a prank. Inside the shower, taking the soap bar to her skin, she more than decided to call a bellboy to get her bags and walk her to check out.

Dressed in a black pantsuit with a pale gray blouse, she looked in the mirror over the dresser in the bedroom, taking inventory of correctness. She reached inside her clutch bag and took out sterling silver post earrings, then put them on—subdued, yet fashionable, and not severe enough to go against medical dress code. She checked the time on her watch, then turned her head to see the time on the nightstand clock. The times correlated. In the next second, there was a light knocking on the door. She walked quickly to the door; then realizing there was the possibility it wouldn't be the attendant from the hotel and could still be the mystery man, she stopped in front of the door and walked as quietly as she could to it, looking ever so quietly through the peephole. A young male dressed in a hotel uniform waited there. She thought it was okay but then pushed her fist towards the door, waving it up and down. I can't go through the day in extreme paranoia. She opened the door and moved her arm in the direction of her suitcase for the attendant to take. She followed him out the door with her bag, a purse, and a notepad in hand.

Checkout went more quickly than she thought it would. A printed bill was already waiting for her as she turned in the key. The attendant looked at her in question as she asked him to help her out of the hotel. Once out the tall glass doors of the hotel, he set down her suitcase on the dark red carpet that led to the building. The coated man there waved a cab for her. Before she could even respond that she didn't want one, he assisted her inside the cab. She worried about the money for the cab fare and searched her mind for the nearest place that he could leave her that wouldn't be too suspicious for taking a cab, someplace close by that a tourist would ask for.

She looked forward to talk to the cabbie. The window between the backseat and the driver's seat was dark glass, so she could only see his outlined image. She leaned forward to knock on the glass to gain his attention and ask him to let her out. Just as she leaned forward to do this, he accelerated, and the jolt from the sudden movement pushed her back in the seat. She spit up; then as quickly as she could, she took a Kleenex from her bag to her mouth. The next thing she saw was the sign of the expressway, and further acceleration was felt. Dread and fright veiled her conspicuous face and body.

CHAPTER 6

What was the cause of this vicissitude? A malicious idiot eliminates, Chris the gang getting a high from a drug overdose and doing something to get on the evening news? Feeling trapped—a prisoner both inside herself and inside the cab—and daunted, vicious cycles of fear rolled repeatedly through her mind, and she remained unmoved and silent. Feeling her heart beat at her skin, it felt as if it was going to jump out of her body. Constrained in fear, she fought to remain in any way calm. The signs of the airport were overhead as the cabbie pulled in the front gates and drove through the parking lot. She breathed out quietly, trying to hide her deep breath. He was just driving to the airport as quickly as he could. Maybe the attendant at the hotel told him I was in a hurry to get there. Well, so much for finding anything else out today. There is still so much I need to find out and know, though.

Just as she relaxed her composure, she realized that she saw no doors inside the main airport, no gates, no attendants—nothing. She was . . . they were in the private parking lot to the side of the airport, and a few smaller jets and hangars were the only things there. She leaned forward, knowing that she couldn't fall back in a parked car, to get the cabbie's attention and find out why they were there or why she was there. No answer came. She knew that he had to have heard her even through the darkened, heavy glass, but no response was transmitted. She again asked him, screaming at the top of her lungs. His response was opening his door and stepping outside the cab, motioning forward, and talking to a heavyset man who then came forward. Instead of getting out of the cab, she turned behind her looking out the back window and saw a long black stretch limousine.

A large silver plane pulled up inside the cyclone fence near where the cab and the limo were parked. An older man was escorted out of the limo by two guards, one on each side of him, walking him to the jet. A uniformed airport worker stood in the machine cart where he was able to push down the door of the plane to release the staircase going up and into it. A dressed pilot ran up the stairs. It looks like I'm going somewhere. What gang am I going with? I'm probably being kidnapped or killed, but what do I know? Obviously, more than they want me to know. Why? Did I do anything? I should have stayed home and not questioned anything. It was like Lauren warned me.

The cabbie talked briefly with the other man who had met them there; then he turned back to the taxi and stood by the side of her door. After seeing the well-dressed older man who got out of the limo nod his head to him before he started up the stairs to board the plane, the cabbie then opened her door so she could depart from the cab. When Dora made no movement to get out, another man walked quickly to the open cab door and, once there, bent inside the opened door and put one foot inside on the floor of the cab and reached for her hand. Before she even knew it, he had a tight grip over her hand and pulled her right out of the cab. She frantically grabbed her bags as she was pulled out.

She stopped momentarily and looked at this man who had pulled her from the backseat of the cab, from the only security she had left. Anger and fear rose up in her, but then it was like a huge weight had been thrown on her when she saw the calm, handsome face of the captivating mystery man from the restaurant. She was still mesmerized by even his appearance. "You work for them?"

He started to answer her out loud then lightly, briefly half nodded his head to her, then looked forward to the jet. She knew he was bound to do as he was ordered, so she stopped her struggle and loosened her grip, but he still held her rigid. She had been caught off guard and relaxed a little seeing him. She knew that he wasn't her lost husband, but there must be a connection somewhere. A lost memory in the resources of her mind had to surface. More than halfway to the plane (the others had already boarded), she thought of asking him; but then she knew that they were probably being watched from the window, so she remained quiet. Walking up the stairs to the plane, she softly asked him if they were the gang that her husband had been a part of. He briefly stopped and looked at the sky, then back down to her as she still had her head turned behind her to look at his facial expression. He replied, firmly, "Yes, yes. That is clear sky atop of us. The morning clouds burned off."

He was given a questionable, almost-dirty look from the man waiting inside the plane for the doors to be closed. He walked in, then stopped before the open door to the forward cabin, and pulled the drapes closed; then he grabbed her tightly and led her to the bolted chair to the side of the closed window on the side opposite the door they had entered through. He proceeded to fasten her seat belt. She observed this, then said nothing. Then she was more than surprised to see him fasten an additional seat belt over her.

"Is this necessary? I mean, where could I possibly go on a closed airplane?"

"We won't be able to put the tracer on you until after we are out of the plane—possible interference with the controls."

"Where are we going?"

He didn't respond to her. He got in the seat opposite her, fastened his seat belt, and looked in her direction as if he was a guard. She thought he was definitely one of the liege men of the older man who must be the leader of the gang who was, as yet, nameless.

The plane started to taxi down the runway. All the shutters were closed over the windows on the side of the plane. The only thing that could lead her was her imagination. She looked straight across from her and to this mystery man. He was trained well—his face was emotionless. She thought she had to remain calm, but not too complacent. Before she knew it, the plane was rising up for takeoff. As near as she could figure, the plane was heading east. They were in Chicago and heading east. New York? Could that be where they were bound to, or maybe Europe? Italy? In that small plane, there was no way it would have the capacity to hold enough fuel to get to Europe. Canada? Get across the border? What were they carrying? Drugs? Were they picking up drugs or leaving off drugs? But then why did they have her? She was involved in the equation somehow. There was the importance of her being there. They had planned it all out, all the way from the hotel. I was followed. Just seeing me in the restaurant that night? Are they headquartered here? Well, yes, they would be—Chris worked for him, them. What is the head henchman's name? Don? Even if it is Don, what is the last name? Miller? That doesn't seem to be the name of an Italian gang, but then what makes me think it's Italian? What if it's Al-Qaeda, and we are going to Canada where they would be much freer to move around? That was the report I listened to that night on the radio that Michael Reagan gave. He talked of all the infrastructure in the country and how there were no laws stopping them from going there or being there.

Oh god, do I miss Lauren and home. Home? Will I ever see home again? Where are they taking me? I see no way of getting out of this. How long will be we up here in this plane? So many questions and no answers. Stay calm, be calm and cooperative. Mystery man over there seems nice. He knows he has me in his web. Maybe he'll let something slide eventually.

Deep into the flight now, there was no noise, no reaction from the mystery man whom she would have to name soon. Debating whether she needed to use the restroom, the feeling was more than clear. She definitely had to use it and soon. Looking at the statuesque hold he had over himself, she was almost afraid to break the silence by speaking. She lowered her head, then looked back up to the ceiling before resting her head at his eye level. She knew that she had his attention, but he made no affirmation of it. Swallowing deeply to make a sound, she then opened her mouth to blankness. He raised his eyebrow in question. That was all she needed. "Oh, this is embarrassing, but it has come to be sort of an emergency. I have to, I need to (he retracted his seat belt and stood up then walked over to her) use the restroom."

He made no verbal remark, just unlocked each safety belt and held her arm, walking her to the back of the plane. She was surprised at getting no remark and surprised at the quick motion he made in leading her to the restroom. Once there at the door, he stopped and released her arm. She was free. She just stood there. "What do you want me to do? Open the door for you or what?" He opened the latch on the door. "It's up to you now. I'm not getting any more involved than this." Embarrassed, she proceeded into the restroom and took care of business.

Opening the door, she found him standing there waiting for her, and she felt further embarrassed. Did he hear each sound that she had made?

He instantly took tight hold of her arm just above her hand and pulled her into a walking motion, returning to their seats. After they stopped, she stood there to the side of him, enjoying the freedom of just loosely standing there. He saw that she made no effort to sit back down, so he pushed her back to a sitting position in the chair. She wiped the surprised look off her face and closed her eyes, frowning at this new way of doing things. "Where could I possibly go? I'm not going to jump off the plane. I have a daughter that I very much want to see again. I don't want to end my life."

He lowered his body closer to hers while he adjusted the safety belts back over her. Then he mouthed words in her ear. "They're listening, and they're watching."

He raised his body up over hers, looking to her as a schoolteacher watching a schoolchild taking a test, wanting to expel her for any reason. She wanted to ask him about Chris. The words were going to roll off her tongue. She started to speak, then quickly realized the danger he was in, so she turned it into a forceful cough. He looked down to her and winked an eye. Then after a long minute, he asked her if she needed a drink. She shook her head yes. He opened the drapes, and she heard noise, but no one was talking.

The other people were behind that curtain. Fear resumed running through her veins. She looked at the drapes, then looked at the floor of the plane. He came back out from behind the drapes, holding a plastic cup of ice water. He walked silently to her, then handed her the cup of water. Without moving her head, she looked up at him and raised her eyebrows to show appreciation.

The plane became off balance with some sudden turbulence in the skies. There was no announcement over the loudspeaker of the plane to fasten seat belts, but it was clear that it was to be done. She proceeded to tighten her seat belts over her lap before the man could even reach forward to do it for her. He grabbed hold of the side of his seat to keep from being lifted off the floor in the shaking, off-balance plane. She knew she wasn't to speak, but she yelled the question to him, "What's going on?"

He remained calm in his composure even through the trembling skies. This only increased the level of her fear. A voice came from behind the closed drapes of the forward compartment. "We're going through turbulence. Stay quiet." Through the rough movements of the plane, she swore that she could feel the plane turn. Instantly, in her mind, she deduced that the turbulence just felt was planned as a decoy so she would not know of the change in direction. She felt uplifted in her heart. Maybe, in fact, they were headed back to the San Francisco Bay Area, and she'd see Lauren again. She decided the best thing for her to do was just remain calm and silent. It would be a long flight. She was going insane. She had to name him. He was captivating and good-looking, and he knew his job and followed the rules. He'd let her in on some truths that were being covered. He was captivating, like James Bond. She then figured she would refer to him as just Bond. That voice from the inside compartment—maybe they were warming up to her, or maybe they just didn't want to hear her scream.

The turbulence stopped. She was quiet but kept her eye on Bond and repeatedly looked at the partially opened drape. Suddenly, Bond looked like he had become unnerved. Whether this change in his behavior was caused by her or by something he was instructed to do, she didn't know. He got up, taking his eyes from her, and looked directly to the forward cabin as if he was already there. Inside, she could hear muffled conversation. Noise came from the galley area between the two cabins. Bond came back to her and placed a tray on her lap. She looked up at him instead of looking at the contents of the tray he had just placed on her lap. "What is this?"

"It's time for you to eat."

"Well, we have been airborne now for a long time. What about you? Aren't you going to eat?"

He raised his stance and became rigid in a guardlike fashion. "I eat after you, and I'm hungry. So hurry up and eat that."

She raised her eyes to him, then breathed out a sigh before looking down at the tray. Well, she thought, it couldn't be too bad. A sandwich, a pickle, and a Pepsi. She opened the wheat bread of the sandwich to see what was inside the bread.

For some reason, this excited Bond. "What are you doing that for?" "I just wanted to see what you want me to eat. It looks safe—an American cheese sandwich. I kind of expected something more or something different, but I'm not complaining." She tried to eat the sandwich in a calm fashion but found it difficult with the stare from Bond. It was like he needed to see every action of her chewing, and she couldn't figure out why. On the very last bite of the sandwich, the corner where each side of the crust met and there wasn't any contents inside, not even mayonnaise, the natural thing for a person to do would be just to leave it; but she knew she'd better eat it. She was scared to think of what he would do or say if she didn't. She picked up the can of Pepsi and gently shook it to find out how much remained. It was a third of the way full, so she knew she had enough soda remaining to wash down the sandwich. On chewing the last bite, she had trouble chewing it. Fighting the inclination to spit it out, she took the soda and downed it. She looked up at him and mouthed the words, "Did I just swallow something?"

He started to raise his head, then stopped, and continued rolling his eyes down. In a firm voice, he asked, "Are you finished with that?" She nodded. He walked forward to her, lifted the tray off her lap, and whispered in her ear, "You'll be out in about a half hour."

She whispered back, "You gave me a sleeping pill?" "Stronger. Placidyl."

The older man, the boss, opened the drapes and walked to her. She swore she already felt groggy, but she still could conceptualize things. He spoke to her. She had imagined him to have a stronger, deeper voice. His voice was actually quite pleasant and didn't carry the firmness that she imagined it would. "We just gave you a Placidyl, a drug in that sandwich. So in about half an hour, you will be out of it and more cooperative with us. You are going on a long trip, but you'll be staying in this country."

He looked at her, half turned his head, then looked back to her, and walked back into the forward cabin. Bond proceeded to check on her safety belts, then put a pillow behind her neck. She reached up and took hold of his right forearm. "Where are we going? Please tell me."

He pulled back, then stood there looking over her, bent down closer to her ear, and touched the side of the pillow; and before taking his fingers from the side of her head by the pillow, he replied, "Go to sleep . . . just sleep."

She then closed her eyes. The rest of the flight went smoothly. She remained asleep through the duration of the flight. Bond was called forward and instructed on the next course of action by the boss. He went back to his cabin as the plane started its slow descent for the landing. Dora was still asleep. He decided to try and wake her for the landing. She opened her eyes after much hesitation. She couldn't talk even though she tried; her speech was slurred. She commented that she felt confused. This was a result of the medication although there were a lot of other reasons for her to be confused right now. The landing went smoothly—as smooth as warm butter being spread on bread. Bond felt glad for this because of Dora's state. She sensed that he felt for her. He must have been one of her husband's friends although she could not remember.

CHAPTER 7

The plane taxied to a stop on the side of a private landing strip on a gated estate on the north coast of Oahu. She was helped out of her seat by the guard, Bond. He held her tightly to support her body and kept standing to the side of her while the boss and his two guards departed the plane first. Once they were down a few steps from the plane, he started walking Dora out of the plane and down the stairs. She had trouble balancing, and he held her from behind and kept his fists over her hands on each handrail. All of them successfully walked along the dark asphalt of the landing area to the side of the estate. The air seemed to pause. Bond knew full well what was to follow, and he lowered his body, holding her to his side while picking up the pace to a run to make it inside the gates of the estate. He yelled for the other guards to be on the offense. Gunfire riddled the air of the peaceful scene.

He pushed her down to the ground. She lay there silently, trembling in fear. He rose to call to the other guard after seeing one of the shooters aiming at them. "Troy, to your right! Cover the boss! Put him down and cover him!" He could see Troy combing over the area, still not putting the boss down. Bond ran to the boss and jumped down, covering him, and then rolled over the asphalt into a green orchid bush. Two other guards followed his movements and covered the boss while the other two returned fire. He ran back to Dora who was still paralyzed on the ground in fear. He couldn't move her at first, then yelled to her that it was him. "Release yourself, damn it! I'm here to help!" He moved as quickly as he could but still heard the oncoming gunfire and was in a dilemma about which way to move to keep her safe and out of the gunfire and still protect himself and both of their lives. She unclenched her body, and he was able to help her up off the asphalt, and they started to run.

Twenty feet from the fence close to the trees, he heard the sound of gunfire projected towards him. His instant reaction was to turn, duck, and fire back; but he was stopped by whom he had to protect. He pushed her into the line of trees just behind the boss and yelled to Troy. He turned towards the glare of the sun in the direction of fire and fired back. The sound of his skin bursting open and the warmth of his own blood hitting his body intensified his anger, and he fired rapidly, shrieking in rage in spite of the pain.

She had been first rolled over and then helped up and was now standing on the raised front porch of the estate by the front door. The boss had already been taken inside. She was being pushed forward into the house, but she had to stop and turn her head to see Bond. Hearing him scream, she cried. She sensed his pain and saw that he had been shot, but she couldn't see any more while being pushed inside the house. Troy told her to go over to the couch and that he was coming and was fine. She looked at him in anger. "He was shot, and you're telling me he's fine?" He sensed her stare, then looked away towards the back of the house to the boss. A man wearing a white lab coat ran from the raised tiled hall behind them into the room they were in. He checked the boss over and handed him a pill, which the boss swallowed with water given to him by one of the guards. The doctor then went to her to check her out.

She pushed him away. "I don't know who you are, and I don't want any more pills."

The boss looked at her. "Relax. He just wants to make sure you have no injuries from the attack."

She looked at the doctor who backed up from her and then went to the boss. "I'm sure that I have bruises, but I'm not going to show them to you. What about Bond? I mean, they shot him. Why aren't you getting help for him?"

The boss looked at her, concerned by the feeling she acknowledged towards Bond. "He is one of our trained guards, and how did you know his name?"

She sat back, perturbed. "What do you mean how did I know his name? He was watching me on the plane and was helping me inside this building. He was the only one who showed any form of feeling for me in this maze of confusion you are putting me through. He never told me his name. I had to give him a name. I just couldn't keep referring to him as 'Hey you.' He is a spy. I don't know—I referred to him as Bond, as in James Bond, the popular spy in the movies. He never did anything except the job that you gave him." The boss heard this but did not reply.

The door was pulled open by two of the guards. Bond entered holding a handkerchief over his bleeding wound. The doctor rushed to him, then walked him into the living room, and sat him in a chair on the side of the couch where Dora was sitting. He unwrapped the wound, then called his attendant for his bag. He cleaned the area of the wound with an antiseptic, then took forceps to open the cut and pull out the bullet that was lodged halfway in. The boss observed all this. "What is your bone made of? Steel? The bullet didn't break it." Bond looked at the boss and replied, "Something like that. An old war injury that seems to be protecting me right now."

"Are they still out there? How many of them were there—are there?"

"They're gone now. They had to pull three of them away. And yes, they are our rivals, the Del Marcos. They still have their style." Dora looked at him, showing a meaningful expression, then quickly realized the boss was watching and was already suspicious of her feelings for Bond. She quickly turned away, and instead of looking back at the boss, she moved her eyes to view the surroundings in this elegant room.

"I am sure that you have a lot of questions right now, questions for me, but you aren't going to ask them. You will be told things as you need to know them. You need protection, and that is what I'm doing. Right now, you are going to be taken upstairs. You'll be given your own room. Don't even think about escaping because there are guards all throughout the property as well as German shepherds. I don't want you getting hurt, so don't even think about trying to escape. I am protecting you."

She rose up from the couch; and at the top of the raised tiled hall by the side of the living room, she took her bags, tightly grabbing hold of one bag in particular. She was escorted up the stairway on the other side of the living room. Just as she started climbing the stairs, she paused, looking at him even after he finished his speech to her. Breathing out, she looked at the stairs below her then to the room, and focused on him. "So you are protecting me—thank you. What about my daughter, Lauren, in California? Is she still there? Is she all right? Are you going to bring her here to be with me?"

He paused, wavering whether to answer her, but then went against his will and answered her. "She is all right and safe. That is all you need to know right now."

A guard followed her up the stairs. She wished the guard had been Bond, but it wasn't. He was hurt, and hopefully, they were letting him rest. She picked up her pace going down the wide hallway, then was pulled back by the guard. She had passed the door of the room that was to be hers. He opened the door, then stepped back; but he put his hand forward, blocking her from entering the room. He went forward and took quick surveillance of the room while holding one hand inside his jacket to what she knew was a gun. The idea of going into a room, and that room being the room she was to stay in, was more than scary. She thought she should be ever so thankful that he was doing this. A house owned by a lead gangster, and there were people firing against them to kill them. Whatever did they do? What is the center of this ongoing war?

After the guard made his inspection, he opened the dark green drapes to the beautiful ocean scenery, then proceeded out to the deck then back inside, leaving the sliding glass door to the outside deck opened. He turned towards her. She remained unmoved. He then took her bags and set them on the floor by the closet, nodded his head to her, and left the room, closing the door behind him. She looked forward to the view and felt the cool ocean breeze waft through the room towards her. Then she turned her head to see the closed door. She had already deduced in her mind that it was locked but turned to the door anyway. It, indeed, was locked. She could not get out. This one room—though large, expansive, and beautiful—was going to be her home for an unknown amount of time. She thought to herself, How did I ever get involved with the mob? She was thinking about Bond, not her husband, feeling the love for her husband and missing him while thinking about another man.

She walked towards the balcony, then stopped by the edge of the bed, feeling suddenly tired; but she went forward and outside to feel the breeze off the ocean and to hear the gentle waves roll in and out. Seeing a chaise lounge and patio chair with thick light red cushions, she sat down, relaxed her body, and tried to relax her mind. In just seconds she rhythmically calmed herself watching the shoreline. *What else are they not telling me, or shouldn't I know or remember? Time is the answer, and that's a scary scenario.*

I'm so tired. I wish I could just make things the way I want them. She breathed out, hoping that breath would bring her an answer. Nothing. *Why, after all this time, is this coming back? I mean, did I never question anything? I lived life like a Stepford wife, happy. I guess I went off the beaten path when I bought that Alice Cooper CD. I shouldn't be punished for that, though. That wiseass young boy checker. He should be sentenced to listening to Lawrence Welk for that one.*

She got up and went back inside the room, then closed the sliding glass door to the outside deck area, wanting to feel safer. Inside the room, she stood with her back to the sliding glass door, then felt unnerved doing so. She went to the right of the door to pull the cord to close the drapes, then inspected the room to see what else was there and how she could figure out her life there. Straight across from the sliding glass door and wall of windows looking down to the beach and shoreline was the locked door through which she had entered the room. To the right of her was a room with a half-opened door, and she went inside to find a large bathroom—a marble-counter vanity with double sinks. *Well, I can wash my face in one and brush my teeth in the other.* There was a large sunken bathtub that had a showerhead coming from above the water faucet, and the toilet was in a small separate room that had a window. It could only be raised two inches then stopped. Dejected, she saw a basket on the counter between the sinks. It contained French-milled soaps, rose water oil, toothpaste, mouthwash, a toothbrush, body powder, and Opium cologne. They even knew that Opium cologne was her favorite. She stood back, disturbed by this. Then she rationalized that they knew everything about her.

There was a knock on the door to her room. She raised her body up, both surprised and scared, then hesitantly went to answer the door. She stopped with her hand halfway to the knob, realizing she couldn't open a locked door. "What do you want? Who is it?" Just in saying the words "Who is it," she hoped it would be Bond. She heard a man's voice but couldn't distinguish if it was his. They wanted to enter and asked her if it was okay. She responded yes and stepped back for the door to open.

To her dismay, it wasn't Bond. It was the other guard who had been in the living room standing next to the boss. His name had been conveyed to her there, but she couldn't remember what it was. He carried a large silver tray and entered the room. She didn't even remember seeing him close the door behind him, but it was closed now. He placed the tray down on the round maple table in the center of the room. He looked at her, watching her look at him questionably in silence. She watched him look down to the tray on the table, unsure of what to say—something she thought odd for these were well-trained liege men. "You don't need to respond. Just go. I am sure that you wouldn't tell me anything anyway. The boss has to do that, right?" He half nodded to her, then backed up to the door, took out a key that was the only one on the key ring in his pocket, and then unlocked the door so he could leave. I am a prisoner here. What about a fire? Well, I guess I can get out the sliding glass door to the outside, but then the dogs will get me. Maybe they'll call them off. I am going crazy. What is on the table? Closed bottles of water were on the table.

She breathed out, then opened and closed her eyes to weighted eyelids. I am tired. She put down the bottle of water, then went to the large king-size bed, pulled back the neutral-colored bedspread, and collapsed on the bed. Her body felt heavy. She was being pushed into slumber. Her mind went in circles, seeing her husband kissing her, then pushing the baby carriage in the park. Laughter filled the skies. Love filled the air. The impermeable feeling of heaven filled the earth. A shattering second-punctured life. A scream ran through the air to unforgiving reality. Her husband fell to the ground, bleeding. Life stopped in a web of dazed confusion and fear. Then Bond was there. He held her, making her safe, safe from the world, offering a torpor to reality. He was protecting her. It was him, not her husband, but why? Chris loved her, and she loved him. She saw him put the wedding ring on her finger; then the scene became shadowed by Bond's face. Was he there keeping them both safe? Did he want her, or did she want him? She wanted her husband but desired Bond.

This is crazy. I'm trapped in a phenomenon of life. Where is the magic cloak where I can just turn things back to the way they were? From life in California, which half of the country dreams of, to the smoky streets in the hustle of downtown Chicago, checking out hospitals, psycho clinics, and, oh, convents! I miss my daughter.

Where is she? I hope she is safe. She took her hands and clasped them to her lips, then lightly turned her head back and forth. Bond, Bond . . . How do I get out of here? She walked to the sliding glass door, opened the curtains, and looked out the closed door. I don't even see any birds around here. She breathed out a heavy sigh. They'd be shot by all these henchmen around here. How do they make money? The days of bootlegging have ended. Prostitution. There couldn't be that much money in that. I mean, to afford this house and wherever else he has forts. Forts. Well, what else could you call them—command centers?

She stopped, then went back to the table and sat down. There is just so much I need to know, like Chris. What is his father protecting me from? She quickly remembered the gunshots fired at her as they departed from the airplane. She sighed deeply, then felt her eyes start to tear up. I should be thankful, very thankful. It's just, just, how does a bird get out of its cage? When are they going to let me out of this room? No phone, no radio, no television, no books . . . no birds. The only thing I can do is sleep. She went to the bed and looked down to it. Sleep, then I'll have more dreams, dreams of Chris or Bond? Bond is probably married with two daughters. Yeah, he is one of the kidnappers who should be the bad guys, but they aren't because they are protecting me from other bad guys who are after them. She lay down on the bed.

Downstairs, the boss sat at his desk in his office—an office that you wouldn't expect to be that of a mobster. A clear window leading out to a porch was on the right side of him by the desk. The door from the house was directly across from the desk. The room was light, and the desk was clear glass. There were oak-stained file cabinets and storage cabinets behind him. A telephone was the only office machine on his desk. A computer sat on a small table to the left of the desk. He was dressed in a beige lightweight cotton short-sleeved shirt and had darker beige long shorts on. He also wore thick brown-lensed eyeglasses.

"Yes, Lorenzo, tomorrow's shipment, twelve hundred . . . what do you mean 'That is robbery'? I'm giving you a break. You are supposedly bringing in coffee. First of all, importing coffee in Hawaii when we have the best here. Now Italian coffee I could see. The flavor is much different.

But plain coffee beans, I guess, for the markets? But I am protecting your ass. I know what you have hidden in the crates of coffee beans. Thank God you have them sealed. They are never to be opened in the warehouse. Do you hear me? Or that is the end. You bring in your trucks immediately, transport them from the ships and onto your trucks, and drive away. I have guards watching the area of the docks so that there will be no interference. I don't believe in what you're doing anyway." He leaned back in his chair, then lifted the phone back to his ear. Finishing the last sentence, he raised his voice. One of the guards from outside came in, looking to him to see if there was anything wrong. He shook his head no, then waved for the guard to go back outside. "Yes, I am still into the horses, and I know you are too. There will be a dead horse in the stall if anything goes wrong here. Yes, and the money will change hands in the usual fashion."

He hung up the phone as Bond entered the office holding a large manila envelope. He took it from Bond, then opened it, taking out typed 8½ x 11 inch papers with no writing of importance on them. Then a computer disk fell out. He told Bond to load it in the computer then for him to leave. He nodded and did this. Right before he left the office, the boss called back to him. "She is going to be getting edgy. I know that she likes you, and the two of you were talking to each other on the plane. Don't think that just because the drapes were closed and it looked like I was sleeping that I was." Bond looked straightforward, trying not to view him in the eye, making no expression show on his face. "This afternoon, you two are going to take a walk on the beach. If the dogs don't like her, I'll have them tied up. I am sure that you will not tell her anything because you know your job." Then in a deeper, hushed tone, he added, "Right?"

Trying to hide any emotion, Bond looked forward, then down and back up immediately to the boss's eye view and nodded his head, responding, "Yes."

Bond left the office, and the boss watched his every move as he walked away. The phone rang, and the boss looked at the phone, mentally counting the rings and answering it after the fourth ring. "Yes?" He heard the voice on the other end and instantly smiled. "You're in Los Angeles?" He listened to the voice respond to him, then answered back, "Good thinking. Make as many contacts as you can. So where are you?"

"I'm at the Koi Restaurant in West Hollywood—the usual table 13. The people who know this place know that this table only goes to the right people."

The boss heard this and was satisfied. Then he heard the sound of ladies' laughter. "So you're entertaining the ladies? You know, you better watch it in more ways than one." He said this with a firm, authoritative voice. The voice on the other end told him that he knew that; he just needed to put up a front while there, and a single man dining alone would draw too much of the wrong kind of attention. The boss didn't like what he heard, but he agreed with him. The boss wanted to remind him that he was a married man but thought it better not to. "Well, I can't tell you what to do anyway. You are too headstrong, like me. Just watch it."

"Over and out, Captain." The phone was hung up on the boss who didn't like what he heard or the fact that he was hung up on and not the other way around. He was the only person who could deal with the boss in that fashion, and the boss sometimes wondered why, but then he knew the answer.

Seeing that the room was clear, he got up and closed the two open doors—the door to the patio and the door to the inside of the house. The room was soundproofed, and they inspected it twice a day for bugs. The boss liked to talk out loud to himself; it made him think better. The East Coast is taken care of, and we still have a hold on certain docks in Europe. He is working on Florida. He stood back, then walked forward and turned. Well, I know we have the docks in Mexico. And if they are in Mexico, Oregon is easy. It's just an inside commute. They take it there themselves. With all the yuppies in Washington, they look for us there. The people that want it anyway. We're just dealing with the transportation, not with the merchandise. We are just the mediator involved with boxes of what we know to be coffee beans. I run a coffee business. That is why Italian coffee beans come into the island of Hawaii.

Upstairs at the outside of Dora's door, Bond stopped and turned around to see if he was being watched. He saw nobody, but that didn't make any difference. He knew that somehow, he or they were being watched. In this business, nothing was easy. He had never had to get himself to come to grips with anything before doing it, but right now, he was having trouble. He felt passion; but was it in his heart for her situation, or was it for her? The boss's wife had died, and in his heart, no woman could ever replace her. It was something that he knew hurt the boss, but the boss never talked about it. He had things that would remind him of her taken from the estate. It wasn't that he was trying to forget her, for he prayed to her every Sunday in church. It was just too painful for him to have reminders. Right now, after the shootings that had just happened right there at the estate, he knew his foremost job was to protect the Mondello family; and Jane was a member, a long-forgotten member who had been given a new identity and a new life. The boss knew that someday, she would remember, and that day was coming near. Did the boss have a plan for this? The boss had a plan for everything. He never divulged any of his weaknesses to anyone except himself.

Bond knocked on the door in a firm, rough, loud knock. Dora looked forlorn sitting on the edge of the bed. She breathed in and huffed at the idea of being checked on again, feeling like a caged animal. I've lost myself, something that until the last few days I never questioned. I mean, how do you lose a person? She talked to herself while walking to the door. Am I Dora, or am I Jane? I am so confused. But mentally, I just want to go back to what I had, what they made for me—the life that they made for me. She breathed in, absorbed her feelings, and answered the door though she couldn't open it. She could just respond that she was there. The door opened, and when she saw that it was Bond, she more than had to compose herself and raise her voice to an even tone before opening her mouth.

In a slow, deliberative voice, he spoke to her questioning glare. "The boss told me to take you for a walk on the beach."

Her heart uplifted, and in a meek voice, she responded, "That would be nice." She started out the door but was blocked by his locked, firm body there at her door. She took her head back, tilted it, and looked at him questionably. "Well, I thought that you asked me if I wanted to take a walk with you, and I responded yes. I thought that meant that we would go somewhere, or do you just want to walk around the inside of this room?"

As if he hadn't even heard her words, he moved his body to the side, leaving the entrance of the doorway open for her to make her way out the door. She didn't even see him move his feet. She wondered how he did what he did but thought it better not to say anything about it. He was by her side until they reached the stairway; then he put his arm to block her movement, and he walked down the stairs first but kept one of his hands tightly over hers until they reached the bottom floor. Then he stood to the side of her in the same fashion as he did at her room.

Seeing the front door, she started in that direction. He pushed her back and told her that they would be leaving out the back door on the other side beyond the living room, the side away from the boss's office towards the kitchen. She was interested in seeing what was there inside the house. The Italian boss's kitchen should be something to see. She imagined bricks and a large iron stove, red flowers, and baskets of fresh fruit and Italian breads. She was quite surprised that the kitchen was plain white, with white appliances and white tile. There was a bowl of fruit, but nothing to reflect in any way an Italian theme in the decorations. On the island of Hawaii, large wood-burning ovens like the kind used to bake pizzas were probably banned. What was there sufficed for the needs of the household.

Bond had her stand still behind him in the kitchen as he opened the glass door to the brown-tiled patio outside. He stepped to the perimeter of the surrounding area holding his handgun. He glanced up at one of the guards standing by a tall palm tree. The guard turned in the direction of another guard and then nodded his head to Bond, signifying that it was safe to go out to the outside grounds of the estate. She observed all this and thought it kind of neat. She was a spy's girlfriend in a spy movie. She then remembered the fear, and the feeling of being in a crime drama flew from her soul. Subdued paranoia captured her nerves as she walked rigidly out the door tightly holding Bond's hand.

It must have been one hundred yards to the beach and the ocean, but it wasn't a direct walk there. First, they had to walk along the porch and then around the left-hand side of the house where the tile patio ended. There were three wooden stairs that you could not see from the house. She felt the mist from the ocean waves, a feeling that usually should have calmed a person along with the serenity of the rhythmic sound of waves breaking on the shore, but relaxation was the farthest thing from her mind. She had desperately wanted out of that room, and the area outside seemed like heaven, but now being there harbored a different feeling far from what she had expected. Bond was there holding her hand too firmly for comfort. She tried her hardest to convince herself it was . . . he was . . . for her own protection, but like the actions of a windstorm, she just wanted to hurl herself out of it—out of the whole scenario, the picture that she had been put in. They stopped, and Bond looked down at her. She felt as though he knew what had just gone through her mind and the way she was feeling. It looked like he wanted to say something to her, but the demands of his job held him back from doing so. She then thought that they were probably bugged somehow and that the boss was sitting back in his desk chair, ready to take notes or give orders on anything that she did or said. She didn't even know what to think anymore. The only good thing she could correlate with this gang, the Mondellos, was her missing husband, Chris. In just thinking of Chris, she heard the gunshots again that had been fired through the air that day in the direction of their baby. Then she saw him moving his body to protect the baby and her from the gunfire. He took the bullet, the bullet that she knew ended his life. The great love that half the world and the country always dreamed of was gone, gone in a shaking, fearful, dreadful, panicked second. Everything ceased—love, meaning—and she was then hurled unknowingly into a made-up life. She now wavered through reality, looking for her subconscious to open the door on the locked truth.

A teeter-totter in her mind jolted her from wanting to know the answers to running back to hide in the safe life that they had made for her. Lauren, she missed Lauren so badly she could cry, but she couldn't let them see that. It would mean that they were winning, but what were they going to do with her, and what was going to happen to Lauren? They must know about her. Maybe she was there or would be brought here. Bond knew that she liked him, liked him too much. She had to make this stop. She felt for him, she needed closeness; and he offered it, but he was part of it. He was one of the ones holding her there, trapped in an inferno in the scenic, unspoiled beauty of tranquil Hawaii. She tried to loosen the grip Bond had on her hand. He momentarily released his tight grip but then tightened it again ever so slightly.

He led her to the soft, sandy beach, and she hesitantly followed him. "Can we just stop, please?" He stopped before taking his next step and held her tight to him, looking at her. "Please, I just want to stand here and relax. You . . . you must . . . what am I saying? Can't you talk to me? I am just supposed to be here but not say anything or feel anything. Just be here, right?" She tilted her head to him. He said nothing, just remained there in silence, passive to her words. "You're not my friend. A friend wouldn't treat anybody like this." He remained silent, looking to the sea. "You probably didn't even know Chris, and you weren't a friend of his or mine. The boss probably just hired you last week and filled you in on a few details. I'll stay here and conform to this doll image that all of you here want me to be. Do you know what it is like to have a life and then get taken out of it? What happens to the people that you love and care about? Can I just forget about my feelings, and possessions? Maybe that's it—I am just a possession. Does the boss get more points for me, for having possession of me? What is it like in this world, the world of the underground, illegal something, hit men?" She stood there waiting for answers, but none came. He just continued to stare at the ocean waters. She breathed out loud through her nose, then shook her head back and forth. She wanted to say something else. Words started to come from her mouth, but then she stopped and remained there standing beside him, looking out to sea. She noticed that they were being watched, watched by the guards at every tree and various other places on the estate.

"Well, we are on the beach. Let's walk." She started out and picked up the pace, pulling him along for a change. He quickly gained his footing and took the lead. In doing this, she knew that she had gotten to him, but he would never let on. Well, that is the way she would play it. They got to the middle of the sandy beach; then he stopped.

He grabbed her more tightly, then twirled her around, pointing towards the side of the house. While doing this, he firmly but quietly responded back to her, "Look, lady, I'm the only one that you have here on this island on your side. Don't push it. You'll find out things when it is safe for you to know." He then pushed her back to the direction of the sea and motioned her to follow him up the beach to the west tree. She looked confused and scared at his sudden, quick motion. In talking to her while in the act of turning, he had shielded his talk from the guards and the boss if they were watching. "Let's go sit down on that bench over there."

She looked to where he pointed. "There is no bench over there. How can we go sit on a bench? There isn't a bench there." She looked at him for a response, but none came. She then looked back to the sandy shore of the beach and saw two guards delivering a wooden bench to the very spot where he had pointed. They were being watched or listened to, and he must have given them some visual sign, but what? You can't turn away for a second. At the side of the bench, he put his hand forward for her to sit there first. She raised her eyebrows at him, then sat down. "What is going to happen next?

Will we be brought piña coladas?" She moved out her hands while talking, and to her surprise, a drink was placed in her hand. It was in a long icy tulip glass, and a paper umbrella laced the top of the drink along with a piece of fresh pineapple and a cherry. She looked quite surprised.

"Well, it's not a . . ." Bond spoke in an eloquent fashion towards her as he had a drink in his hand too. "It's a lLonge Island Icd tea. There is liquor in yours, but none in mine." She looked at him questionably. "What other liquor would there be on the island? Rum. I know you'll like it, so drink it."

"Well, I will then, just so I won't offend you." If there was ever a good excuse to drink, she just gave it to him. After taking a swallow, she wanted to breath out an "Ah" of relief and "Oh so good" to the taste, but she wanted to remain calm and quiet. Oh, what the hell. "It is good. Thank you, Bond. Bond—that can't be your first name."

"Why would you need to know my first name?"

"You're right. I'll stop asking you questions. I'll just relax and enjoy this drink." He leaned back, then regained his posture in the chair, and smiled at her. "Is it okay for you to talk now? I mean, I won't ask you anything about the supposed gang's activities." Just as she finished this last word, she thought better. She should not have said anything, especially this. She just decided to keep it low, quiet, blend in to what they wanted, and try to pick up on everything that she could.

Bond looked at her assertively. "I thought that you thought it better to play it low?"

She started to twist her neck to him after hearing this comment from him. How could he know—know what she was thinking in her mind? He was a mind reader. That is why he was assigned to her, that and the fact of his persona. She would melt, being captivated by him. She was a single woman who had urges, but they were just opening up, and her husband was not there to fill them. Was this part of the gang's plan—to get her teamed up with him, keep her quiet from her emerging feelings and knowledge? She thought it best just to stay silent.

Bond looked at her in an even temperament, calm, relaxed. Before he verbally responded to her, she looked away back to the quiet, sweeping ocean tides. "There is a lot that you want to know and a lot that you will be told. The main thing for you to do right now is just wait, and let it happen. Things will happen. You will be told things that you need to know when you need to know them. Don't be concerned of your daughter's safety." He stopped his conversation almost abruptly. He had divulged too much information to her. She knew this but remained calm and quiet, knowing that if she showed any emotion, he would close up on her. She felt she had regained his trust. He did feel for her. She didn't know now to hold her feelings and emotions towards him. She definitely felt for him. In just that moment, she envisioned holding him, touching him, and how his skin would feel; but then she thought quickly to change her thoughts, feeling that he picked up on everything. It was scary yet comforting at the same time. Why didn't she stay in Chicago longer to find out more before they took her? She was fleeing something, maybe an inert feeling from the past that was telling her something. Maybe this was the best place for her to be right now for her safety and her daughter's safety, keeping her out of danger. The gunshots vibrated through her mind once again.

She took another sip of her drink and smiled at Bond. He looked at her like he knew her feelings. She wanted to be receptive and had much difficulty holding back and keeping herself calm. "Things will get better, and I think you know how to play things right." She leaned back, composed by the sudden calmness that filled the sky. If he did know her feelings, this was going to be risky, keeping her feelings for knowledge and her feelings of desire under wraps. He moved his relaxed composure away from her on the bench just inches, enough to read into the movement and what it represented. A strictly Platonic relationship was all that could emerge and maybe not even that with the presence of the boss, which was transmitted through everything surrounding life there on the island.

She thought she should immediately spring into dialogue to keep him there in that instant, mostly so that she would not have to return to the room upstairs and be held prisoner. "What island are we on? I know that we're in Hawaii, but there are four islands, aren't there?"

He looked at her, smirked, and then looked into her eyes. "No, there are actually eight islands here in Hawaii. You are on the north side of

Oahu. The state tree is the kukui, the state flower is the hibiscus, and the state bird is the goose."

She pulled back her head and closed her eyes. There is no small talk with this guy. A goose. "You've told me that I will have a long stay on this island. I will need some more clothes."

"Yes, that you will. What size are you?" She retracted back, thinking it a personal question—you never ask someone their clothing size, especially their shoe size, unless they're an underweight fashion model. He noticed her hesitancy. "Come on. You have to know your size. Do you want me to read the label on the back of your blouse?" She lifted up her eyes, then thought, Well, that is one way to get close to him, not the right way though. She breathed out, took a sip of her drink, then swallowed, and composed herself. "I am a size 12, dress, top, pants—the whole shooting match. And shoe size 9½ m, underwear size 6. And I hope you don't need a bra size." She was embarrassed and moved her head down trying to conceal it.

He laughed inside himself, then looked at the beach. "I'd say a 36B."

In an even tone, she responded, "C."

"You will have them on your bed tonight."

"You are going to go clothes shopping for me?"

"Well, I don't know if it will be me, but one of us here on the estate."

"How will you know what to buy, what I like?" She looked to him for an answer, but there was none forthcoming. "I hate purple. Nothing purple. I don't like orange either."

"Yeah, I agree. You look too fat in orange, don't you?"

"Yeah, kind of like a melon." They both enjoyed the light moment but knew that there couldn't be too many of these.

"So basically, am I just supposed to eat, drink, smile, and remain quiet and behave?"

"Basically, that's it. And believe me, you want to do that. What you have to do now is establish trust. What swimsuit size are you?" She looked at him, defending herself from this invading question. "Well, you are here in paradise. There is a private beach out there. You will want to go swimming if you know how. It will be one of the few things that you will be allowed to do."

"Well, yeah, that would be nice. I do know how to swim. I wear a size 12 like I told you earlier. And as for the suit, a one-piece, please. No bikinis."

He looked at her and smiled. "Bikinis. Aren't those only for fashion models?" She smiled and nodded her head to him.

He rose up and took her by the hand. "Don't tell me that it's time to go in already."

He turned them back to the direction of the house, already leading her to the back door. "It's time to go in now, but if you behave, you'll see some of the inside of the home. Don't ever go to the master's den, though. All of us, including me, only go there after we are given orders to."

She looked around closer inside the kitchen. The double ovens had a GE monogram on them. She squinted trying to read the monogram on the refrigerator. He could see her trying to read it. "It's a Kenmore."

"The boss has a Kenmore?"

"Don't talk about things like that, and remember what I told you about being quiet and your behavior. Now is the time to prove yourself. I will not be talking to you. The boss is watching." The boss walked into the kitchen and led her out the door to the next room with a large dark-wood dining table. He sat at the middle of the table with his back to the wall, and he motioned for her to sit down opposite him. He nodded his head up to Bond, who immediately left, like a trained pet. The nonverbal communication that was carried on here was scary, something she didn't know how she would ever master or decipher the meanings of.

Behind the boss was an area the size of a china cabinet, but there was not one there. There was a raised wooden bar with the same stain as the table. A large copper cappuccino machine was in the center of the bar. The cabinet underneath held a stainless steel half refrigerator. There were espresso cups to the side of the machine as well as a glass sugar jar and a religious metal figurine of the head of Jesus. To the side of that was a metal figure of the Mother Mary with a halo over her head.

He was handed a cup of hot espresso, then given the sugar jar. She watched, observing everything, and was surprised that the guard standing behind him did not do this for him. He spooned one spoonful of sugar into his coffee and then was handed a plate holding a freshly peeled and sectioned orange. He looked at her face though held back from looking directly at her. He offered her coffee, but she declined. She was fearful and trying to hide her trembling, racing body the best she could, not wanting him to sense this, yet knowing full well that he did. She wanted to run the length of the island to release the tension and escape, but she sat there silently, unsure of what to do.

"You are here because I want you to be. You went to Chicago, and why you did that . . . you were supposed to have forgotten everything. Treat everything that you remember as a dream. It is just that. You have no proof of anything that happened. When you need to know something, anything, I will tell you." He lifted a piece of orange and put it forward, offering her some. She put her hands up, signifying that she didn't want any. He shrugged, recoiled it backward to himself, and ate it. "You will never taste an orange sweeter than this one." She didn't want it but decided to put her hand forward and take some to please him. That was what this whole play was going to be—doing everything and pleasing the boss in every possible fashion, which she hoped would be peaceful and legitimate.

She wanted to ask him about Chris so badly. It was just how to approach it. He told her, Bond told her, that she couldn't question anything; but he was the one love of her life, her husband, and their love had been so deep. Songs were written expressing the need, want, and desire for the love that they had; and now it was gone. No one denied that the marriage existed. Chris was real. Could he still be alive? It was just such a deep and emotional issue. The boss had feelings, too. His only son. He had already lost his wife. He didn't talk of her and certainly made no emotion or talk of Chris. It was just too painful. She thought that she shouldn't dare mention it or him. The answers would come to her as she needed to know them, just like they told her. What was she doing defending them? She was scared; but more than just being scared, there was a strict demeanor that she was going to have to follow, and she knew it. It was just how to keep her thoughts inside herself.

The boss looked at her, expecting her to say something to him. The floor was open for her to make conversation, and she knew it. "You just told me, and told me previously also, as well as being told by your man Bond, that I cannot question things—during my stay on this island, this place of yours, which is a very nice place to say the least. The boss. I know that you are the boss. Believe me, I do and will respect you, but to call you boss? You must have a name, a name that I can address you as." She looked at him hopefully and a little reluctantly, fearful of his response.

"No one here calls me by my name. That is because I have no family here. You are related to me—by marriage to my dear son." He stopped and looked sorrowful after saying that, which led her to think of Chris's demise. He didn't know what else he should say to her right now. He didn't want to make her feel too comfortable.

He started to respond back to her, thinking that he'd tell her. Well, if she didn't want any coffee or fruit, she could go back to her room; but the boss would never open a sentence with a preposition. He finished another wedge of orange, then drew back his head, and took a small sip of espresso. "You don't want anything. You will go upstairs to your room."

She was surprised and didn't like this option. She quickly retracted. "Is the option for coffee still open to me? I would very much appreciate a cup and the presence of your company for me to listen to and not to question." He liked what he heard but still did not trust her. It just proved he was dealing with a smart woman, and he liked that. His guard came up to his side and poured her a cup of coffee, then handed her the cream and sugar. She looked to the boss in appreciation but reveled in how the guard got there without ever being seen. How was he given the order to serve coffee to her? She was definitely being watched. The boss had some way of knowing these things and conveying the message to his staff, guards, and servants. But how? Finding the answer to this mystery was intriguing all by itself.

The short cup of espresso was placed in front of her. She normally always put creamer in her coffee, but she thought that doing this might not be welcomed by the boss, Vincent. He was a proud man, and coffee was his business, so she had better just savor the cup of freshly brewed espresso and savor it with all the gusto she could contrive. She swallowed, and her immediate reaction was to wince at the strength of the brew. It was far different from the dishwater with milk Italians would call American coffee. She changed the look of bitterness to conjure up a look of surprise and delight in the aroma of the potion.

The boss laughed watching her. "You know how to act it out. You'll get used to it—the taste. You will get used to a lot of things, things the way they should be. I will arrange to have your American brew made for you. It will be on the table in the morning waiting for you. Breakfast here is served at seven o'clock. You might think that is early, but God has given us this beautiful part of the day, and we are to make the most of it." She nodded her head to this comment, then thought of a man so religious who goes to church, prays, commits himself to the Lord, yet kills people. Was it righteous for these people to die? Only God has the will to judge people. Their lives were given to the earth by him. How could we take possession of that?

To break the stillness of the moment and not have him try and read her mind, she asked him for a piece of orange. The guard handed her the plate containing the orange sections. She took one of them, then motioned for the guard to give it back to the boss. She took a bite into it, and it was as sweet as candy with the most penetrating orange flavor—delicious. It was the boss's, so it had to be good. He probably had it flown in from Italy on the jet that morning. Not wanting to drink any more of the coffee and to get away from the discomfort of the prying silence of the room, she put her head up to his direction to speak to him. "I know my only other option is to go to my room. It's just that I did enjoy the peacefulness of the outside so much and the fresh air. I know there is probably obvious trouble in me being out there, but you seem to have guards. Could you appoint one of them to watch me? I will just sit out there quietly and unmoving." She was smart in the way she asked this question.

He looked to her and huffed. Whether it was that he didn't like the new way that she was handling herself or that he knew of the clever way she conveyed the question to get the answer that she wanted was unclear. He raised his head to the side where another guard stood, one that she hadn't seen or met yet. With the guard at his side, the boss stood up and whispered words that she could not hear in his ear. He then told her to go outside to the patio with the guard. She was to stay there on the patio and not go out any farther, not to the beach or anywhere but only the patio that adjoined the house; and if she did not follow these orders, she was never to have any say in what she did again. She nodded her head and got up and walked outside to the patio with the unnamed guard.

Outside on the patio, she moved to the table and sat down on one of the large cushioned chairs. The guard did not sit down. She looked behind her where he had positioned himself. He looked to his wristwatch and touched something on it, then looked at it like he was reading a response. This whole new world was something new to her, but it was the ever-increasing push in technology of today. She had to gain acceptance corresponding to the will of the boss, and gaining trust was the key. She felt tired, like a weight was pushing on her—the weight of fear, uncertainty, and having to overcome the urge to fight being dominated. She had to drop her hard will and grasp at something, something to move ahead. The weight moved heavy over her eyelids. Silence prevailed over the world. Rest, rest. Before she could even think her next thought, she was asleep sitting upright in the chair. The guard observed all. She was safe.

CHAPTER 8

Bond came back in the front doors of the house. The boss could hear someone enter and asked one of the guards to find out who it was. The guard went to the front door and saw Bond who took the covered clothes to the upstairs bedroom to Dora. The guard went back to the office and told this to the boss. The boss nodded and waved him away. Both guards were in the office with the boss as he read through the latest information from the computer papers placed on his desk.

Upstairs at the entrance to Dora's room, he set the flat covered vinyl garment bag on the floor and took the key to the door from his pocket. He then opened the door and picked up the bag from the floor and grabbed four paper store-named shopping bags, then walked to the bed, and set them down. He breathed in that something did not seem right. She wasn't there, but still, something was different. The room and the estate were guarded. Nothing could be there. He froze his body looking forward. What was behind him? He felt a presence. He shielded his movement as he was trained to do and took his revolver from his inside lapel, then turned in one swift motion, stopping rigid directly to the back of his former view. He made instant focus straight in front of him. There was nothing there. Then he looked to the floor without moving his head. Nothing. He turned his view to the ceiling. It was there. His heart stopped, but he could not surrender to the laughter he felt. A bird had flown in the room and was flying in circles against the walls, trying to find a way to escape.

He went to the bathroom, took a long beach towel, then snapped it towards the bird, leading it to the open sliding glass door out to the deck so the bird could make its escape. He then took his pager-cam and pressed buttons and left a message for the staff to come to that room and clean it. He went against his better judgement and walked to the open window and looked outside. He was not to be seen in this room, but he had the inclination to check it out anyway. Everything looked as it should be. He then saw Dora sitting on the patio chair. His eyes checked for the presence of a guard even before his brain could tell his eyes to do so. She was covered, safe. He then saw her look up and spot him. He turned his body away from the deck and window in a stealthy motion. She took a second look and saw only emptiness but still wondered. There were still emotions—and hope—in her heart for him. He made tracks as though in flight to leave her room, leaving the door to the room unlocked for her return without him having to be there to unlock it for her. His trained mind knew of the danger of the insurgent forces.

Dora sat there quietly so as not to have the guard take her back inside the house. Her mind rallied for things to do, anything. She felt like a pawn. If she moved in any way, there would be a capture of her by one party or the other. She had to blend herself in with the organization, this new way of life. She had only seen this in movies and heard about it in history. She felt like part of the supporting cast in *The Godfather*. Women did not have a good outcome. She would change things. The only problem was she didn't know how yet. She fought with her overwhelming need for rapture from Bond, which, at the present moment, seemed to overshadow the need for the truth. Passion had just absorbed her soul.

The boss sat back at his desk, resisting the suggestion from his guard to go upstairs to his bedroom and lie down. Instead, he sat back in the chair, leaning his body down, transfixed in thought. He saw the guard still seated at the computer station in the dark room and waved the guard who stood by the patio door over to him. "Help me upstairs." The guard stood to his side as he had trouble lifting his body up and off the chair. It seemed like he should have been helped up, but everyone knew not to help or touch the boss unless he asked for it, and he never did. The only exception was Chris. Chris mattered above all else. He was the only family link to the boss.

The guard opened his bedroom door and took a quick sweep of the room and connecting bathroom. Everything was clear. The boss signaled the guard to leave, then gave a slight smile to show his appreciation, something not normally done by him. He went to sit on the side of the bed. He reached for the lamp on the nightstand and turned it on, then opened the drawer, and took out a framed picture of his dead wife. He held it up and then placed it down on the nightstand. He lay down on the bed, then instantly turned to his side to view the picture. Oh, Christina, what have I done? I know that you miss him too. I need him. He is the only thing that I have—my son, my only connection to you. The Lord took you too early, but it was my fault. You just went to tend to your garden. It was such a beautiful day. The sun was shining, the birds were singing, and all troubles had ceased. I even lost my consciousness to my life, the life that I put you in. One bullet from the unguarded hillside above the garden on a Sunday afternoon. You didn't stand a chance, and no one heard it until it was too late. I miss you. Tears fell from his eyes. He did not wipe them; he just turned to the side, looking up to the ceiling, looking to the direction of heaven. I know you are there. You just can't have him yet. He closed his eyes and tried to find sleep for his worn-out body.

In the jungles of Venezuela, Chris ran fast though carefully as he could hear the sound of weaponry behind him aiming for him. He was much more than an interloper. He was a trespasser and a spy. The jungles were dark with few areas of welcomed sunshine. The ground held poisonous snakes that could swing from tree branches and wrap around your body, coil up around you, and strangle you before there was even time to fight them off. Blood was running from his shoulder wound more swiftly, making him more of a target, but there was no time to feel the pain. The force for self-preservation overwhelmed every feeling, every nerve in his body. He was running towards the light, but there was danger in doing this. He didn't know what he was running towards, but the option to turn to either side with trees that were closer together offered no less danger and little chance of camouflage or opportunity to outrun his pursuers. Slow the pace. I don't know if the path will drop off ahead or if enemy fire is waiting there. It took all his will to come to a stop with the sound of gunfire behind him.

More exposed now, he was a clearer target. He tore off his undershirt, making a wrap, and tied it around his shoulder. He grimaced in pain, then quickly readied himself for what lay ahead—a tall steel petroleum tower.

He looked down below him and saw that there was a drop of about two hundred feet, making a jump or fall prohibitive with large gray rocks on the ground below. To his right was decayed wood, meaning a fall and the ground beneath it would be unstable. To the left were trees. He looked to the closest tree at the edge, then jumped to it, catching a branch; but the branch snapped off. He fell, holding the branch. The fall was instantaneous, he rolled before the branch hit the rocks, and he landed on top of the branches that now covered the rocks, then rolled over and off it. He stood up but was unable to run from the direction of the gunfire. It was everywhere. He ran to the tower knowing that the tower contained petroleum; and if they fired at that, the explosion would cover all of the surrounding area in fire, and they would lose thousands of dollars. The government would be after them and instantly be there since the government kept 70 percent of the profit from the sale of the petroleum.

The petroleum was being put on oil tankers that were left there on different roads out from the area. He observed the movements of each worker, the order in which they did things, and the speed at which they did them. He made a quick calculation in his mind, then ran for the right side of a tanker away from the middle view of the operation. The men chasing him observed this from the top of the hill where they stood with their guns and machetes. They fired at the oil tanker, the tanker blew, and it ignited into flames. The screams of the dying, burning driver filled the air. The workers scrambled for the water line and opened it to a powerful streaming flow, putting out the flame before it could travel to the other reserves. They were successful; and two tankers, only half filled, drove away and left the site to flee the danger. The gang up on the hill was satisfied in seeing the tanker holding Chris's body explode. They laughed in delight, then observed the site for a few more minutes before turning back in the direction from which they came.

One of the policemen at the site ran to the side of the half- extinguished truck and visually swept the site as best he could. Before being seen, Chris jumped on the side door of the truck. The workers fighting off the fire pushed the policeman back away from the danger of the flames and told him to leave. He explained the reason why he was there to them. They told him anyone who had been there was now gone. He still went back to the side tower and radioed ahead what had happened and that there was a possible trespasser on the road to the trains.

The sky suddenly became darker, and the workers looked up to the skies. The most logical explanation was the black smoke from the fire, but indeed, there were rain clouds that now covered 70 percent of the sky. The rain was welcomed by them and helped extinguish the blaze, but the rains made it more difficult for the trucks leaving the site. They had to slow and take the curves more carefully. Chris was gone, gone in the explosion. He had been successful in fleeing from the forces firing at him and survived the drop from the hill, but the truck . . . how could he have survived the explosion and kept the engulfing inferno of flames from consuming his body?

The trucks increased their speed as they were now on the paved highway that led to the *autopista*, a ten-and-a-half-mile long freeway that cut through rocky mountain terrain that would lead them to Caracas. The first tank truck led the way at a speed that seemed unsafe to be traveling in the rain, but the weight of the vehicle enabled it to maintain a steady pace. The second truck left a safe distance between them, knowing that nobody should have the nerve to break in between these two trucks. The second truck driver noticed something on the passenger-side door of the second truck and radioed to the second truck driver. This second truck was minus its second driver who normally filled the passenger seat that most of the other trucks had; and it was reported to Carlos, the driver, that he had a passenger, most possibly an unwelcome passenger, hanging from the side door on the outside floorboard.

Carlos lowed his truck, radioing the two other trucks that he was doing this. The man hanging on the outside of the truck reached up to the handle and balanced his weight on the open door and then pushed his body inside the truck, swinging the door closed as quickly as he could to fight the force of speed hurling him off the truck. Carlos looked to his newly arrived passenger and was in the process of taking his revolver out from his belt when a wad of five one-hundred-dollar bills appeared in front of his face. Carlos dropped the gun and left it on the car seat as he took a turn, then smiled back to the passenger. He saw this man's bleeding arm and passed him the first aid kit. He started talking to him quickly in Spanish. Speaking Spanish fluently, the new passenger answered him and asked him where they were bound. He was told Caracas. He told the driver that was perfect, just where he wanted to go, and that he'd rather not talk. Carlos looked at him, smiled, and nodded.

Chris looked out the window to the sites they were passing but said nothing, trying not to look like a tourist. When the truck stopped by the side of what looked like a warehouse on the outskirts of Caracas, Carlos told him that he was waiting for the police to pass inspection of the truck before they could go any further. The passenger got off after he heard this and told the driver that this was the end of his travels with him and thanked him.

He had to escape from Caracas immediately. He knew that the drug runners would not call off their search for him. They had to have gotten wind of the fact that he was in the truck, and now there would be an inspection of the truck. There was a record of everything by this government, and news traveled fast. The smell of death was in the air, and he had outrun it. He needed to get to the coast, and the closest town with a shipping port where he could try and somehow board a boat—unnoticed or noticed, depending on the situation—was La Guaria. The journey there was roughly ten miles. He knew he could not walk; and more importantly, he knew that with this shoulder wound, he needed penicillin. It was just where to get it without questions and with American money.

On the roads to the warehouses, he saw more trucks approaching the cyclone-fenced area surrounding the buildings. He acted out a fall, but he knew that none of the drivers would stop to help him. Once down on the ground, he held one hand over his shoulder wound and rolled his body down the hillside of the entrance road to the warehouses. His roll picked up speed. He had to find some way to stop or slow down before rolling off a mountain or into a building or truck. He didn't know what was ahead. He remembered his father always told him that when in an unknown situation, back off and do nothing, but do not retreat, for that showed resistance and weakness.

In the course of gaining velocity, he pulled his body to a side direction away from the momentum of the roll. This didn't stop the roll, but it slowed him down. He was able to stop his body but was still fearful of being spotted, so he stayed on the ground. He kept his body flat and moved on all fours, traveling almost as a snake, viewing only the cold darkness of the dirt beneath him. At the end of the row of bushes, he stopped his body at a clearing, then rose straight up in a stance against a tree. He had no idea what kind of tree it was, but at this point, he really didn't care. He closed his eyes and breathed out a silent, heavy breath. Either he was going to have to take another fall or jump and a roll. There was still the option of calmly walking down the hill and being an open target. The jungle had ended, but he was still in an open field of danger and not yet in a town. Not that a town here could offer safety anyway. With his bleeding body, he decided against the option of a jump or a roll, and he crossed to the other side of the unpaved road through the clearing that led down to another grove of trees. In the open, he stood strong and composed, yet he felt fear run down his spine with every step he took.

Then at the bottom of the clearing, the half-mile journey ended. He entered the forest and crossed back to the left side. He walked through the forested area. He was in pain, holding his wound for what seemed internal miles and endless time.

He came to a plateau but had trouble focusing his eyes with the sun's rays piercing his vision. He was so tired and in pain from his wound. His body begged for sleep, rest, healing, and comfort. He strongly forced himself to keep going. In closing his eyes to shield them from the sun, he slipped and was startled by this. Then he tried to stop his body, but it was too late. He slid down the slope and could feel each roll of his body until suddenly, he felt himself stop, and his heartbeat resumed. He opened his eyes but could not clear his vision. He closed his eyes again and kept them closed, seeking moisture for his dry eyes.

When he reopened his eyes, he saw the high white stucco wall of the back side of a building. In panic, he grabbed on to a jade plant and lay still on the grass at the back of the building. He opened his eyes to a fuzzy, glaring sun vision; then he closed, opened, closed, and opened his eyes again, trying to refocus his vision. He saw a garden hose and a shovel. The shovel was closer, and he was just two fingers away from being able to grab hold of it. He grimaced, loosened his body, and reached forward with all his might. He took hold of it and tried to roll his body further in its direction. He now had a hold of it six inches down from its top. He then heard the sound of people running towards him, and the yelling sounded like female voices.

He looked up and saw several women standing directly over him, crying out in what he believed to be Portuguese, different from Spanish although close to resembling it. They helped him up. He said nothing, just looked confused. He thought it best not to speak, for he didn't know who they were or where he was. They took him into a room in a school, a nurses' office, and he turned to view the woman who had run alongside of him. She was a nun. He had rolled into a Catholic school. Next, he saw a woman wearing a nurse's uniform fill a needle; then she held his wounded arm tightly to administer the medication. He held back, looking at the needle. What were they injecting him with? Were they on the other side? He focused on the vial the nurse had used to fill the needle. They were giving him penicillin.

He sat there no longer fighting their actions. He expressed a thankful look to them without saying anything. They thought that he was the gardener on the school grounds. It was a perfect alibi. He no longer had to worry about his wound and how he would get it taken care of later. Now it was a matter of getting out of there before the real gardener returned. But why did they not know the real gardener? Was this a setup? He had to make a quick exit. The older sister from the adjoining office was bringing in a clipboard with papers on it. He realized that they had commented that they would need his signature on these insurance papers, getting injured while on the job.

He thought of the perfect fast getaway with no questions asked. He would do it. He sprang up from the chair and grabbed his stomach, making his body look queasy, and asked for a bathroom. They were in shock and did not want a mess in the office. The nurse started to take him to the bathroom in the office, but the older sister said no; they didn't want him to dirty that bathroom. That bathroom was only for the sisters. She told them to take him or direct him to the outside bathroom, which was to the left behind some tall hedges. He still couldn't conceive how perfect everything seemed to be playing out. Around the hedge, he could no longer be seen by them. Instead of going in the bathroom pit toilet, he ran around the garbage dumpster and then saw the traffic on the street in front of the school. He made his escape walking out on the street in front of the school into the noisy crowd that continued for several blocks to the north.

CHAPTER 9

ora felt the coolness of the ocean breeze become too cool. It was hard just trying to relax, doing nothing, saying nothing, and having a guard standing behind, watching her every move and having omnipotent power over her behavior. She couldn't stand being sequestered from her life. *I can't even seek bail. At least upstairs, I'm alone, and I have my privacy.* She turned to look at the guard who was unmoved by her action. She tilted her head, thinking of his guardlike, uncharacteristic rigid stance. "I'd like to go up to my room upstairs now if it is possible, or do you have to get permission from somebody to let me up out of this chair?" He stepped to the side, then walked to the sliding door of the house, and left it open for her to enter the house. He stood beside the open door and said nothing. She rose up out of the chair and went in the house in one movement. Once inside, she turned to him, stopping his movement. "I know my way upstairs, so you don't have to lead me. I am sure with all the guards here, no one could have possibly entered the house or the estate without your knowledge." He followed her upstairs and stood by the side of her door anyway. She stood back while he opened it and took inspection of the room, then returned to the hall, and closed and locked the door.

She walked to the middle of the room and turned her body in a circle, then raised her arms to the ceiling, stretching them as high as she could. *I just want to scream and run out of here and back to my life. I don't care what the onetime life I had was. I want to go back to the life that I know.* She relaxed her body and walked over to the window and closed the drapes, seeking solitude but wanting to escape from it at the same time. *I'm lost* in a maze of confusion with no way out . . . I'll have to make a way out. I'd better not say these things aloud since this room could still be bugged by them—to make sure that I don't have . . . what? A Game Boy with a pirated cartridge? She sat at the end of the bed, putting her hand back, and she felt one of the paper bags. She stood up, scared and surprised by feeling the bag there. Bond! Bond went shopping for me. What did he buy me? She ignored the paper bags and unzipped the garment bag. Letting the garment bag fall to the floor, she held up the clothing—pants, blouses, skirts, and dresses. My god! I never dreamed of having clothes like these. I mean, I dreamed of having them, but that is all I could afford to do. I just never perceived that there would be any way that I could wear clothes like these—the cost! These are off the New York runway—designer clothes! My god. Maybe there is something good about being here after all! For the next two hours, she tried on the clothes and unpacked the bags containing accessories.

Belts, scarves, jewelry, stockings, bras, underwear, a one-piece bathing suit trimmed in gold accents. God, can I keep these? There was even another bag that contained makeup. It wasn't her shade but darn close. There was even a bottle of cologne. I hit the jackpot! She stood up looking at the bed that held all the clothes and goodies. Well, there's a closet over there. I'll start hanging everything up. She walked to the sliding door to the closet, opened it, and took out some hangers, then walked back to the bed. Picking up a black-and-tan dress, she proceeded to hang it up. Walking it back to the closet, she said to herself in her mind and then she said it out loud, "My daughter, Lauren. How is she? Is she safe? Does she know that I am gone? What have they told her, if anything?" She stopped, then walked back to the table, and sat down. Grabbing a box of Kleenex, she started to cry.

There was a light knocking on the bedroom door. She ignored it. A minute went by; then she heard a louder knocking. She dried her eyes, then threw the Kleenex in the wastebasket at the side of the table. She got up, fighting the force causing her to do so. She stood still behind the closed door. "I can't open the door. Who is it, and what do you want?"

The man standing behind the door swallowed, then replied back, "It's Bond. I only wanted to know if you found what I bought you is acceptable."

"Oh, please open the door. I want to thank you for everything. It is . . . they are . . . everything is just right."

"Well, I don't have to come in. I do have to tell you that dinner is in an hour, and you do have to dress formally for dinner. May I suggest the flowered dress with the short sleeves and the matching throw?"

She nodded her head back and forth. She started to talk, then breathed in her words instead. "Thank you for the FYI, and thank you again for the clothes. I will take your suggestion. Will you be the one who will come and get me to take me to dinner?"

"I don't know yet. It depends on what the boss wants."

She raised her voice and responded through the closed door, "What the boss will tell you? Don't you ever get . . . ? Never mind. I guess I will see you sometime around here soon. You're the only one other than the boss whose name I know. Everyone else is just the guard. How many of you guards are there anyway?"

"On the usual days, there are twelve. But on holidays, there are more. You see, the other bad guys would think we have our inhibitions dropped on holidays, but those are the most dangerous days."

She relaxed her mood. "Thank you, Bond. Thank you. See you later."

He turned and started to walk away after hearing her say good-bye to him. *That woman can't help but make me smile.*

She pulled her body from the door. Every time she encountered Bond, she felt something. *I know I should still be mourning my husband, Chris. He's not just missing. He's gone. I hardly remember him though. But that's just it. These new memories that just resurfaced. Is that what happened or what I am being made to believe? In Chicago, two people acted like they knew me—knew me by the name Jane, not Dora, the only name that I know. Relapsed memory. I still get these overwhelming headaches. I attributed it to the effects of the drugs that they gave me during the long plane flight—the change in temperature, the insecurity, the loneliness, not knowing of my daughter, the heartache, the loss . . . the clothes. Chris is gone. Why, after all these years, did they hunt me down and tell me that they are doing this for me, for my life? How deep was my involvement? Did I work for them too?* She went over to the bed and sat on the edge of it, and a forlorn look came over her face and weakened body. *He was my husband.* She took her hands to her temples and pushed in, feeling pain and pressure. I feel as though I've been thrown into a pinball machine. When will it end? I wish I could just turn on the stereo really loud and just jump around and . . . I've got to be two people . . . well, that I am, but the person that they want to see. Don't question anything anymore. Gain their trust so I can have my freedom for the other me, the me that I won't let them see.

She went to the bathroom, fixed her hair and makeup, and regained her composure. Going to the closet, she opened it, already knowing what she was reaching for. And now to put the dress on, she held up the flowered dress. It was an A-line and high waisted. There were four buttons at the top of it and a high scoop neck. She checked herself in the full-length bathroom mirror and nodded her head at what she saw. A pair of gold earrings will complement this dress nicely.

Downstairs, the dining room itself was dressed for dinner. The dark wood of the long oval table was adorned with a dark red runner and two crystal candleholders with white candles inside. The centerpiece was a crystal bowl of red hibiscus. Michelangelo silverware, bone white china, and crystal wineglasses graced the table. Soft orchestral Italian music surrounded the room. It was definitely not the atmosphere of Hawaii, but rather the atmosphere of an Italian country table. Refined elegance circled the atmosphere.

Two guards, one of them being Bond, escorted the boss to the head of the table against the back wall and china cabinet. The opposite end of the table was open to the doors of the room. The table was set for three people. Dora walked down the stairs after the door was opened for her to exit by an unnamed guard, the same one who had watched her outside on the patio. He left her side at the bottom of the stairs and directed her to the dining room. She stood in the doorway and looked at each side of the room, then to the boss at the head of the table. She nodded to him, and he nodded in return. Before she stepped up to one of the set places, she stopped, looking at the third place. How could he bring Chris back from the dead? Was he going to sit there? The boss watched her actions and said to her, "You can't sit down from way back there. Come here and take this place." He motioned to the seat on his left. She hesitated, then nervously went to the place, and sat down. Being nervous and not wanting to have eye contact with him, she looked down and took the cloth napkin from the ring and placed it on her lap, then looked to the dinner plate in front of her. The boss, Vincent, looked to her and the fact that she was not making eye contact. He swallowed loudly, then cleared his throat, making this noise so that she would have to make eye contact with him, which she did. "I know what you were thinking." She thought, Why not? He knows everything that I do, think, or feel. And that is a dangerous situation. "I am sorry to break the news to you, but Chris is not joining us for dinner. I am not that powerful . . . Another man will be joining us, though." She relaxed her composure and the elevated feeling that ran through her spine, thinking it would just be another guard whose name she didn't know. He would watch her pick up her napkin off the floor to make sure that she didn't try and run away through the trapdoor under the table. The boss took a sip of red wine, then breathed out, savoring it. He turned his head up at the arrival of a well-dressed man in a black formal suit.

Dora turned her head, but not far enough to fully take a look at this gentleman who just pulled out the chair at the other side of the table from her. She was surprised and delighted but instantly took the joy off her face, not wanting the boss to pick up on the fact that she was happy about seeing who sat there. It was Bond. She wanted to retract from him, but she was mesmerized by him. I can't feel this way. I have to keep in control and feel the loss of Chris. She closed her eyes, feeling a torrent of unbalanced jingling in her mind. Her uneasiness was picked up by the boss. "Young lady, are you all right? Drink some water."

She opened her eyes and shifted her body against the back of the chair, then tenderly lifted the glass, and took a small swallow. "Thank you. I feel better."

"I just made the suggestion. I didn't drink the water or make it, the Lord did." She nodded. She didn't want to go into any notion of having to express feelings or reasons for her actions.

The boss lifted his hand, and a guard brought them dinner. The portions were already put on the plates, and the full plates were placed in front of each one of them. Dora looked to this and thought it odd. The dinner did look good though it was not what she expected. The class of the estate and the room made her expect more. The dinner was pasta; and long spaghetti noodles covered by lightly crushed tomatoes and garlic and freshly chopped parsley, leaf lettuce covered with olive oil and red wine vinegar, and garlic bread graced the plate. A nice-looking dinner, but not having serving bowls of food on the table made her feel that she was eating a Weight Watchers' frozen entree.

The boss noticed her skepticism. "I don't cook here. Everything is brought in. I own two restaurants on the island. No one would suspect that every meal has to be brought in to a home like this. A home like this should have at least one gourmet chef. That is why I don't have one or any. Just the simple necessities are kept in the kitchen, and they are checked repeatedly." She said nothing in response to what she just heard. She thought about what he said, that this course of action and eating this way was for the best, and then she wondered about the significance of the danger she was in just being there and welcomed the idea of guards always following her.

She made it through dinner with the least amount of conversation possible, and she made little or no affirmation of Bond. After dinner was finished and their plates were cleared from the table, a plate of fresh fruits was put in the middle of the table. Most of the fruits on the plate were not native to Hawaii. She declined the fruits, and so did the other two. The boss pushed his chair out and said that he was going to retire early that night. He left with the guard who had stood by the sidewall through dinner. She tried to hide her nervousness, but she knew that Bond was picking up on it, and it was probably making him snicker inside. The tension was like when two strangers who want to meet each other very badly are in an elevator trying to figure out what to say and how to say it before the door opens, and they step out.

"Come on, Bond. Break the moment. I more than feel the antinomy. I am Dora, but I have to behave like Jane, whom I have nothing but reemerging memories of—painful memories. I mean, in more ways than one—the headaches, painful reflections of time, the truths that I am supposed to shield. I realize that this is being done for me, for my benefit, my life. And I should shoulder the responsibility since I am the one who transposed my life. But you see, I need ownership. I don't feel I control my own destiny." He sat back, then got up from his chair, walked around to the back of her chair, and pulled it out for her. Then he placed his hand out for her to take hold of, and he led her out of the room.

He then walked her up the stairs and turned in the direction of her room. She was silent all through his every motion but was very inquisitive of the outcome. He pulled out his key from his jacket pocket and unlocked the door to her room. He made a quick inspection of the room. Her eyes went to the direction of the bed, and he noticed that. He did not release her hand and led her to the table and sat her down there. He sat on the other side of the table. She laughed and looked up to the ceiling. "So all this was just to take me from one table to the other. What is the difference?"

"Privacy."

"But you aren't doing anything!"

"Look, I am going to say . . . some things to you that you should not be told or know yet. Maybe you knowing these things is not part of the boss's plans, but it will make my job easier." She looked at him with her full attention. "Everything that he, we, are doing for you is going to come out right. The reason for all the security around you is the fact that you were married to Chris, the boss's son. He was shot at. You and your daughter would have died too if it wasn't for the fast thinking by Chris and you. You had the sense to run. He pushed the baby carriage away from his line of sight and made himself a target. He got it, but you and your daughter survived. Another onlooker was there and pushed the carriage to a safe place where you later received it and your daughter. You underwent psychological treatment to lose your past memory so you could start a new life. It was when you went back to Chicago and played Nancy Drew that the other rivals, the ones responsible for the shooting, caught wind of you there and brought on this sudden will for your death. The boss has moved out of Chicago, but there are still ties there that could lead to his arrest. He is no longer in the illegal activities that he once was. And before you worry excessively about deaths and horses' heads, he was involved in gambling, illegal gambling, there. A death, maybe a few deaths, did happen in one transaction—a death of a family member of the other family. We are a sworn enemy, bound to revenge. We are protecting you for your life. They want to kill you just for—"

"They want to kill me just to even the score?" "Basically that is it."

"I don't like the games that your work plays, but my new identity?" "Not enough was done about it."

"So I am just to stay trapped here under scrutiny until you kill all the other gang members off, or how is this going to work?"

"Right now, the boss is working with a judge and someone in the police force to bring this family down."

"Okay, what . . . Let me get this straight. You are working for the Mondello family, which is an Italian, maybe Mafia family." "Used to be Mafia."

"Okay. I just want to get this straight. A family that was involved with some questionable deals that were, at the time, illegal. The boss, the only remaining family member, is now legitimate because all he does is move coffee beans around the country. And he is not aware that illegal drugs are packed inside these cases of coffee. And a judge knows this, and a police officer or someone with important standing in the police force does. And there will be an arrest or murder or the blowing up of a building that, of course, all the rival family members will be in. And the boss will have no part in that. It just works out for him. I cannot go anywhere because I am dead meat if I am seen anywhere since the gang surely knows that I am here. I mean, they already fired at me leaving the plane. Okay. Thank you. Now that I know all this, I can easily sleep at night. No biggie!" She sank back in the chair, let out a huff, opened her eyes wide, and gave a half smile.

Bond slowly shook his head. "That is basically it. You just have to keep this from the boss because it is my ass on the line about this." "Don't worry. I won't say anything. Just call me Jane. I mean, I have to conform to who I was. It is who I am supposed to be now, but isn't there going to be anything for me to do but stay in this room and look at the walls all day? Oh, and the back caning of that chair you are sitting in has thirty-seven rows of caning across it. I guess tomorrow, I can count the vertical rows. Then I have three other chairs to look forward to. I have to be able to do something. Just how much should I know?" Bond looked excited and scared at what she just said. "Don't worry. I would never divulge to anyone what you just told me. It's, I mean, guard 1 or guard 2. I have to start naming them. Even the little men on the Pac-Man games have names. There's

Blinky, Pinky, Inky, and . . . ah . . . um . . ."

He looked relaxed watching her struggle. He waited another minute, seeing her aggravation in not being able to remember the name of the fourth Pac-Man character. "Sue, its name is Sue." She looked at him like he took the last bowl of good breakfast cereal and left her with stale cornflakes.

"Thank you. This doesn't sound like a spy novel, discussing video games." He thought to say at least none of them had guns but remained silent instead. She could tell by his undertones, and he started to motion his body off the chair. "Please, don't go yet. You are the only sanity that I have."

He wanted to stay, but he had to fulfill the duties of his job and knew that he had already overstepped them. "Don't worry. You will see me tomorrow." He stopped before opening the door, then held the knob, and looked to her and smiled. "Good night, Jane."

She remained in the chair. "Good night, Bond."

He packs drugs in coffee. No wonder coffee doesn't taste good anymore. Well, at certain times, it does. You just have to ask for the coffee without drugs. Oh yeah right. She got up, went to the bed, looked to the sliding glass door and window, and thought of how good the night air would feel. With the knowledge he just gave her, she thought twice before going to the window or opening the door. She did get up to it to make sure that it was locked. The only thing to do now was go to bed. In only minutes, she was in bed, dreaming. She tried to daydream the dream into being with Bond, but the never-ending dilemma in question overshadowed it—the walk in the part, the sky, the peacefulness like a Hallmark greeting card, the sudden gunfire, the cries, the screams, and the fear of death. She tried to change the thoughts and woke up from sleep sweating, panicked, trembling. It's over, it's over. I'm safe. Now it's me. Something happened before that. Why can't I pull that out? All the feelings, the emotions, a never-ending love that is gone; and I'm left alone, literally being scared for my life. Bond, I have to think of you. There is a reason that you are here in my life now. Protection. Please, for me, it has to be something more than that. She sat to the side of the bed and held her chin in her hands, holding her fingers over her face. I have to have you.

The next morning, she was already dressed and looked ready to go somewhere. She put herself together very well. When there was a tapping on the bedroom door for her to leave, she was standing on the other side of the door, ready to make her departure. The guard who took her downstairs wasn't Bond.

Downstairs, the guard sat her at the table. The boss was already seated there. She took coffee from the machine, then turned to the boss, and handed a cup to him. This surprised him. "Well, I am going to be here a while, so I might as well make myself comfortable."

He held the cup of coffee in his hand but stopped in the motion of taking itto his mouth and said, "Not too comfortable. I'll still be on guard." She sat down and nodded her head at what he just said.

CHAPTER 10

He waited until he saw a large crowd of people making their way up the side street to the side of the building towards the pier. Then he walked into the crowd, keeping his distance but still at some close proximity to the group of people. The men and women were dressed in regular day clothes as well as work clothes from different jobs. The crowd increased as more buildings of various businesses lined both sides of the street. He stood to the side against a building to get out of the increased pace of the crowd. He was feeling the pain in his arm now, but at least, he knew one positive thing—he knew infection would not set in.

He had to get out of these work clothes and fast. The afternoon was setting in. Across the street and up two stores, he saw a bar. He waited until another crowd of people passed before him, then blended back in with it. He stopped to the side of the raised embankment used as a sidewalk to walk along the street. Two cars and a truck passed; then he ran across the street and jumped to the raised embankment on the other side, not losing his momentum. At the door of the bar, he stood outside observing what it held. Various people, mostly American tourists, sat at ten different tables next to the door. The bar was straight ahead in the middle of the room. There were five people sitting on the barstools drinking beers. One of these men was dressed in an American navy uniform. The pier was just up the street two blocks. He wasn't aware that it was a stopping point for the navy, though. He would have to check this out and find out more, and the only way to do that was to go inside. Once inside the bar, he stood to the side at the entrance to make way for an American couple leaving. They were busy in conversation and made no note of him. He looked at their table and saw that no other eyes in the bar were watching him. There was a piece of uneaten chicken left on one of their plates, and he took it off the plate and then turned his head away from the direction of the bar and quickly ate it.

Sitting on a bar stool two seats away from the sailor, he saw the bartender stop in front of him and ask him what he wanted. He took hold of his throat, raised his eyebrows, and made a noise like he was trying to get something out. He saw the bartender tilt his head back in disgust. Then he pointed to the tall frosted draft beer glass that another patron was drinking at the bar, and the bartender then gave him a beer.

The sailor finished his drink and looked at his watch. It was a naval watch, and the navy seal was right on the band. He then got up. Chris watched this but did not turn his head to see where he went until he was out of view. He had gone to the bathroom. Chris then placed money on the bar to pay for the beer and left. He walked to the entry door; then once the bartender took the money and turned away from watching him, Chris walked back to the bathroom where the navy man had gone. Inside the bathroom, the stall door was closed. He looked down below the stall and saw navy shoes. He then turned to the sink and turned it on as if washing his hands, but he did not get them wet. The sailor left the bathroom stall. Chris turned from the sink, then motioned the sailor to go there. The sailor did; and Chris walked up behind the sailor, put his arm forward, bending it at the elbow, and rammed it into the side of the sailor. Then he reached under the back side of the sailor's neck and pushed in, and the sailor collapsed. Chris then dragged the covered garbage can over to block the door. A Swiss army knife was in the pocket of the sailor's pants. Chris opened the knife, raised his arms, and shaved off the hair under his armpits. Then he opened the first aid cabinet on the side of the sink and took the tape and taped his gun under one armpit and his watch under the other armpit. Then he put the rest of the uniform on followed by the sailor's watch.

He washed his face, wishing for a razor to shave but thought he looked like he just sported a five o'clock shadow. Satisfied with his look, he moved the garbage can back, then walked out and saw a half-finished glass of beer and two not-yet-finished whiskey cocktails on the bar tray in the hall. He took them and walked back into the bathroom and poured them over the sailor. The sailor would smell of beer, so him lying there on the floor of the bathroom would mean that he passed out from intoxication when somebody found him. He made quick, firm strides leaving the bar and walked up the street to the pier.

Only small fishing boats were tied up at the pier or leaving it. The navy ship, a repair ship, was pulling out to sea. It was too far from the pier now to try and jump on board and too far away to try and swim to. The Caribbean. It was headed for Puerto Rico, an American-controlled island. The ship had to be heading there. A likely place that Chris would be headed for, and right now, it was just the escape that he needed.

Natives on a fishing boat ready to leave the dock saw his dilemma and yelled for him to hitch a ride. They could take him by the direction of the ship. He jumped aboard the departing fishing boat and thanked the men on board in Spanish, which was the language they spoke. They laughed when he told them he missed his ship because he was having a beer in the bar.

On board the wooden utility boat, he had trouble balancing his first steps on the boat out on the ocean waters. The three crew members laughed at his unsteadiness. A navy officer should have better sea legs. They laughed at his loose footing, blaming it on the alcohol he had consumed. Out from the lip of the dock, halfway out to the flat seawater ahead, one of the crew members turned and looked back to port and saw the half-gale flag go up. He yelled the news to his shipmates, and they tightened hold of the boat, moving in the direction of the currents so as not to capsize. The rising waters did blow them off course; but once the waters subsided, they were able to change their course to the nearest island, Isla de Margarita. It was an island under Venezuelan rule, so there were no problems being that they were a fishing vessel.

They pulled out far enough from the harbor of Porlamar to still be able to fish and see the happenings at dockside on the island. Chris noticed a large cruise ship docked there, an American cruise ship. He pointed to the cruise ship on the island, gave them a handful of money, and asked them to let him off. They pulled up anchor and went into shore to leave him off, then returned back to sea. His clothes were more than grungy and smelled like the sea. He slid into a side street with various tourist shops and found one without the usual swell of tourists. Speaking Spanish, intensifying the American accent on purpose, he bought a man's flowered shirt, white Bermuda shorts, white cotton ankle socks with a bright blue band around the top of them, and basket weave sandals—signifying a typical middle-class American tourist. He held a plastic bag over his shoulder that held the gardener's uniform he held earlier. The only other change he made to his appearance was to wear a disposable camera around his neck.

Looking in the direction of the wharf at the placement of the cruise ships, he looked and memorized each of the ship's numbers, then went to the side loading dock, and took inventory of the shipments and their contents that would be put on the ships. A few of the items were what some of the tourists bought on the island; most of the other items were food supplies for the ships. There was no way to get in through any of these shipments. Returning to the side pier, he aligned himself with a group of tourists posing and taking pictures. One couple stood out from the others, not just because they were the couple standing closest to him but because of the loudness and contempt in their voices for each other. They were in their late fifties, both overweight and pale in complexion. She held shopping bags galore and was trying to take pictures of the ship they would be boarding. She was telling her husband to come over to her and get some of the bags that she was holding so that she could focus and take pictures better. He complained very loudly to her of the money that she had spent buying all these things on the island and how she was going to be messing up their house and make their trip terrible with all the crap that she was buying and that he would have to get a second job just to pay for everything. For every complaint that he made loudly to her, she, in turn, said something right back to him. Chris took this as his opportunity.

He swiftly went to the side of this woman and took the bags from her hand. She jumped back in surprise. "Miss, let me help you. Give me the opportunity to hold these bags for you while you take your pictures."

She smiled at him, expressing a thank-you, then turned and sneered at her husband before taking the pictures. She giggled and stepped towards him, holding the camera. The boarding call on the ship sounded. "Thank you."

"Oh, you are welcome. It was my pleasure. You have such beautiful fair skin, such beauty."

She smiled and giggled more. "Well, we don't get too much hot weather. I'm from North Dakota—long winters, so I mostly am in the house."

Her husband, who stood in the background, raised his eyebrows and grunted, "Mister, if you like her that much, you can have her." "Let me walk these aboard for you." She stepped to the side for him to walk alongside of her up the ramp to the ship. Right when the crewman asked for the tickets to board, he turned around and knocked the passenger holding a wad of tickets in his hand—the leader of a group of tourists. Still holding the bags, he helped pick up the tickets, expressing an apology, and conveniently held one of the tickets back in his hand to show the crewman so he could board the ship. Before entering the door to the inside staterooms where she was heading, he gave her back her bags and told her what an honor it was to have seen her, and he hoped that he would enjoy her company again on the journey. She giggled some more as her husband came up from behind, heard this, and replied, "Oh Jesus!"

Seeing that he had the attention of the purser aboard the ship, he moved quickly, but not too quickly to be noticed. He walked in the direction of the elevator and took it to the lower cabins. He noticed he still had the attention of the purser walking behind him. He saw an open cabin door and went inside. An older middle-aged woman was inside taking things from her suitcase. She turned around seeing Chris standing there. He walked towards her, smiling. She smiled in return. The purser stood at the open doorway to the room. "There you are!" He then hugged her and placed his cheek up to hers, making the squeeze tight enough so that her words could not be heard. She did not repel him; instead, she enjoyed this hug from a handsome stranger. The purser watched this, then left the room, closing the door. Chris still waited to pull back from her, and once he did, he immediately started a conversation. "I hope your stay here is comfortable. Is there anything else that I can bring you?" She stood back, confused. "I see your hesitation. I know that you need your privacy. I will leave and give that to you. Thank you." He stood back from her, opened the door, and smiled at her before he left. She stood there silently in the room, confused but elated by what had just happened to her.

There are a lot of lonely souls on this ship looking for me. I better watch it before I have to create so many identities that even I forget them all. First thing is to find out the coordinates of the ship's travel and when the next stop will be reached. I have to make contact with Dad and get rid of the phone that I have. He went to the end of the hall and moved towards the direction of the ship's kitchen downstairs. Right as the waiter walked out of the kitchen, Chris slid in the open door and quickly moved to the end cargo hold of the kitchen.

Inside the room, he ripped the gun off from under his armpit and swallowed the pain from ripping off his skin and hair follicles. Then he took the phone off. Once the phone was free, he looked around the surrounding area for a place to dispose of it but then thought better of it. Knowing what he would do with it, he placed it inside his pocket, then searched through the contents of the various drawers on the wall that contained different foodstuffs. Most of the drawers he pulled out and the cabinets he opened contained food supplies that he knew would be eaten. He stopped and almost put the gun in the back of a drawer that contained pitted prunes, but then he thought better of this idea knowing about all the retired people on the ship. At the bottom of a cabinet containing what looked like survival items, he placed the gun on the bottom of an open box of expired baking soda.

Next, he went back up to the deck of the ship and waited until they had pulled deep into the sea while standing at the side of the ship viewing the ocean. He was sure that he had onlookers; so he moved to the front mass of the ship, away from the view of those seated on the lounges, and looked for the placement of the sun. After waiting a brief moment, he walked back to the side of the ship in a crowd of people, then took a cell phone out of the jacket pocket of one of the older men passengers. He walked back to the end of the ship and punched in the number of his father in Hawaii. His father answered on the usual fourth ring. "I'm in the Caribbean. Don't say anything. Bye."

His father listened patiently, wanting so much to talk to his son and ask things, but he knew that he couldn't. He was very relieved to find out his son was all right. His heart beat slower and more steadily. Chris knew that the call had been picked up, and now they would know where he was. Any one of the crew could be the traitor as well as any of the passengers. He needed to either lie low and hide out or make himself highly visible.

The ship had 1,299 passengers according to the ship's log. He had hidden out in towns smaller than this. It was just that there was no going up the mountain or down the coast or hitching a ride on the side of a big rig to escape. It seemed like hiding out in a prison. He had to find some place on the ship to make his home, but for how long? He didn't even know the duration of the cruise. He looked out to the deck. I've got the answer right here. I just have to take advantage of it.

In the next ten minutes, he was lying on a lounge chair in the middle of a group of retired ladies, sipping a margarita. They fought over which one of them was going to rub suntan lotion on his back. He felt more than protected. He asked them where they were all from. The majority of them were from Wyoming. Only one was from southwest Montana. Chris listened to stories of their hard winters and how Jamie's restaurant (which they all knew about, but they were not really close friends) had been featured on the food channel. He had trouble keeping an interest in their conversations but pretended to pay close attention, for they were providing his free ticket out. When they asked him what he did, he thought of telling them he was a doctor from southeast New Mexico but then quickly changed his mind, fearing they would all bombard him with medical questions and dilemmas. He told them he was a dogcatcher from Arkansas. None of them asked him questions about his business or home.

To end their silence, he told them he had fought in Desert Storm and that it was a sore topic. He didn't want to recount his memories of that. They all shut up, him being a war hero and all. They did ask him, however, if he sustained any injuries there. He noticed two men looking in his direction. He told the ladies that he had suffered an injury to his feet. They instantly raised his feet and started rubbing and massaging them. In the process of them doing this, they hid his face and kept him from being seen as they clustered around him. The men asked each other what was happening over there. One told the other, "It's just a group of old ladies. There can only be ladies there." They then went to the lower main deck to find what was there.

The next stop would be the island of Puerto Rico. He wondered if it would be safe to stay aboard or if he should make his departure on that island. There was an airport there—flights to Florida—but what would they expect him to do? As far as work went, he wouldn't be able to do any more. This whole area had become too hot. They wanted out of Florida because of the increased security. That was it. They would be doing business there. Make it legitimate. I have to get back in touch with Dad somehow and tell him this. The airwaves are unsafe. Urgency is of the utmost. It will be another day until we dock in Puerto Rico.

He got up from the group of women and told them that he would be right back. He was just going to use the poolside restrooms. They were very concerned that they were losing his company and prepared to follow him away from the pool until they learned that he was going to stop at the men's room, and none of them were that brave.

He was tired from the trip there and told them he was going to his cabin to rest. He asked them for their company at the early dinner. They smiled and accepted his invitation. He then went to the main information center of the ship and faxed a message to his father's company on the docks in Hawaii.

Need to get opposition to back off. Too suspecting. Plant legitimate shipment to force the police to confiscate, in the docks of Nassau, the Bahamas. Repeat, just coffee aboard. JC imperative. Planted decoy. CM TO VM.

He sent one more fax to a bogus address in California. The fax did not go through, but he had planned it that way. He made believe he was a naive tourist to gain the attention of the ship's employees. If anyone did ask what he was doing, they would tell whoever asked that his transmission had failed.

The men who were following him, watching his every move, traced the call that he had made on the stolen cell phone. Their phone rang back to them to tell them that the person who received the call made on the stolen phone was in a pizza parlor in Kansas City. A pizza parlor? Could they be doing business there? They then phoned back to their leader. Straw Hat Pizza in Kansas City, Missouri, was now going to be checked out.

Chris observed the men who had been following him but did not let on that he had seen these men in the act of tracing the call, and he heard what they found out. It was hard to cover up and swallow the laugh, but he did. The problem of what to do for the evening perplexed him. He wasn't going to share the room of one of these ladies, but he would be found out as a stowaway with no room for that evening, and he had to shield his identity.

He would stay on the deck until midnight or in the disco bar until two in the morning, but he had to have his wits about him for the next day when he would be departing the ship and heading to a new island. He knew that he already had followers that he had to elude. Recalling the layout of the ship in his mind, he visualized what he would need to do, and he didn't have to wait until midnight to do it. He would have to get a knife, however. A fishing knife would be most practical, and it would do the job he needed done. Surely, there would be a fishing knife somewhere on this ship, and the kitchen would be the most logical place to find it.

He made straight, determined tracks to one of the ladies' staterooms that he had the key for. When he sat with them earlier, he had taken a room key out of one of their tote bags. In front of the door, he stopped to look at the key and at the doorknob. Anyone observing this would just think that he was getting ready to open his door. He did this to make sure that no one was watching him. He stepped inside and closed the door ever so slowly and quietly.

He used the shower and went through the travel bag on the bathroom counter. He took a disposable ladies' razor out of the bag and shaved his face. Then he combed his hair and wiped the comb dry afterward before placing it back in the bag. He looked out the peephole and found the coast clear. He left the room and made steady tracks back up to the deck. He tossed the disposable razor covered in tissue in a trash container beside the door on the deck and then held the door open for a ship's attendant who wheeled forward a rack of the ship's uniforms. He took off the last one hanging on the rear of the cart and held it over his arm, then went immediately out the door, and took a white beach towel from the open shelf. He rolled the uniform inside the towel, then walked across the deck, and went back inside the hall on the other side of the ship. He then went into the closed and dark dining room and stood to the side of the decorative trees and plants by the reception station and put the waiter's uniform on. He covered the clothes he was wearing in the towel and placed them at the back of the potted plants. Inside the busy working kitchen, he blended in, moving his body down the row of busy chefs. He stopped only long enough to observe the actions of the other waiters. He then took a rack of wineglasses out of one of the dishwashers and placed it on the roll cart to go out to the dining room. As he did this, he watched the chefs and walked behind where they were working and stood to the side to make room for another waitperson to roll a cart to the dining room door. While standing to the side, he walked sideways to the cutlery drawer, opened it, and took out a fish knife and a carving knife. He handed the carving knife to a chef who was turning to get one. The chef nodded in appreciation. He then walked back outside to the dining room, holding the fish knife by his outer side. He went back to the potted plants and changed back into his tourist clothing and placed the knife in his side pocket.

He went back outside to the deck and climbed the stairs to the upper deck. The whistle just blew to announce the first seating for dinner. He observed the time on his wristwatch, then walked over to the side railing of the ship and relaxed, looking out to the ocean and watching the beautiful calm sunset over the ocean swells. A crewman asked if he needed help. "No, thank you. I'm just relaxing looking at the ocean. You know, I didn't see any information on evacuation procedures for the ship if there were some sort of accident. Praise be that there isn't, but what would the procedure be?" The crewman smiled at the question, but it was quite clear that he was bothered by this question, not wanting to take the time to explain these proceedings. Chris smiled like a tourist listening, then acted like a big shot in saying thank you to the crewman.

The rafts came down automatically on each side of the ship. On the right side of the ship, there were windows, and they could be observed from the officer's steering port on the front of the ship. The only ones not able to be seen were the last two on the left rear of the ship, and these were usually the last ones to be dropped, but they couldn't be dropped automatically like the others because of the electricity running through the center of the walls outside of the row of boats. It was explained that children and the handicapped should be given the first consideration. Chris thanked the crewman and then told him that he wasn't hungry yet, but a drink sure sounded good. The crewman bowed his head, then left, ever so happy to be away from this questioning tourist.

Well, I can't wear a waiter's uniform or tourist shorts at the captain's dinner, so it's back to the ship's shops to buy a suit for dinner at three times the price it would normally sell for. What is my other option? He reluctantly walked back to one of the shops on the main level of the ship and was happy that there was not a female saleswoman there to flirt with him. There was just a middle-aged man who was trying to pretend he had a foreign dialect but who was quite unsuccessful at it. Chris picked out a plain black suit—not their cheapest suit but not their most expensive either, one right in the middle price range.

He bought the suit, then took it in its bag to the showers at the side of the swimming pool, and changed there. He slowly promenaded to the side of the ship where the life rafts hung from the left side of the ship where no one really visited. There was no need to. He placed his bag on the deck up against the side of the ship, then looked at his watch, and went back to the main floor for the first dinner seating.

The ladies watched everyone who entered the reception area of the main dining room as they sat observing all actions from a bar table. He caught sight of them, then shook his head no to the hostess, and walked up the three steps to the bar area to join the ladies. They smiled feverishly at his arrival. He explained that he was famished, and they were seated at the middle of a large table. He was starving, but he was very careful not to eat too much knowing the journey that he was facing that night.

Outside, it was the midnight hour. He went back to the cabin deck and stood in front of one of the ladies' doors. He took off one of his shoes and left it in front of the door. He then picked the lock of the door, placed one of his dress socks in the doorjamb, and closed the door until it latched. He then quickly left that hall and deck, going back to the left side of the rail area where he had left his bag and looked down the ship to the hanging life raft. He cut the rope that tied the raft to the side of the ship, and the raft dropped to the water, making only a small splash. He then lowered his bag onto the raft and left it tied by a rope to the bar under the deck of the ship. He quickly left, going to the lower deck on the other side of the ship. He opened the kitchen door, then lit an oiled rag on fire, and threw it under the stainless steel workstation counter. He left the room and almost ran out of the kitchen area.

Once on deck, he did run. He had changed back into the waiter's uniform and shoes so it would not raise suspicion if he was seen. The fire alarms sounded throughout the ship, putting an abrupt end to the quietness of the night. He went back to the deck with the raft on the left side of the ship, cut the rope, and then swung his body over the rail and dropped into the raft. All the commotion on the other side of the ship should momentarily steer their attention away from the fact that they had lost a life raft. He caught the tip of a swell and paddled with it, distancing himself farther from the hull of the cruise ship. The moonlight was not bright enough to light the dark waters of the unknown abyss. The Caribbean did not have very deep water he thought, but there was also the mystery of the Bermuda Triangle. The moon seemed to rise higher above him, and the water became more choppy. He tied himself to the inside of the raft by the paddles. Not knowing the way to the nearest islands, he decided to let the pull of the water guide his course as it usually did lead to islands. There are hundreds of islands in the Caribbean although few are inhabited in the five-hundred-mile-wide sea.

He fought the swells out on the open water and fought the sleep trying to take over his body at the same time. Hope kept him afloat. He remembered Homer's journey. Teach me humility. Then he thought of Charles Darwin, man and nature. Survival was the key. Survival and safety. The hours on the cold dark sea felt like days passing with no reason.

The bright rays of the morning sun slowly warmed his face. The swells had calmed, and shadows rippled over the water. He lay lifeless on the floor of the raft, unaware of the fact that he was rolling with the tide to the shore of an island. The bouncing of the raft hitting the sandy beach on the island instantly awoke him and caused him to open his eyes and turn his head. He held each side of his face to steady himself. He had a bad feeling of motion sickness, and delirium was more than apparent.

He hurled his body out of the raft into the water pounding the sandy shore of the beach. He grabbed the rope on the front of the raft to pull it farther out of the water and over the sand so it would be above the high tide line on the beach. He sank to the sand and lay still for a minute, trying to balance his body on the solid, unmoving ground, reaching in any way possible to find equilibrium on land. His skin was pale but had a green tinge to it. He felt nauseous with a sinking feeling in his stomach. He wanted to throw up, but he had already thrown up three times in the raft. He did throw up again although nothing came out. He gathered all his strength to turn his body over on the sand, and in one motion, he stood up. He felt like he was going to fall, so he bent his knees slightly but remained standing; and then he raised his hand over his eyes, shielding them from the rays of the sun. He looked to his left, then to his right, and saw tall palm trees and foliage on each side of him. He balanced himself and sidestepped to his right and leaned against a palm tree. A coconut fell just inches from his foot. He wondered if it fell because of the force of his body leaning against the tree or if it was just in line to fall. He thought of the meat in the coconut, but not relishing the thought of eating anything, he thought of the milk or juice of the coconut to alleviate his thirst. He made his way back to the raft and leaned his body over to grab his bag while anchoring his feet to the ground as deeply as possible for balance. He opened the bag and took out the fish knife, then took hold of the coconut. He looked at it twice, trying to visualize it without moving. He then sat down on the sand and, taking hold of the knife, pierced the three holes on top of the coconut. He pulled his head back and raised the coconut to drink the juice. It was a welcome liquid on his tongue. He winced at the sweetness of the coconut milk but then closed his mind to the taste and swallowed every ounce he could get from the fruit. The sound of a bird crying in the forested jungle caused him to look back towards the trees. He grimaced in pain at how he felt and the idea of braving it on a deserted island like Robinson Crusoe.

It was still early morning, but he was already thinking of cover for that night. He looked up to the sun and sky to see if there was a possibility that the moon could still be visible as sometimes would be the case in the early-morning hours. There was no sign of the moon. He knew that it was probably too late. It was sometime in the morning. Then in his delirium, he remembered his watch and raised his ripped shirtsleeve to see the time. It was 8:30 a.m. He had slept through a lot of time that morning.

Walking up the beach towards the trees, he talked out loud to himself. I don't suppose I'd find a good man Friday on this island, Daniel Defoe. It was Friday when he had found him, so he named him Friday. I don't think being called Wednesday sounds that nice. Is it still Wednesday? He stood back from going into the jungle, then made his observations, and took his compass from his other pocket to pinpoint his location for his return. He looked to each side of the area on the coast where he had landed and thought of walking around the island; but that would be impossible since to each side, there were sharp, protruding rocks. He then went back to the raft and pulled it in off the coast some more and tied the rope to a tall tree with a thick trunk.

Walking back to enter the inland jungle area of the island, he said to himself, Now to go find Wednesday. Even the company of a monkey wouldn't be so bad. He watched his footing, making sure there were no snakes where he set his feet down. He cut some of the hanging vines with the knife he held in his hand; the other hand he held open as if to strike anything that flew towards him or tried to jump him. He came to a clearing near what he thought might be the middle of the island. Rocks were laid out in a circle. Walking closer to the rock formation, he saw deadwood ash. A fire had been lit there, but it had been at least two weeks since that occurred. The island had been visited by man, but was this man or were these men still there awaiting his arrival? The wood ash was so old, he knew they had moved on, but what was on the other side of the island? A Holiday Inn? He laughed at the thought of that one.

He cleared a path through the vines and trees on the other side of the old campsite. The noise of the animals and birds seemed to get louder with each movement he made towards the other side of the island. He wondered if it was just his imagination working overtime, and he proceeded without fear, looking to see what was lurking on the other side of this remote island. He stopped feeling heat. Apprehension caused his body to freeze. Then he fought the fear that was constraining him and went forward only to find that the forested vines had ended, and he felt the sun pierce through the sky on the other side of the island. His ride through the adventurous land was over, and he was rather disappointed he didn't find anything, disappointed too because he found no other way to get himself off this island. He still wasn't sure how safe it was for him to be there. It was too easy, and that made it time to be wary.

He walked to the beach on this side of the island and saw fish swimming in the shallow water offshore. He remembered reading on the cruise ship about rock fishing on these shores. He took a fallen branch from a tree and rolled it over the rocks, trying to smooth it. The bark peeled right off, and he was left with a smooth core. He then tied the point of the knife to the end of the pole then sheepishly walked into the shallow water along the beach. He stood there motionless, holding his breath. A whisper would have pierced the aura surrounding him. He jabbed a fish with the pole and then took it out of the water and walked backwards up the beach. The fish was still fighting for survival but becoming weaker with each passing inhalation of air. Watching this troubled him. He took a fallen palm leaf and wrapped the fish in it, then untied the knife from the pole, and put it back covered in his pocket. He then went back through the jungle towards the other side of the island.

In the middle of the island, he again stopped at the rocks that encircled the old campfire and thought of the ease of lighting a fire there to cook the fish. Then he thought better of the idea and returned to the shoreline on the other side of the island. He dropped the fish wrapped in the palm leaf on the sand in the middle of the beach, then looked up to the sun. He envisioned the progress it had made across the sky since he had first looked at it earlier that morning; then he resorted to looking at the time on his wristwatch.

By the shadow cast down by the sun and the change in its direction, I estimate it to be about 12:30 p.m. He then looked at his wristwatch and raised his eyebrows at what he saw. The actual time was 12:35 p.m. A little off but not too bad. I'm sure that I will have plenty of time to work on perfecting this. He proceeded to work on making a fire to cook the fish. He thought of sleeping there that night, but the logical thing to do would be to sleep in the middle of the island and have a fire for warmth there where it had previously been made. However, right in the direct middle of the island, he was a sitting duck; and if any form of rescue happened by, he wouldn't see it, and they wouldn't see him. It was true that he needed shelter from some of those who might find him, but he still needed to be in the open to see who was approaching.

It was the season for flash storms in the Caribbean, so he had to have some sort of shelter from the elements just for survival. He didn't know what creatures would come out in the evening, and he envisioned sand crabs biting him, an idea that was not welcome. He instantly thought of the solution and went back to the raft and riffled through the supply chest. He then took the hammock out and tied the ends to palm trees that were roughly six feet apart. He still had the other clothes in the bag to wear over what he now had on for warmth from the cool ocean breeze.

He formed rocks in a circle, then packed down the center as flat and solid as he could. He went around that area of the shore to find anything that would burn that was the right size to put in the middle of the fire pit he had made. He gathered two solid, firm sticks and rubbed them with enough force for the friction to cause a spark. Then he rubbed them harder to create a fire. He had it lit but had to run back to it a few times when he thought the wind might put it out. He gathered more firewood and kept a steady blaze going. He already noticed the darkening of the sky and approaching clouds. It was too early for evening to be setting in, so a storm must be brewing. He gutted the fish and cooked them over the fire and ate them as quickly as he could so that he would be ready with all his resources about him to try and battle any weather predicament that came along.

He squinted at seeing a large black swarm of something flying towards him. As the apparition got closer to him, he was able to determine that it was a giant swarm of mosquitoes. He had no cover and no repellent. Using his wits, he quickly dove into the water, away from the direction the swarm was traveling, which was towards the coast. Once in the water, he swam to the deeper water along the shoreline by a large rock formation. He was getting low on breath, but he was not feeling it was safe yet to pop his head up for air. He swam closer to the large rock formation and saw that he could swim under the rocks there to a small area in the middle of it. There was a small cave inside the base of the largest rock, and he popped his head up, gasping for air. Then he quickly slowed his breathing, not knowing how much air this cave contained. A black oil-based substance shined over the enclosed rocks. The nearest he could conclude was that it was the ink of squid or jellyfish. Something must have killed one or several of them that only the ink remained. He smelled what he wiped on his left hand, but he could not determine the nature of the smell. Then he quickly thought of how they sprayed swampland with oil to keep the mosquitoes away, so he rubbed his face and upper body with the oily substance that didn't wipe off with water. He couldn't reach his lower extremities, but he was able to extend his feet up to the top of the water in that small space, and he rubbed his feet and lower calves with the substance. He then filled his lungs with all the air he could hold before he lowered his body back into the now-colder ocean waters. He remembered the swimming motions that brought him into the cave, then traced his way back out. Just as he popped his head up from the water, he saw the giant swarm of mosquitoes fly off into the forested area of the jungle.

He made his way back to the fire pit and threw more branches over it to keep it going. Now especially, he savored the warmth of the fire but did not allow his body to stay too close to the heat of the fire, not wanting any of the heavy oil-based substance to leave his body as he needed his body to be covered to ward off the mosquitoes. Now is not the time for weakness to show. I am a Mondello. I have no weakness. Be strong. I can't lose my perception. There is strength in honor. Yeah right, Tom Hanks, with his crew and vending machines, and Steven Spielberg there watching him marooned on the lost tropical island in *Cast Away*. That was Hollywood . . . I am in reality. There has to be a corny line to finish this sentence. Yeah, it's called practicality and life. Jane . . . back to the hammock to turn in for the evening.

CHAPTER 11

She sat at the table, silent and nervous, not knowing what to say or how to act. She caught herself and straightened her composure, not wanting to show any weakness. She knew there was a strong man sitting next to her, a man who knew everything, especially a woman's vulnerability. She thought of a different person to show, and she had to keep with that person's character. It would be a long, slow process; but then so was this stay on the island, and it had only lasted two days so far.

She split open a roll, then took the plate of sliced fruit, and filled her plate. "Did you send out for this too?"

"Why do you need to know?"

"Okay, so we're playing that game. Well, for lunch, I want a hamburger, no lettuce, with cooked onions on it. I figure I might as well put in my order now. That way, you can give your henchmen the time to figure out how to get to the burger stand and back here to the estate undetected." This last statement from her bothered the boss, but he showed no sign that what she said had bothered him. Feeling further unnerved, she saw nothing to do or say, so she just took another sip of coffee.

He read the newspaper but kept it down on the table instead of holding it up so he could still see her. "I'm not going to be comfortable locked in my room all day, and my body will just atrophy. There is all this land surrounding your estate. With all your guards and maybe air patrol too, couldn't you arrange for me to go outside and at least get some air for some of the hours of the day, air and exercise? I don't see that you have a swimming pool, but I see there is a roped-off area in the ocean next to the shoreline of the estate. Would it be possible to go for a swim?"

He took his eyes from the paper and looked her square in the eye, which caused her to drop her head and look down to the table instead of at him. "I will get you a boom box for your room, and I'll have one of my . . . henchmen . . . bring up some of those hard rock CDs that you young people like. You will not do anything until I tell you to. Your safety is a factor. Do you want to dance against gunshots shooting at you? I have some paperwork to do this morning to transpose some information. I am expecting a very important transmission. I will have to leave the estate for an unspecified amount of time. I know that you like Bond. He will be back to watch you, but don't lose your heart to him. You should still be grieving for Chris. You were and still are married to him."

She nodded her head, then thought of how he was protecting her from danger, and she was thankful; but why did he bring up her dead husband? Was she supposed to pacify her emotions with his memory for the rest of her life? She sat quietly and ate some breakfast, then got up from her chair, and stood there silently until a guard came to her side and escorted her back upstairs to her bedroom where she was, once again, locked in.

To her amazement, they had put a television in her room. Maybe it was a reward for following orders. She turned it on but found poor reception and only limited channels. They probably blocked anything of importance, she thought to herself. She turned the dial repeatedly, and in doing so, she saw a brief picture. She turned the dial back to that station where she had seen the color. Well, surprise surprise. Bob Barker and *The Price Is Right*. He ought to get an award for the longest-running television show. He is still on it. Well, at least you don't have to dress up as a chicken to be on the show. You have to act as stupid as one, though. She sat herself down, made herself comfortable, and watched the show.

The show ended; then a soap opera started. She turned the television off, thinking of how she didn't want to be pulled into the torment of being a prisoner to a soap, but she knew that eventually, she would. She walked to the sliding glass door and opened the drapes more than the few inches they were open. She thought of how she could go outside and sit on the deck and watch the sea pull back and forth, but then she thought differently. There would be plenty of time for that. She missed her daughter so much, she felt like crying. The boss, Vincent, must know this; but he hadn't said anything about it to her. She didn't know what to say. She had said something once, but she didn't remember his response. He said that she was told some sort of lie, that she had run away from her, run away from life. Well, she did feel that she ran away from her life—that she never had a reason to doubt. Was Mr. Mann still calling Chicago looking for her? Boy, would her hotel-room bill be big by now.

She went to the table and grabbed a notepad, then walked around the room taking notes. She made notes of things that she would need to make her stay more comfortable. Now for the first time that she could remember, she felt an emptiness, a loss, a heartache, a longing for a lost love; and he wasn't there. Bond is a replacement, but the boss warned me about losing my heart to him, which I know I already have done. I don't know what to do. Write a love song; a long, slow ballad; a country song about losing my life and my heart? She got up and slowly walked in a circle. In those songs, they sing of wanting to end their life then because their cousin shows up with a crossbow and tries to kill them because they're in love with the same woman; and there was a car crash or somebody threw someone else off the bridge, so he had to down a bottle. Now he's drunk and with a gun, singing his heart out . . . stay away from the South. She laughed as she circled the room thinking of things that could be put in the room to make it feel more like her own place instead of the inside of a hotel room on a long trip—something, anything, to ease the burden of loneliness.

In the bathroom, standing at the mirror looking at her worn-out body, she put her index fingers to the sides of her eyes and pressed just hard enough to feel the sensation of skin on her face. The caged bird sings. I have a cracked voice. My daughter made me quite aware of that. She grabbed some of the various sundries that had been left for her by Bond. She picked up some nail polish, then looked at her fingernails, and saw that three of them had the polish chipped off. She sat down on the bench at the side vanity. Let's see. I'll take off the existing polish and repolish them with this new polish. How long can I make polishing my fingernails last? Chris?

At the docks on the west side of the island, the boss got out of the back of the limousine. Then a guard opened the door for him after he found the coast was clear. With a guard on each side of him and one in front of him and one behind him, he went into the building where supplies to be transported were held. He looked at the packed brown wooden boxes, then turned the corner, and went into the back office. It was lit with fluorescent lights, making the office appear much brighter. He had to take a moment to adjust to the color and brightness in the seemingly colorless room. A short slim Hawaiian man stood up from the desk, then nodded his head to the boss, and left the office. One of the guards closed the door after the man left the room.

One of the guards lifted the fax and handed it to the boss. He adjusted his glasses and read the fax. His eyes were moving over the transmission, but he showed no emotion at what he read. He took a handkerchief from his lapel, then sat at the desk, and reached for the phone, holding it in the handkerchief. He dialed the head of transportation for his coffee fleet that was still headquartered in Chicago. "Yes, Timothy, it's Vincent . . . Oh, everything is all right. I need to make a change in the shipments. You'll have to get two ships. Pack them full of crates of raw coffee beans. Make four of the boxes in one of the ships different. Plant a smell in these four boxes but nothing from an illegal source . . . put spices in them. They'll be a different weight, color, and container size to arouse suspicion . . . Yes, a planted decoy. How soon can you get these ships to the dock? . . . Two days?" He hesitated, wanting to say sooner but then thinking that the rush would arouse more attention than he wanted. "Okay, two days. Fax me back the information here when you can tell me what happened. Ciao."

He rose from the desk and walked towards the door, then stopped. One of the guards listened at the door, then opened it slowly, drawing his gun to his side, then walking out to the hallway and looking in every direction. He then motioned that it was clear to depart and go back outside to the limousine. The only stop made on the way back to the estate was at one of the restaurants he owned. They stopped in the back of the delivery zone of the parking lot, and a guard ran in the back door of the restaurant and came out only a minute later with a bag of food. The boss saw the bag on the seat next to him, then nodded to the driver to return to the estate.

Stopped in the portico at the front of the house, he waved his hand up to Bond who was perched on one of the towers. He started his way down the side ladder of the tower after he saw another guard waiting there for him to come down. In less than a minute, Bond was at the boss's side, and the other guard was now manning the tower. The boss handed him the bag of food and waved him away. Bond left then went into the house and upstairs to Jane's room. The other guard there stepped aside as Bond knocked on the door. He heard her voice and then opened the door with the key from his pocket. She smiled brightly at seeing him and waved him forward with her arm to sit down at the table with her, which he did, placing the bag of food in the middle of the table.

At the table, she smiled at him as he pushed the bag towards her. She took it and removed the items from the bag. She smiled in delight seeing the hamburgers. She took the wrapper off one of them and pushed the other to Bond. He smiled, thanking her. It was just the way she wanted it—no lettuce, mayonnaise, and grilled onions. She held it up and was in the act of taking a bite when she saw Bond. She put it back down, then took the plastic knife, and scraped the onion off the burger. She then picked it back up and took a bite. He took a bite after watching her do this. "This is good. Thank the boss for me."

"That is not for me to do. That is for you to do." She made no comment to his remark. "You are talking to him, aren't you?" She still made no comment to him. "It would be or will be a lot easier for you to just conform to things. There is a nice life for you here." She was ready to snap at him, thinking of her limited appearance and no freedom to do or say as she wanted and not even able to take a swim in the ocean for fear of snipers; but she caught herself from an emotional outburst, pressed her lips together tightly, and remained quiet. She then took another bite of the burger. Bond watched her do this, then made a half nod, and spoke up. "That was a good idea that you just had—biting your tongue and keeping silent."

She tightened her posture. "How do you guys do this? I said nothing. Your boss knows everything that I do and feel, and now you let me know that you do too. I mean, do you have a spyglass into my soul or what? What did you do to me when you had me drugged on the plane? What is the purpose of me being here and playing patsy? You are protecting me, but I didn't need any protection until the Mondellos showed up."

He looked to her, relaxed, and then responded to her, "You were the one who found us, remember? Why does a person who lives in California, the paradise destiny of the mainland, go to the smoky, crowded city of Chicago? And think about that one before you respond back to me in your high-pitched fashion. Look, I am only trying to be your friend in this situation. I am going above and beyond what I have to do for your benefit."

She put her eyes down to the table after he finished this response. She remained quiet for ever-passing seconds, then responded back to him, "This is a good burger. I will thank the boss, and thank you for the company." He squinted to her and then smiled and went back to eating the burger.

When they finished eating, he put the empty wrappers back in the bag and left it on the table. The quietness of the room was uncomfortable. He broke the stillness of the moment with a question. He leaned back and relaxed in the chair. "Say, have you seen any good movies lately?"

She found comfort. "No, I haven't, but I saw a really good episode of *The Price Is Right*." They went into comfortable daily conversation of no particular matter and stayed away from politics and any connection to the Mafia or the rival gang following them. He told her that things were pretty calm and that later in the evening, they might take a walk on the beach.

He left the room taking the empty bag from lunch. Her heart dropped as he left, but she made no sign of emotion. She listened to the door lock, then went back to the mirror, and looked at herself. More than anything, she wanted to change her looks, her appearance. Was it because she wanted to hide who she was or because she wanted to hide who she was becoming? She loosened her clothing, then took off her blouse, and put on a tee shirt and sweatpants. In the room in a clear space next to the sliding glass door, she started exercising; and then she thought of how she wanted the change, the change to herself. For the first time, the more she exercised and perspired, the more she just wanted to do it. She drove herself and found comfort in it at the same time.

She dressed nicely in one of the Ralph Lauren dresses for dinner and sat there calmly through dinner with the boss and Bond. After dinner, the boss went into the living room and listened to opera music while smoking a cigar. She and Bond did go out to the beach and took a slow walk along it. She enjoyed the outdoors and his company very much but made no comment. She remained in an even and calm temperament. Bond enjoyed the lack of conversation and not having to defend himself or the Mondellos. He did nothing but enjoy the change of colors of the sunset in the calm ocean waters. The only thing that he did other than just walking was occasionally looking over to her at his side and smiling at her as she, in turn, did the same.

As soon as they were back in the house, the boss set his eyes in their direction from a sideways stare. It wasn't a direct look, not enough to acknowledge, just enough to make them feel edgy. "I know the procedure by now. You take me upstairs to the door of my room. I stand back while you open the door and make a sweep of the room. Then you step aside for me to enter. I go in and stand at the doorway inside the room, and I look at you. You then look at me, put your head down, then close the door. And I stand there until I hear it close and lock." Bond said nothing. He looked straight-faced at virtually nothing, but he was absorbing everything.

The boss still did not make eye contact, but he replied to her, "Yes. That is right. Now go to bed."

She turned towards the stairway while Bond followed her. Upstairs, in front of her door, she stood farther back while he motioned through the room. Only after they changed places, with her inside the room and him in the doorway, did she speak to him. "I did this willingly and without any comments. I am obeying. Do I get any Brownie points for this? Do they accumulate up for a reward at the end?"

Bond smiled at her and held in his laugh although she could still hear it. "Good night," he said. Then the door was closed and locked.

Instead of going to the sliding glass door to open it up to let in the breezy night air or turning down the bed, she went into the bathroom but left the door open. She just stood there with her face to the mirror, examining herself. I don't like what I see. I see someone who is not me. I have to change, but change into what? I want my life back, the life that I was put into—the created life, the safe life. I want past memories, not of me but of Chris. I want the Chris that was in my life now. Then there would be reason, but would he want the new me? Or is it the new me? What about Bond? Why do they or the boss or the Mondellos—I only see one of the family, and that is Vincent—want me safe? I cannot carry on the family name. What about my daughter? I deserted her. What kind of mother am I? What does the church think of me? I left her there for the pastor and his wife to take care of, and I left. What lie did they create? I just didn't come back. Am I still in Chicago? Or Arizona for that matter? I have to find some way off this island, this estate. I have to get word to them that I am okay. I have to leave. Bond, I really need you now, but a different Bond, a fighting Bond. Unfortunately, for me, I know who I would be rooting for. And that Bond would not be the Bond that would work to my advantage.

Before turning in for the evening, the boss made a brief stop in his office. Bond stood by the open door. He made sure that the glass door to the outside patio was locked, then stood dormant but observant by the door, looking at nothing but seeing everything. Then he took the phone to his ear and dialed a number that he had no trouble remembering. "Yes, it's Mondello. I have to have a planted decoy in Malta. Make it known, but under ranks . . . You don't need to know where I'm hiding anything. I need them to look there. You know the routine and procedure. He came from the Caribbean to intercept a shipment of the new gold . . . right." He hung up the phone, looking straight ahead, but the picture that engulfed in his mind was of his family.

He got up and made a brief stop beside Bond. He released the hold over his body and turned his head halfway to Bond, then pulled away, and motioned with his hand for Bond to follow him to his bedroom to check it out before he went in. Then the boss could go in and close the door. He wanted to say something to Bond but couldn't. He didn't know whether it was because the time wasn't right or because he just could not let himself make known this information to him yet, and he thought it was probably a little of both. He got into bed, turned on his alarm for the morning, then started to pull open the drawer of the nightstand, but stopped, pulled his hand away, and turned over with his back to it. He left the drapes open with just the sheers covering the window. As soon as the light from the sun filled the room, he was up looking to the alarm and waiting for it to go off. He still set it every night, though, just in case there was the remotest chance that he would, indeed, sleep in.

CHAPTER 12

"Look guys, gals, there are hordes of you. So there has to be both unless you are self-duplicating or asexual. Let's get this in unison. All of you have to croak at the same time. Do it quickly, and get it over with because I have to sleep, and Now! Sorry I raised my voice at you. It's just that I'm going a little crazy here." There was no response or noise back from the frogs. He waited there like he was expecting something from them. He turned around, looking back to the ocean, then turned, and made his way back to the hammock. Okay, I'm getting back into bed now. So if you have anything to say, get it over with now. He got into the hammock, and all was quiet for a minute or so when a loud forceful chorus of croaking started, and it lasted for two minutes. Then all was quiet. He smiled to himself, then closed his eyes. One minute later, one frog started croaking. He turned his head and put his hands over his ears. The other frogs did not join in, and the one solo frog stopped. There always has to be one wise guy in the crowd.

The quietness of the evening ended about three hours later as the frogs started their chorus again. He woke up sleepy, then tried to find the comfort of sleep again. He whispered to himself, "Tomorrow, I am going to have to open coconuts in the evening and place them on the shore on the other side of the island. Females are always attracted to sugar, and where the girls go, the males will follow. Tomorrow—another night and day here. I have to devise a way off."

He closed his eyes and instantly envisioned her—the two of them together, holding each other while the music of their song played through his mind, "Looking for Love" written by David Coverdale and John Sykes and recorded by Whitesnake:

I'm tired of waiting an' closing my eyes. I'm asking myself, why is it all my horizons are so far away. I look in the mirror, don't like what I see. In my reflection, a stranger is staring at me. Looking for love. The love of a woman, the needs of a man. I try so hard to believe, but I don't understand. The search goes on, but over the mountains, across the sea, I know love is waiting. I hear it calling to me. Calling my name. I'm looking for love all around me. Looking for love to surround me. The love that I need to rescue the state of my heart. Alone again, it's always the same. I've just been making my time since the day I was born. With no one to blame.

The candle is burning. It's way down low. I just need someone to show me the way to go, which way to go. I'm looking for love all around me, looking for love to surround me. The love that I need to rescue the state of my heart. I'm looking for love an' finding only heartache. Looking for love an' finding only heartache. I'm looking for love to rely on. Looking for love, a shoulder to cry on. I'm looking for love to rescue the state of my heart . . .

The morning sun streaked across each grain of sand on the shore and sparkled on random grains. The water seemed to be transparent in the shallows of the sandy beach. The morning call of the birds broke the sound of the drifting ocean tides. He moved his head to the side and half opened his eyes, then jumped to attention, not recognizing any of his surroundings. He then lowered his head and moaned when it registered in his brain where he was and the predicament he was in. He shifted his head in each direction but made no motion to rise up out of the hammock to face another day on this island. He locked his view on a bird on the branch of the tree closest to him. He looked at the bird, took in his expression, then looked straightforward to the bird as he rose up out of the hammock and stood, stretching his body. He wiped his forehead, then looked again to the motionless bird. I'll have a double espresso, one sugar. The bird flew away.

I know he didn't leave to get me the coffee, and I've got to get some water. Anything but coconut milk. How many days has it been? Well, not counting yesterday, it makes it one day. I have to stay away at least three days. After three days, the coast guard mostly gives up looking for anyone.

I know that the raft has been reported missing from the cruise ship, and the ladies will surely make my disappearance known. They are probably going through every cabin looking for me. What are they going to tell the girls back in Toledo or wherever they were from? He went to the shore and waited for the tide to pull in, then bent down and cupped his hands to hold water and then splashed his face. He was shaken at seeing his darkened skin, then remembered he'd camouflaged his body with the oily substance the night before to keep the mosquitoes off him. I'd better leave it on. There is no telling when the swarm will return. He went back to the raft and bent over it, lifting out his bag. He pulled out the cell phone, and he opened it just to make sure that it was off, which it was. He could not risk sending a transmission from the island. Anything could be picked up, and he still didn't know if he was alone on the island. He went back to his hammock, looked at it, then gruffed, "This is home. It's no penthouse on Broadway, but at least Donald Trump doesn't own it. I don't have to pay rent. It's definitely a studio. There is no time for this foolishness. I've lost my wits. I have to start devising the rest of my plan. I'll go check on the raft again and get my bearings for the departure, which will be in two days." He left the shoreline with the compass and a small pair of binoculars. He didn't need to worry about a pad of paper and a pencil because all the information that he needed for his departure was in one place—his mind.

CHAPTER 13

He hiked through the middle of the island, making careful strides—fearing not only the unknown, but also the known rivalry against the family. He marked the direction of the sun with each look at his watch, then remembered the direction of the moon the night before. Once at the beach on the other side of the island, he checked the map that he had. He made calculations in his mind. I'm somewhere in the Lesser Antilles. The route of most cruise ships is up the west side of the Lesser Antilles until they reach the waters off the coast of Puerto Rico where they stop unless they weigh anchor at St. Kitts or St. Croix. That's it! The outer west St. Croix—I'll intercept a ship there, just not the same ship.

He stopped walking, seeing something shine off the side of the large boulder kissing the water on the cove on the right side of the shoreline. He stood quietly and as rigid as a deer for a few moments; then he gathered his thoughts and walked forward to view the shining object that was attracting his attention with its glare. Just steps from the object, he looked over the rock to his side, balancing on his tiptoes. There was a glare reflecting off a boat. Someone else, indeed, was on this island. He stealthily went into the water around the cove and saw an outboard cruiser anchored there. Its view was hidden from the island. He had company. He swam forward to the boat towards the back of it where the motor was.

He took out his knife and ripped the rotor off the back of the engine. Then he swam to the opposite side of the boat from where he was able to first view it. He slammed the knife into the side of the aluminum alloy boat just high enough so that it would still float on top of the water but wouldn't penetrate into the inside of the craft. He knew once it became water bound in deeper water, just the weight of the boat would cause it to sink lower in the water. Add the weight of the crew, and the boat would sink to the bottom.

He swam back to the shore, and just as he bent his body to stand back up, gunshots were fired at him from the depths of the jungle. He bent down again, running along the beach, listening to determine the direction of the bullets; then he ran straightforward into deeper water. In the now-darker ocean water, he noticed a shark's tail on the floor of the ocean. This didn't necessarily mean the shark was dead because they can regrow new body parts, but this was the decoy that he had been looking for. He splashed his body up in the water and into the gunshots, then screamed out in fear, attracting their attention even more. They now knew his location. He took hold of the tail carcass of the shark where the skin still remained and balanced it in his hands while giving the men onshore one more view of his face. They heard a cry and a scream from beneath the water and saw a raised shark's tail. Chris popped open one can of Pepsi, and another shade of darker fluid poured out into the water near the shore. The gunshots stopped, and laughter filled the air.

Chris inhaled all the air his lungs could hold, then dove deeper into the ocean water and swam to the right, which would take him around the coast to the other side of the island. Approaching a group of high boulders underwater, he heard the sound of the waves crashing on them; so he briefly surfaced, breathing in three times, then resumed swimming under the water. In what he thought to be fifteen minutes more of swimming under the surface and rising briefly to the top of the water for more air, he noticed the water was getting shallower. That was it—he was on the other side of the island. He rose up out of the water and ran in the direction of the sandy shore to his raft. He never stopped, even to look and see if the gang was approaching. He just followed his gut instinct, which served him right.

He ran, pounding the sand, only stopping to remove the rope tied to the tree to release the raft. The sound of the foliage moving up ahead was filling the air, and his heart raced faster. He ran, holding the raft to his side, and pushed into the water not yet deep enough to carry his weight and ride the current out. He ran deeper into the water and pushed the boat to the side, then jumped up, and landed stomach first in the raft. The raft sank down in the water with his weight. He took hold of the paddles and rowed as fast as he could turn his arms. He was powered by fear and the overwhelming desire to win. He saw the next wave rising up, then pulled the boat to the side to try and ride out from under the swelling current. He leaned the weight of his body to the side while paddling to get away from it, not wanting to be swept back up to the island. He could see a strong wind gust pushing to his eft, the wrong direction from where he needed to go, but it was a way out. He rode it and got in it and found himself fighting to stay afloat riding the gust. He fell out of the boat, and it moved away from him, but he was still within an arm's reach of it. His fingertips felt the side of the raft, then pulled back. He was losing it. It was pulling away in what he feared was a hurricane. He pulled into a swell at the side of the raft and lunged back inside of it while pushing water out of it. He rode it out of the swell but still had to fight with the current to keep the boat balanced.

With a deep sigh of relief, he came to an even current and somehow, in the circling motion, found that he had been blown back on course and was even closer than he predicted he'd be if he hadn't gotten caught up in that torrent of angry ocean currents. Balanced in the raft, he looked up to the sun and smiled at it. The splashing water of the angry current had washed most of the oily substance off his body. He didn't relish the idea of mosquito bites but then thought that this was good because he would most likely be reaching an inhabited island soon. He pushed his hair from his face. *That last bullet gave me a haircut.* He took the map out of the Ziploc bag, then looked at it and to the direction of the sun to figure his course. Occasionally, he had to row the raft back in the right direction. Luckily, the water and weather were calm on a now-peaceful seventy-two-degree day. The only thing that changed the calm expression on his face was when he moved and felt his overwhelming thirst.

He made plans to dock at St. Kitts, but the winds were blowing against him. Pangs of hunger and thirst consumed him. He knew that if he just stayed on this course where the winds were pushing him, he'd reach St. Croix. He looked repeatedly at the ocean water, looking for anything to wash up to the raft, ideally foodwise. He got to even wishing for a dead fish, but there was nothing. He swallowed in slow swallows, not wanting to feel the dryness of his throat. The evening moon was a half-moon. One side of the moon, he thought, looked like it was hiding, only giving the moon the appearance of a half circle, but he knew the other half was there. But if you looked at it in just the right way, you could see the dark shadow revealing the rest of the moon. *What is hidden on the moon? It looks mysterious tonight.* He didn't want to drift off to sleep, thinking he'd be lulled to sleep, and then a giant quiet shark would swim by and swallow him. He knew that these relatively shallow ocean waters would not harbor man-eating sharks, but there was still the possibility of a shark taking a bite out of the raft, leaving him for dead meat. He would not be able to swim to land since it was still so far away. He did lull himself into a short nap that refreshed his body. He woke up surprised by the idea that he had fallen asleep. He checked the time on his watch and was glad he'd slept only for a short time. He kept his eyes on the stars but was unable to name the constellation he saw. He guessed it was Sagittarius. *I bet it's Sagittarius, twenty to one odds. I'm a gambler. Yeah, wouldn't I like to be in Monte Carlo right now . . . Waitress, I'll take a Grey Goose vodka martini with a twist, shaken, not stirred . . . and my wife, out of the line of gunfire, that would be heaven, and my daughter—correction, our daughter—it's been so long, thirteen years. I still yearn for her. I wish that I could stay faithful. Where is she?*

CHAPTER 14

The following morning in Hawaii, the boss skipped breakfast and went right to the office. Bond had not reported for work yet. He took another one of the guards from outside the front door to his office to stand at the wall between him and the glass door to the outside patio. He didn't wait to have the computer turned on for him. He did it himself. He went to the Florida docks file, looked the picture of the dock over, and then got on the telephone to his man watching over dock 18. The Del Marco shipment had been stored the night before on the adjoining dock.

The man there had been surprised by the force of the police busting open the office door. They told him that they had received a tip from an unknown source that there were drugs being shipped in the coffee beans. The boss told him to remain calm and to let the police comb through anything that they wanted. It was also vital to get all the journalists he could down there now to cover the story. He hung up. Minutes later, the boss turned on the twenty-four-hour news station on the television. Dock 18 in the port of Miami was being shown as it was being searched by the police for drugs. Four boxes were pulled out in an open circle in front of the chief of police and military police as well as Mondello's man who worked in the dock space he owned there. His man looked cowardly and afraid, unaware what was going on. The four boxes that were put there in the circle were obvious since they were of different colors and weight than the other boxes. Another difference in these four boxes was that they were labeled HEMP on the outside. There was a definite odor that emanated from these boxes. The top of one of the closed boxes was pried open, and the chief of police smiled and began his pose. The top-ranking military policeman pulled out bottles of cinnamon and vanilla beans as well as bottles of colored sugar used to decorate cakes/cookies. Everyone in the building laughed. Then two more MPs stood on each side of the boxes and pulled out more of the same. The police chief's face fell as Mondello's man started laughing. Then a few more in the crowd laughed. The police chief stood there with a swollen, embarrassed facial expression. Then the story went back to the announcers behind the desk in the newsroom. "Well, April Fools' Day came early to some today."

The boss turned off the set, smiled, and then went to the dining room for his morning coffee. Jane was already seated at the table. She nodded to affirm his presence but said nothing. He had noticed the change in her behavior but said nothing. He poured himself coffee and then took a plate of fruit and opened the paper, commencing to read it. She looked ahead and to her side but at nothing, like a trained guard. Bond stood behind her, but she made no reaction to his presence there. The boss thought, What is this new game she is playing? She got up, pushed her chair in under the table, and took a side-view glance at the boss. "I will need a few more things, and I would like to pick them out myself. Will you arrange for one of your servants to escort me out to the town so I can get these things? I will behave. The only thing that I want is my daughter back. I'll change my life to whatever you want me to act out. I will cause you no problems."

The boss sat back, conservative in his expression, and thought, Why this sudden change of behavior? She has something planned out in that female mind of hers. He lowered his head out of her view, then responded back in solemn words, "Maybe tomorrow . . . Bond, take her outside and walk her around or something." Bond turned, facing the door, waiting for her to take the lead. She looked at the boss, lowering her eyelids to him, then turned, and walked out of the room. She heard Bond's footsteps at her side but said nothing to him either.

Bond was also suspicious of her behavior. He wanted to ask her the reason for it, but he rationalized that was what she wanted him to do. They were now walking on the stretch of beach, and he knew that the longer he held back any verbal response to her, the more it would make her crack. With each unspoken word, she felt more and more like screaming. She needed to release it—all of it or any part of it. She knew that he knew that his silence was tormenting her. She took her hand to the front of his body, holding him back from walking any farther. He snickered inside, thinking she was going to crack and that it hadn't taken as long as he had thought. She looked at him, circling her eyes to the outline of his face. "What time tomorrow do you think we'll be leaving?"

He emotionally fell at her response. That wasn't what he expected to hear from her. He looked at her straightforward, directly in the eye, with a guard's expression. "You'll have to ask the boss."

"The boss. I like that!"

Hearing this surprised Bond. All he seemed to hear from her was her wanting her other life back and crying. What sparked this change in behavior?

She more than sensed his change. "Come on, you can talk to me. We're from the same world."

"No, we're from different worlds drawn together at the same time but for different reasons—the same world."

Now more than ever, she wanted him to elaborate on what he just said and ask for the meaning, but she held back her need and desire to jump in and demand an answer. "If that's what you say. I suppose."

"The boss will determine when you find the answer to this." Skepticism and curiosity lured her overwhelmingly to want to demand an answer, but she swallowed and kept quiet, walking closer to the waves on the beach. She was teasing the water, stepping within its grasp, then pulling back right before it rose to cover her now-bare feet. Bond watched this and thought she was playing the same game with the water that she was playing with him. He watched her with quiet and silent observance. She knew more than ever that he wanted her to say something, anything, and she wanted to talk more than she thought she could contain herself; but with all her female charm, she held back dialogue and kept suspicion aroused in the air. She turned to him as he made immediate eye contact with her.

"Isn't it usually about this time that you have to turn and take me back to a bolted-shut room? Come on, let's go." She walked away from the beach and focused on nothing except the ground below her feet while walking back to the estate. Bond turned, watched her, then stepped forward, and quickened his pace to catch up to her. Once at her side, he slowed his footsteps but exerted no change in breathing. She swallowed her laughter at the good job she was doing. She wanted to look up to the windows of the house to find out who was looking at them, observing this behavior, but then she didn't want to be so obvious. She opened the door; then a hand went over hers and stopped her. She jumped.

Bond turned to her, showing anger in his facial expression. "You know better than that. I am always supposed to open doors before you and check the area before you go anywhere." He held her back, then went inside the door, and did a visual sweep of the room. Then he took her hand and pulled her inside. He motioned to the guard who stood at the side of the bottom of the stairway. The guard came forth. He told the guard to take her upstairs and put her in the bedroom. He took the key from his pocket and gave it to the guard. He looked no more to her, not wanting to see or have to react to her expression or anything she would say to him. The other guard held her tight by the arm and took her back to her room. Bond waited until they were out of view; then he stood back behind the open door of the boss's office and waited to be called in. The boss gave him a side-glance, looking up from what he was reading sitting behind his desk; and Bond walked forward, stood in front of the desk, and waited for him to nod his head. He sat in the chair in front of the desk, then waited for an additional nod before speaking.

"She's getting to a dangerous point. She is changing her behavior. I know this is to gain our trust, but she is already planning something." The boss waved his hand forward, motioning Bond to stop speaking. "I know this. Just let her play her hand. She has been conspiring with a scheme. I am fully aware of that. We're onto her, but we can't let her know that. You and I shall act pleased though verbally not saying anything about it. She wants to fit in as part of the family." Bond moved slowly and uncomfortably in the chair, saying nothing but expressing everything. "I know you are losing your heart to her—don't." The boss spoke these words solemnly and forcefully.

"When will Chris come back? Will he still feel the same way about her? He has the life of a playboy—gambling casinos, houseboats, luxury spas and hotels, life on the run. Women are suckers for that. I mean, will he . . ."

The boss slowly shook his head from side to side, then lifted his hand just inches atop of the desk. Bond knew the signal and also knew that the quieter the command, the more it was meant. "Chris is living a life, creating airs, of a different man. And he has handled himself quite well doing it. He is around these women, surroundings, but he knows his limitations. He doesn't know when he'll be coming back. It could be days, or it could be years, but I strongly doubt it would be the latter. You are Chris's brother." Bond covered his body with surprise and mistrust. The boss instantly read this. "I know you are speechless. It's life, an unexpected turn that you just have to take, but you are still on the same road. You see, you cannot allow yourself to get consumed with this woman. She is your family."

"But I was not conceived by Mother."

"No, you weren't, and I know that I will pay for that in heaven. I am your father, but there was another woman. You do not need to know her name, but she was your biological mother. My wife knew the truth, and she still raised you as her own."

"Is that or this the reason why I am your closest guard? I mean, you do treat me like family. I am still within the dangers of the job though, but so is your real son." He stopped after saying this, hoping for the boss to blow, saying how much that he loved him or something to that effect; but there was no response from him. He just looked straightforward, looking past Bond while still looking at him.

"I know that you talk to her a lot, things you shouldn't say. But you will say nothing of this, or you won't be my son any longer."

Bond felt the chill of these words on his nerves. He wanted to release himself in any way possible but found nothing, no way that he could. He silently rose up from the chair and returned to his guard duties, leaving the room and giving no response to the words that had just made a noose around his heart.

The boss sat in the chair unmoved by what he had just seen. He looked to the direction of the ceiling as though he was looking to his wife, seeking solace, but he felt no redemption. He did the only thing that he could. He lost himself in his work—checking the dock records, where his shipments were and where they were bound to. He had warranted off the police at one docking station, but there were others. Some of the chief points he didn't have to worry about because he had the whole assemblage involved and paid off so nothing would happen, and they knew if they tried to intercede in any of the shipments, the reward for doing so would be the loss of their lives. Protect to be protected.

Checking through the coffee records was starting to remind him too much of Chris. Where was he? He couldn't send help for he had no idea of his whereabouts. He closed the file on the coffee business, placed it back inside the side drawer of his desk, and took out the file on a cigar business he owned. He picked up the phone and dialed the number of the man who watched the shop there. The phone was answered, and he instantly started conversing with him in Italian. In only an instant, he was laughing and forgetting the complexities of his family.

Bond reveled in his thoughts, feeling unloved and becoming unrestrained in his composure. He made his way to the outside right-hand side of the patio opposite the beach and talked to the guard there. The guard nodded and called for another to watch the side door of the inside of the office, and Bond went into the house, then came out only ten minutes later dressed in sweats. He looked at the ocean and the overall view of the beach; then he clasped his gold cross necklace and placed it inside his shirt. Then he took off in the direction of the beach at a quick run, undaunted by reflections of words. He had lost his onetime wife and family to a divorce asked for by her. He was lost in the ring of his job, unknowing that it was his family. He had lost the love of something that he had found. Now knowing the truth of his real family, he felt no warmth, no encircling of love. He felt removed from it. He heard a person running up behind him. He didn't want to know or find out who it was, resisting his guard training.

He glanced to the side and saw that it was Jane. He looked to the side of her, wondering why she had been let out. He figured it had to be by orders of the boss, further punishment. He no longer felt the desire to talk to her or be warmed by her presence. Opening her mouth to speak to him, then feeling his contempt for her, she changed to silence, then smiled at him, and picked up her stride, passing him up on the run down the beach. He looked ahead and saw her, knowing the happiness that this must have given her in doing this. He was further entwined in the circle of distrust and resentment for what had happened to him in his life. It wasn't his life. His life had been the boss's version of his life, but what could he do now? Hope that when Chris did come back with someone else that he would be there to catch Jane, the understudy? That was mostly what he felt like now. No pride, no honor, no worth, no dignity—everything had been ripped right off him. She was playing a role. He felt that he could too. He changed his mind to feel what he had felt for her and not what the boss, his father, had told him to feel for her. There was still a chance that she would fall in his arms and not Chris's. He ran in a circle, then went back to running in her direction. He saw her watching him do this, and she smiled even more brightly.

When he got to her side, she asked him why he ran off. He told her to build up steam so that he could outrun her. He quickened his pace and passed her up. She started to catch up to him; then out of breath and panting wildly, she stopped, bending over to try and catch her breath and slow her elevated heart rate. He still ran to the tree that ended the stretch of open beach, then ran back to her at a slower, leisurely run. "Couldn't catch up to me?" He smiled at her, saying this as she was still too out of breath to respond back to him.

She bent her body back up. "No, just you wait. You will be so far in back of me that it won't even be funny!"

"The funny thing is you telling me that. That day will never happen!"

She smirked at him. "Women are a lot stronger than you think." "Oh, I know that. A woman can drive a man to drink." He looked back at her, thinking full well he had the last word in on the matter and had won the argument.

"The woman knows that she caused the man to drink, and this stupefies him. So in the long run, she wins anyway."

He shook his head to her. "I am not going to engage you with words on this matter any further, and silence drives you women crazy."

She gave him the evil eye because there was just no way that she could respond back to him on the words he had just said to her. She ran back to the house, then stopped on the patio, and sat on one of the chaise lounges. He sat down ten feet from her on a patio chair. They both remained quiet, knowing the bounds of the house rules.

After two hours of resting in the sunlight, they were told by the wave of another guard by the door to the house that it was time to go back in. At the top of the stairs, standing back behind the now-open door of her bedroom, she stood still, having only one foot inside the room. Turning her head to the side, she looked both at Bond and the other guard who stood to the side of her door, "I don't know when lunch will be, but I don't feel the slightest bit hungry, so you won't have to come and get me for lunch. I am reading one of the novels that was left in my room last night, and I want to finish it. I see that two more bottles of San Pellegrino have been left on the table as well as a bucket of ice. I'll be fine." He looked at her, feeling warmth but then catching himself to remember the new knowledge he had of the situation and of how he couldn't lose his heart to her, but he already had. He nodded to her as the other guard then closed the door, pushing her inside the room instead of walking her in the room. She didn't change her expression although surprised by his actions, reminding herself of the new life she had to live through to gain her freedom.

Inside the room, she poured herself a glass of water from the bottle, then huffed out. Looking at everything in the room, which still seemed sparse, she reminded herself of the life that she wanted. She took another swallow of the water, then stood up almost at attention in the middle of the room, then started a course of vigorous exercising. Catching herself in the middle of side leg lifts, she slowed her movements, knowing full well that if she continued exercising at this vigorous rate, she would burn out before she could make it halfway through the amount of exercising she wanted to do. After one and a half hours of exercising, she stopped, walked to the table, and gathered her breath, slowing her breathing before taking a swallow of water. She turned abruptly and walked to the bathroom and looked at her body in the mirror above the vanity sink. She opened the drawer of the vanity and took out a measuring tape. She measured her arms, then her bust, waist, and hips. She made no written record of the measurements, just remembering them in her mind, and thought of how much each of the measurements was going to have to come down. Looking at herself in the mirror, she brushed her hair with her hands and moved it in different directions, trying to think of a new style. She nodded her head, coming to a conclusion about her new look and making mental notes of what she would have to do.

The boss went through every business dealing that he presently had going. He was able to half forget about his missing son and revealing the truth to his other son. He knew he had stayed back from feelings, expressing nothing to Bond. He was strong, and he was conveying this. It would make Bond stronger too. This business did not work with emotions circling in the air. He left the office, going outside to the side deck patio. The guard was surprised seeing him go there and stay there. He had never visited that patio before; he only looked out to it through the open door. He liked feeling the air of the breeze from the open door. The guard expressed nothing but the trained, secure, heavy stare, observing everything and feeling nothing. The boss looked to a cloud rolling by in the sky above him; then overwhelmed with the silence and lack of motion, he took a cigar from his vest pocket and leaned forward for the lit match that the guard held in his hand for him. He puffed in but wasn't able to breathe in on the cigar. Then he realized that he had not cut it before trying to light it. He blew out the dying orange heat from the tip of the cigar, then took out his cutter from the same pocket. He cut off the tip and dropped it, not looking to the ground to see where it went. He was usually very picky about things like that, and seeing the tip of a cigar on the brick patio floor would usually have driven him crazy. If he did not reach down to pick it up, he would have instructed the guard to do it, but he did neither; and this action did not faze him at that moment. The guard then relit his cigar; and he took the first breath of it, coughed it out, then stood still, gathering his thoughts and concentrating on nothing but the smoke that would be inhaled from it and the enjoyment felt from the dark tobacco of the Montecristo number 5 cigar. He stood there smoking the cigar and watching the sky without showing remorse or feeling for anything. The overhead clouds turned to shades of gray tinted with a brown contrast. He thought it odd the change in color of the clouds, then remembered the tropical climate and thought of the oncoming rain that would shower over the land of the estate. He did not hurry in smoking the cigar, thinking that if the rain did start, he would still stay there trapped in the raindrops expressed from the clouds while smoking that cigar. Crying from heaven is what he emotionally felt in feeling every light raindrop from the shower storm hit the flesh of his skin. Inside, he was crying, feeling each drop. He stood there strong and proud, feeling the drops tingle on his skin. He dropped the cigar to the bricks and stepped on it, putting it out. Then he looked to the guard looking straight ahead but still at him, and he went back inside the office and closed the door to the outside patio. Inside the house, he went to his bedroom.

CHAPTER 15

The boss sat on the side of the bed and pulled open the drawer of the nightstand, taking out the picture of his wife. I guess you know that I told him the truth today. I know, why did I? He had to know. I had to tell him eventually. He would have found out, somehow, some way. I am getting too old to be traveling all around the world. I am making our home here in Hawaii my permanent home. I'll sell Chicago. Our place on Lake Como in Italy, I'll pass that down to Chris. But Bond, what will I leave him? Chris, I hope and pray, will come back eventually—the sooner the better for my heart. I miss you. I miss you greatly, more and more each day, and I cannot wait for the day that I see you. But it is too soon. There is still much for me to do, much that I have to do for us, for our children, Bond and Chris. You know that they are both in love with her. One of them will get her. He started to cry and took a handkerchief off the top of the nightstand, wiped his eyes, and blew his nose. I know I have to be strong. I am the father, and I am the boss. I . . . He stopped talking, feeling that telling the dealings of the business was not something to be telling his wife in heaven. I love you, and I will do my best to make everything right for you.

He lay down and closed his eyes to take a nap and wondered how he was going to make it right for himself. He knew that he controlled lives, the lives of his workers and business partners; and occasionally, he encountered interference and had to order that lives be lost. Now he wondered, were they the lives of the bad or just the lives of those bad for his business? He stopped himself in this line of thinking. He was the boss of the organization. He could not think like this. It showed weakness, something he was never allowed to feel. He reassured himself that Chris was all right. He knew how to handle himself. It was just Bond. He would have to get him away from the estate for more free time. Maybe then he could meet a woman who would capture his heart and not break it. Maybe he could find love again. He would have to give him standing in the family, the estate, the business. He already had a part in that, but a part just the same as all the others. He would have to reveal the truth to all of his employees of his shortcoming and that Bond was his son. He would be displaying weakness, something a boss like him was not meant to do. Let time absolve all things and see what comes to be or deal with it straight on and be thought little of. He could not turn to either side for an answer. He thought he would do nothing. He would give Bond a raise, a step-up in the job, a better standing. Bond had been there forever and a day as far as the others knew. That was the answer for now anyway.

She dressed for the evening meal. She was used to doing this by now. It was a formal occasion though the only ones there with her were the boss and usually Bond. Of course, they were watched by additional guards. This home was not a place where one could drop his guard. The rules were strict though both the boss and Bond were comfortable with this lifestyle. The knock on her door was never more than five minutes from the time of the night before. Sometimes, it would be a different guard than Bond; but tonight, she was sure that it would be him. She was aware of a change in his behavior, but then he reverted back to his previous behavior. She thought, well, she had changed in her behavior too. And he was aware of it but made no verbal acknowledgment.

She was dressed in a dark green satin dress with three rows of velvet at each side of the bustline, and the dress hung just below her knees. She wore black velvet sandals that wrapped around just above the ankles. The only jewelry that she wore to accent the dress was a pair of silver circle clip earrings. She went lighter on the shade of lipstick, not wanting to go red or bright pink to offset the color of the dress. Instead, the lipstick just highlighted the natural color of her lips, leaving a glowing shine. She stood behind the bedroom door looking at the second hand sweep on the face of the watch, counting the seconds until there would be a knock on the bedroom door.

The knock came only four seconds past the first minute of the five-minute time frame she had estimated, and she was more than surprised that it was not Bond who would accompany her downstairs. She recognized the guard. He had accompanied her downstairs before, but she made no verbal response to him. She just immediately went down the stairs and to the dining room. She stood back from the red area rug that went under the table and out from the chairs. She stood there waiting for the boss to nod his head, giving her permission to enter the area of the dining table and sit down. She was surprised, but then not too surprised, seeing Bond already seated at the table opposite from her seat. He was wearing a black dress suit and looked more than handsome. She wondered why the formal dress, a change from his usual guard attire, but she made no response after seeing this. She just pushed out the chair and sat, then sat up to push the chair back in under the table, something that Bond himself normally did for her.

She needed an answer for the racing, questioning wheel revolving in her mind. She did not want to look at the boss, for he had a way of knowing what she was thinking, and she wanted to remain calm and unquestioned. She turned her head to his side after hearing him unscrew the cork of a bottle of wine. He poured the three glasses before him each three-quarters of the way full, then looked to Bond who reached for one, then handed one to Jane. He made a toast, and they each took a sip. No words were spoken by either of the men, which she thought odd, but she said nothing and made no uplifting response to the silence. Next, she saw a salad before her, and she didn't even notice the server had come into the room to deliver the salads to the table.

The next course was grilled mahimahi over a bed of rice with a lemon butter sauce and a sliced, curled lemon on top of it. All remained quiet through dinner with the exception of an occasional smile from Bond when he looked at her. She wondered if they were setting her up for something. There had been no recent encounters of fear from the other gang or bullets ricocheting off the walls or through the windows. The anticipation of the moment had become more than she could bear, but she knew that she could not jump off the walls, which was the way she currently felt. The boss was compelled to comment on her feelings, feeling how unnerved she had become. He was prepared to tell her that Bond was his son, but then he contemplated whether this would make things worse.

Recognizing her fragile state of mind, he thought better of the fact of releasing the truth, but he could see no option. "You have probably noticed"—she turned to look at him as if she thought he was telling her that she had just won the lottery of a million dollars—"that Bond here is very close in my operation." She said nothing but nodded her head. "Well, there is a reason for this. A very good reason and an important reason. You see, Bond here is a relative." She turned from his face and looked at Bond who was looking at the boss. "He is a relative of the family."

"A relative of the family?"

He raised his tone and composure to a very strict and formal appearance. "Bond is your missing husband's brother and my son, though not by my departed wife. And you are not to say anything about the latter, and nothing needs to be said further on this matter. You will stay in his guard . . . as you behaved before."

She was taken aback by hearing this news. Then she thought of her missing husband who haunted her thoughts and dreams. Bond is Chris's brother. The feeling she had towards Bond, then. Was this incest? Bond was Vincent's son. Why hadn't he told her this before? That is why he treated her like family—because they are family. She sat back in the chair and made a deep sigh, feeling her heart race. She couldn't look at either one of them and felt both of them looking at her. She took another breath and heard no words spoken by either one of them. They were waiting for her verbal response, which she couldn't give. She just sat back in her chair, planted her feet firmly on the floor, and pushed back her chair. Then she got up and turned around, looking away from the table to the direction from which she had entered the room. "I am going upstairs to my room. I am not feeling well . . . I am just going to my room. I am sure that there will be a guard at the base of the stairway. There usually is. I know that he will take me upstairs. Please, the two of you just stay here." The last words she spoke were barely audible to either one of them as she was out of the room and halfway upstairs.

A guard did take her up the stairs, and she stood back from the door as he entered the room and made a sweep before she entered. She went in the room, transfixed in state, never looking at the face of the guard. Inside the room, she stood with her back to the door and waited until she heard him lock the latch from outside. Feeling weak, she felt as if she was going to fall even while leaning against the door. To avoid the inevitable, she slid her body to the floor, sitting with knees bent and her feet forward. She cried and took off her sandals. In a hurried, angry motion, she threw them at the wall. Then they flew off the wall, after making a scratch on the wall, and fell to the top of the bed.

I am being treated like a lost treasure with no life of my own. What am I? A missing piece on the golden chessboard of the family? The Family. She thought in her mind that she had to get out. She rose up from the floor, feeling strength from the angry state that she put her body in, and she unzipped the back of her dress and just threw it on the floor and went into the bathroom. She came out five minutes later dressed in pajamas. She looked at the bed, then turned away from it, and turned on the television and started exercising, running in place, while devising her strategy to leave the island and flee the estate.

She could feel her body gasping for air, more than air, but she couldn't release herself from the hold wrapped around her body. She slowly slowed her motions, then collapsed her body to rest on the bed while rhythmically breathing. She gazed at the view of the television screen and saw the color of the screen, but she couldn't make out the vision that she saw. She closed her eyes and took her fingers to the side of her eyes, pressed against her nose between her eyes, then reopened her eyes, looking down to the plain backdrop of the bedspread, then straight ahead to the picture glaring from the television screen. She laughed. Well, what do you know? *MacGyver*. I've got to listen to this. I might learn something that I will need to know. She sat watching the show with the utmost interest, forgetting about that the facts she had just been told, which grabbed her like a noose, constraining her and limiting her life.

At the end of the *MacGyver* show, she turned off the television, then took the notepad off the table, and wrote out a list of things to get the next day when she was going to be taken out shopping. She knew that writing this list was not a safe thing to do. The boss seemed to know and predict everything, but she couldn't take the chance of forgetting anything that she needed as now she knew how she was going to make her escape. She knew most of the plan anyway. There was still the problem of how she would get off the estate. She was going to have to gain trust and be given more leeway on what she could do there. She thought she had handled herself pretty well that night. Silence was killing her, and it would kill her even more, but that was the only current thing that she could think of—that and the exercising diet. She was going to have to lose weight and keep the fact that she was doing it from them. She could pad her clothes with towels, sheet covers, anything. I am determined I am going to make it out of here. She held her hand open under her chin and the side of her face and whispered, "Bond . . ." She got under the sheets, turned on the alarm clock, turned off the light, and went to sleep.

CHAPTER 16

The sun commanded the sky over the island, banishing every cloud from the sky. A person's image was mirrored over the clear waters on the beach. A more pleasant day could not have been asked for. A music CD of Jim Brickman played throughout the house instead of the usual opera music. Jane took a sip from the espresso coffee cup at the kitchen table. The boss watched her from the corner of his eye as he usually did. She smiled, then wished him a good morning. He was happy that she was in a good mood, or at least that is what she conveyed through her presence.

She passed on the biscotti and instead reached for an orange from the center fruit bowl on the table. All her attention was concentrated on peeling the orange, so she didn't notice Bond come to the table and sit down across from her with a cup of coffee. She knew that he was there but made no affirmation of him, keeping her eyes locked on the orange. While peeling the fruit, some of the juice sprayed on her face. She immediately pulled the napkin from her lap and covered her eye, biting her lip from the pain of the citrus stinging her delicate eye. She didn't even see him get up, but Bond was there at her side. He dipped a napkin in the glass of ice water on the table in front of her and then dabbed it on her eye. She looked to him surprised and felt thankful but only nodded in appreciation.

Moments later, she and Bond were sitting in the Hummer on their way to the shopping mall. He was more than surprised when he turned on the radio, and she didn't change it to a different station.

She wasn't even voicing her usual sarcastic wit through the confined air of the SUV. There was a definite change that he was aware of and wondered if it was an actual change or if she just wanted to gain his trust and attention.

In the parking garage at the mall, she sat inside the SUV reluctantly until he came around to the outside of her door and opened it, holding her arm while she got out. She made him hold her hand while they walked inside the mall. He wondered about doing this and why she wanted him to but then thought it was safer on his part. She would have more trouble trying to lose him.

The first stop they made was at the Gap. She took two pair of size 12 blue jeans with a pair of black slacks size 10 sandwiched in between them. On the way to the fitting room, she stopped at a rack of hanging tee shirts. She moved the wire hangers quickly, just stopping long enough to read the size tag under the collar, and she took out three tee shirts. The two on the outside were bright pink; and the one in the middle, all Bond could conclude, was a dull beige.

He stood outside the entryway to the dressing rooms. She tried on a pair of the size 12 pants and a pink tee shirt, and they fit. She didn't try on the others because she knew that the matching tee shirt and pants would fit. The others she was going to have to work on. She walked out of the dressing area and headed straight to the cash register. Bond stood to her side, and she nervously nodded her head down upon seeing him. Then she grabbed a wrapped plastic bag of crew socks and placed everything on the counter in front of the cashier. She said nothing to the cashier or to Bond, only turning to him and looking at him, wondering why he had not given the cashier payment for the merchandise. He quietly snickered and took the company credit card out from his wallet for payment. The cashier commented on whether that was the reason that she brought him along on their shopping trip, just to pay for things. He commented back to the cashier that his "wife" was definitely a woman who knew things like that.

Back inside the mall, she seemed to drop some of her guard or nervousness, but he still could not figure out the reason for this new behavior. She took hold of his hand again but this time, took hold of his flesh almost gingerly. He thought that was intriguing but peculiar behavior. He asked her where she wanted to go next, and she pointed to Victoria's Secret. He nervously followed her there and walked inside the store with her, looking away from the smiling saleswomen. He looked to the wall where ladies' thongs hung, then turned away from both views and saw a mannequin wearing a low-cut front-closure bra. He whispered in her ear that he would be waiting on the bench in the mall outside the store. All smiled and contained their laughter as they watched him hastily exit the store.

She got underwear, bras, and nightgowns in both her size and one size smaller. She then signaled him, and with reluctance, he reentered the store and gave them his credit card and signed for her merchandise. He looked at nothing except the ceiling while back inside the store. He walked out by her side but would not hold her hand. They walked through other stores just looking at things—a poster store, a music store, an art boutique. They stopped at the food court of the mall. She sat down at a white shining Plexiglas table in a black plastic metal-bottom chair and relaxed. He stood in front of her and asked her what she wanted as he took a twenty-dollar bill out from his wallet. After hearing her answer, he left and only went to that one café that had what she wanted, and he got his lunch there as well.

He set the tray down on the table as she pushed the shopping bag back down to the floor, giving him room to set down the tray. He pushed an ice tea and the carrot-raisin salad that she had asked for in front of her. He had a small shrimp Louie salad and a can of Diet Coke in front of him. She thanked him, and then they went into the course of eating and light talk, which contained laughter—back to their usual behavior.

He noticed that at the front gates of the estate, while they waited for them to be opened, she changed her behavior back to the same behavior she had expressed at the breakfast table that morning. He also changed his behavior back to the behavior of a guard on duty. The boss watched them as they got out of the Hummer. Bond took her bags out of the back; then she grabbed them from him and followed a predetermined path inside and up the stairs of the house. Forgetting the locked door, she stood there silently and waited until the boss told another guard there at the front door to go up and let her into the bedroom. He watched Bond walk in through the front door, then motioned for Bond to follow him inside his office. Bond closed the door behind him, then sat down opposite the boss at the desk.

"How did it go?" Bond expressed a look of unrest and uncertainty through his closed persona. "What did you do, or what is she planning?"

"That's just it. I don't know. Her behavior—she was definitely different in her behavior last night, this morning, and at the start of our trip. But at lunch in the mall, she loosened up back to her usual self. At the front gate, it was like something just came over her, and she reverted back to this new image she has created for herself."

The boss looked at Bond skeptically. "Do not lose yourself." Bond looked away from his view and to the side, then lifted his head up from looking at the floor, knowing that displayed weakness. Looking to the boss but not at his face, he stopped moving his body and direction of eyesight and opened his mouth, clearing his throat and gathering the boss's attention. He masked the nervousness but showed humility. "Why didn't you ever tell me that I was, that I am your son? I mean, I am your blood. I am part of this family."

The boss felt a torrent of anger rip through his nerves. He lowered his eyelids halfway down and showed contempt in his eyes. The first thing that rolled of his tongue was the answer, "Guilt". He made a hard swallow. "You have been raised by me and my dear departed wife. You have always been a part of this family and taken care of. You have been in danger in this job, but not as much danger as my son, my other son, Chris." The boss raised his hand to his mouth and took his index finger to his mustache area. He wiped his finger over it twice, feeling the top of his lip. Then he took his hand from his face and reconfigured his body to sitting upright in the chair. "I kept you from the truth . . ." He looked away from his son's eye view. "I feel that you are able to handle this knowledge now." He got up from the desk and took a pitcher of water, poured himself a glass, and took a swallow. With his back to Bond, still sitting in the chair, he went on. "In five minutes, you have to guard the right tower on the shoreline." He paused, still holding the glass of water. Bond showed hesitancy, deliberating on what to say or do; then ten seconds later, he got up from the chair, walked out of the room, holding the door open, then looked back to the floor of the room, and closed the door. The snapping of the latch when the door was closed echoed through the air.

The boss sat back down at the desk. A tear welled up in his eye. God told me to tell him the truth. He breathed out, lifting his head up. This family is going to be kept together. He reached to his roll-dial directory and thumbed through it, stopping at the name of the shipyard in the

Caribbean on the coast of Jamaica. He talked with the head shipman at the port and explained about his shipwrecked son.

They need to find him. The only fear that he was aware of, other than dehydration in a lifeboat, was that of the Cuban drug runners finding him. There wasn't much chance of being captured. It was more like being killed. The boss swallowed more heavily upon hearing that said to him. He mentioned a great reward—cash-value reward—for finding him. He left his number, something he had never done before. Usually, he used transmissions over the computer. He had gone against his instincts this time because his heart was growing weaker with each passing second of not having contact with his son.

Upstairs, Jane moved in a calculated path, putting things away from the shopping bags. In the closet, she put the smaller-size pants and the smaller tee shirt away to the right side of the closet out from the middle area where the other clothes hung. The bottom middle drawer of the dresser is where she kept the smaller lingerie as well as a bottle of reddish blonde hair dye. It sure was good that I commented to that saleswoman in Victoria's Secret that I loved her hair color. I talked her into selling me that extra bottle of dye that she had in her tote bag to have her hair dyed that day in the beauty shop in the mall. I just have to devise the right time when all of this is going to happen. I have the airline flight schedule that I picked up at the information desk in the mall, which I covered up with a map of the mall, and I have my credit card number memorized. Timing is the essential key. I have to exercise more. Lose weight so I'll fit into the tighter clothes, dye my hair, wear these dark glasses . . . change my identity. I'm getting pretty good at doing that. It's just a matter of timing and not making them suspicious that I'm doing it.

She closed the drapes and put on her sweat clothes. Turning on the stereo, she put five CDs in the player—Cher, followed by Meat Loaf, then Aerosmith, Led Zeppelin, and, Whitesnake. David Coverdale, you are still the finale. She bent to the floor and started leg lifts to the sound of the song "I Bet Your Wife Tells You That Every Night." Hearing herself say the word "wife," she fell into a silent, lost mood, then regained her strength and moved her body in the motion of the music, thinking of how badly she wanted this change.

CHAPTER 17

Hovering on top of the ocean waves, he lay with his body rigid in the raft. He felt to be in a delirium from the heat of the sun and the parched dryness of his throat. He squinted, then raised his arm over his face, and looked at the time on his watch. Okay, it's two o'clock in the afternoon here in—he laughed—the paradise of the Caribbean, somewhere in the Caribbean. According to my watch, I am heading north, but I've been heading north for two days now. He saw a shadow fall over his body; he knew he was still on the ocean and not on treasured land. He wondered what entity had caused this shadow; he wasn't really afraid, but fear showed apparent over his tired body. He took all his strength and raised himself to sit up in the raft, in the middle of the raft for balance. He looked to the sky and saw one single cloud roll over the sky above him. I feel like the losing party in a sad love song, the song that you hear in an elevator that makes you want to run out and take the stairs. He squinted further after seeing a color-craft vision over the ocean waters to his east. He squinted, then reached down to the half-open dark cloth bag and pulled out a pair of binoculars. He saw land—the island! He sat upright in the raft and used the oars to reach the island. He swallowed his weariness and sat tall, balanced, and strong making his way to shore.

He arrived at the wooden dock and grabbed hold of a line, pulling himself and the raft in. There were some people watching him, but no one helped. Standing on the dock, he turned, looked at the raft, and then just walked away from it.

On the other side of the pier from where he had landed, there were cruise ships docked. He went away in the opposite direction, mostly fearing that he might be spotted by his adoring fans on the cruise ship he had been on earlier.

He was in Puerto Rico, an American island, and language here was no problem. Being familiar with the docks, he knew that he was in the city of San Juan, the only place where boats could dock on the island; and the Bacardi Rum Distillery was there, as well as a large U.S. national park El Yunque with twenty-eight thousand acres of rain forest, the best sports fishing, and the home offices of many American banks. This will be an interesting stay, he thought. The first thing to do was to find a hotel to stay in, but under what name should he register? He was not out of danger—yet. Here, on this American island with no restrictions, it was easier for everyone, including the enemy. Then he realized that the most natural place for him to go would be to the coffee warehouse, his father's coffee warehouse.

He needed a place to think out of sight. The most logical place to go would be an American hotel, the Hilton. In the lobby of the Hilton, he saw other workers from a cruise line enjoying themselves at the bar. That was it—this was his out. Then he thought that this avenue was getting stale since he had already used that route before on the other island. He had to keep an alibi. He peered closer inside the bar and noticed laughter, then looked up to the television on top of the bar counter. The television show *Will and Grace* was on. He had never watched that show; the only thing that he had heard about it was that one or two gay guys were living with a straight woman—typical New York humor. But that was it, that was his alibi. He checked into the hotel under a fictitious name; and when asked for identity, credit card, driver's license, anything, he reached out and grabbed a clip of hundred-dollar bills. He smiled at the man behind the check-in desk. "How much is this room, $400 a night?" He raised his shoulders and spoke in the closest approximation of a woman's voice that he could master while expressing a woman's mannerisms. He took another hundred-dollar bill and pushed it in front of him over the counter and placed it in the clerk's hand. "I don't want any interruptions, if you know what I mean. Bill and I have had a long"—he reached up and gently touched his face and then batted his eyes—"well, it's been a long week. And

Bill and I just need to relax and be left alone, if you know what I mean." The clerk quickly retracted his hand from the counter and pushed a key card in his direction, then told him that he would have no interference. Chris took the card and ran his hand behind his back butt cheek, then turned around, and winked at the clerk.

Chris waited until he saw a man walk to the elevator, then ran up alongside this man, following him into the elevator while the clerk watched this. He shook his head. "We are definitely living in a new age," he said and lowered his voice, "beyond the Age of Aquarius." Chris exited the elevator on the eighth floor at the middle of the hallway. He read the sign showing the directions of the rooms. He read the numbers to the left and the numbers to the right, but he didn't know which way to turn, not having paid close attention to the room number when the clerk handed him the closed paper containing the key card. Nervously, he opened the paper containing the key card and read the number, room 805. He went down the left hallway. He was glad the room was down the left hallway. He had noted that the rooms on the left side of the hallway were always better, with the exception of that suite at the Sheraton Palace in San Francisco.

He ran the card down the strip on top of the doorknob. It flashed green, and he instantly opened the door. He quickly closed the door behind him while he stood looking over the room. He hadn't expected that $400 would have bought him a suite of that proportion, but it did. The room was very large. The wall straight ahead was all window with a glass sliding door to the deck outside, and lounge chairs dotted the deck. Thick gold drapes were pulled back over white sheers that swayed in the breeze coming in through the half-open door. The furniture even looked expensive, far from the normal hotel-room furniture. A small bar was to the right side of the glass window. The wall to the right of the room was solid. There was a half counter with coffeemaker, small refrigerator, and kitchenwares to the left side of the room and a half bath by the door as one walked in. The bedroom was to the right of the small kitchen area at the left side of the room. Two wooden double doors opened to the bedroom. The colors in that room were gold and red with wood-stained walls to the side of the bed. The room had a romantic feel though it still possessed a masculine air. The bathroom with a sunken bathtub and walk-in shower were to the left side of the bed. Well, Bill and I would have a good time in this room. He laughed.

Then he sat down at the end of the bed to start thinking out his plan. He walked to the refrigerator and lifted his eyebrows as he took out a can of Pepsi. He opened it and took a sip, followed by two more. Aahh. America! Pepsi, money, and gays though I forgot the most important thing—freedom, which presently, I do not have. He took another drink of the Pepsi, then went back to the bedroom, and sat down on the end of the bed again. Somehow, sitting on the end of the bed always helped him think. He would have to rise up from the bed to do something, anything. He rose up and walked to the wall opposite the bed to the side of the entry doors of the bedroom. He changed his clothes to a casual tourist outfit, then headed out of the hotel, and down to a street of tourist shops.

He bought a Jamaican hat and a map—a typical one that a tourist would buy, showing all the points of interest on the island. He also found a store with a professional photographer where he could get his picture taken, developed, printed, and miniaturized. After shopping, he stopped at an outdoor bar—a watering hole filled with tourists—and ordered a tall glass of ice tea donned with an umbrella, a wedge of pineapple, and a cherry—totally tourist.

He half finished the drink, then got up and left the bar, and went back to the hotel. At the front of the hotel, before entering, he observed people who went inside and the people who were already inside. There was a desk area enclosed on three sides where it was darker. There were five computers for hotel guests to use gratuitously. The clerk who had waited on him earlier had just been relieved by another worker. Chris stood outside, then looked up to the sun, and smiled like he was just enjoying himself. He counted down the minutes in his mind. Five minutes later, he entered the hotel and went immediately to the elevator. He waited at the elevator for it to fill up, and he stood aside for all of the people who were waiting to enter it. Now it was full, and he told them that he'd wait for the next one. They waved to him, looking sorry like they weren't going to see him for a long time when they didn't even know him. The next car opened its doors right after the first one left. He instantly boarded it and pressed the button for his floor, pressing the close-door button right after he entered it, hoping for a quick ride to his floor. He was successful. He went right to his door and unlocked it with the key card in one motion. Inside, he let loose of all his shopping bags.

He took the blonde wig out and a pair of scissors, then grabbed hold of one of the bags, went into the bathroom, and stood in front of the vanity mirror. He placed the wig on his head, then had trouble adjusting it in just the right way. Once satisfied, he took the scissors and began cutting. With body powder, he lightened the tone of his facial skin and eyebrows. Then he took out a small box and placed blue contact lenses in his eyes to change his eye color. He fought to ignore the pain of putting these foreign objects over his pupils and took a tissue and held it against his tear ducts to dry his tears before they could fall. He took a black button-up shirt and put it on, then inspected himself before buttoning the final collar button. He nodded his head, pleased with his newly changed appearance.

He felt for his wallet, making sure it was in his pants pocket, which it was; and then he left the bathroom, grabbed the key card from the table, and left the room. Instead of going to the elevator, he took the stairs. He knew that the hotel security cameras were observing this. It just lessened the chances of somebody picking up on him. At the second floor, he boarded the elevator to the main floor where he got out and looked at nothing except the open doors to the street outside.

He made tracks to the photography shop that he had scoped out earlier. After his picture was taken, he stood back in the supply area of the front of the store between the cameras and printed postcards of the island. He thumbed through some of the selections but stayed away from the front of the store where he could be viewed through the large window.

When his picture was ready, he paid for it and thanked the man who had waited on him. He walked to the door, then returned to the counter, and asked for a miniaturization of the picture, like it was something he had just thought of and not something that he had been planning since he first spotted the photography shop. The man at the counter did this for him, and he now had a picture, the perfect size for a driver's license picture or an identification card. He paid the man and nodded his head in thanks. At the door, he paused then waited for other people to walk down the sidewalk before he opened the door and joined the group of people passing by the photography shop. At the end of the block, he turned, then crossed the street, and made his way back to the hotel where he went directly to his room without looking at anyone or anything inside the hotel.

Inside his room, he went to the bathroom and very carefully removed the wig and placed it back inside the plastic shopping bag, then set it away from the sink where it would not get wet. He washed the powder off his face, then turned to the shower, and thought of the luxury of one but knew he didn't have the time. Something he would do later. He left the room and took the elevator to the main floor where he went over to the area with the computers for guests to use.

He logged into the correct program that he sought. He knew the precise codes to enter, and bingo, he was in the files holding the central financial records for large investments and holdings. He knew there would be twelve pages of data that would come up, pages with warnings on matters of security regarding steps that needed to be followed in dealing with American holdings in foreign countries. He remembered this code from a previous time when he had to retrieve information on a case. His mind was a steel trap.

After the twelve pages of information came up, he entered another code to access the financial record report. He came to the files labeled Inspectors for Government, then entered the Del Marco Corporation business file name. Three accounts popped up on the computer. He tried to open the first file, but the question of why the information was needed was instantly displayed on the screen. He paused, then caught himself, knowing that the slightest hesitation would be picked up on. He entered the answer: IRS information on this company was needed. He instantly typed the number of a fictitious agent that he had used before. The computer then showed enlarged pictures of these files, then asked him which one he wanted to access.

He went through each of the three files with separate information. He only looked through them long enough to get an overall idea on the accounts. The most important reason he accessed these accounts was to get the account numbers, which he got. He wrote them down carefully in his leather notebook in his jacket. Then he switched the files on the computer to inspection accounts, and he entered these account numbers on this page, then pressed the Print button. After the files were printed, he closed these files. While the computer was in turn-off mode, he crossed the numbers on the screen. The computer stayed on with a blank screen; then he pressed Escape, then went into an identity release file, which he accessed through his government employment record, then entered the same number as the FBI agent.

He left the hotel lobby area and returned to his room with a printed copy of the needed information. The wheels were now in motion, and tomorrow was going to prove to be a very valuable day in more ways than one.

Back in his room, he did feel hungry now, so he took a bowl of sliced pineapple from the refrigerator and quickly ate it. Food was the least of his concerns. He stopped eating with only two bites left and went into an almost-combat state of mind, freeing himself from any constraints he could feel mentally. He moved his body, exercising and releasing his mind, moving as a trained master of martial arts. He had studied it and was versed in the movements. He composed himself for his new developing encounter.

He relaxed his body into the deeply cushioned chair. He wiped the sweat from his forehead and then raised his head, gathering all the oxygen he could into his lungs and then slowly breathed out. When relaxation should have been overwhelming him, he stopped, looking straight ahead to fear. I almost forget. I'm slipping. Don't talk about it. Just do it. He changed his clothes and went down the elevator to the overpriced lobby shops. In ten minutes, he was in and out of the gift shop holding a dark brown alligator-skin briefcase. He looked at himself holding the briefcase in the lobby hall mirror. He frowned. Instead of going back to the elevators, he went, instead, down the hall to the boardroom doors, looking for any to be open. None were. He did the only thing that he could do, knowing that the security cameras were probably fixed on him. He stood there to the side of two of the doors and waited. He opened his briefcase and took out the page thanking the buyer for purchasing that briefcase. He read it while looking at his watch. The doors opened to two of the meeting rooms just an instant later. He watched the businessmen come out of the meeting rooms while he held this piece of paper.

One of the last men to come out was a rather docile-looking man, professionally dressed, skinny, and wearing thick eyeglasses. Just his actions made a person think of Jerry Lewis in a comedy, awkward and clumsy. Chris hit him with his briefcase while turning, making it look like he was also walking out of the meeting room.

He made quick apologies while straightening the man's posture so that he wouldn't fall. He explained to him how he didn't feel very well and was a clumsy mess. The other man really liked hearing this, thinking he was not alone in his clumsiness and awkwardness. Chris told him how he just could not get used to this new briefcase and asked him if he would mind exchanging his scratched black vinyl briefcase for this alligator-skin one. The man was overjoyed; and they went back inside their meeting room so he could take out his papers, calculator, etc., and put them in the shiny new briefcase. Chris asked him if he wouldn't mind giving him some extra file covers and any extra papers that he didn't need any longer. He got both, and they both left happy. Chris headed back to his hotel room.

He reached in the nightstand drawer and took out the telephone book, opening it to Banks. Let's see. Banks that would hold large business accounts. Well, three of them are obvious—American banks with large accounts as well as stock holdings doing business in Puerto Rico to save on taxes, but there are these European banks also. No, maybe that would be too . . . I'll go with the American banks. How can I go into these banks posing as a government agent to look at the holdings of this company if the accounts aren't even in that bank? He took his index finger to his cheek, then blinked. I won't be going in the bank on that premise. I'll make a printed list of companies thought to be evading other tax loopholes. I just hope that they don't ask me too much about this because I don't know . . . Security. He got up and stood in the center of the room, then moved his body, conforming to motion and balance, exercising with martial arts moves, releasing stress and strengthening his level of mind control.

Later that evening, after about an hour of concentration and movement, he showered; then before turning in for the night, he thumbed through the tourist map that he bought earlier and compared it with the listings of the banks in the phone book, planning his course of where he would be going the next morning. Above all, he had to be very professional in every respect.

CHAPTER 18

The next morning, he woke before the alarm sounded. He had left the drapes open just enough for the morning sun to shine on him while still having them closed enough for privacy. In rhythm and balance, he got himself ready for the day, putting the wig back on. He hesitated before powdering his face, then putting the contact lenses in. The only stop he made before exiting his room was at the left side of the refrigerator to take a swallow of juice. He then left the hotel making no eye contact with anyone. Down three blocks and to the right, he saw the sign on a large high building—the foremost bank in the United States of America. He made no pause of any kind, knowing that he was being filmed on camera—a security measure. He only thought of looking astute and professional. He knew that downstairs was just used for street accounts and that the second floor was strictly for personnel. He went to the elevator and told the guard there that he wanted the fourth floor while taking out his government inspector's badge and flashing it at him. The guard took his cell phone out from his uniform pocket and then called the offices on the fourth floor. The guard then opened the elevator for him to enter; and he took his key, turned it over the buttons, then pressed the number 4 button. The guard then exited the elevator before Chris rode up to that floor.

On the fourth floor, Chris walked by the secretaries' desks and went right into the office of the accounts manager. Two secretaries ran by his side while he did this. He flashed his badge to the manager; then the manager waved for the secretaries to leave the office and close the door behind them. Only ten minutes after the door was closed, it was reopened with the manager walking out and Chris sitting at the lead computer for the bank. The Del Marco accounts were not listed under the Del Marco name but were listed under the names of the businesses that they held individually, but they were linked together with the Del Marco family being the controller of the accounts only after going through the first major company of their holdings, Crown Liquors; and of course, the major liquor produced by them was Jamaica rum.

Chris wanted the records of this company and where the holdings were in the United States of America. He got this information and listed it on his laptop, listing it through codes that were well inscribed in his mind. After getting all the information that he needed, he knew that he could not just dissolve their assets then and there. That would be too dangerous and obvious, so he moved the company's holdings from one company to another, enough to screw things up for normal business operations. Then he closed that file and returned to the lead file of the bank and closed that screen. He got up, closed all his belongings, and then opened the door of the office and stood to the side of the door until the manager greeted him. They shook hands as the manager opened the elevator and unlocked the buttons inside to send him back down to the bottom floor.

Chris knew that it would be too obvious to go back to the hotel now, and he didn't want to risk going to another bank; so he went in the direction of a Starbucks across the street and to the left, only two stores away. He stood in-line holding his briefcase, then ordered an American latte. He held the cup by the bottom of the saucer and found a table at the outside corner of a roped-off street section of chairs and tables. He sat down with his back to the end of the street and looked as nerdy as he could make his body look while he drank the latte.

Now at noontime, the sun streaked through the island sky, causing him to squint to shield his eyes from the blinding rays. He took his sunglasses out from his pocket, then stopped himself before putting on the Ray-Bans because he knew that he would be wearing them later in the day while assuming another identity. He finished the last sip of his latte, then was sorry that he had done that since it was now cold; but he did not make any affirmation of it, wanting to show no emotion. He picked up his briefcase and knocked it over the rope sectioning off the restaurant from the street—all the more a nerd, he thought. He then took very slow and careful steps and managed to get to the center of a crowded sidewalk and moved along with all the people, never establishing closeness to anyone. Down about five side streets, he exited from the main street and made a quick turn into a side street, then went down a side alley as though he knew where he was going. He crouched down behind a dumpster, then looked up to the side of the building to see if there were any open windows where he could be observed from, but there weren't any.

He took off the wig, then took his handkerchief from his pocket, and wiped the powder from his face. He opened the lid of the dumpster and was blown back by the heavy garbage smell that emanated from it. He compared the smell to that of rotten fish and boiled cabbage, then threw in the wig. He took a handkerchief from his pocket and wiped his face as clean as he could get it. From his briefcase, he took out a pair of light blue swim trunks with a dark blue stripe across the top right under the waistband. He put these on and then put on a worn white tee shirt. He doused his body with suntan oil, mostly to just give off that distinctive smell. Now he put on the Ray-Bans and took out a flat folded beach towel, then tossed it up in the air while still holding one corner of it to fluff it up and get it back to its normal thickness. He looked at the steady stream of foot traffic going down the main street and waited for a slight break in it, then walked from the alley and then the side street and back into the crowd. Two more side streets up the road, there was a large open area with access to the beach. He walked down the concrete steps, tripping on the first step. He grabbed the towel to his body while he supported his weight against the rail and regained his footing. Then he continued down the stairs and made a turn to his left at the high raised beach lockers. He took some change out of his pocket, put the money in the slot, and turned the key to open the locker. He placed his briefcase in the locker and took out the key. He placed the key on the gold cross necklace he wore around his neck, then walked away from the locker bank with the beach towel folded over his right arm. He walked in the direction of the water with admiring ladies watching him. He got a surfboard from the rental stand after telling the attendant his name and room number. He signed the name of the person he had registered under, then took the board down to the waterline.

He walked out into the water with the surfboard, and then when the water was deep enough, he put the board flat on top of the water and rode it out to deeper water to catch a wave. He caught a wave, then rose up, balancing himself on the board with some difficulty. He rode out the wave, then leaned to the side, and caught the board before the wave finished, not wanting to show the appearance of falling off the board. He returned out to the deeper water for two more rides, still unable to really ride a wave all the way to shore. He took the board back out to deeper water once more and rode it as close as he could to the shallow water of the beach, then took the board under his arm, and walked up to the dry sand. He placed the board standing up in the sand, then walked to the other side of it on the beach a safe-enough distance away. Here, he dropped the beach towel, then lay down on the sandy beach to get a tan, lying on his stomach and on the gold cross that held the key to the locker.

He was deep into getting a tan and felt the sun gently baking his skin. The warmth of his body almost felt as if he was getting a massage by the sun's rays, but he still felt the cold and the hurt in his bones from the coldness of the island waters. A dark shadow passed over his body, lowering the intensity of the warm sun; and he almost shuddered, wondering if he should look up and find out who caused this shadow. Was it someone who would compel him to lie more, or was it someone to run for his life from? He did have the option of not recognizing this figure and just of pretending to be asleep while getting a suntan, but playing possum was against spy rules, at least in this case. Before opening his eyes, he moved his body to the side to make it easier to gain his footing should a fast getaway be required. While moving his body and his legs, he took his hand and held it under his neck, sliding the key to his back so that it would not be seen by this person.

The body standing over him was that of a very tanned young woman who couldn't be much past her teens. She did have a figure, but she would be an unwelcoming presence for him to be seen with. She was midheight and thin with not too much of a figure, but she definitely had the jewelry—three necklaces and a ring on every finger, including both thumbs. She smiled and moved her head back and forth seeing him look at her. He decided against rising and standing next to her. He twisted the ring with the crest of his family on it to the back of his finger so that it looked like he was just wearing a gold band, a wedding ring. "Can I help you? Are you lost?" He said this coldly as if questioning a schoolteacher, thinking she would identify with that.

She sheepishly moved her body, trying for an innocent expression. "Sorry, I thought you were Mike. I need a surfing buddy." She laughed after saying this.

"Well, I'm not this Mike person you are looking for. The surfing instructors are over there where you rent the surfboards. If you need any other assistance, I think that woman over there would be able to help you. Good day." He pointed to a mother sitting on the beach with her four children seated around her. He then turned back on his stomach, closed his eyes, and resumed his suntanning.

He was good at judging time without looking at his watch, and he knew that it was time to make his escape. He still had to show his mask of gayness around the hotel since any one of the employees he had encountered so far during his stay could just happen to walk down on the beach and observe him. I am too known here, he thought. He got up, went back to where the surfboard stood in the sand, picked it up, and then walked back to the attendant to return the board to him. He noticed a woman's flowered sun robe over the back of a chair, and walking by holding his beach towel, he picked it up and rolled it up in the towel. He made his return to the front desk of the hotel and noticed that the first clerk who registered him was back on duty, so he wrapped the sun robe around himself, then took out a carnation that was in a vase on the table in the hotel lobby, and walked up to the clerk. He gained the clerk's attention, then batted his eyes, and wiggled his hips at the same time. He pushed the flower towards the clerk and told him it was for him. He then looked sad and spoke in hurt words, telling him that his boyfriend had just broken up with him and that he had to check out early. He said that he would have to have some time to freshen himself up though and winked right after saying this. The clerk looked at him and his actions as he spoke these words to him, then he grabbed hold of another clerk who had just stepped to the back of the registration desk. He pushed this clerk in front of him so he stood in front of Chris at the other side of the desk and said, "You wait on him. I'm leaving. I'll take an early lunch in the back—employees only." Chris then signed the checkout bill and went back up to the room.

Inside the room, he went immediately to the bathroom sink and washed his face, still feeling residual powder over his tan complexion.

He combed his hair, then leaned forward, took in a deep breath, and made note of his reflection in the bathroom mirror. He noticed the start of wrinkles. Despondent and not wanting to face the reality of what he did, he then realized that he was born into this job and never had any thoughts of seeking anything else. He was now at an age when memories played with him, and he sometimes wondered but then quickly realized that this only made him weak. He shined the mask over his body to what he had to endure and show in all respects pertaining to his life, his job, his family, and his career—a prechosen path with no escape but death.

He went to the table, stopping only long enough to open the refrigerator. The Pepsi supply was out. Nothing but overpriced beer remained in the refrigerator. He closed it, frowning, then went to the coffeemaker, opened a coffee pouch, and placed it inside the coffeemaker, filled the pot with tap water, and, with reluctance, turned on the Brew button. He sat down, then looked to the coffeemaker sideways to see if it had started brewing, and it had.

Where do I go next? I don't feel like playing the role of a drunken sailor anymore. He lowered his head into his hands, which he supported on the tabletop; and he bit his lower lip, then ran his eyes to a side-glance at nothing. He looked at the open newspaper on the table. A rich yachtsman needed a sailor to steer his boat to the Bahamas. I'll go down to the docks, but I have to stay on the west side of the ocean and avoid the waters around Cuba. They know me there and will kill me. The operation stashing drugs, cocaine powder in coffee bags—correction, burlap-covered coffee sacks. How did the rackets make money before drugs? Gambling? This you can do everywhere now. Protecting politicians? There is always money there— but there are usually drugs there too but not always. Hookers? There are usually high-call hookers there. He got up and took hold of the coffeepot, then grabbed the plastic cover off a plastic coffee cup. He smelled the coffee while taking it to his mouth for a sip. He closed his eyes after drinking it and made an unfavorable expression. Well, the only thing that I can say for it is that it is wet—a liquid. What it is I could never say, though.

He sat back down, then suddenly grinned. Sports—we have to get into sports. There is big money in that. He took two more sips of coffee, then got up, folded and put everything back in the bag. Then he put the sailor suit back on. He taped the leather money fold to his calf, then rolled the crew sock up over it. He adjusted himself, then grabbed the bags, and left the building.

He watched the pier where the private yachts were docked and lowered his cap, then set his bags down at the end of the pier. He took quick formal steps towards a yacht with the English name of Stewart painted on the side.

He watched as a French seaman walked aboard carrying something that he could not make out down to the galley; then Chris also boarded the yacht. A whistle blew announcing the arrival of a cruise ship, and most of the men there moved off in the direction of the docking ship, knowing that American tourists would be exiting the boat. They would be there to help with bags and directions and have their hands out for tips. Chris took a handkerchief out from his pocket, then sprayed it with a can of bug spray sitting on a rail outside the ship's boarding gate. After spraying the handkerchief, he walked into the galley and stood silently behind the French sailor, putting the cloth over his nose. The sailor passed out. Chris saw an open bottle of rum there in the galley. It was probably used for cooking since it was in the galley, so he splashed some of it on the uniform of the unconscious sailor. He then pulled the sailor back to the dock and laid him over the bench at the beginning of the long boarding ramp.

The owner of the yacht walked by and saw his crewman lying there on the bench. He called to his man, but there was no response. The owner's wife leaned towards him and instantly smelled the booze. She explained to her husband that this man was drunk. "Great. What do we do now? We have to meet the Elliots in the Bahamas. That very important dinner is in three days." Chris walked up, looking stern and professional, to the side of the couple and saluted them. Then he told them that he was Tom Johnson and would be taking the place of their regular employee for the voyage. He took the bag the wife was holding and escorted them both onto their yacht. He undid the lines securing the yacht to the dock and headed out in a northeasterly direction for the islands.

Chris was well versed in nautical travel and handled the yacht in a professional manner. The seas were calm, and he had no worry of capsizing or encountering bounty hunters. These waters were fairly well traveled, and passing boats were plentiful. In looking at the charts up by the yacht's helm, he judged that it would take roughly three days to get to the Bahamas; and from there, it would take an additional two to three days to get to Key Largo, their final destination. He liked the idea of jet travel much better. You can get there at least three times as fast. They had left the dock behind and were now out in the open ocean, away from the view of any neighboring islands. He thought about the pros and cons of sailing all night or anchoring somewhere and turning in for the evening. He desperately needed sleep, but he knew that he could show no weakness. Feeling secure enough to leave the helm for a momentary pause, he did. He went down to the galley, heated up some water, and blended in some instant coffee crystals. He paused only long enough to stir the cup before going back to the helm to guide the yacht to Nassau.

He stood at the helm all through the night in a half-asleep mode. He was shaken awake at seeing a gleam of light coming in over the east side of the yacht, and he watched it closely until he realized he was watching the sunrise. He breathed in a sigh of relief and gratitude at seeing the dawn of a new day. Just about ten o'clock in the morning, Mr. Stewart took over the helm, and Chris retired to the lower berth to grab a few hours of much needed shut-eye.

He slept longer than he expected to, opening his eyes at four in the afternoon. He stroked his forehead, then got up off the berth, straightened his composure and posture, then brushed the wrinkles from his uniform. He walked up to the deck where Mr. and Mrs. Stewart were relaxing on lounge chairs, enjoying the sun on the deck and watching Chris as he took over at the wheel. No words were spoken, and Chris just went to work and stayed there at the helm until the next morning.

At eight the next morning, Mr. Stewart's wife brought Chris a cup of coffee. He thanked her and kissed her hand as she smiled at him. He took a sip. It was strong and not brewed to his taste, but he was thankful for the much-needed caffeine that it contained.

CHAPTER 19

The next two days went by much the same as that day had with little or no talk exchanged. The shores of the Bahamas were well in sight, and Chris radioed in to find out which dock to tie up at. He steered the boat into the outlined area of the docking port, and then two seamen grabbed the line and pulled the yacht into the dock. The Stewarts stood on the deck of the yacht, anxiously awaiting the docking and the opportunity to place their feet on dry land once again. Mr. Stewart looked apprehensive when Chris took his hands from the wheel and left it to go and help the missus by holding her hand while she got off the yacht. However, just the look in her husband's eyes conveyed to Chris that he should, instead, stop dead in his tracks. As he left the yacht, grabbing hold of the tail end of the line that secured the yacht to the wooden dock, Mr. Stewart turned to Chris and handed him a piece of paper with writing on it. Chris nodded his head to Mr. Stewart, then took the paper from his hand and used his other hand to shield the sun from blocking his view of the paper he had just been handed. He quickly scanned the document, then paused and read it again. Chris looked up and saw Mr. Stewart walking down the dock. He glanced back and noticed the bewildered look on Chris's face, so he stopped in his tracks and stood forthright, looking at Chris. "Well, the yacht needs supplies, and the missus and I are on vacation. You are now a paid servant of ours, and I know that getting supplies for the yacht is in your job description. Look in the jacket that you left down below at the side of the dining table. I placed in your jacket pocket all the cash that you should need to get these supplies. If there is any money left, you can buy yourself a beer. We will not be back until much later this evening. You will need to fuel up, and then after you do, try running it around this side of the island to test the engine. I think that either there was something wrong when turning to the left, or else it was your steering."

Mr. Stewart was now at the end of the wooden dock. Chris did not look at him, but he did not look down at his feet either. He wanted more than anything to be free—free from the confines of this yacht, the confines of the Stewarts, and the confines of his present situation. Again, he was going to have to worry about being seen. There was the possibility of running into them, so a disguise was out of the question. He didn't know the layout of the island or surroundings. It was just going to be a matter of quick judgement and being quick on his feet and in his actions to get back to the yacht as quickly as possible. He went down below and took the jacket containing the money, then looked in the bathroom mirror, and combed his hair. He made sure of his appearance before leaving the yacht and that all the doors and controls were locked and covered.

At the end of the wooden docking area, he sat on a bench looking relaxed in the warm tropical climate. He observed where people were walking and what they were carrying. They came from the right side of the port with shopping bags. Some people walked down or back and forth on the road straight ahead, but barely a person was seen walking on the left side of the pier; and if they did come or go from that side, they held nothing. He stood up, reached up to the sky for a long stretch, then swung his arms back down from the stretch, and turned to the right and started walking down the road to the right of the pier.

Wearing his Versace sunglasses, which had a mirrored finish so that anyone's reflection was put back in their own face, his eyes were not visible. As expected, the first half of the block was just tourist gift shops. It was a question of whether to remain walking up this street in hopes of finding more of a city or to head down one of the many side streets in hopes of finding a more suitable place to get the needed supplies. It was also a matter of how long he could hold back the fear of being spotted. He felt as though he was stuck, defenseless, down at the end of a dark alley. This feeling was more than unwelcome. With the overwhelming feeling he was being watched and something was lurking nearby, he slowly stopped when he no longer heard anyone walking behind him. He turned and went into the lobby of a small hotel. The male receptionist there was talking on the phone and paid no attention to him. Chris walked right to the elevator and pushed the button to the top floor. He rode alone on the ride up and showed no emotion as he planned out his course of action. The doors opened when they reached the top floor. He stood back and remained in the elevator, listening for any noise signifying people might be on this floor. No sound echoed from the hallway, and the elevator door started to close. He pushed his arm forward and stopped the door from closing. The door offered resistance, so he quickly pushed the button to open it, and the door then opened wide for him to exit. He quickly exited the elevator, then reached back in, touching the button to the bottom floor. The elevator door closed, and he stood in the hallway and observed the lights above the elevator door flash down to the number 1, signifying the elevator had returned to the main floor where he had come in. He stood apprehensively and motioned like he was carrying a gun in his inside jacket pocket although he wasn't as he turned and looked down each hallway.

The hallway to the right just had rooms and doorknobs on each side and was a dead end. The hallway to the left had a window at the end of it and another hallway with a sign that read Roof Access. That would be too easy. He climbed out the open window, then kicked his foot to the outside black iron ladder that ran up and down the side of the building—the fire escape. He did not go down but went up instead. His heart raced faster at each noise that he heard from the street below. On the top step of the ladder, he swung his body over the side and caught one foot on the bricks covering the edge of the roof. His other foot fell, and he fought with all his strength to keep from falling and to move his body in the direction of his mounted foot. He just stayed there, hanging from the roof, dangling in what he felt was midair over the top of a six-story building. He swallowed and then counted to three in his mind and swung his dropped leg up with all his strength towards the roof. This motion swung his body on top of the roof. He looked puzzled and surprised but only smiled after forcing himself to hold back uncontrolled laughter.

He sat up on his bottom, Indian style, steadying himself; then he rolled to the center of the roof and stood up. He took a moment to gather his equilibrium at this height, then swallowed and composed himself. He briefly looked down from each side of the roof, knowing he was on top of the tallest building in the area, so he could easily be seen. He had to move quickly so if someone thought they had seen something or someone peering down from the roof, he would be gone in the next second when they blinked.

He saw more commercial stores on the road straight ahead. He didn't feel like climbing down the risky fire escape on the building, so instead, he opened the door to the hallway on the top floor. In just the second it took to open the door to go inside, he realized he set off an alarm—not necessarily an alarm that he could hear, but a silent alarm. The only thing he could do or use now was speed—quickness in action and thought. Inside the building, he did not ring for the elevator but instead went down the hallway without the window at the end. There it was, the last door on the right-hand side—the door marked Stairs—Emergency Stairway. But it would not open. It was locked.

He knew he did not have time to try and dismantle the key lock. He stood back, then with a quick and forceful action, kicked the door in and ran down the stairs, stopping at the floor just below the bottom. He went into the hallway, breathing heavily. A side-room door had just opened, and he heard tourists conversing in rapid French dialogue. He slowed his actions, then nodded to them as he passed them in the hallway. They turned down the side of the hall, and he heard them signal for the elevator. He went to the window at the end of the hallway and put his feet out the window on the stairs and went down three steps. Then he heard people yelling, so he jumped to the road and landed with his knees bent. That took only a second; and he repositioned himself to a standing position, then ran to the end of the side street, and worked his way into a crowd, falling into the pace at which they walked.

Down the length of two more side streets he went, then turned down the next side street, and went down it, making his way back again to the main street. He went into one of the two main stores there and got the supplies on Mr. Stewart's list, and he did have enough left over for one bottle of beer, which he got for himself—a bottle of imported Bavarian beer.

Back at the yacht, he unloaded the supplies, then took off his jacket and his shoes, and relaxed. The sun was just going down. He took the yacht out of the harbor and started to the north to circle the island as Mr.

Stewart had instructed him. Outside the dock area, he stopped at the side entrance of the bay surrounding the island, awaiting clearance to circle the island. He twisted off the cap of the beer and downed two swallows. He opened his mouth wide looking to the peaceful overhead sky. He lowered his face, then set down the open-beer bottle, feeling a shiver go up his warm, sun-drenched spine. His senses called him to attention as quickly as a trained dog starts to bark when something is wrong.

Chris forced himself to calm down and listen for the sound that had caused him to come to attention. He heard the ticking, the same sound of the ticking of a wristwatch, but his three-face TAG Heuer wristwatch was silent. It wasn't his watch making this noise. His well-trained ears sensed the ticking countdown of a bomb. He jumped from the top deck of the yacht and walked towards the bow. Hearing nothing there, he made his way back to the stern next to the motor, and the sound resonated from there.

CHAPTER 20

He drew his ear closer to the sound, then heard the sound grow louder—the final twenty-second countdown of a bomb. He had set enough of them to know. He ran to the center of the yacht and grabbed an air tank, hose, and goggles; then he climbed the rail and jumped into the water. He was pushed farther away by the force of the explosion, and pieces of the yacht and flames flew through the sky. He swam swiftly away from the wreckage.

He dove down towards the bottom of the ocean, feeling he was submerging himself down the drain of a sink to find refuge. As he surfaced again, a board from the yacht hit him in the back. He grimaced in pain, but he could not let himself feel the pain, or it would slow him down. He realized they now knew where he was—this was overwhelming proof that they had found him. It was no longer a choice of swimming to the other side of the island. It was a matter of swimming completely away from the island, a long swim he knew from driving the boat to the island earlier that day. There were no neighboring islands to the south, east, or west; so his only choice was to swim to the north as far out from the island as he could.

He tried to think of alternatives and other possibilities. The option of being able to get aboard another ocean liner was a dream, an unconscionable dream at this time. He had only the cash taped to the leather carrier on the side of his calf. Where was Dad? Dad had to know where he was. He would surely hear of the explosion that just happened, but it had only been a brief few minutes since the explosion. The main thing to do now was to swim away from the island and keep his body as rested as he could in his life-sustaining swim.

He felt his legs getting numb even though he was still moving. It was essential that he rest. At that moment, even the idea of a floating corpse that he could rest his body on was a dream. His eyes grew heavy because he was so tired, and he felt himself growing heavy and sinking into the ocean depths. He closed his eyes, then forced himself to reopen them, fighting to stay strong. His right leg, injured in the blast, grew heavier; and he thought, This couldn't be it—this couldn't be the end. It was just the middle of his life, but it was also the line of work that he was in. This was one of the hazards of this line of work. Suddenly, he could feel the sandy bottom of the ocean floor, and his head was pounding but not just from the pressure at this depth. He felt like the back of his head hit something. He could only envision a large heavy ocean boulder, but what was it? He gathered all his remaining strength and turned his head and body, which was dragging behind him, opening his eyes again to see what was in front of him.

A sunken submarine! He opened the top hatch, then closed the lid again once he was inside. He waited for most of the water to drain out through the sides, and then he opened the second hatch lid and climbed down the ladder to the main level of the sub. It was deserted from the looks of it. He wondered how this could be. Was it planted there? It was very old, a combat submarine. He thought it was an old wartime submarine from World War II, but what was it doing there? The war had not been fought in any part of the surrounding area. Could it have been dragged there by scavengers? How could that have happened? More than likely, it was another planted diversion by the opposition. The doors would not open for him to leave, and he would be trapped inside with lack of oxygen. However, it was well maintained with no marine life inside. It was cared for, so someone or some people must be using it, but where were they now? On board in some other part of the submarine? He wanted more than anything to relax and sleep on the side cot, to rest his tired, aching body. Instead, he carefully surveyed the compartment of the sub. A fresh food stash was present in the galley. He relaxed, thinking that if the other party was on board or would return in a short time, he had no way out anyway. He opened a can of tuna, then pulled open a box of crackers, and relaxed at the dining table at the side of the galley. He only rose long enough to look for something to drink. He found a plastic bottle of water, and he took it back to the table with him. He then sat back down and opened it and downed a swallow as he finished the tuna and the box of crackers. He got up, relaxed his body in a stretch, then went to the controls of the sub to see if any of the controls or the radio still worked.

All of the submarine's front board control panels were functioning. He thought, well, they had to be. A submarine this age was not nuclear but relied on batteries for power. The way that they would charge the batteries was to rise to the surface and open the conning tower seal to get the fresh air and the ability to charge the battery. That was it—that was his escape. He looked down at his feet, hearing and feeling that he was hitting something. He leaned the chair back, then bent down, and picked up a piece of paper.

It was Cuban. It displayed the different times of pickups and deliveries. There were drugs in the storage compartments of the vessel—a lot of drugs. No wonder nobody was looking for this sunken treasure. The police as well as the government knew about it. This was a treasure trove of wealth. He was the interloper, and there could be no call for him. He wondered why he wasn't dead yet. He knew that very soon, he would be. If he hadn't already been spotted on this vessel, there was a plan for his disappearance. He had to think fast and move—and now.

He left the front control area of the submarine, then found a flashlight, radio, and life jacket. He found silver wrapping tape in the side cabinet of the galley, then returned to the front control panel of the submarine. He stopped at the ladder to the conning tower, climbed up the ladder, and started to open the screw latch. It turned, and he could feel the pressure of the water against the opening. He stopped and went back down the ladder and back to the front controls of the submarine.

He set the control panel mechanisms to rise to the surface. He could already feel the jolt of the motion rising up from the floor of the sea. Air was filling in the compartments. The motion of climbing was felt. Now up from the chair, he was ready to make a quick run forward. He stopped and lifted his air tank, then put it back down, and took another full one sitting there on the shelf. He put the goggles back on. They were hanging down under his chin with the strap around his neck. He ran to the ladder of the conning tower, then climbed up while the submarine was rising to the surface. He broke the seal, and water poured in. He stopped the turning motion of opening the seal and was jolted back by the pressure. He knew now that the submarine had surfaced. He finished opening the hatch, then jumped up from the ladder, and took a brief moment to get his bearings before jumping off the top of the submarine and into the water. His biggest fear was sharks, but then the force of the pressure of the rising submarine should have driven them away. There was a helicopter overhead, and someone in it was firing at him. It was meant to kill him. He rose up in the water, then plunged down into the depths, and swam away from the submarine.

He swam countless yards underwater, still in a northerly direction as he had planned in the course of his escape back to the American waters off the shore of the Florida Keys. Still not knowing how safe it was up on the surface, he had to leave the safety of the depths of the ocean waters to find out. He rose to the top and removed his mask and opened his eyes wide. The whiteness of his eyes would shine brightly against the dark backdrop of the dangerous deep ocean waters, a scary vision of sharp contrast. He lifted his body up just enough to notice his surroundings. He did not see the helicopter or anything else for that matter. That made him realize he should suspect something, so he plunged back into the depths of the ocean waters.

He still counted the yards as he swam, but he stopped counting at 3,250 yards, knowing that this was two miles out. He knew that they would be canvassing a five-mile radius looking for him. Perseverance, ambition, drive, and thirst for survival and winning kept him going at an even stronger pace than before.

He surfaced just yards past the five-mile radius. Exhaustion overwhelmed him. He fought the temptation to pant for breath to recuperate from his narrow escape. He kept himself calm and fought the desire to take in rapid full breaths. The sun's reflection shined brightly over the water, especially in the direction he was looking. He wondered what he was seeing. Was it delirium having him see this, or was it real? He put the mask back over his face, then dove back down but not as deep as before. He stayed just below the surface so he would not have to worry about being spotted in the water.

He saw land—the coast was near. It was just a matter of swimming there; but he felt so tired, overwhelmed, and hurt. Just then, a lifeline was thrown to him and landed only three feet from his head. He hesitated on turning to see where this came from and who had thrown it. His first thought was that it must be the enemy, the Del Marcos, but why would they want to save him? They would want him dead. The police? Perhaps they thought he was responsible for the explosion. His father? But how would his father send a lifeline to save him when he didn't even know where he was?

He closed his eyes and turned to the lifeline and then started pulling himself in with it while someone was pulling him to his right to the course of the rising sun. The waves became higher and higher from the motor of the boat. An American crewman on a fishing boat pulled him on board, and another crewman came to assist with the rescue. They pulled Chris onto a bed inside the first aid section of the boat. Chris breathed deeply and thanked the Lord with every breath that he took in while trying to slow his heart rate. One of the crewmen gave Chris a bottle of water and cautioned him to drink it slowly, only a sip at a time.

The boat approached the outlying islands of the Florida Keys and docked on the central shore off the coast of Miami. One of the crewmen made a call, and minutes later, help arrived. Chris was transferred from the boat on a stretcher, and an ambulance took him from the dock area to the Miami-Dade hospital.

CHAPTER 21

Back on the island, Jane knew her plan for escape but was very careful in the timing. She knew that anything planned too quickly would fail. Careful execution had to be planned in mastering this scheme for the return of her freedom. She had some reservations for brief moments, liking the fact of not having to work and having no responsibility, just enjoying the estate of a millionaire; but she felt bewilderment and loss having to be confined in a locked room for hours each day, and she did miss Lauren greatly. She had just made no affirmation of it or let it show. She felt she had gained more trust but still felt there was a lot more that she had to acquire.

She had to control her rebellious attitude and to swallow hard, but she also had to remain strong in her inner emotions and keep her will in a secretive manner. Walking around the locked confines of the estate in the last two days, she was surprised at the apparent lack of guards watching her. She had grown quite accustomed to Bond being behind her everywhere she went. They were still watching her character, but this was apparently a matter of having gained some of their trust, but for what reason? Chris was dead. They had already gotten all they wanted. What was the reason for getting her, especially after all these years? Was it to weaken their enemies' power? It was all a game of power. With men, it all boiled down to power—who had it, who wanted it, and who could steal it—to leave the enemy weak. She felt that she was just a pawn on a chessboard, and her presence or lack thereof was the key to the next move.

At the side of the front of the house, she carefully walked in front of the six-car garage. There were no windows at the side of it or at the back. On the top of each of the six automatic rolling doors, there was a window. She walked from the right side of the garage and then went forward along the drive going into the garage, so she had a full-length view of the entire garage structure. The last garage door on the right side was raised halfway. Should she dare contemplate walking inside? The dogs were at the beach making their daily runs. There was no fear now of getting bitten by them. She felt there was a reason for the half-open door. Was it some type of further testing of her? she wondered. She slowly walked to the half-open door, then bent down, and ducked inside the garage.

The car that usually occupied that stall was gone, hence the half- open door. To the right of that car's stall, there was a step up into a room with a large glass window giving a full view of the inside of the garage. There looked like there was some kind of desk inside that room. Seeing no reason to want to see the contents of that room, she turned to her left and walked down to the area behind the cars. Two of the cars were a deep jet-black; the other cars were each a different color but nothing much away from being a neutral shade of grayish white. All of the cars shined either from a fresh coat of wax or from never being touched. Who would have the nerve to touch a Ferrari 550? She walked down to the other end of the garage, enamored with the grace and beauty of the machinery. It took her breath away, and she was awestruck, admiring the cars and the wealth it took to acquire and maintain each one. She remembered her neighbor's Corvette; even when it was parked in the garage, he was so very protective of it that you had to walk three feet away from it. She remained in the protected area away from the cars and thought, Oh, to sit in one of these, the thrill. I wouldn't dare though. Not one of these is the bright red of Magnum's. He was in Hawaii. Could you imagine all the onlookers if a red Ferrari was spotted on the island? Everyone would be looking for Tom Selleck.

After saying the name of the movie actor, she brought herself back to the reality of her present situation. She was no longer enamored with the Ferraris although she enjoyed looking at them very much. She was surprised that her presence in the garage had not set off any alarms. There must have been cameras in the garage although none were visible; however, with the nanotechnology of today, one could have easily been hidden just in a speck of paint on the wall. She turned and walked down behind the cars to the half-open door to make her exit, thinking of how wonderful it would be if Bond offered to take her for a ride in one of these. Then she thought of the confines of the locked bedroom and told herself how much she wanted out of there. She knew her route of escape. It was just the vital timing that was the current problem with her escape plan.

Away from the garage now and halfway back to the house, she tilted her head when she heard a car driving on the grounds of the estate. It was the missing car from the garage. She was surprised seeing that it was not a Ferrari; it was the Hummer that Bond had driven when he took her to the mall. Gee, too bad, odd man out. Feeling the light breeze of the sun-kissed day, she didn't want to be subjected to the inside of the house, so she remained outdoors.

Walking around the house, she was now at the back patio, looking down to the beach. She stopped and looked for the dogs, still fearful of being bitten. As usual, there was a dog at the bottom of each tower and a guard posted at each one also. Neither of the guards were Bond. She hadn't yet seen Bond today and was getting worried, not just because she missed this man whom she had become accustomed to but also because she feared for him in this job of his. Was he in the line of fire somewhere? Then she thought no because the boss had already lost one son to the dangers of this lifestyle. She didn't think that he could ever bear the thought of losing another son, his only remaining offspring.

Maybe he was just sick and was in bed, but where did he sleep? Well, it had to be somewhere on the estate. There were still areas that were out of her range of view. She'd be trespassing just in walking to undisclosed areas of the house, and she didn't even want to imagine what the consequences or punishment for doing that would be. She would lose all the trust she had gained. She changed her mind and forgot about going to the beach and instead lay down on the chaise lounge on the patio and worshipped the sun.

Rattled awake by voices and footsteps behind her becoming louder as they approached, she was not surprised. It had been quite a while since she had been under their scrutiny and dominance, and she was fighting opening her eyes, fearing she would be ordered to return upstairs to her room and once again locked away in subjection like a good little girl—something she could no longer verbally question or be sarcastic about. She swallowed the feeling weighing on her mind, knowing she would have to follow their orders without question.

She opened her eyes and saw Bond, and an instant smile came to her face. Then she saw the boss standing at his side, and immediately, she lowered her smile to a straightforward glare. The boss had already picked up on this. The man saw and sensed everything. He was the closest thing to God imaginable in pure power. The thing was, he didn't even have to lift a finger to show this power. There was just an overwhelming aura of power surrounding him.

Bond lowered his dark glasses to just under the whites of his eyes and winked at her, then pulled them back in place. The boss sat down on a patio chair and noticeably made noises while making himself comfortable in the chair. He stopped the movement once he was comfortable. The only reaction from Jane was that she gave him her full attention, and he breathed out heavily and drew in all the air that he could before he started his speech.

"I know that the news of . . ." He lowered his face, then turned his attention to the waves on the shoreline. He took a moment looking at the ocean, then turned back to her. Though not looking directly at her eyes, he was still looking at her. She got nervous with the lack of speech from this aristocratic aged man. "Your behavior has definitely changed. Whether you are doing this deliberately for some reason I am uncertain, but you are showing that you know your place here, and that is good . . . Time heals all wounds. I don't or can't say that this is true, but it helps . . . time that is. Wounds never die. They just heal." He looked to his side at Bond who was standing at full attention, taking both of them in as well as all the surrounding area as a guard would do. He straightened his relaxed composure and resumed speaking, "You and Bond will dine out tonight. I am giving you a quick release from the strain of being here. Maybe this will soften your composure, but don't think that this will be a common occurrence. It won't be, and it's not. You will dress in a quiet and subdued manner yet with a grace of class and rich composure. I am sure that you know what I am talking about." He sat there straightforward, showing no emotion, yet it looked like he carried the weight of the world in every atom of his body.

He whistled for one of the guard dogs to come. One came, and the other was held back by the whistle of the watchtower guard. She grimaced in fright at seeing this trained attack dog run to them so rapidly. The dog ran so fast you couldn't even see its feet touch the ground before they were in the air again. The animal stopped right before the boss's feet. He looked forward at the animal, then drew forth his hand, and held it in the air in front of the dog's nose. He lowered his clasped hand to the side of the dog's mouth, then lowered his hand to pet the dog's chest. He moved his hand down, then to the side of the dog's stomach, and the dog started wagging its tail. They were friends. He was the master of this animal. She observed this and thought of how the boss was just further showing her his control.

Bond remained locked in his guard stance, and the boss still showed a feeling of something being wrong but said nothing. He just kept his hand locked on the dog. The moment was more than uneasy. She again felt her heart beat at the back of her neck and the muscles of her body beat against her skin. Why couldn't he say something so she could leave? There were unspoken words filling the air around them. She thought, What, what could I say to break the uneasiness of this moment and make my escape? She welcomed the solitude of the locked bedroom and desperately sought to retreat there. She wanted to breathe out a heavy sigh to relieve the moment, but she wanted no attention drawn to herself. She kept still, then raised her eyes to Bond's view, keeping her eyes locked on his face. She knew that he noticed this, but he remained quiet and unspoken. Feeling her heart sinking, she drew her body up, but then the dog came to full attention. The boss grabbed the dog tighter, keeping him locked in his stance, then moved his head to his side, pointing in her direction for her to go. Before moving, she glanced at him and thought of expressing a word of thanks, then thought better of it, and simply walked away, making her way back into the house and up the stairs to her bedroom. She stood there looking at the locked door and waited for a guard to come and unlock the door for her so she could enter.

Inside the room, she stood to the side of the bed and noticed a change. She had made the bed that morning, but it was different now. The sheets were tighter, and the bedspread was tucked underneath the mattress and did not hang out over the box springs. Somebody or someone had been in her room that day—in her room while she was outside. That room was her only place of privacy and seclusion, so this invasion was more than unwelcome. Anger overwhelmed her although she knew she could not convey it. Her plans for her departure that she had made and worked on for days—had they been discovered and taken away from under her? Was that why the boss had to see her yet remained unspoken, not knowing what to say? She clenched her fingers closed, then pulled her arms upward and pushed at her head. It took all of her willpower to constrain herself and not scream out. She went to the side vanity in the bathroom and bent down to the bags that she had placed there with her needed papers inside. She unzipped the gym tote bag and seeing the rolled tee shirt still inside, she relaxed her composure, fell back, and took a deep breath. She pulled herself upright, grabbing the rolled cotton shirt. She closed her eyes hearing a slight sound from the hallway in front of her bedroom.

Her first reaction was to roll the shirt back up and place it back inside the bag and push it underneath the counter, but then she thought of the time it had taken to find out if the papers were still there. How much longer would it take to put it all back—a second, a minute? They had always knocked before they came in the room, but what if they had found the papers in the bags? Her heart raced, and she shivered, consumed with panic. She fought the force keeping her still, and she pushed the shirt in front of her and swung it open. A paper with the information about the plane flight fell out. Seeing this, she breathed out and gave a laugh. Then she remembered the noise from the hallway, and she quickly took the ticket and the papers and rolled them back up in the loose tee shirt. The rest of the contents were on the bottom of the bag; and she placed everything back inside, then zipped the bag back up, and pushed it back underneath the counter. She quickly ran out of the bathroom area and went back to standing at the end of the tightly made bed, still trying to find a reason for it.

Hearing a pounding at the door, she practically fell off her feet. The pounding continued in a more pulsed and louder knock. Her name was called. She stood still, fighting to grab even a breath to calm her racing body. She could feel the sweat pour off her face. At the side of the nightstand, she grabbed a Kleenex, wiped her face, then made quick steps to the door. About three feet before the door, she slowed her pace, knowing full well whoever was behind the door would be able to hear her run there;

and she did not want her rush to the door to be known. "I'm here. Who is it?" The voice that penetrated the air on the other side of the door was Bond's. She heard him say that it was him. She was fearful. He couldn't be here to take me out already, could he? He knew something.

"Jane? Is there anything wrong? Are you okay? Can I come in?" She breathed in, then stood back. "Yes, yes, come in."

He came in and did his usual sweep before relaxing to talk to her. "Your sliding glass door isn't open. It always is. Is there something wrong?"

"That is what I wanted to ask you. When I left my room this morning, I left the sliding glass door open for air as I always do. Well, when I came back to the room this afternoon, there was a definite change. The bed is different, and the door was closed. Who has been in here?"

He more than noticed the apprehension in her tone. He relaxed after hearing this from her. "Did you go inside the bathroom?" She tilted her head to the side, then felt the fear of someone finding what was in her gym bag under the counter. She said nothing. "You have fresh towels too. The maid was in here today and changed the linens on the bed," he said.

She walked towards him, breathed out, and laughed. She moved forward to let her body fall into his. She stood back, puzzled that he did not catch her in a hug like she had planned and they had done many times before. He changed his stance yet remained where he was standing. "I'll be back in two hours to pick you up to take you to dinner. I hope that will be enough time for you to get ready. Bye."

He turned from her view and left the room without looking back to her. She stood still after observing this, not knowing how to comprehend what she had just seen and felt. She looked to the floor as she heard the door latch shut. I am fatigued and perplexed. I can't put blame on anything for any reason, but what is the reason? I can feel my heart run in circles in my chest. It even feels like I am swallowing it at times. I have to keep breathing to stay alive. I was his wife. I gave birth to his child, but it wasn't a boy. She rolled her tongue over her lower lip, then took her hand to her lips, and clasped it shut and breathed out, closing her eyes again. She moved her head to a side view, focusing on nothing, then clenched her fists shut with force and trembled, shaking them. The only thing that I can do now is get dressed and look as nice as I can. I may be dressing for my funeral.

She started towards the bathroom to shower, dropping her clothes off as she made her way there. She turned on the pulsing jet of the shower. She thought she'd wait a few minutes for the temperature to regulate before getting in the shower and fumbling with the controls. She looked in the mirror at her naked body. She had lost some weight, but there was more to lose to mask her identity for her escape. I don't know what to do. I don't feel that I can camouflage myself much longer. I had the strength, and now I have to regain it, but for what reason? I see no end, but I am fearful of it. Inside the shower, she felt the water on her skin. She turned the jets to hit her back, then quickly turned back to face the shower, and adjusted the heat of the pulsating jets cascading over her skin.

CHAPTER 22

Out from the shower, she dried off; and still holding the thick, plush white cotton towel around her body, she opened the door of the closet and visually swept the clothes in the closet. Quiet, understated, and subdued. Am I dressing for dinner or dressing as an attorney going to court? I don't like lawyers—they always want money. What do you mean $550 for a phone call? It's five hundred dollars for the phone call, and he charges another fifty just for picking up the receiver. She took six different garments on hangers out from the closet, then threw them flat on top of the bed. She stood back from the bed and looked over her choices. Let's see. Will it be gray or neutral beige? Boy, this is an exciting decision. She picked up the gray skirt and top and put them back in the closet. I don't feel like being gray.

She proceeded with putting on the beige dress and the accessories like she was a saleswoman in a Beverly Hills dress store. The solid beige dress had a high neck and a lighter, softer fabric draping down the long sleeves. She placed a gold drop-front belt around the waist. She fought the desire to place a gold necklace over the dress or place a pin to the side of her breast. Instead, she opted for thick gold circle clip earrings and pulled her hair around her ears. Sandals would not look good with this professional yet fashionable outfit, but she couldn't get the dark shoes to contrast the color of the dress. Her only shoes were either black or light brown, which still would not look good. Fighting the force to resist sandals, she pulled out the burlap wedge sandals; and after trying them on and checking herself in the mirror, they looked good. She was pleased. She then returned to the bathroom vanity mirror to do one final check of her makeup. She picked up the lipstick and ran it over her lips one more time, then took a tissue and pressed her lips into it to seal the gloss. She flushed the soiled tissue down the toilet and returned to the bedroom and looked at the closed door. She stood back and fought the desire to go to the sliding glass door and look out. The drapes were shut, and she wanted them to remain that way. She sat down at the round table and tapped her fingers over the tabletop waiting to hear Bond's knock. She checked the time on her wristwatch and started to worry about his lateness. Checking the time, he wasn't late yet. She was just early. He still had one minute. Wouldn't it be good if he was late? I could razz him about that all night.

She looked back at her watch while walking to the door and standing behind it while counting down the final ten seconds . . . seven, six, he's not going to make it, hah! Three, two . . . At just that second, someone knocked on the door. "Sheesh. Damn it."

The voice on the other side of the door said, "What?"

"Nothing. Come in." The door opened, and he looked at her, smiling and nodding his head. He liked what he saw but said nothing. She, in turn, was impressed by him with his dark brown suit; but neither of them said anything to the other. Somehow, they had orchestrated themselves to match each other in color without even knowing what the other was going to be wearing.

In a gracious yet still somewhat professional manner, he took hold of her hand and walked her down the hall and stairs then out of the building and stood with her outside. He released his hold on her to take the car keys out of his pocket. To her utmost surprise, they weren't going to be traveling in the Hummer. A shiny white Ferrari was parked in front of the house. He unlocked the car doors, then opened the passenger door, and held her hand as she sat in the absolute pinnacle of automobiles. He got in, then looked to her, unspoken and still. "You can breathe now. The boss watched you marveling at these automobiles in the garage. He told me to take you out in one tonight instead of the Hummer. I hope you don't mind."

She tried to keep from marveling at this vehicle while being held captive in it. "No, I don't mind." He laughed at her after she said this and put the car in gear and drove out of the open gate to the highway.

Inside the front lobby of the restaurant, obviously owned by the boss, she was at first surprised that it was an Italian restaurant. She had expected something more along the tropical or Oriental theme in the Hawaiian Islands. This place reminded her of something along the line of the Olive Garden restaurants. The host came to them and seated them at a booth to the side of the room. The booth had a raised side offering some privacy in this open Mediterranean atmosphere with a tiled floor and dark-stained wood.

The waiter came to them, and Bond smiled, nodding his head while still holding the menu. The waiter nodded back, and the next thing she knew, a waiter was putting a wine bucket to the side of the table. Another waiter placed stemmed glasses in front of them, and then the other waiter popped the cap off a bottle of champagne and poured some in each of their glasses. Bond held his glass up in her direction for a toast. She clinked her glass to his, then took a sip of this bubbly liquid. At first, she thought of Dom; but then after taking another sip, she realized it had a strong balance.

He noticed her thinking. "It's Cristal."

She half shook her head, then looked at him smiling at her. "It's good." He smiled, then laughed to himself. They opened the menus then to decide what to have for dinner.

The waiter came back with pad in hand to take their order. She ordered the mussels from the appetizer side of the menu. He ordered the swordfish with a side of rice pilaf and fresh vegetables. The waiter left a salad bowl, two plates, and a basket of garlic bread sticks on the table, then left them in their privacy. She breathed out, smiled at Bond, then bit her lower lip, and smiled again to him. He loosened his collar. "Don't tell me. I know. You wanted to stay home tonight, didn't you?"

She smiled, then took her right hand, and placed it behind her neck, then lowered it back to the table. "Oh, I'll make it through this, don't worry."

They started on the salads and bread. The waiter brought them each a glass of ice water and left. He took the salad plates after they'd finished, then refilled the bread basket. Another waiter brought the plates to the table. A large oval hot white plate was placed in front of each of them. The waiter held a towel between his hands and each plate to keep from getting burned by the hot plates. The mussels steamed in the air, and the aroma was marvelous. She could see a slight sprinkling of paprika as well as fresh parsley shaken over the open shells, and a faint whiff of garlic adorned the aroma steaming off the plate. There was a fresh basket of soft bread sticks placed on the table to be used to soak up the tasteful liquid from the plate. His swordfish was thick and showed the grill lines on it. Parsley adorned the top of the rice, and the fresh vegetable was four spears of fresh steamed asparagus. Little talk was expressed through dinner as each enjoyed the food. At the end of the meal, they passed on dessert but enjoyed a hot cup of tea and the opportunity for conversation.

CHAPTER 23

njoying their tea, the talk, though relaxing, was of nothing more than past movies or books that they had read or funny memories from their youth, mostly at school. On the ride back home, no music came from the car, and no talk was exchanged. The only noise was the hum of the motor. Back at the estate, he helped her out of the car; then another guard who stood at the side of the front door took her hand and took her inside while Bond put the car away in the garage. Inside the front door, she stood still, waiting at the base of the stairs; and the guard returned to his position outside the front door. Light beamed from the half-open door of the boss's office. She felt no desire to talk to him and felt no need for closeness. The relaxed feeling that she had enjoyed through the course of dinner and the company of Bond was lost. She knew that if she just stayed there, that would be reason enough for him to come out and see her, and that was something that she wanted to avoid at all costs right now. She took hold of the bottom rail of the stairs but hesitated before starting the climb up the stairs and to her room. No guard was there to accompany her or to unlock the door of her room, but she knew that there must be cameras or something throughout the house because everything she did seemed to be known.

She started up the stairs, quickening her pace with each step to the top. She wanted Bond's company more than anything, but right now, she felt the need for seclusion since he wasn't there. Stopping in front of her door, she looked to the shiny knob and thought that it looked brighter than before. Well, the maid was there in her room earlier that day. She probably came back to polish the doorknobs. Feeling dreary from the change of company and the labyrinth of the estate, she dropped her shoulders. She heard footsteps walking up behind her but felt no need to turn around and look. It would just be someone who would, once again, lock her inside her cage.

The doorknob turned, and the door was pushed open. She made no effort to walk into the room, knowing that the guard had to do his usual sweep of the room first. The man behind her stood to her side, and when she didn't go into the room, he said, "What are you waiting for? I'm not going to carry you in. I enjoyed dinner with you, but . . ." She quickly turned her head and was overjoyed at seeing Bond. She then walked in and stopped at the side of the bed. He walked in and closed the door behind him, then went to stand beside her by the bed, looking into her beautiful brown eyes.

Looking into each other's eyes, the silence of the room was noted. It was just them. No other thoughts but each other went through their minds. Her lips were full, and he softened his hard composure, sinking into the rapture of the moment. They both leaned their bodies forward towards each other, then loosened their arms, and wrapped each other in an embrace. She looked up at him as he lowered his lips down to hers—a slight touch against her lips at first, then with increasing pressure as they held each other. She wondered if she should fall back down on top of the bed or wait for him to make the motion. He turned the hold he had on her to the side so that they would both fall to the bed beside each other. Their feet became locked together, and their legs were firm against each other as they fell on top of the mattress, feeling the softness of the quilted pillow-top comforter. She loosened her body for him to overwhelm her while still locked into a deep kiss, which quickly became an open-mouth kiss. The only sound beside the beating of their hearts was when they gasped for air. She loosened the notch on his belt as he placed a hand on top of the bed, balancing himself as he lay down over her; and with the other hand, he took off her top. She reached down and took off her belt. He then started in motion for them to turn over to the middle of the bed, giving them room to further take off their clothes. Each drew a deeper, harder breath with each passing second, consumed by passion, lust, and wanting. She moved her pelvis forward into him, feeling his hard penis touching her. He unzipped his pants, then stopped the motion of taking his pants off, lusting forward in another deep kiss while running his hand over her breast. She slid her hand down the side of his pants, then abruptly stopped. Her mind was consumed with Chris's image looking to her, the image of his face, his smile.

She looked down to him. "I don't think so. I can't, not yet. Not here. Please, just leave." She turned her back to him and walked towards the drapes over the sliding glass door. She stood by it but did not move the drapes to look out. She looked at nothing, not even focusing on what was in front of her. He got up from the bed and said nothing. He just put his clothes back on and walked to the door, but he stood there looking at the doorknob before he put the key into the keyhole and turned it. He had the door open just an inch, then started to turn his head to look to her and opened his mouth to say something. She could feel him do this. The brief pause seemed to last forever until he grabbed hold of the door and pulled it open, then left. She didn't hear the door being locked but then thought, Did it matter?

She walked back to the side of the bed and looked down at the impression in the down comforter. She could envision the outline of their bodies and felt him, felt his touch and his pounding heart. She began to cry, then stopped herself, and lifted the pillow, throwing it with all her might back onto the comforter. She began to scream, then stopped herself, knowing full well that one of them or all of the guards followed by the boss would be inside of the room and would be giving her the third degree about what happened. She swiftly turned her body away from the bed and started in a rage to the bathroom. She threw off her clothes and pulled on her sweat suit from the side counter of the vanity. Then she returned to the bedroom and stood to the side of the sliding door. She stopped just long enough to turn on the boom box, listening to the music that vibrated through the air before starting a forward lunge. She pulled her body out from the downward stretch and walked back to the boom box. The CD that was playing was Journey. She stopped it, thinking to herself that it was a song to be listened to while making love, and she wanted to forget that right now.

Not wanting to scour through the stack of music, she recognized a CD cover and put in the Whitesnake CD. She moved with each step, swinging her hips, raising her shoulders, and moving her arms up and down. She didn't pay any attention to any of the words or the lyrics. She moved her body in rapid succession to release herself from the torrent of emotions and the ones that she had to keep locked inside. Then she stood still but moved her legs, bending them up and down. It's a good thing I stopped, she thought to herself. I would have been cheating on my dead husband. This life that they have put me in makes me feel like I am dead. How am I going to behave around Bond now? How should I act in front of the boss, the wise old man who knows it all? I feel like running, running away, but where would I go? Where is my life? What is my life? Chris, my husband. I feel like you are talking to me. Well, maybe you are here. Ghosts aren't visible, but ghosts are an entity. He was my love, my angel sent from above . . . shit, now I sound like a Hallmark greeting card. She moved her body to the motion of the music and wiped the sweat from her forehead. Back to the plan. Don't lose face. I'll just ignore what happened and behave towards Bond as the trained guard that he is. In front of the boss, I won't speak until spoken to. They had cameras in the garage, and they watched me. They watch everything I do.

She went into the bathroom to shower, then dried off. She left the bathroom and headed to the bed; but just before stepping away from the front of the vanity section of the bathroom, she stopped, then grabbed a nightshirt, and put it on. She feared that he might make an appearance again during the night. Sitting at the right side of the bed, she tried relaxing her mind. This is driving me crazy. Number one, I am a person who can't leave a project half finished. It's just not in my nature. It has to be complete; or at least, if it isn't, I have to have proof in the way that it will be finished and when it will be finished. I don't know what they want from me. Their excuse is my protection. Maybe it's not the enemy who wants me dead. It's them—they are the ones who want me dead, but if I exposed them, what would my benefit be? Lauren? No, Dora is the mother of Lauren. I am Jane.

She crawled under the covers, then turned off the light on the nightstand. I wish I had a sleeping pill. She rolled to the other side of the bed, then hit the pillow, and rolled back to where she had been. She opened her eyes and looked to the side, looking at the door to the hallway. She wrestled with the bedsheets, then got up out of bed, grabbed a chair from the side round table, pushed it up to the door, and placed it behind the doorknob. She looked at it, then thought, This wouldn't stop anybody. It would just buy me time. The motion of moving the chair would be heard and maybe give me enough time to at least get out of bed.

She got back in bed, then moved around, and pulled at the covers trying to find comfort; but she couldn't. She finally lay still in the bed and laughed. I am now Jane. Tarzan and Jane. Tarzan is Brendan Fraser. Now that's a thought. She regained her composure. No, after what just happened, I have to get my mind off that. He does have a hard body, though. Oh god, now I really wish I had a sleeping pill. I have to go to sleep. I have to have plenty of energy these days. She closed her eyes and thought, Energy to stay locked in this room? She did finally fall asleep but never to the deep third stage of sleep.

In the morning, she dressed as plainly as she could—dark brown jeans and a plain white tee shirt. She stood back from the breakfast table and took inventory of who was there and what they were doing—trying to gauge the mood in the room. The boss had his eyes to the newspaper but was still aware of everything around him, as usual. Two guards were standing at each corner of the room. He usually had only one guard by him in the room, and he was usually sitting at the table with them. She suddenly felt fearful with this added security. Was the rival gang close by? Being locked in her room was now safety that she wanted.

She pulled out the chair and sat down at the table. Looking across to Bond, she was surprised that he did not get up and pull the chair out for her as he normally did. She got comfortable and thought it best not to say anything to him or look towards him. She didn't know what the boss knew about the night before, and she hoped that he knew nothing about it. Breakfast was the usual, biscotti and fruit with espresso coffee—no surprise there. She turned to face the boss, and he turned to her at the same time, their eyes locking to each other. She blinked, then looked at him again. "Would it be possible to get something else? I am not a fan of espresso. Could I get—"

He interrupted her. "What would you like?"

She was surprised at his attentive words. Bond must not have said anything to him, or maybe it was what he had said. "I would like a latte."

She waited, not saying anything more because she wanted to see how he would react to her saying this.

He snapped his fingers to the guard who stood to his right. The guard nodded, then went into the kitchen and came back in a minute, and placed a latte in front of her. She nodded to him in thanks, then took a sip. It was good. That's all that she had for breakfast, but no one said a word to her about why she didn't eat anything. Uncomfortable with the lack of conversation and tired of looking at the empty coffee cup in front of her, she got up and walked out of the room. First, she was surprised that Bond didn't follow her up the stairs as he always did. She waited and stood still; then not sensing him coming after her, she continued up the stairs, not wanting her pause to be noticed.

Something definitely had been said because now, at the top of the stairs, she turned and walked to her room and was very surprised to find the door open. She apprehensively went inside. There was no one else there. She stood looking to the open door and did not know whether to close it or not. Then after thinking it over, she walked forward and closed the door, knowing full well that if they wanted in, then they could easily get in. Had she gained more trust, or did they just leave the door open after they went through her things? Did they install a camera to watch her?

She feared that she had to stay locked in silence and fear. Her usual outlet was turning on the stereo, but she didn't feel like doing that now. She went to the sliding glass door and opened the drapes and then the window, standing there only long enough to feel the breeze enter the room. Then she walked away and sat in front of the TV. She turned it on, then sat back to see what was on the screen, not even feeling like waiting until she found something to interest her. *The View* was on, so she sat back and listened to the hosts gossip to each another. She looked dead to the world.

She thought it would just be a period of waiting—waiting for her life. Just sit back and stay focused. Swallow all that comes against me, and graciously accept becoming this new person and assuming this new identity, living a life of fear and crime. She turned off the television, then took the large decorative pillow from the top of the bed, and delicately put it on the floor. She bent down to a yoga position, then hummed to herself, seeking the redemption of relaxation from yoga, hoping that she would never come out of the relaxed trance that she hoped she could put herself in.

Downstairs in the office, the boss sat behind his desk going through reports from his many business ventures. "You'll acquire the coffee-distribution operation, and I will completely take over the car-parts business. I want out of Chicago. Old ties there that have to be broken. The new businesses I'll be acquiring are in California. We have to have this completed today . . . Yes, I know the procedure. The papers will be to you by noon, and I expect them to me here by then too . . . Deal." He hung up the phone and got up from the chair, then opened the side doors to the outside, and looked out at the rippling ocean waves. "It . . . the ocean is like life . . . it is always in motion, unpredictable at times. But you always know that there is constant movement, feared and peaceful at the same time."

CHAPTER 24

Jane spent most of the day locked inside her room. She already had her plan in motion in her mind. Now it was just a matter of timing. Thoughts of Bond went through her head repeatedly though she tried to convince herself that they didn't. She would think about other things; then halfway through writing the correct word on a crossword puzzle, the mental image of him on the beach, driving the car, in the restaurant, talking to her at the table, or in bed with her would fill her mind. She closed her eyes tight and tried everything to forget about him. She wanted out of this life and out of this family. Besides, the boss had told her Bond was family, but her husband was dead, and she was no longer part of his life or their life. Then there were the bullets, which were a part of this life. Where was her life? She wanted it back so badly that it left her with a virulent taste in her mouth, which she had to free herself from by thinking about what she was waiting for, and the answer to that was a safe time to initiate her plan. When would there ever be a safe time? she wondered. The plan of action was now. She scoured the room, then went to the door, and listened for any noise. Sure, they usually knocked first, but what was to keep them from just bursting into the room and taking her somewhere else? She felt feverish just thinking about this, and her nerves played with her. She clasped her hands and squeezed them, trying to release the pent-up emotions so she could get herself to freely concentrate without emotional interruptions.

She turned on the television and turned on the stereo, then pulled it all the way over to the TV. She pulled the clock radio off the nightstand

and placed it by the TV and stereo. She turned all of them on and got the information that she needed—she had to be at the airport for the flight that was to take off at six o'clock. An hour before—not too much time. They'll track me. She put the plastic baggie that held her money and the needed information inside her bra; then she walked over to the side area of the vanity and took out the gym bag that she had there. She grabbed a beach towel from the bathroom cabinet and knocked on her door. She waited for a guard to come and open it, feeling the blood pound in her body from the nervous tension. She had planned out each prethought movement that she'd make for the plan to work. The guard knocked, and she told him that she wanted out. He pushed open the door and stepped aside for her to exit. She walked down to the beach and was surprised that she wasn't followed, and the usual guards weren't at each tower along the beach.

Jane opened the entrance door of the tower on her left. She changed into the wet suit and covered her face with the mask. The plastic bag containing the needed change of clothes and information regarding the flight she strategically placed inside one of the pockets in the wet suit. She went all the way down to the water on the left side of the beach. A rocky cove blocked that side of the beach with large boulders. She walked down beside these large rock formations into deeper water and farther out into the middle of the water so as not to hit any of these rock formations. She knew the distance in her mind until there would be a break in the heavy wire net that lay below the surface of the water and up against the boulders. She felt along the rocks and measured each movement of her hand, looking for the opening. She reached out and felt along the rocks for so long that she almost gave up hope of finding the opening. However, she persevered, wanting the feeling of freedom that would come from her escape. Ah, an opening. Her left hand went through to open water. She shook it back and forth, then thought it better not to do this. She didn't want to attract any attention by stirring up the peaceful water inside the cove, an action that might attract the attention of the guards or the boss himself.

She managed to enlarge the opening in the heavy wire net blocking the way out to the ocean waters. She freed her chest and the midsection of her body, feeling the freedom of a bird fleeing the confines of an egg, but then she felt an abrupt halt to her progress and viewed this with both skepticism and fear. She bent back behind her to find what had hold of her calf. The broken wires had caught the skin of her wet suit and her right calf. She saw what had happened and relaxed so she could pull back to free herself from where she was caught on the wires. In doing this, she pierced the skin above her right wrist and saw blood enter the clear ocean waters. Then in one motion and with a vengeance, wanting desperately to be free, she pulled the heavy wires from her wrist. The only thing that she felt was the power of escape and the overwhelming drive to do it. Now free from the confines of the cyclone net, she lowered her body back down into the ocean and turned left, swimming her way to the open beach by a coffee shop that adorned the coastline at a more central part of the island. If she was seen by anyone there coming out of the water in a wet suit, it wouldn't even be noticed since surfers and deep-sea divers commonly navigated these waters.

Feeling she was in shallower water now, she placed her feet on the bottom of the sandy beach and walked out of the water. The sunlight that made her pupils contract as she took off the goggles was welcomed by her smile. She caught herself from showing any emotion, then made instant tracks to the restrooms outside the coffee shop. She changed out of her wet suit in a bathroom stall. Now dressed in dry clothes, top, scarf, and pants, she took the wet suit out from the stall and placed it on the cement tile floor of the restroom just under the hand dryers. She walked over to the sinks and checked her face, then straightened her hair, and applied more lipstick. She left the bathroom, and outside the restaurant, a bus had just pulled to a stop. She boarded it and sat down on an empty bench, looking out the window at planes in the sky. She knew she was still going to have to transfer to another bus to get to the airport.

Outside the front boarding area of the airport, she shook her head to the men taking the luggage from the bus and tying stringed tags on the bags. She explained that she only had a carry-on bag. At the ticket counter, she gave her memorized credit card information and got the paper ticket. She was ready to board, but the flight wasn't scheduled for boarding for another thirty minutes. She sat in the seat by a pay phone to the side of the boarding area. She didn't make a call but still held the phone, making it look like she was having a conversation so she could have some privacy. The boarding call was finally announced on the loud speaker.

She fought the natural inclination to run aboard the plane. She waited until it looked like most of the flight had boarded; then she got up and stood in-line to board. She gave her ticket to the attendant, then went aboard the plane, which appeared to be only half full. She liked that feeling of openness. To the left in the fourth row in the middle section of the plane, she saw her seat.

It was the middle seat, but she didn't feel that crammed and pushed and shoved feeling since no one was sitting to either side of her. She fastened her seat belt and felt comfort in a relaxed state. The flight attendant just announced that the skies were clear, and it would be an easy flight to California. She heard the doors being pulled closed, but then she had a strange feeling even though the plane hadn't moved. A tall shadow fell over her. She looked down to the floor of the plane in the aisle and saw a pair of feet. She saw a pair of men's sandals and thought it was probably a tourist. She had lost the freedom of having no one beside her, but they were men's sandals, so maybe this could be something good. She looked up to his legs, and they were long, tanned, and bare. He was wearing tan shorts. She looked further up to his body frame—nice hips, slender, definitely a tourist shirt from the islands, up to his face. Will it be a young model's face or the face of an older male tourist? She looked at his face, then froze in fear, shock, and disbelief.

He smiled at her. She closed her dropped jaw, swallowed, and then asked him how he knew. "Why do you think that it was so easy to get off the estate and get here, hmm?" The attendant then came to his side and asked him, pointing to Jane, if that was the person he was looking for. He nodded his head, then reached down, unlatched her safety belt, took her by the hand, and led her from the plane. As soon as they got to the open boarding gate door, the door to the plane closed, and it headed down the runway for takeoff.

She looked around and saw that they were alone, and she proceeded to talk to him. "You knew everything that I did, didn't you?"

He looked at her and raised his eyebrows, then nodded. "I've been here at the airport most of the day waiting for you. Why do you think I wasn't at the estate?" She could find no response or reply. She followed in his tight grasp outside the airport where a limousine waited for them with an open door. He pushed her inside, then got in, and closed and locked the doors. Then the chauffeur drove away and went back to the estate.

She tried not to look at him but finally turned her head, looking at him face-to-face. "How did you know? I mean . . ."

"Oh, it's not too hard to know when you're up to something. You give yourself away."

"I give myself away? How?"

He turned and looked out the window, then back at her eyes. "You are quiet. It's dangerous when you are quiet." She looked at him, then swallowed, and closed her eyes and leaned back in her seat feeling like a watched caged bird. What could possibly be the next course of action?

He looked to her wrist and noticed the dried blood from the cut just above her wrist bone. He reached forward and opened a panel on the wall to the side of the rear-facing seat. He pulled out a first aid kit. She made no confirmation that she had observed him do this. He already had the cotton bandage unrolled and was ready to apply it to her skin. With his other hand, he sprayed the antiseptic spray on her wounded wrist. She shrieked in pain at the spray and turned to look at him in a hostile way. He pulled her wrist tighter to him, then wrapped it up. He tore the tape with his teeth and placed it over the bandage. He replied to her that he wasn't doing that for fun; it was for her benefit. She knew the truth to his words but did not let on any thankfulness for him doing that. He looked at her, rolled his eyes, then asked her if there was any other place where she was hurt.

"There is, but you are not touching that area."

He pulled his eyes back but looked directly at her. "Do you want me to close my eyes or turn around while you tend to it?" She looked at him seeming to have dropped some of her guard as she remembered how much of each other they truly had seen on their night together. She looked as though she wanted to say something but just held the bandages and tape in her hand, then raised her pant leg, exposing the open wound on her right calf. He observed this from his side view, then turned all the way around, looking to the driver through the half-open darkened glass.

She sprayed the red area of the wound, about a two-inch- circumference oval area scraped down to the very first layer of skin. She had to touch the area very carefully so it wouldn't start to bleed again. The dressing she applied made it feel much better indeed. She was surprised that he didn't ask her how that happened, how she had cut herself; then she thought they had probably been observing her as she did it. Oh, the pleasantries of facing the boss after this.

The iron gates to the estate opened. In turning to see the view out the side window, she saw dark storm clouds covering the sky. Rain was evidently coming although not here yet. A more fitting welcome for what she was about to face could not have been planned. The limo parked to the side in front of the main door to the house. The boss wasn't standing there to welcome her back with a whip in his hand or standing behind the window to spy on her as he always did. His absence should have been cause for celebration, but his not being there just stirred the pot of pent-up emotions yet to come. Somehow, his absence made matters worse. The driver got out almost running as did Bond. He ran from the car while yelling to her to stay in the car. She didn't hear this, but she just stayed there and waited for the door to be opened for her. When it wasn't opened for her, she opened the door wide but then stayed in the car, waiting for a hand to reach in and help her out. When no help was forthcoming, she slowly climbed out of the limo but saw no one standing there waiting for her. There was no one in sight. The front door to the house was wide open, but no one was there. She sheepishly walked inside the house and still saw no one even though the door to the boss's office was open.

She was not in an adventurous mood and didn't want to go in and confront him. After standing in the open foyer for a few minutes, she found no option but to go upstairs to her room. She didn't have a guard to accompany her there, and she wondered as she climbed each stair who would be there to let her in so she could remain inside a closed, locked room for an indefinite period of time. Upstairs, standing at the door to her room, she saw that it was open. It had been kicked in. Wood fragments hung from the doorframe, and she was fearful to push the door open and see what was inside of her bedroom waiting for her.

She reached for the thought of Chris being there to protect her. She had envisioned his death so many times in her mind; and it made her shake from head to toe, thinking of that scene in the park—him falling, the gunshots, the baby crying. Where was Bond? She locked her body in a frozen state while standing at the open door, afraid to move it in any direction, as if the noise of her doing this would cause the person on the other side to fire their gun. The bullet would plunge into her, rip her skin, pierce through her warm and throbbing heart, pinch her nerves, then move through her bones, fragmenting them into pieces. Then she'd fall to the floor crying in intensified pain. The irony of this was that if she was dead, the story would be over.

Her only other option was to turn and face the loneliness of the house and walk back down the stairs to the further unknown. There was no sanctity. There was only the fear of the unknown, the overwhelming, piercing fear of the unknown. She closed her eyes and tried to conceptualize an answer as to what to do—to face fear or turn away from it. She took a long, deep breath, then swallowed it, and held it while pushing the door all the way open. The room looked clear—no madman or bomber came forward to grab her neck or put a gun down her throat. The wind was blowing in through the open sliding glass door and caused the drapes to move violently back and forth. She took another breath and went inside the room. She thought, Is this another warning? Locked in fear in the middle of the room by the side of the bed, she felt her nerves race through her body. It was the fear of death, the dry feeling of parched skin, a dry tongue, and trembling flesh—weakness in not being able to defend herself from what she felt was the inevitable. She pulled her shaking hand to her mouth, then heard a loud stabbing sound that shattered the skies. The dark flash of a body ran to her and pulled her down, then rolled her to the side of the bathroom away from the flying bullets that riddled through the sky, coming from a helicopter right outside the grounds of the estate.

She closed her eyes and, through this motion, hoped that she'd awake from a bad dream; but reality was more than there through the consuming pain and fear of her racing heart. Under the vanity at the side of the bathroom, she opened her eyes and saw that it was Bond who was pressed against her chest. He looked at her with eyes wide open, not in fear but taking in the reality of what they were facing. He didn't need to say anything. His expression said all that needed to be said. She was quiet and pushed herself further under the vanity.

Bond counted the bullets that were fired, then raised his body from under the vanity. He shielded her, then ran through the bedroom to the open door where the drapes blew in the wind. He stood with his back to the wall beside the open door to the deck and cocked his gun, holding it out with his arms held rigid to counteract the force of the gun and get a clear shot. As the helicopter gained altitude making its departure, he fired at it.

He clipped the side of the open door of the helicopter where the gunmen had fired at them. One of the men pointed his gun in Bond's direction but fired a blank shot. Bond fired back at him, hitting him in the arm; and the gunman retreated back inside the helicopter, holding his wounded arm. The other man fired at Bond who dropped to the floor and rolled, but instead of rolling back inside the bedroom; he rolled outside onto the deck, then stood up in the clear open space, and then fired straight up at the helicopter. He shot the gunman once, then fired three more times, hitting him with each shot. The gunman fell from the helicopter and landed in the swimming pool below, and blood flowed through the clear water of the pool. The helicopter flew away. The guard dogs ran to the pool and barked at the bleeding body turning the crystal blue water to a pool of red blood. Bond stood up and walked back into the bedroom. Jane came out from under the vanity and ran to him as he fell to the floor at the side of the bed, panting in exhaustion and pain.

Many thoughts bombarded her mind. The first was to make a sly comment asking him if this was the reason why he was in a rush to get home. Then she thought better of that. She could not find anything to say. She just remained silent and held him. This man, her husband's brother, was indeed her savior. She felt passion for him and also trust and security. Now it wasn't a matter of how to get off this island; it was a matter of how to stay alive and how to get him. Jane looked down at him as she felt his grip tighten on her hand and felt his look penetrate through her. She lowered her head and looked at him while supporting his upper body in her hands. She found that she had trouble looking directly into his wide-open, tearful eyes. She closed her eyes, composed herself, silently breathed out, then bent down and kissed his forehead. He slowly opened his hand, then closed his eyes. Worried, she immediately checked his pulse at his carotid artery. He was still breathing but in labored breaths.

She got up to go get help but first pulled his body up so he was lying on the bed. He blinked to her, and she covered him with a blanket, then touched his head. He moved his head ever so slightly, telling her to leave;

and then with one hand, he waved her out. She left running at first but then thought of him and how she wouldn't be there if he needed her. But it was a matter of his life, and before she even knew it, she was at the bottom of the stairs. She swung open the office doors and was very surprised when she did not see the boss there. Was he all right? Oh god, what do I do now? She heard a rustling behind her. The sound was moving away from her, but she still froze in fear. My life too. Oh god! In one movement, she turned her body around to look out the office door and to the base of the stairway where the noise came from. She didn't recognize this man who ran up the stairs carrying a large dark leather bag, but she remained deadlocked to his view. Seeing the next man who followed him up the stairs at a run, she clasped her hand to her chest, then moved her hand over her racing heart, and tried to move her trembling body and shaking, wobbly legs. She had trouble moving them and almost fell on her side. She caught herself and ran after these men. She didn't know who the first man was, but the second man was the boss. They only stopped when they got to the door of her room. The boss had no guards beside him. He was the one who took a gun out of his vest pocket and swept the room before they entered. They all ran to the bed, and the doctor got there first. He ripped open Bond's shirt, saw the blood, then took up his wrist to get his vitals. While the doctor went on with his medical care to save Bond's life, the boss took hold of Jane's hand, something he had never done before; and she was surprised that he was doing it now. They had never touched before.

"So now do you know why it is so important to do what you are told to do here? I'm not playing a game with you. It is your life. I don't have much family left, and you are still part of it—the family that is. Don't ask any more questions, at least not now."

She looked over to him, feeling embarrassed and somehow guilty. She bit down on her lower lip, then shook her head to him, and held his hand. "Thank you."

"Don't worry. My doctor is very good."

It turned out that the bullet had just broken the skin and grazed the tissues over his chest. There was some skin loss. The doctor covered the wound with gauze and left pain medication for him as well as instructions for his care. He would be staying there, right in this bed, that night; and Jane welcomed the opportunity just to be near him, to care for him.

She stayed in the room with him that afternoon and all through the evening. Fearful of lying in the same bed with him, thinking that in her sleep, she might roll into him or cause movement that would hurt him, she took one of the deep-cushioned chairs from the table and moved it over to the side of the bed, then covered herself with the spread from the bed. She could hear him breathing, but that was a very welcome sound to hear.

She turned circles in her heart thinking of how she was giving up on Chris and was now completely entranced with Bond, his brother; but she was in that life now, and he was there, so it seemed like destiny—a Mondello to the core. What of her daughter, Lauren? She felt her heart break, wondering what her daughter must be thinking when she didn't return to her. She was a rebellious teenager, but she was her own flesh and blood, the daughter she had given birth to and had held through the night as a baby and as a child. She was Chris's blood too, a tie to him. Then in the same turn, Lauren was now out of the line of fire, which Jane was definitely in now. She felt happiness knowing that her daughter was out of danger. I'll see her again soon. I just won't be able to see her as her mother. Mother—something that I feel I was made to be. I didn't feel complete until I was a mother. This is something that I am committed to.

In talking to herself, she fell asleep in the chair as the sun set through the still partially opened drapes. The morning light woke Bond up. He tried raising his body up in the bed; then after moving from his waist up, he grabbed his chest and pulled his hand over his wound, then shrieked in pain. He looked to the partially opened drapes covering the sliding glass door. He was surprised seeing that he was in Jane's room, then felt the empty bed next to him, lowered his body back down, and breathed out a relaxed moan. In turning his eyes to both sides of the bed, he saw her still asleep in the chair beside the bed. She was snoring, a soft snore, and he laughed when he heard this from her and thought of how he could razz her about that. She moved her neck, then stopped the snore. She pulled her head farther back in the chair, then pushed it forward, and cupped her cheeks with her open hands and bent her head down. In an exhausted voice, she mumbled, "It's morning. It feels like Monday morning."

Bond looked over to her and said, "Well, I see you are nice in the morning. Will you cheer up after your shower, or will it have to wait until your morning java?"

She looked at him, then licked her lips, and straightened herself in the chair. "Well, I see you are feeling better and in the boxing ring already. Are we going to start every day like this, throwing insults to each other?"

Bond laughed lightly. "It appears so."

She stood up, then reached her hand over to his forehead, feeling for a fever. "Well, you don't appear to be hot. No fever. It just appears that there will be a long healing time. No Olympic tryouts for you."

"Well, you're the one who keeps me running around all the time." "Bond, pretend that you are an Indian, and we just compromised on a peace treaty. All right?" "Yes, Mother."

She held out her hand and stopped him from saying anything further. "Please, I'm not prepared to hear that." He realized what his kidding dialogue meant to her and then apologized. "The first thing we have to do is get you to the bathroom and then get some liquid in you with another pill. Then if you can handle it, something to eat." She helped him out of the bed and took him to the bathroom. Once there, she closed the door and leaned back against the wall, waiting for him. She was surprised that he had made no remarks to her when she had helped him to the bathroom; then she thought that he still might be feeling uncomfortable about the comment he had made earlier. She helped him back to the bed and got him in and covered back up. There was a knock on the door, and before she could even respond with a "Come in," the door opened; and the boss and a maid appeared. The maid had a glass of apple juice for Bond and put it on the nightstand. Then she stood back and handed Jane a cup of coffee, then left the room. The boss walked over to the other side of the bed.

He didn't open his mouth to speak until the maid left and closed the door behind her. Bond had already smiled at him, and he had smiled in return. Jane got up from the chair, then walked over to the table, and sat there drinking her coffee, offering a limited amount of privacy for Bond and his father.

He asked Bond how he felt, and Bond replied that it was painful, but there was a tone in his voice that was lower than his usual tone. His father told him that one man from the helicopter was dead and explained how his body had fallen into the swimming pool. He looked at Bond, then put his hand out towards him, and held his arm. Bond knew what this conveyed since his father was not a man to ever tell anyone that he loved them. This was his way to express love without the words. The boss looked to him, then looked up to Jane sitting at the table. He could see she was contemplating whether to swallow the last sip of coffee from her cup. Bond called to her, and she came to him with cup in hand.

The boss told her to go downstairs to the kitchen and get a refill and then find a guard to take her outside to the patio to get some air. She made no response to him but just left the room with her cup in hand and firmly closed the door behind her. The boss listened until the sound of her footsteps grew fainter and then completely disappeared before he spoke to Bond.

"I changed some of our vesting." Bond opened his mouth to speak, and in just the way he was breathing, his father could tell that Bond wanted to say many things. However, his father stopped him, regaining control of the conversation before Bond could get a word out. "We're out of Chicago and now mostly California. We are in partnership with the luxury sports car dealership in the Los Angeles area, and there is one more dealership that we have to acquire." He took a deep breath, giving Bond the opportunity to jump into the conversation. Bond thought about this but said nothing in response. His father was silent, but he remembered everything, and nothing went without closure. Bond made no comment, opening the way for his father to finish his train of thought.

"In two weeks, you should be healed. After that time, you will be taking a trip to California. I will be staying here doing paperwork for the takeover of the various businesses. You'll leave here, and your first stop will be the Los Angeles airport. Then you'll take a connector plane to Oakland, and a limo will pick you up at the airport and leave you off at the wharf parking lot in Vallejo. There, I will have someone waiting for you to take you through Napa, but you won't be staying there. The driver that you meet there will inform you and take you to meet a man named Jake. He will provide your transportation while you are there. He will take you to a suite at the Sonoma Mission Inn.

"Sonoma is a valley away from Napa separated by hills. The Sun Haven Winery is located there in the heart of the wine country. One of the owners of this business is the Del Marco family. The other partner just died, and he has no surviving heirs to pass the business on to, so this winery will become the exclusive ownership of the Del Marcos. This year has seen a record-producing crop of wine grapes. One of his wine tasters who goes to the tanks at night to get the samples will not just be taking fluids out in the tubes for testing. He will be putting another fluid in the vats, all the vats, poisoning the record year's grape harvest for that winery. This will financially knock them out of business. They will still have all of the needed workings for a vineyard, but the business will be broke, wiping them out. Another domino will fall to break the Del Marco family.

"I know that Jane really feels for you right now. And I know that you, in turn, feel for her. And so far, you have kept everything right and in control. I don't know how you are going to keep her interested in you and stay far enough from her at the same time, but I know that you will find a way so that nothing will happen." He stood up from the bed but never took his eyes off Bond's face. "I know you will make this happen. You are my son." He moved away from the bed and walked to the other side of it. He stopped and retraced his steps back to the side of the bed. He saw that Bond was looking straight ahead and not at him, but he knew that Bond was observing him as he had been trained to do. He grabbed his son's hand and held it between his own hands. He said nothing and then left.

CHAPTER 25

At the bottom of the stairs, the boss stood there motionless. It was more than obvious that he was still thinking about everything that was going on. He had a planned course of action but was still worried and could never let this show to anyone. Then he felt angry with himself because he was not able to hide it from himself too. He went forward, stepping into his office, but he saw no guard inside or standing to the outside door of his office, so he turned around and left. He wanted to sit down, concentrate, and meditate in his thoughts; so he looked to the large open living room at the center of the house but saw no safety in this large open area either. He went to the dining room and pulled a photo album out of a closed cabinet—an album containing pictures of his family and himself from back to the time of his marriage.

He turned the pages past the marriage to his long-departed wife, then turned back three more times to one picture in particular, a picture of his wife and himself standing under the altar locked in their first kiss as husband and wife. He closed the pages of the book. That was far away and long ago. It is just the memory of a family, what we had and what we were. I can't bring her back. Now I just have to keep the other two alive. He heard footsteps nearing him, so he placed the album back inside the cabinet and took up the newspaper that he had already read earlier in the day. He looked at the feet, then up to the body of the person who was approaching. It was Jane. He looked to her, then back down to the paper.

She came forward to the table, then pulled out her usual chair, and sat down. She took an orange from the fruit bowl but just held it in her hands and moved it around like it was a worry ball. She knew that he knew that she was there. It was just the fact that he made no affirmation of her that annoyed her so. She wanted to lash out at him, screaming that she would appreciate it if he could just show her something but then thought it was just a new way of life she would have to be learning. She gathered her strength from her stomach and felt it move all the way up her torso to her throat. Once at her tongue, she let it out. "I feel that I have become quite resilient in this matter."

"Yes, you have." He lowered the paper and looked at her. "Bond will be leaving soon on an important assignment. He will be going away, leaving this island. Maybe he will be going somewhere else in this same country, or maybe he'll be going to a different continent. You will not know nor will you be told."

She tensed her body, then tried to relax, but felt her blood move through her veins and her heart pulse at the back of her neck. She opened her mouth, then shut it, and rose up from the table and quietly pushed the chair back under the table. She then moved away from the table and started out of the room. Just two steps from being out of the room, she stopped abruptly and turned back to face the boss, tapping her feet to make just enough noise so that he would look up at her. It was impossible to get the attention of this man. "I can't believe you. You can just tell me anything, anything—pass you the salt, or duck out of the way of speeding bullets. Then you tell me that the man that I love, seemingly the only thing left in my life, you are sending away. And you won't tell me where or when. I know that wherever you are sending him and whatever you are sending him to do, his life will be in danger. I already lost my husband, and it took me years and a whole new life to get over that, and I don't feel that I have gotten over it yet. But there is nothing that I can do to change anything that happened. I just have to accept it. And now the man whom my heart has found to take his place—no, no one can ever take his place. But Bond, this new man I feel for in this empty life you put me in . . . how can I feel no emotion, no emotion whatsoever?"

He held the paper, then shook it to further open it; and he looked down, then back up to her. "Are you quite done?"

She looked to him, raised her eyes in anger, then replied violently, "Yes."

He looked back down to the table and held up the paper, folding it noisily, and then he looked up directly into her eyes. In a straightforward, loud voice, he replied to her, "Good." He then moved his eyes and face back down to the paper he had already read and became transfixed in it, completely blocking her presence out of his mind. She could feel his anger as he did this and felt at a loss for words, so she left the room and went out to the hallway and up the stairs. She stopped at the closed door to her room long enough to calm herself before going in to check on Bond and stay there with him.

He looked to her, smiled, then resumed reading a book that he held. She thought that was a good idea and then took a book that she had been reading from the table and sat in the chair beside his bed, opened it up, and became instantly engrossed in it. She did feel a comfort in being with him; and she, in return, hoped that he felt this. Then she wondered what his father had told him about how to behave towards her. She knew that he must have said something and feared what it was.

They each read their books in hand. The lamp was on where it stood on the nightstand even though the sun was coming in through the open drapes. Bond smiled over to Jane. She was reading but felt his eyes on her and looked up to him and smiled back. He moved to the side of the bed, then grabbed a walking cane to help him up from the bed. Then he went into the bathroom, closing the door behind him. Jane watched him do this but didn't offer to help because she knew he had to do this on his own to get stronger. There was a knock on the door, and then it was quickly opened by the boss. He came in the room with the doctor and looked at Jane. He turned his head towards the bathroom just as Bond opened the door and came out. Bond was surprised that his father was there, then caught himself, and changed his line of thought before he said anything. He stood still and remained quiet so his father could initiate the conversation.

He moved aside, signifying for Bond to get back into the bed, and then walked over to Jane who was sitting on the chair reading. He took the book that she held in her hands up to his eye level and focused on the cover, then removed it from his view. He looked back up to it again, showing an unwelcome expression. "*Disclosure.* She would be reading something like that. She keeps us busy, that's for sure." After he placed the book back down in her lap, she moved, then opened and reopened her eyes; then she started to get up out of the chair. He put his open hand firmly on her shoulder and prevented her from getting up out of the chair. She took her hands to straighten the hair around her face. Bond had the sheets folded back over his body as he lay in bed. All were quiet, awaiting the boss's word.

He looked at Bond and said nothing, but the look was full of love. The doctor stood to the side, quietly, and then the boss looked at the doctor and cleared the way at that side of the bed by stepping out of the way. Jane looked up as he did this, still surprised that he had no guard by his side. Was everything in the estate okay? She worried, then made a motion that she wanted to get up from the chair. The boss saw this, then swivelled her chair towards the sliding glass door, and motioned for her to go out there. She did but still felt scared going out in the open. She wondered with each step that she took if there was a guard at each of the towers outside. Were the guard dogs on duty? Then she thought of the dark red water in the swimming pool and cringed thinking of that, but she stood to the side of the sliding glass door and looked out, standing behind the wall and to the side as if she was a guard. All was clear. There were more guards than usual outside, and the dogs were running up and down the beach. The water in the pool was now clear, and there was no sign that anything had just happened out there. Then she thought, What did they do with the body? She tried to imagine, then stopped herself from thinking along those lines. There was a limit to the involvement that she wanted.

The doctor took the bandage from Bond's chest and examined the wound carefully, checking for any sign of infection at the site as he expected bullet fragments had entered this area where the skin was torn off and blood was exposed. His father did not like seeing this worried look on the doctor's face, and he knew that the doctor would prefer to care for Bond in the hospital, but the family could not endure such exposure. The doctor asked Bond if there was any pain, and Bond said, "Well, I just got in a gunfight for my life. They missed me, and that's the way it's going to remain." His father nodded his head hearing Bond say this. Standing at the window, Jane could not hear that well, but she didn't want to hear anyway and hummed the lyrics of a song in her mind instead to try and block out what she might hear.

The doctor stood back from the bed and spoke to the boss. "Well, he seems to be in good spirits. And the site is not swollen or infected, and he's not complaining of any pain." The doctor looked down, then repositioned the bag he held. "I . . . he's good to go. I know that's what you want." The doctor looked up at him, then held his bag tighter to the side of his body, and left the room.

"Bond, do you need help getting up out of bed and dressed? I can send a guard in here from outside to help you." He looked at Jane standing with her back to him as she was looking out the window.

"No, I can do it. I will be and I am fine."

He whispered to Bond, "You know you can't get too close to her. Watch it." Bond showed no emotion to what his father had just said to him, but he felt like he just swallowed his heart having to bury the emotions that he had for Jane. He made no verbal response to his father who stood there looking to him; and after a long moment, his father turned and left the room, closing the door behind him.

Bond called Jane over to his bedside. She went there quickly and waited for him to speak to her. "I'm feeling better, and I got a clean bill of health from the doctor. I am going to get up and dressed. Can you throw me over my clothes? I want to get out of these pajamas that the doctor helped me into last night."

"Do you want me to take your clothes into the bathroom for you, then help you get there?" She said this showing a smiling and helpful face. He looked at her, then thought that was too obvious, and managed to get to the edge of the bed by himself; but then he held her hand to make certain of his balance before trying to walk on his own. He took his clothes from the chair by the round table, then went into the bathroom to dress. He then left the room without looking back at her. Her happiness vanished after watching him leave. I'm back to square one now. Be quiet. Don't say anything. Don't react. How in the hell do I do that? What do I feel? I'm sure they will tell me.

That night at dinnertime, Jane went down the stairs and down the hallway to the dining room by herself. She stood outside the open doors to the dining room with no guard in sight but felt no fear now because at that moment, she could find no reason to live except for pure self-survival. The boss was sitting at the end of the table as usual. He wore a wool scarf around his neck. Perhaps he was trying to ward off a cold. She didn't feel like asking. Bond was seated at his usual spot. She quietly went to the table and sat down. The only thing that she wanted now was distance, distance from all of them. She once again yearned to have her former life back.

Bond had not helped her to her seat or even verbally acknowledged her. The boss never acknowledged her presence, with the exception of viewing her sideways, which was always more than disturbing. Dinner had already been placed on the table. A covered serving dish was in the middle of the table, and both Bond and his father had already helped themselves to the salad and dinner rolls. She found it difficult to be sitting there between them with the boss to her side and Bond across from her, without acknowledging them or saying anything. The two of them had already versed themselves in all that they needed to know, and she felt that they were somehow communicating with each other without the use of words. Bond rose up from the table, and she relaxed, thinking that maybe he would be coming to her side to make sure that she was all right or somehow say something to break the silence of the moment. He stood up and took hold of the open bottle of white wine, then reached across the table, and poured some '95 Napa Chardonnay in her glass. The anxiety of the moment passed, and she mouthed a soft thank-you to him.

The boss took the silver dome lid off the main dish for that evening—grilled mahimahi steaks on top of a bed of fresh papaya and pineapple salsa on steamed rice garnished with mint leaves. A plate was passed to her, they said a dinner prayer, and they both waited for her to start eating before they did. She thought about the courtesy of their actions, then thought that perhaps she was just the taster, and they were waiting to see if she was going to die before they started eating. She took a bite of rice laden with some of the salsa and fish on her fork, then nodded her head to them. The boss snickered, then began eating.

The next five to ten minutes went by with no conversation. It was apparent to her that this did not bother the men, and she tried her best to keep her emotional uneasiness at bay. Bond finished chewing a bite, swallowed, then wiped his face with the cloth dinner napkin. He looked at Jane, then glanced at his father before looking back to Jane. "It was your scar, the scar on your wrist that gave you away. I mean, you didn't expect me to check out every person who went in the airport, did you? I stood by the security cameras that photographed the passengers before boarding." She looked questioningly. "Okay, when you had to put your handbag down and walk through the metal detector, they zoomed in on the scar on your wrist. That's what gave you away. I then knew the gate number and what plane you boarded."

She looked down to her right wrist and saw the red scar that she had gotten from trying to swim through the jagged wire fence at the edge of the cove while making her getaway. Three different comebacks went through her mind in response to what he had just said, but she decided to remain silent instead of answering with bitter or sarcastic words. When she remained silent, Bond knew that he got her.

She ate very little at dinner, mostly from being so uncomfortable. The plates had been cleared off, the usual basket of fresh fruit was placed in the middle of the table, and a pot of coffee was passed around. She passed on the fruit but did pour herself some coffee. The first thing she noticed was that the usual bone white Italian espresso cups were not on the table, and the pot of coffee was larger than usual too. She filled her larger cup up just halfway, expecting the strong rich taste of espresso. She had grown so accustomed to it that she had stopped putting milk in her coffee and instead put in one teaspoon of sugar. As she put the teaspoon of sugar in her coffee, she noticed both of the men were watching her; and she stirred her coffee while eyeing them both, wondering what they were conspiring to do now. She took a large swallow of coffee, then closed her eyes, and grabbed her throat. "My god! What did you do to the coffee?"

Both men laughed, looking at her then to each other and back to her. They both opened their mouths at the same time to tell her something, but then Bond closed his again, giving the floor to his father. Bond softly laughed, and his father said, "We are no longer in the coffee business. All of the remaining coffee that we had here on the estate has been disposed of. And right now, young lady, you are drinking canned coffee." She pushed the cup towards the middle of the table and said that she would pass on the coffee. She rolled her tongue over her lower lip, then moved her eyes to the ceiling, and said no to them. She sat quietly, waiting until they finished and until the boss got up from his chair. She then left the dining room but remained in the hall area, waiting for one of them to tell her or suggest to her what to do now. She waited for both of them but really wanted to see only one. The boss walked past her without even giving her the usual sideways glance, but Bond stopped walking as soon as he reached her side.

He showed no change in his demeanor towards her. It felt as if she was hopping on stone tiles over a deep lake not knowing which one of the tiles would be a false step, and she'd sink, but she had to keep moving and keep her fear under control. He paused and looked at her, then looked down to the floor. Somehow, she sensed that he was nervous, something she was sure a Mondello was never supposed to show or succumb to. "Well, after what happened earlier, taking a walk outside is out of the question. And I don't feel like the two of us . . . going up to my room"—she rocked her head from side to side—"my domicile." With all the glass on the windows of the living room, going in there would seem like walking into the bull's-eye at a firing range." She saw that he was watching something either on her or near her, but he was not watching her. She looked at him, questioning him with her eyes. "What is it?" He motioned for her to be quiet. She stood rigidly but still watched his eyes. He took his handkerchief from his vest, then shook it open down by the floor, loosening the fabric. Then he made an open circle with it and caught something that had been on her shoulder. She watched him do this, then watched him open the front doors of the house, and shake the fabric loose to free the living creature he had captured. She feared what it might be, mostly thinking it was a poisonous black widow or imagining something far worse. "What was it?" she asked him, trembling.

"It was a fly. He's free now. Somehow, I just can't bring myself to kill them." She caught herself from falling back as this was spoken by a man who killed people day in and day out just to survive.

They stood by each other in silence again, neither knowing what words they were searching for. "I don't suppose that you have a bedroom?" She put her hand out in the air. "Somewhere where we could go? Or is your room like an army barracks with a small twin bed and weaponry to the side?"

He took a step back from her and tensed up his relaxed composure. "You know, before you said that last remark, I was ready to take you there, but not now. You are going upstairs to your domicile as you call it." He grasped her arm tightly as he led her up the stairs and to her room. He pushed her inside the open door, then remained outside. "You'd better just watch it because at any moment, I will put that lock back on this door, and it will not come off again!" He slammed the door shut and left, leaving her alone in the empty, lonely room. She made no response to what he had just said to her.

CHAPTER 26

She kicked off her shoes, went into the bathroom, took off her clothes, and then put on a pair of pajamas. She sat on the pillow up against the wall and assumed a comfortable yoga position and started chanting to relax her wary heartbeat. Her pulse slowed, and her breathing came easier. Then she drifted off to her haunting past, searching for any way to envision Chris—the peaceful park, the sunny day in Chicago, even the rock group Chicago sang through the air. The only thing that caused her to take her eyes from Chris or their baby whom he was pushing in the carriage was the occasional sound of a bird cawing as it flew by. The feeling was so peaceful and serene; it was almost as though it was in heaven. Then came the explosion, and her entire world changed. The bullet hit Chris, and her heart seemed to stop beating as time stood still. She opened her eyes, body trembling, feeling nothing but coldness, fear, and panic. She took her hands and held them over her mouth; then she shook her head from one side to the other and stopped as she relived that moment in time. There is nothing left. He's gone. I don't want to live anymore, but I cannot take my own life. I am afraid to die. God, just take me so that I can be with him, please. I just want to be with Chris.

She rose up, then lowered her body down on the bed, looking only at the darkness of the room and saying her long-gone husband's name repeatedly out loud until sleep overwhelmed her. Deep into sleep, she dreamed of being in that room, the room where she now was; and bullets shattered the glass door, blood covered the floor of the room, and she saw a body on the floor. The body was covered by a blanket. She trembled, afraid to pull up the blanket and see whose body this was. The bullets were flying everywhere. She trembled, then screamed, and sat up, eyes wide open in the bed. My god. I can't do this anymore. She got up out of bed and covered her cold, trembling body with her bathrobe.

She went to the hall door, stood back, then swallowed, and opened the door. To her surprise, the hallway was lit. She moved her foot forward, then stopped, feeling something under her foot and hearing a rattle. She leaned over and picked this item up. It was a pill bottle with sleeping pills. They know what's happening. They are watching me. She turned back into the room with the pills in her hand and was so thankful for them. She swallowed two pills with half a glass of water, then turned in for the night, praying for sleep.

In only twenty minutes, she had fallen into a deep, restful sleep. Her bedroom door was opened, then quickly closed so as not to admit any light or noise from the hallway that might awaken her. The gentle footsteps neared her bed, and the shadowed body bent over her and kissed her cheek, then covered her with the comforter. He stood straight over her, then took his hand to his mouth, covering the sound of his breathing. "I do love you, just not in the way that you expect me to. Soon, soon, you will feel the togetherness that you long for." He turned away from her, then went back to the door, and left, closing the door ever so quietly.

The following morning, she was dressed and ready for the day. With great reluctance, she went down to the dining room and to the table and sat there with fruit and a breakfast roll. She pushed the coffee cup forward and said that she'd rather have tea. The boss told her that Bond would not be there for a while, and she was not to ask about him etcetera—the usual talk from him. She listened but made no show of emotion to his speech. It was back to playing the game, and she wanted the power of the queen. She waited until he was through with his speech and his breakfast before she spoke.

"I would like to do something else." She more than had his attention now. "Remaining quiet in my room all day with only the television and the stereo . . . you know, it does get kind of boring. Oh, I know you left me a nice selection of books to read, but I want something else."

"Another yoga mat perhaps?"

"Oh, you know that I do that? Well, why not? You know just about everything." He looked at her with a not-too-pleasant stare. "Oh, the only thing that you don't know is perhaps what year the actual pyramids were finished being built. I mean, you do know everything else." The features on his face softened ever so slightly as he stared at her. "I haven't done it for ages, but I would like a paint set, you know, watercolors. I mean I do have a wonderful view out of the bedroom window. I know it seems rather foolish. Why would I want a painting of the scenery when I have it right there at my disposal every day? That is a question I cannot answer. It is just something that I want to do."

He leaned back in the chair, then relaxed, rising up from the chair. He stopped and stood behind the chair, looking at her. "My wife was a painter, and I still have all of her supplies put away. I'll have them brought to you sometime today. Thank you. I'll see you at dinner." He moved the chair in closer to the table, then stopped as he walked out of the room, and said, "And as for the pyramids in Egypt, the Pharaoh Khufu built the Great Pyramid in 2600 BC. About eighty Egyptian pyramids are still standing today. Most of them are in groups at various points on the west side of the Nile River."

As for the news about the pyramids, this man did know everything, but the news about the painting came as a blow to her. If she had known about his wife being a painter, she never would have asked for these supplies or even thought of doing it. Then she thought over his words to her. What did he mean when he said "Thank you"?

She got up and left the table. Through breakfast, she had more than noticed Bond's absence. Then she thought to herself that this might have been done on purpose to get a reaction from her. She didn't care, at least that was what she told herself. Going up the stairs, she thought that he was probably on a mission of some sort. She opened the drapes over the window just enough, maybe eight and a half inches, so she could see the view but still remain in privacy. In the next hour, the canvas board, stand, and paints, as well as a tarp for the floor, were brought to her. She arranged everything and was now in the midst of drawing and painting. She started with the sky and the blueness of it. It was void of clouds and birds, so there was nothing to paint or draw as far as that went. Palm trees lined the side of the open shallow beach on each side of the sand, but the top leaves were so high that they couldn't be drawn on the board, only the bases of the trees. The tide was not rolling in just then, and the water remained relatively still, only coming up to the very tip of the sand and then instantly retreating. She looked out the window, then stepped to each side of the view, looking perplexed. Okay, how do you draw sand? This is pointless. She took her sketch down, then started another with her pen to the board. She closed the drapes and just drew from the image in her head. She did this with rapid strokes as she had already had the image in her mind.

The boss's phone rang. He waited for the usual number of rings to go by, and the guard traced the call to its origin—in Florida, the call was traced to the airway in Florida. The call was being broadcast on an open line. The call was from Chris telling his father that he was in the Miami-Dade hospital and where he would be next. He ended the call before two minutes had passed.

He was in the hospital, but instead of being seen in the emergency room where instant computerized tracking of patients was done, he was taken to the geriatric department and pushed into an empty room. The door was closed and locked. An emergency medical team was already in place there to check on his condition, and all the necessary instruments had already been assembled.

Dehydration and pure exhaustion were the obvious symptoms. His pulse and breathing were good, but there was a concern over his lowered blood pressure. They would keep him there for observation in that room with a nurse and a guard by his bedside. Right now, this measure would keep him out of the line of fire. It had already been determined where he was going next, but Chris had a spirit that could not be harnessed. Sometimes, even his father wondered if Chris himself knew where he was going or how he was going to get there and fight off any obstacles in his way. It must have been in his blood that he always escaped. There was just one thing that still had bondage over his heart, and Chris hoped that this situation would soon be rectified so peace could return to his soul.

He rested up in the hospital through the night and into the next morning. Then he was taken out of the hospital in a wheelchair wrapped up with a loose wool throw and a hat covering his head and face, posing as an elderly gentleman. He was escorted into a van with the name of Shady Palms Rest Home painted on the side. The van went up Highway

41, which intersected with Highway 123, then took Highway 131 to the airport at Fort Myers. Chris boarded a small passenger plane there and took it to St. Petersburg-Clearwater International Airport. He took a tourist limousine from the airport to the coast where he got on a boat and took it to Safety Harbor, Florida, with a typical group of retired tourists.

He registered at the front desk using his usual fictitious name and was handed the keys to his suite. One of his father's usual guards was there, and Chris recognized him but made no affirmation of his presence in the side hall by the registration desk. He had Chris's luggage and was waiting to take him down the outside corridor to his suite. He opened the door and made a sweep of the room, then placed the luggage in the bedroom, and returned outside to stand guard. Chris opened the French doors to the outside deck and the private garden.

CHAPTER 27

Two pit bulls raised their heads up to him. He whistled in a high pitch, and the dogs instantly sat. He reached down, unafraid of their bite, and petted the head of each dog. Well, they did say that small pets were allowed with an additional fee. He smiled seeing a hammock and two girls in their twenties with tanned skin wearing swimming suits with sarongs wrapped at their hips. One held a frosted martini glass in her hand. It was his drink—a Grey Goose vodka martini with a twist. The other girl held a Japanese fan to wave above his head and keep him cool. He lay down in the hammock and was then handed the drink and fanned in the private shaded garden of the suite. He relaxed himself, then took a deep relaxing breath. Sometimes, life is good.

He took a slow sip of the martini and savored it, caressing it on his tongue before swallowing. I'll rest up here for a day. The lady who held the fan over his head started rubbing his shoulders. He relaxed his shoulders and breathed out in relief. Maybe two days, then I'm off to Japan. Hopefully, I'll end this ongoing war with the Del Marcos once and for all.

On the island, Bond was resting in his bedroom and working at the computer, getting needed information. He checked the time on his wristwatch, then got up, took the water pitcher from the side dresser by the closed dark wooden shutters, and poured enough water into a glass to swallow an antibiotic pill. Then he returned to the computer. He was reading about the wine-making process. I know full well what to do. It is just a matter of getting to someone that works for this winery to do this. Or would the person who would be doing this job be working for more than one winery? But that would be too obvious, knocking out the competition. The wine taster and the wine tester would have to be one in the same, but both processes are done in different stages, so that will be a factor. I have to see the process there and see how it works first. It is just a matter of knowing the right people, but that is what this business is all about—knowing the right people and getting rid of the ones that do not need to be involved.

He went back into retrieving information on the computer, then closed the screen. He took out a wire-bound notepad and charted out what he would have to do. He read it over, and then in his mind, he made a synopsis of the events that would have to take place. He then got up and ripped up the papers with his writing on them plus five pages underneath those pages where the encryption might still be traced. He stood over the metal trash can and lit a lighter, and a deep orange flame shined in the dark room. He lowered the flame to just above the top of the trash can, then took the papers to it. He bent back far enough to be away from the flame, but he still felt the penetrating heat of holding the lighter to the burning papers. He felt the flesh over his fingers soften but would not let himself be fazed by the heat. He only dropped the papers loose in the trash can when there was only one-half inch left to burn. He watched the fire turn the paper black and then engulf the remaining white until it just disintegrated invisibly into the air. He then felt the need to hold his hot finger and thumb but resisted the temptation of handling hot flesh and went into the bathroom and held his finger and thumb under the cold running water from the faucet instead. He looked up to his dark reflection in the mirror and looked deeply into the face that was watching him—his own. He closed his eyes, then opened them to a face showing no emotion in the mirror. I know what to do now. Chris, are you coming back? Coming back to Jane? Nobody can tell what you are going to do. I guess I am the predictable one with the even temperament, and you are . . . you. He closed his eyes and left the room without even drying his hand.

Bond left his room to go check on his father who was in his office with a guard, as usual, sitting by the computer at the side of the room. Much to his surprise, he found that his father had a laptop at his desk that he was working on. He raised his eyebrows up to Bond who nodded and sat down in the seat across from him at the front of his desk. He noted the concern in his son's eyes.

"Don't worry. I am on the same line as the other computer. He is just making sure that no one intercepts this line. I have been going through the annual reports of all the new holdings we've acquired." Bond shook his head at what his father had just told him, thinking that it was good that he was doing this and keeping his mind off Chris.

"How are you?" Bond cut in on his father's dialogue. He knew that his father did not like to convey feelings. By him breaking in the conversation, it was making it easier for his father.

"I am doing fine. Don't worry about me. I just went over the new phase of the operation in the Napa Valley. I will need to have the 'right' legmen there in order for this plan to be carried out and to succeed." His father nodded his head, and they proceeded to discuss everything that would be done. He already knew, of course, each new phase that Bond told him about and the necessary steps of getting the right people to make this happen. After they finished their conversation, his father was on the phone making all the necessary calls to set the plan into motion. It was now just a matter of time—time for Bond to heal and time for all of the pieces of the plan to fall into place in the right order for the plan to succeed in the Napa Valley.

Upstairs in her room, at the easel with the drapes closed, she outlined the vision she saw in her mind—it had a solid bottom with no particular form, and the remainder of the area was the sky with peaceful white clouds. A giant egg, but only the bottom of the egg, was shown standing straight up on the ground. A lady with long flowing brown hair was trying to push her way up and out of the egg. Wings sprouted over her back like she was trying to fly away from the egg. She wore a dark dress with an indistinguishable design and no particular form. Her grief and determination and struggle were expressed in her facial tone. The bottom half of the egg would not break free and let her fly out to the freedom of the sky and the clouds.

The next few days went by with Bond greatly limiting his actions. He allowed his body to heal by getting the rest he needed, and his father kept to his usual routine of doing things. Jane spent much of her time working on her drawing and painting. She was on her third drawing, and in each drawing, the woman in the painting was closer to breaking free and out of her shell.

At the nightly dinners and morning breakfasts, she and the boss each tried to outdo the other in wisdom that was learned from books, newspapers, or television documentaries. They found much enjoyment in this contest. They discussed everything from the Great Pyramid to how to best get rid of a cold.

The talk through the evening's dinner became almost numbed, and the boss explained the meaning of cold feet. "It was because frozen feet were common among soldiers of the nineteenth century. A man who had cold or frozen feet could not rush into battle. He went slowly or not at all."

Jane swallowed, then took a small sip of her coffee before responding back to him with a smile. "Crocodile tears, this expression comes from a tale from ancient travelers who said a crocodile cries when he eats, signifying that he is sorry. This isn't true at all. When a crocodile eats, he cries because when his mouth is full, the food presses on the top of his mouth. And this releases tears from his lachrymal glands."

The boss countered back even faster with another explanation of a phrase. "Ancient Romans believed that six or eight of the hottest days in the summer were caused by the Dog Star, Sirius, rising with the sun and adding to its heat on these days. They called these days the dog days."

Bond turned his head from his father, then to Jane, and back again. "Wow, you got three of them today. You two better stop and rest up. You better not get too carried away, or you won't have any left." Neither Jane nor his father responded back to him. He had gotten the upper hand. So neither Jane nor his father had won, but they didn't lose either, and this satisfied them both.

All of them left the table and went their separate ways. The boss went to his office, and the first thing he did was go through the morning newspaper one more time, trying to find any bit of information that he could have missed to use it at the next meal when he encountered Jane. Bond went to the open patio area and breathed in some fresh air. He was a bit apprehensive in going out into the open at first; then he swept the perimeter of the backyard with his eyes and saw a guard at every post as well as the dogs out.

Somehow, he still did not feel safe though. He went back inside and then headed to his bedroom, convincing himself that he was feeling fear. There was no room for that, at least that is what he had to tell himself. He thought of how nice it would be to go upstairs and razz Jane, but then he thought of the closeness factor, something that he knew that she wanted. He did too, but he could not give it.

Jane was upstairs in her bedroom. She looked at the yoga mat, then quickly walked away, and went to the easel. She felt she wanted to free the captured woman some more, but there was something in her mind that kept her from doing this. She looked down to the floor and saw a stack of blank canvas. Another painting could always be drawn. She took the brush tip to the paints and started painting in the colors of the woman, keeping her skin in a neutral tone to the backdrop of the blueness of the sky.

CHAPTER 28

Chris slept through the night without the use of any painkillers or sleeping pills. He felt in a relaxed state, and he now knew what he was going to do to totally eliminate the Del Marcos, his and his family's longtime rivals. The next morning, he took a bulletproof limousine to the airport, but not the airport in Miami. From the airport in Atlanta, Georgia, he took a plane bound for Los Angeles. Atlanta was only a short trip from the northern part of Florida where he was. It was probably closer to Atlanta than Miami.

That morning at breakfast on the estate, the clouds were dark, and rain poured down on the island. Jane thought of the odd feeling happening in paradise. It seemed spooky to her, and she felt almost unnerved by it. She anxiously awaited breakfast, but the boss was not at his usual head-of-the-table place at the dining table yet that morning. Bond was there, and he smiled and poured her tea although he offered no conversation to her. The feeling through the room between the two of them was friendly and balanced. The boss came in and sat down at his usual spot at the table without a sound, but he was well noticed.

He took a sip of coffee, then opened the paper. Quiche was served to them by a servant; then they each quietly went through the motions of having breakfast. Jane was still a little disturbed that no one talked during the course of the meal. The plates were cleared; then the boss lowered his newspaper and passed a smile through the room. She nodded to him, then started conversing with him. "Wild goose chase—it was once a game. It was a horse race in which the second and each succeeding horse had to follow the leader accurately and at a definite interval. The horses had to keep their positions like geese in flight. The chase was called a wild goose chase. Since this was not a race, for no one could win, we adopted the phrase to describe a person following a course that leads to no goal." She finished the last word with a smile on her face to him, waiting for him not to be able to show her up.

He smiled at her, then quickly replied back, "Happy as a clam—we say this because clams appear to desire nothing but to be left alone, and since clams are gathered up only when the tide is out, they should be very happy at high tide."

This last remark from him conveyed two meanings to her—the meaning that he showed her up and also that he wanted to be left alone. Bond countered back, "Well, you spoke for the clams. But as for the oyster, the world is his oyster. That makes you think of Chris, doesn't it?" Neither of them responded back to him. They only lowered their eyes and thought about how much they missed Chris. "Through the hardened shell, there is a treasure inside." His father looked to both of them to see who had said this, and they both had said it at the very same time. Dismayed, the boss left the room; and Bond helped Jane out of her chair, an act that he just at that moment had resumed doing for her.

They walked out of the dining room side by side, then stopped, and she looked perplexed when they reached the end of the living room and the base of the stairs. He reached for her, then slid his open hand down her arm, and stopped at her wrist. He instantly relaxed. "I know that we have gotten used to doing things differently around here lately." She swallowed, then looked further to his face, agreeing with him. He took her hand in his, then told her it would be nice to have a talk outside. This surprised her because usually when they had their talks, they were upstairs in her room. Then she thought with the recent events between them that talking outside was probably a good idea.

They stayed in the outside patio area instead of going for a walk on the beach. He did take her all the way to the left end of the patio before they stopped beside a cement bench. Outside in the open, they didn't have complete privacy, but he still wanted to somehow be as far from his father's view as possible. He held his hand out to her, then pulled her to sit on the bench beside him. She liked the returned feeling of closeness to him, but something was different now, and she feared what he was going to say to her. "Today I will be leaving." She showed an expression of surprise and fear. "Calm down, I will be all right. I will not be alone. I will be going to California." He wanted to tell her more, but he couldn't. There was still the veil of disguise that always had to be there. He then quickly changed the sentence to tell her that he would be staying with some friends there. "Don't worry. Everything will be fine."

"Why should I worry?"

"You won't. I am just going there to get some work done for one of our cars."

She looked to him, turning her eyebrows down to him, then scratched the side of her head. "One of the Ferraris, I presume. I mean, surely, you could get the necessary work done here, couldn't you? What kind of work do you need done?"

"You're right. The work is for one of the Ferraris."

They were both quiet, watching and listening to the gentle sounds of the surf. "Question—if one of the Ferraris needs work here on the estate, wouldn't you just have a mechanic come here and look at it? I mean, you aren't going to take the whole car to California, are you?"

He laughed. "No, I'm not. The work to be done is for the engine, and there is a car dealer that we have worked with for years in California. I'll be going there and picking up the part. My father does not want to have it sent here because of the possibility that someone may get hold of the needed parts during shipment over here and do something to the part. I mean these cars . . . well, they are . . ."

She looked to him, still not satisfied with the answer, but she thought what else could she have said about it. "They are Ferraris, so you have to go there." He looked away from her and down to the cement of the patio. "Bond?" He looked up at her. "Be careful. You know you are all I . . . we have left."

He hugged her, then stood up, and stepped away from her, not to take his leave from her but to stretch—he stretched out his arms and waved them to the sky. "I just had a tightness in my back, that's all." She stood up, then looked to the beach. "I know, don't get too close. I will stay out here as long as you need me."

He turned his body away from her, then turned halfway back around to her view. Then he took a step back towards the house. "We all need you. You make sure to take care of yourself while I am gone."

"When are you leaving? You talk like you are ready to leave now."

"I am. I am just going to go back to the bedroom and make sure that I have packed everything. I will be leaving this afternoon. I won't be here, so take it easy on my father, okay?"

She tugged at the side of her neck, then made a small laugh. "Okay, I won't always win, but you know I have to keep it interesting for him." Bond smiled at her and left. She looked back to the beach, then saw the dogs start their run, and she went back inside the house and up to her bedroom to work more on her painting.

That afternoon, Bond boarded a United flight to get to the Los Angeles airport where he would get a connector flight to Oakland. The flight that took him from Hawaii to Los Angeles went smoothly. He was not seated next to a noisy or overtalkative passenger. In fact, he had nobody by him in the first-class seat, which he savored. In the busy terminal in Los Angeles, he did notice someone, someone very familiar. As he walked down the central hallway of the airport, he noticed a familiar person there, and that person made note of him also—Chris locked eyes with Bond only for five seconds, but they both knew that things were going well in seeing each other. But that was all that could be, seeing each other for those few brief seconds. Bond wanted to turn and see what boarding gate Chris was heading to, but he knew the danger if he turned his head—that would make Chris's identity there known if someone had seen or recognized either of them. They could never be seen together—that would be too dangerous for both of them.

Bond boarded the flight to Oakland. There was no first class on this connector flight, and he was seated between a married couple who were fighting with each other. All they did through the whole flight was talk and talk by throwing insults at each other from past memories of when each of them somehow screwed up. He more than wanted a drink—a drink of alcohol. But he needed to have his full senses about him when he landed, so he opted for a soda instead.

Through the course of their fighting, Bond actually took sides. At first, he was on the woman's side upon hearing how the husband screwed up by getting drunk on their first family Christmas together; but then he quickly changed sides when the wife mentioned she had offered her husband's car to the neighbor's son, who was drunk and banged the car up so badly that it was in the shop for a week. In putting their tribulations through his mind, he was glad he wasn't married. Hearing the flight attendant announce that seat belts needed to be fastened, he thanked God and prepared himself for landing.

CHAPTER 29

He walked out of the airport to a line of limos waiting for passengers. He walked down the line, then stopped by the chauffeur who had the same type of Versace sunglasses as he did and had a Hawaiian lei on. He walked around to the driver's side of the limo, and the chauffeur opened the back door for him. Bond got in, and then they left for the bayside city of Vallejo.

They entered the parking lot adjacent to the ferry line that traversed the San Francisco Bay. Vallejo was on the north side of the bay from San Francisco. Driving down a regular city street, Bond was surprised when the driver took a left instead of a right to get to the wharf. Then after making the turn, he saw that he had to turn left before he could take a right and go to the pier. It was a medium-sized parking lot with the road on one side and the ferry building and launching area on the other side. Bond barely noticed the cool breeze off the bay or the heaviness in the bay air.

He departed the limo in front of the ferry building, well aware that he was wearing a bulletproof vest under his clothing. People walked by him on the way to their cars as he scoured the parking lot for the pickup vehicle that he was told would meet him there—a jet-black Escalade. He spotted it at the far end of the parking lot. He observed the other people around him, making a quick surveillance scan of the scene. Seeing no thing or person that might bring danger to him, he walked over to the Escalade. As he approached, the doors were instantly unlocked for him, and he opened the side door and threw his bags inside. He got in the front passenger seat and buckled his safety belt, and the car then drove away without either one of them saying a word.

They took Highway 29 up to the central part of Napa. Since it was already evening, they stopped at Marie Callender's and had dinner. The restaurant was crowded and noisy, and it was also a place that any person of stature would not be expected to frequent, especially in such a pristine valley. Although he felt in need of a cup of coffee, he still passed on it as the waitress asked them what they would like to drink since Marie Callender's had become infamous for their bad coffee. He stayed with just ice water with lemon as did his associate. They told the waitress they would both have the Frisco burger, medium. They were seated at an enclosed booth that offered some privacy.

Nightly, on a regular basis, a person would go to the different vats containing the wine as it aged and collect samples, just enough to fill a vial. The vials would be dated, and the information was then given to the winery on everything from what wine was to be produced, the date on which the sample was collected, the date of maturity, the date of harvest, the type of grapes that were being aged, and the anticipated yield. As with every business in the world today, information could be bought or, in this case, changed. The man whom he met and discussed this with was simply known as Jake, and that is how Bond would refer to him.

He had a copy of the collector's routine, but this man who collected the samples nightly feared involvement with the police if caught. He agreed to collecting the samples as he did his regular job. In this particular case, there would be a handoff before he placed the samples back in the truck and took them to the lab. The planned interception would take place before those samples were put in the truck, so the samples the truck would take back to the lab would be from another winery and would be clean. It was just that the day before bottling began, a discovery would be made that would result in the loss of thousands of dollars, and the reputation of the winery would be lost, resulting in a further loss of over a million dollars.

They paid the bill and left. The man left Bond off in Sonoma, known as the Valley of the Moon. He would be staying at the Sonoma Mission Inn, a rich, very upper-class hotel where privacy and discretion were honored by both the staff and the guests who stayed there. This was a haven—a retreat—for massages, body relaxation, and the enjoyment of the fruit of the valley where wines were thoroughly enjoyed. Checking in under an assumed fictitious name was not uncommon. He checked in using his real name and identity for he knew that he would be protected.

In the second-floor room of the Spanish architecture building that formed a square around the retreat gardens and trees, he closed the shade without even looking outside to the view. Sitting down at the love seat by the window, he reached for the pamphlets describing the massages and various body treatments that you could get there. He scanned over them, then set them back down, and grabbed accompanying pamphlets describing the different tasting rooms, vineyards, and tours that could be arranged or the road directions on how to drive there. He took special interest in the Ferrari-Carano vineyard for the simple reason that he was supposed to be there on this trip getting the Ferrari fixed. They have a large Italian kitchen on the estate. How nice. He breathed out, laughing, as he placed it back on the table. In one motion, he took his palm pilot from his pocket and called the estate in Hawaii. His father answered the phone after the usual number of rings, and Bond told him that he was there and that things were under way. There was no assurance in his father's voice, which made him leery of the events to come; but then he quickly reassured himself that they were the ones in control, the ones who had the ultimate power. And that was what this struggle was all about, plain and simple power—a word that spoke volumes with every meaning.

The hour was late, and he could think of little to do. He felt tight and wound up and sought a release of some kind. The natural things to do there would be to relax and get drunk. The bottle of Domaine Chandon that was in the room sure looked inviting; but he fought the temptation to have a drink of any kind mainly because he was too wound up already, and he needed to have all of his resources about him, not knowing what to expect. He fought off the idea of a relaxing shower because the natural thing to do after a shower in the late evening would be to go to sleep, and he would now be on a new work schedule that would not start until late the following evening. So tomorrow, he would need to sleep during the day. He did not know how he would manage to sleep during the day since his normal routine of doing things started with the sunrise and didn't end with it. He went to the bathroom, combed his hair, checked his appearance, then put his shoes back on, and went outside to the grounds and surrounding areas of the inn for a walk in the peaceful night air. In the Valley of the Moon, he thought to himself, I'd like to see the moon.

Once downstairs and outside the hotel building itself, instead of walking around the inner courtyard, he walked to the sidewalk outside the hotel. It was peaceful, and the only sounds were those of occasional cars going by on the street. He looked up to the moon, and it was directly overhead. It almost seemed that you could reach up and just touch it with your hand. It was an overwhelming feeling.

From behind him, he heard the sound of car tires approaching. Cars had passed him before, but this sound was somehow different. The car was just about thirty feet behind him when it stopped. Why would the car just stop in the middle of the road? There was plenty of space on the side of the street to pull off and read a road map if someone was lost. Next, he heard a car door open; then a person stepped out of the car and cocked a gun. Bond fought his reflex to grab his own gun to shoot back in self-defense because he had forgotten to bring it with him. He lunged to the right and fell into the hedge surrounding the building. Then he heard the gunfire. It was meant for him. The Del Marcos had found him. Well, they owned a winery in the area; and naturally, they'd be around somewhere. He ran along the outside wall of the building, dodging bullets, trying to get back to the building entrance. The gunfire stopped at the sound of another car approaching; and the sound of a siren, a police siren, then wailed through the air. Bond heard footsteps running back to the car. Then he heard the car door slam, and the car sped away.

Bond knew that this was all the more reason to quickly get back inside the building and hide somewhere. The police would be searching for the victim of the gunfire to see if anyone had survived or if someone was hurt. He ran inside the building, then dashed inside the first door to his right. He was now inside the sauna. He did not stop but went through to the changing room, threw off his clothes, and then entered the sauna wrapped in a towel. He stayed there for twenty minutes, and those minutes seemed more like hours. Now dressed again, he went back into the hallway in the front of the lobby; and at the registration desk, he checked out, giving the reason that an old girlfriend he wanted to stay away from had found him there.

He asked the bellboy to go up to his room and get the bags that he had never even unpacked.

He hailed a cab and fell asleep on the drive to the small sleepy town of Yountville, seven miles north of Napa. He had the cab driver leave him off at the small shopping area—Vintage 1870 shop. There was a restaurant with an outside bar where people sat talking and drinking. Then a black Escalade revved its engine and started towards Bond. He got in, and Jake nodded to him; but neither of them spoke as they drove up the once quiet two-lane highway now busy with constant traffic—trucks, semis, and cars. Fourteen miles up the highway, Jake took a right and veered off the road and parked behind a storage garage that housed unused tractors. "They found you." Humiliated at having been discovered, Bond sank a little lower in the seat. "The Del Marcos are good. We'll get this over with as soon as we can. Gasoline—we'll use gasoline in the wine vats, and we'll do it tonight. But now, you and I have to get some sleep. I'll be traveling up this highway and onto another highway, and we'll be staying at a hotel on the lake in Kelseyville. It is by no means deluxe, but it offers peace and quiet and a bed." Bond shook his head in acknowledgment, then closed his eyes to get some sleep on the drive up there.

The black Escalade hugged the sharp curves up and down through the hills with tall trees along both sides of the road. The road finally straightened out just before they made a turn to the right. They drove about a mile straight down, then turned to the left and saw a very welcome sight—a lodge with cabins on the hillside and a small motel and lake to the west. A small parking lot separated the hillside cabins from the lodge where the restaurant and registration desk were. The lodge was busier than they expected because they had an outdoor stage, and concerts were performed there—mostly rock concerts—and that night, Lynyrd Skynyrd was to perform.

In the lobby at the end of the registration line, Bond worried about getting a room, but Jake told him that four rooms had already been reserved for him under the name of Smith. Bond thought Smith was the obvious or standard name, but then he thought that this name might be a deterrent. He registered and paid cash, leaving fifty dollars extra for any added fees. The clerk smiled at him and handed him four room keys. They moved the car about a half mile to the motel and went up the stairs to their rooms, which were in the middle of the second floor with outside entrances. They had a nice view of the deep blue lake. All was quiet on the lake. The only movement was an occasional jet boat speeding by with a water-skier.

They took the two inside rooms, then talked out on the deck, adjusted the time on their wristwatches, then turned in, and closed the rooms up to try and get some much-needed rest. Inside, it was a standard motel room—a bed, television, dresser, nightstand, telephone, and bathroom. Quite the ordinary room. Bond took off all but his underclothes, then pulled up the sheets, and turned in for the afternoon. At check-in, he inquired about the concert and gave that as the reason he was there; he even bought four tickets to it with seating in the open, higher area where there were no designated seat numbers so that his absence there would not be obvious.

Later that night, at 10:00 p.m., Bond's wristwatch went off; and he rose up out of bed and met Jake outside. They could still hear the sounds of the concert going on, but they knew it had started at 7:00 p.m. and would be ending soon. They quickly left the motel and made it back through the tight turns to Highway 29 and took it south. Upon getting to St. Helena, they both knew that the drive to the winery itself would not be much farther. They went to a dark, barely paved side street off the highway and met Roy, the man who gathered the tasting samples from the winery.

The three men rode in Roy's truck to the Sun Haven Winery just above Rutherford but not quite far enough north to be in St. Helena. They went the back way into the winery as the front iron gates used for tourists were locked. They traveled down two unlit residential streets; and in the quiet, peaceful darkness, Bond was apprehensive that the sounds of the truck tires would be noted. Then he thought that the residents here were more than used to the sounds of trucks at night going to the winery for testing. Right now, it was only the three of them who knew that something was going to be different about collecting the samples tonight.

They drove past the paved street and turned left at the end of the block that was posted with a Dead End sign. They noted headlights driving out from the back supply yard and storage rooms of the winery; and the two of them ducked down, leaving only the solitary driver, Roy, visible to any eyes looking towards the truck. He slowed down as the truck bearing the winery emblem also slowed down and opened the driver's window to talk. It was the foreman from the winery who explained that he just finished making one last check on the vats of wine for a report that he had to submit to the county in the morning. Roy nodded his head and drove in as the other truck drove out. Bond's heart rate slowed as the truck parked at the back side of the dark building. All three of them got out and quietly walked to the front of the building where Roy took the key out of his front pocket and unlocked the chain on the doors. Then he punched in the correct code to the alarm system to temporarily turn it off.

CHAPTER 30

Bond bent down and pulled the burlap material over his shoes to cover them. Jake watched him do this, then turned back to Roy, and watched him open the door of the large room that held the wine in steel vats. The wine was in its final stage of production before it was to be bottled. With Bond now at his side, they each held a large flashlight and shined it through the area of the building, seeing all that the room entailed. Jake pushed his head forward to Roy, signaling for him to hurry and gather all the necessary clean samples. Bond and Jake quickly walked to the back of the truck, opened it up, and then took out the bags of a copper-arsenic-mix pesticide that used to be sprayed in the vineyards here but was now illegal in this country; so it wouldn't be detected until the bottling phase. If present in high levels, like those that would presently be in the wine, it was lethal. Systematically, they opened each vat after the wine sample had been collected and added some of the copper-arsenic-mix pesticide. They watched the time on their wristwatches as they did each one.

They were now down to just two remaining cylindrical steel barrels. These two containers were smaller and contained the signature wine of the Sun Haven Winery. Bond had trouble releasing the cap from one of these vats so he could open it and pour the little remaining gasoline into it. Jake sensed his trouble and stopped opening the barrel that he was trying to work on. Roy stood nervously outside the room. There was added security on these two vats containing the signature wine,—a trigger with a coded lock. The alarm was now ticking as he had set it off. Panic overwhelmed him; then in one breath, he fought for control and ran outside to Roy and told him what had happened and asked him if he knew the code. Roy ran to the truck and opened the glove box, then took out the small folding binder, and rummaged through it, trying to find the code. The ticking now became louder. It was down to the final twenty seconds before the alarm would blow, signaling the owner and the police that intruders were there. Bond took the code from Roy's hand, then ran back into the building to the signature wine containers. His fingers trembled. They were down to the final eleven seconds. He wondered if they could just run out of there and make a getaway quickly enough. Then he closed his mind to every thought and pushed his finger forward, hitting the right side to disengage the alarm. At the final second, the clicking stopped; but then in one heartbeat it started again, a half tick, then stopped. He poured the little remaining gasoline in the barrel, then ran from the building. They all headed to the truck, and Roy brought up the rear since he had to lock the building back up.

They drove away; and in his nervousness, Roy went faster than usual, above the speed limit for the rural neighborhood streets they had to drive down to get back to the main highway. Bond reached his hand over the wheel and told Roy to slow down. A screech sounded as he stepped hard on the brake; then he quickly let up on the brake pedal and drove more slowly down the rural road. He stopped at the entrance to the highway and waited for every headlight to pass before he pulled out.

Four miles down the highway, Bond had Roy turn off, and they all got out of the truck. He then told Roy to continue making his other collections as usual and to just breathe slowly. It was over, and everything was okay. Roy was paid; then he smiled and drove off. Bond and Jake got back into the Escalade and drove out of the Napa Valley, then east on Highway 12 to Interstate 80, which they took all the way to Sacramento. The morning sun peeked through the dark clouds, and a few stars were still visible. As they traveled the freeway, the sun became larger in the early-morning sky. They stopped for gas at a truck stop. There, they were able to shower and change their clothes. They drove on to the Sacramento airport where Jake left Bond off with his two bags and drove away without even looking back. The Escalade was out of sight as Bond entered the airport building and headed to the boarding gate.

He bought a ticket for the next flight to Portland, Oregon, then went to the coffee shop, and had breakfast. He more than noticed women watching him. They were either single or traveling alone, away from their husbands or boyfriends, and were looking with interest at him. While waiting for his order, he grabbed a newspaper from a table where a previous patron had left it, and he folded the paper open in front of his face and started reading. His order of fried eggs, potatoes, and toast was delivered to him; and he concentrated on eating his breakfast and reading the paper while still keeping his attention focused on the time when his flight would take off. He reached down to his ankle and scratched the torn skin over it where the burlap used to cover his shoes at the winery had torn his flesh. Then he thought of how the burlap coverings were now in the garbage can in the dressing room at the truck stop.

Bond slept on the short flight to Portland, and upon arriving at the airport, he wondered what to do now. He knew nothing of the city, and he had no contacts that he cared to see there. He took a brief walk around the airport and made note of the destination at each boarding gate. In just about an hour, he was aboard a flight to Seattle. From there, he took a boat to San Juan Island and stayed at the Friday Harbor Inn. He more than welcomed the peace and serenity offered on the island. Rest and sleep were what he needed most. He did not call his father for he knew that no news was good news, and he didn't want the feeling of being tracked again. He enjoyed the peace, privacy, and seclusion and got some much-needed sleep.

Back on the Mondello estate, the boss saw very little of Jane. She was at meals, and they each tried to outdo the other finding definitions of words and meanings of various sayings. They both kept their minds sharp. She mostly stayed in her bedroom and worked fruitlessly on her sketches. It was the same sketch, but it seemed to change in some way with each passing day. He spent most of the days in his office sometimes going through the same paper repeatedly. Nothing about it changed, but it was just somehow satisfying to do it. His heart had gotten lonelier—not just in the loneliness of missing his wife, but also of worrying of not having either one of his sons there with him on the estate. It was the worst feeling he had ever experienced going through his heart right now; it was planted deep inside him, a feeling worse than betrayal or even worse than when he had been wounded by gunfire.

He went against his own rule that he had abided by since his wife's death and went alone outside and sat on the same bench that he had sat on the day his wife had been shot. He remembered it so vividly in his mind, and he retraced every movement that she made. He watched her planting a new flowering plant. It was yellow, as bright as the yellow sun. He looked at her; then she looked up at him as she kneeled down on the ground, wearing a tan canvas hat that was tied under her chin with a sheer pastel scarf. He looked at her and smiled, then looked down to a book that he only pretended to read. It was in that one brief instant when he took his eyes from her that she had been shot. She didn't scream in pain; she only breathed in and then fell forward in death. By the time that he or anyone else there on the estate realized what had happened, the gunman from the Del Marco family had gotten away.

He dried the falling tear from his face, then went back inside the house. Jane had just walked down the stairs and was at his side. She sensed that something was wrong. She stood there at his side, but he made no comment and spoke no words. It took all of her might; but she reached over and took hold of his hand, then walked with him to the dining room, and sat down at the table with him. She gave him a glass of ice water; and as she set it down in front of him, he thanked her, then took hold of her hand for a brief moment. She was surprised by this but said nothing. She only held his hand in return.

On board the jet plane to Japan, Chris went through tourist pamphlets containing information on the island country of Japan. This steered him away from having to talk with any other overzealous passengers and relaxed him at the same time. He knew that every piece of information that he gained could and would be vital to his survival on the island so he could accomplish his goal. His mind kept drifting back to the days in Chicago when he was married to Jane. Then he thought, When I *was* married to Jane? I still am. What does our daughter look like now? The person who sat to the side of the row he was sitting in turned his head to look at him to see whom he was talking to, but there was no one there. He looked back to him and smiled, then continued reading the pamphlets. The overhead announcement that they were about to land was made in three different languages—Japanese, American, and French—and there were many French people aboard this flight. While fastening his seat belt, he thought of how the one announcement in all three languages was made by the one Japanese stewardess. He thought of how he was told that when the Japanese graduated high school, they were versed in at least two languages, and one of these was always English. They were a very well-educated people. The ultimate goal was to get into college, and there was a special preparatory school just to take the test to get into college. Six years of elementary school were followed by three years of junior high, then three years of senior high school, then competitive and rigorous testing before college. The cost of living was very high in Japan, and the unemployment rate was less than 2 percent. Their average workweek was fifty hours. A house was referred to as a rabbit hutch; and a small house, very small by American standards, went for over 1.5 million dollars if one was even available to purchase. Most of the people who did own homes owned them because they had inherited them from generation to generation. The goal was to be a salaried employee, and once a company hired you, you were guaranteed that job for life. There was very little crime in Japan. They strove for the best in everything that they did—the lessons of Confucius—and remained busy. He proclaimed "What you do not like done to yourself, do not do unto others" several hundred years before Jesus pronounced the Golden Rule, and his goal was to develop a moral responsibility towards others.

The plane landed, and all the passengers got off and went into the very busy, hustling metropolis of the airport. The natives were very quick and preplanned in all of their movements. Chris took a bus to the hotel and only went to his room to place his bag there before leaving to see the city and get his bearings.

Back at the estate, the boss looked down to the table as Jane sat down to the side of him, yet he said nothing. She had learned to leave the floor open for him to initiate the conversation or to decide the topic of the conversation when he did resume speaking. There had been times of awkward silence before, and she hoped that this time would not prove to be one of those. Feeling fidgety, she took a glass of water and immediately drank some while his glass just sat untouched in front of him. Somehow though, just having that simple glass in front of him brought him the leverage he sought, and he did then start to speak.

"I got word from Chr . . ." She turned her head instantly to him and raised her eyebrows and eyes, feeling all the joyousness in the world on hearing these words. In his deep, silent mood, he caught himself. "Sorry, I didn't mean to upset you. A different Chris—I shouldn't call him by that name. It is someone who works for me. I've been sent the needed information, the information I need or the family needs to bury the Del Marcos . . . a record of transaction numbers from all of their offshore accounts . . . I am not going to follow this any longer. I want no part of it." He placed his hand over his chest at just the spot where his heart was. "It shouldn't be that much longer." Jane motioned her head to the side, wondering what he meant by saying "It shouldn't be that much longer."

In each passing second, he seemed to fall deeper into the hole he was letting his body fall into. She thought of helping him to his room, then thought differently. Being alone was not what he needed right now. She more than wished for the mere presence of Bond just to give her strength right now to deal with this. She did feel for him and more than just in a man-woman capacity. It was just the aura that he gave her in just being there, but right now, she needed to be with his father and give him all of her strength. She helped him from the table and sat by him in the living room. She put on the opera music that she knew he loved on the stereo. She felt the mood called for something deep, so she picked a CD by Johann Sebastian Bach, the Fugue in D Minor; then she sat back in the deep-cushioned sofa to the side of him and listened to the music in silence.

Walking the busy streets of Tokyo, Chris knew he'd be an easy target to spot. Although the crime rate was not high in this country, he was still nervous about the possibility of losing his possessions or his life. How would his rivals know that he was here anyway? Then he remembered seeing Bond at LAX, and he thought his presence there was probably planned by their father to throw the Del Marcos off his trail. Trying to blend in, Chris quickened his pace to keep up with the busy locals. Hunger caused his stomach to rumble, and he took his hand to his stomach, fearing someone had heard it. He sidestepped to a busy stand, selling noodle soup and sake, and ordered and paid for his food. Then a bowl of soup and a cup of sake were immediately put in front of him. He pulled up the spoon, then leaned back, hearing the other Oriental patrons sitting at the counter beside him slurping their soup in a noisy fashion. He then leaned forward and ate his soup in the same manner. In seven minutes, he was done with his meal and left to get lost in the hustle of the street again.

Five blocks down the road, he saw a tourist shop to his right, and he dodged into it. It sold clothes, postcards, and tourist maps in all languages. He found a map printed in English, then bought it along with a silk scarf, which he put in his pocket. He walked the streets and dodged in and out of shops and buildings for the remainder of the day. He scoped out all means of transportation, then returned to the hotel, went to his room, and stayed there until the following morning.

The next morning, he took the food tray placed outside his hotel room and placed it on the table but did not eat it. Instead, he took a power bar from his suitcase and grabbed a can of Coke from the vanity next to the ice chest. He opened the wrapper of the Power Bar and took a bite, washing it down with three swigs of soda. He finished the power bar while repacking his bags. He put all of his possessions into one bag and then opened the other bag and put in steel netting and a steel box with small toothpick-sized airholes in it. Inside the box was mesh and leaves. He placed that in a backpack also containing jungle clothes and a head mask. He left the hotel and hailed a cab to the Bureau of Land Management.

Once there at this building, he talked in the native Japanese tongue to a scientist and a guide. From there, they took a high- wheeled, covered Jeep up to the mountains of Nagano. At the bottom of the hill, they all changed into their protective suits, then climbed to the middle of the mountain. They briefly rested there, then proceeded with the climb to the top of it. Before reaching the top of a plateau, the sound of buzzing was overwhelming. The flying creatures moved in unison with one another, and they looked like a black plague traveling through the skies. The three men stood to the side of the stone cliff and waited while they received information from the scientist. Chris had the bag open, then walked forward towards the Japanese hornets, and waved a black cloth. This attracted them as hornets are aggressive and attracted to the color black. He opened the case, and about thirty flew in. The guide immediately closed the case and locked it, and they then made their way back down the mountain and back to the Jeep.

Chris paid them; then they gave him a ride to the airport. He didn't board the jet, however. He waited at the terminal, avoiding onlookers and the security that covered the grounds of the airport. He went to the bank of pay phones and dialed his father's business number that he could intercept at home. His father answered the telephone after the usual number of rings. When he heard Chris's voice talking to him on this open line, he was curious but then knew that Chris wanted this call to be traced. Otherwise, there were numerous ways he could have made the call safely. Chris told his father of his whereabouts and that he had drugs worth thousands of dollars—a sure tip-off for the Del Marcos to run after him. Chris waited there at the airport for another two hours, then went to the section of the airport where one would board smaller private planes. He was just steps from the boarding ladder to the private jet that he had told his father he was going to take when he was grabbed from behind by Japanese airport guards. He immediately started conversing with the guards in their native Japanese language. He told them that the Del Marcos, whom he had just said good-bye to, well, they had forgotten one of their pieces of carry-on luggage. He had just seen them at the metal detector, and they had left the box there (he pushed the steel box forward for the guards to view). The box had their name stamped on it, and it had a Passed Security sticker from the airport placed over it. The guards turned away from Chris and conversed with each other. Then one of the guards used his walkie-talkie to call someone, and they chatted briefly. One guard then took the steel box from Chris, and the other guard thanked Chris in Japanese and bowed his head. Chris, in turn, reciprocated, then turned, and walked away, leaving that section of the airport and heading for the main gates.

Chris got in-line for a flight that was just leaving for Hawaii. The airport guards were at the Del Marco jet, which was almost ready for takeoff, and the outside door to the plane was about to be shut by a uniformed airport worker. The guard yelled to the worker who stopped from giving an okay for the Del Marcos to close the door. In that brief moment, the box was given to the worker. Then a hand from inside the plane took the box and nodded to the worker; then the door was closed, and the plane proceeded to take off.

The Del Marco plane was now airborne and could still be viewed from the airport. One of the guards on that plane was asked by another guard what was in the box. The guard holding the box then broke it open and raised the netting and leaves covering the hornets. A black cloud of hornets then flew out from the box and stung everyone on board, including the pilot, releasing their deadly venom. Without the proper antidote, a person would die from the sting in just minutes.

Chris was now aboard the plane bound for Hawaii. The stewardesses walked down the aisle, checking all of the passengers in their assigned seats, making sure that everyone had seat belts fastened. The overhead announcements were being broadcast to the passengers, but Chris paid no attention to them. He was sitting at a window seat where he could view the smaller private jets landing and taking off. He paid particular attention to one plane, one with a red stripe across the side of it with an emblem painted on the stripe—the emblem of a family, the Del Marco name. This plane was gaining speed traveling down the runway and had just taken off when there was a sudden movement, almost a jolt, seen in the sky as the plane was now airborne. The plane moved to the left, then jolted quickly to the right, almost looking like it was trying to wave; then a sudden noise catapulted through the sky, and the plane nose-dived and crashed on the edge of the main landing strip. All heads turned to watch this spectacle, and different languages pierced the sound waves aboard the plane. Some screamed, some cried, some covered the eyes of their children from viewing this disaster. Guesses flew through the inside compartment of the plane, making it loud and almost unnerving.

The overhead radio told the passengers on the plane to sit back down and remain quiet. They would have to remain in their seats, and the plane could not take off until it was determined what had happened to the other small jet plane, announced the captain. It might have been a terrorist attack; and in that case, the passengers would have to return to inside the airport, and the flight would be canceled. In fact, all flights in and out of the airport would be canceled for the day. Upset voices filled the locked compartment of the plane, complaining and protesting. Others remained locked in their seats in fear. Chris sat calmly and looked for the stewardess to offer them drinks. A stewardess did come down the aisle offering passengers drinks. He took one vodka martini, which he paid for and gave a most gracious tip to the stewardess. He relaxed in the upright airline seat, looking remarkably comfortable for being in such a tight, enclosed space during a time of crisis; but no one made note of this with everyone being so worried about what the outcome of the situation down the runway might be.

CHAPTER 31

The press was informed, after the investigation of the plane and the remaining contents that weren't burned, that investigators found that the plane was owned by and, at that time, was being used by the Del Marco family, who was well-known for its illegal activities. All the people aboard were dead, not just from the explosion and crash of the plane, but they also were eaten alive by the deadly Japanese hornet. It was illegal to have these creatures, and the authorities were amazed they had them aboard without the hornets getting loose and attacking them earlier. These hornets were so deadly that a person once bitten by them could only survive for minutes before dying. There was an antidote, but it had to be administered in just a matter of seconds after the bite, and it wasn't guaranteed to work. In Japan, they knew that people would die every year from attacks of the hornets. The Japanese were working on developing a new breed of killer bees that could attack and eat the hornets and wipe them out. Chris knew about how deadly hornets would be to mankind. He stopped himself from thinking about this as it was a sign of getting weak, something he could never allow himself to do.

He looked out the window to the site and saw the fire department's truck leaving the scene. It looked like most everyone who was there was now leaving as a large disposal truck pulled up to the site and started picking up the pieces of the crashed airplane. The overhead announcement was then heard with news of the plane crash. They were told by their pilot that a steel container of the dangerous, deadly

Japanese hornets had been found on board the plane and that all the people as well as the hornets had burned in the crash. The authorities did find, in the bottom of the steel box used to carry the hornets, a substantial amount of cocaine. The authorities believe that had something to do with the hornets and that the Del Marcos didn't anticipate that the hornets would be so deadly to them. One of the passengers on the plane must not have known about the situation because after his body was found, he was thought to have been the one who had opened the box. Because of the delay and the number of flights waiting now to take off, Chris's flight was going to have to be rerouted to the island of Guam. There would be an overnight stay there before the flight would leave the next morning for the island of Hawaii. Ohs and complaints were heard throughout the plane before it was explained that the passengers' stay at the hotel on Guam would be covered by the airline—they were sorry about the course of events that had taken place, but they could do nothing to change the current situation.

Bond woke up groggily, almost fighting the force in his body that caused him to rise up from the comfort of the white percale bedsheets. Halfway up, he collapsed back down on the mattress and rested his hands on the fluffy white comforter enveloping him and the softness of the mattress. He more than enjoyed the rest of his stay on the quiet, peaceful island of San Juan, off the northwest shore of the state of Washington. He never even left the peacefulness of the inn's room. He found himself fighting with the force of having to return to the reality of life. His stay here had definitely ended, and he knew it. He had to return to the estate and his family and work in the game of his life—one eye looking forward and the other looking in every direction to shield himself and the family he belonged to from danger and death. He opened and closed his eyes while circling his pupils, reminding himself of the game of life.

He rose up from the bed, letting the bedding fall from the upper part of his body and feeling the cold chill of the air. It was not cold in the room—it was just feeling the difference between the air in the room and the comforting warmth of the bed. He immediately circled the area of the room, searching for anything out of the ordinary as a trained spy would do. He walked to the bathroom to shower and dress for the day. Halfway there, he momentarily collapsed himself in his uptight composure, feeling resistance to the facts of his life; but he caught himself and then planned his course of action and the events that would have to occur in the course of this day.

He ran his fingers under the pulsating jets of the shower, then adjusted the temperature of the water on the shower control, and waited a few seconds before getting into the shower. Then he lifted his face up to feel the pulsating water and wiped the sleep from his eyes. He turned and felt the pulsating water hitting the skin on his back; it massaged him as he slowly moved in each direction for the water to hit every point on his back side. Moving back to face the water, he shampooed his hair, then rinsed out the sudsy water from his head, and got out of the shower; he then kissed his skin with the fluffy warm towel and wrapped it around his lower body and went to the sink. He looked at himself in the mirror but showed no emotion at what he saw. He only reached for the razor and started shaving his face.

Minutes later, he left the room dressed casually like a model in a *GQ* magazine, wearing his Versace sunglasses, a black polo shirt, and loose tan slacks. He carried a small leather suitcase only slightly larger than a briefcase and left the island and returned to the airport in Seattle where he boarded a direct flight to Hawaii.

Aboard the plane, he was more than happy and pleased that the person who sat next to him for this long flight was a priest dressed in his cassock. This man's identity was more than known to all who would see him, and Bond knew that with the lifestyle of the twenty-first century, not too many people would want his company or have him listening to their conversations. Bond smiled at him before takeoff. They introduced themselves to each other; then the priest started a prayer while holding the gold cross necklace that he wore around his neck under his garment, only pulling it out to hold it during the prayer. Bond saw this, then bowed his own head in prayer with the priest. He saw that the priest observed this from the corner of his eye but did not show that he had observed Bond's actions. At the end of the prayer, he held Bond's hand, then said amen to the Lord. Bond returned in saying the amen, then turned and smiled at the priest.

During the course of the flight, Bond found himself in conversation with the priest whose name was Michael. They discussed passages from the Bible and expressed different views on the interpretations. When the priest, Michael, asked Bond what he did for a living, Bond was baffled about what to tell him. There was no way he could lie to a priest, so what was he going to say to him? Thoughts of different things that he did in the course of his job ran through his mind, and he realized that the time it was taking him to give the priest an answer had grown considerably too long. He faked a cough, the standard way out of a situation like this; then he thought better not cough too long, or he would have the attention of the entire plane, and a stewardess would be right by his side with a medical kit. That was it! A medical kit. He told the priest that he was an in-home aide for the elderly. He smiled at himself after telling this to the priest as he honestly felt that he did not lie. The priest smiled at him and told him that it was gracious of him to be in such a profession. He was surprised when the priest changed the conversation to sports, and he laughed at himself but took an active part in both listening and conversing with him.

CHAPTER 32

Jane noticed that there was caring and warmth in the boss's heart, which were shielded by the cold facade he surrounded himself with. There was danger in trying to break this cover, even in a moment of compassion. She remained quiet though she tried to express her presence there as boldly as she could. The music had ended, and the silence was more than noted by both of them; but neither of them spoke, not even making idle comments just to be speaking. Clouds covered the bright sun that had been shining into the living room, and they could see the beach and the ocean waves. The darkness and gloom provoked by the clouds covering the sun were felt by Jane in every sense as she waited quietly and patiently for some sign from him. Fear then flooded the curve of her spine, and she cringed just trying to remain still and unmoved by it. She feared something had happened to someone, someone close to both of them. Could Bond be in danger? He wasn't there, and she didn't know where he was or why he was gone. She couldn't believe the excuse he had given her. He could be anyplace on the earth or just on the other side of the island for all she knew. Lauren—was she all right? She kept telling herself it was nice being away from her rebellious teenage daughter, but her absence more than filled Jane's heart. It felt to her like a piece of her heart was emotionally breaking off, more and more each day that she was separated from her. Then she thought of Chris and envisioned them in the park. The sound of bullets pierced through her mind, and then she closed her eyes and shivered, trying to relieve these emotions. She felt her body grow weak, weak from the torment that she felt—that deep, haunting emotion that kept returning to her, the feeling that just consumed her flesh and nerves, leaving her heart trembling.

The boss turned to her, looking her square in the eye. She felt him do this even before she turned to see him looking at her. He almost winked, only slightly closing one eyelid; and then he swallowed and sat back, looking out to the darkening sky. Her mind raced, searching for what he was going to say next. "Don't think of Chris anymore, and don't try to reply." He cut off his own speech, and his voice grew softer with each word he spoke to her as he pulled away from looking at her.

She looked at him, then pulled away, and looked out to the darkening sky. The rain was now falling. "Chris is dead. I know I am, and we are, still reminded of him each and every day. But that is just it. He is in heaven. I mean his job . . ." She swallowed deeply, fearing these last words that she just said. She was not only talking to his father, but to the mob boss who was also his boss; and it was quite clear that this man, Vincent, was a religious and proud father. There was no wrong in his life. "I meant the danger of his job. I know it eats at my heart too, but I have to think of him in peace in heaven and looking over us." She stopped abruptly from speaking, mostly not knowing what else to say and not wanting to sound sanctimonious and also still fearful of what the boss's reaction would be to what she said.

He got up from the couch; but she remained seated, looking at him for only a few seconds before taking her eyes off him, then looking back to him and away again. He stood in front of the open window and looked at the view. This surprised her that he would put himself in possible danger by an open window. He had expressed fear, but evidently, there was no fear around the estate, at least not at that moment. "You should get rested up. Look nice tomorrow. That pink-and-white trimmed, ruffled dress that you have—wear that and"—he clasped his hands together and rubbed them, almost like this was giving him strength—"just look nice and feel good thoughts. The danger isn't over yet, but it will be soon."

She looked away from him and then closed her eyes and reopened them again, viewing the floor, puzzled by what he had just told her. The danger wasn't over yet, but it would be soon. What was happening? She felt even more fearful now. Bond, whom she had come to wrap her heart around, would he be coming back? Or in what condition would he be coming back? She turned to look at the boss to see if maybe he would say something more to elaborate on what he had just told her, though she knew the probability of that was slim. He was gone, or at least gone from where he had been standing a moment ago. An arm reached over the top of the couch where she sat. She turned her head slightly to see what she had only felt happen. The pillow on the back of the couch dented in, and she saw his hand. She lifted her hand up to touch his, and then he withdrew his hand, and she heard him walk away.

He spoke but only to remind her of dinner at six thirty. She breathed in and then out, making a sighing noise, then went up to her bedroom where she had a host of things she could do. She knew that none of these activities would free her mind from the torment she was going through, but she might get a slight release from the mounting tension, a momentary escape from the deep, raging thoughts and feelings overwhelming her.

Inside her locked bedroom, she welcomed the thought of the confines of her room. The first thing she did after locking the door was to walk quickly to the side of the drapes where the cord was and close them. She looked to her easel and saw the picture that she had drawn and had already started painting with color. The woman now was fleeing from the broken shell of the egg. The top of the egg was completely broken off, and it had fallen to pieces on the ground beside it. The sides of the shell had once been intact, keeping her prisoner in the casing of the hard shell, but now it was wearing away; and with her hands, she had pushed the shell loose and was now starting to fly up to the freedom of the sky.

Somehow, this newfound freedom, which she previously strove for, now looked dismal and bleak to her. She tried to convince herself that in her heart, she still wanted this freedom. She put down the paintbrush on the easel by the painting and went over to the stereo. In one motion, she took a CD, placed it in the machine, and turned it on—something to fit her mood as she usually did. But instead of listening to pounding, rhythmic rock 'n' roll, she listened to the soothing sound of Etta James singing "At Last." Standing in front of the painting, she looked at it, raising her eyes to it and smiling, then took up the paintbrush again. In only minutes, she had relieved herself from the previous torment she felt in both her heart and her mind. This might even get finished tonight, she thought. I'll just have to make one stop to have dinner with the boss, but

I won't tell him about this painting. I'll remain quiet like he seems to want at the present. I better stop thinking of him and the family, or I'll return to that dark, silent mood again. She then thought of him saying that last comment about the danger not being over yet but that it would be soon. She pulled the painting on its stand closer to the side of the window so she was standing behind the sidewall of the drapes instead of being in front of the window, even though the drapes were closed. After moving, she took a brief pause, then returned to the creative state of art, expressing herself on the canvas.

CHAPTER 33

The boss was in his office, and he told the guard who sat by the side of the computer to turn it off. The guard was puzzled by this but said nothing, and corresponding with his boss's wishes, he turned the computer off. Going against his better judgement, the boss took the palm pilot from his desk drawer and dialed Bond's cell phone number. The sound of the phone ringing buzzed through his ear. He was happy hearing the sound of the ring. Bond woke from his airplane seat, feeling the buzzing of his phone. He looked to the priest who was sleeping in the next seat, then took the cell phone from his lapel, and opened it, looking at the identity from the incoming call. He saw that it was from his father. At first, he was alarmed, then thought maybe, just maybe, the old man was checking on him being that he had not heard from him in a while. Bond then wondered about Chris, then wiped that from his mind, and did what was procedure for a situation like this. He turned the phone on, punched in the numbers to spell out the word "plane," and then hung up, and placed the phone back in his pocket. He noticed that a girl was looking at him, turning around from her seat in front of him and to his right. Instead of looking away from her and ignoring her, he smiled at her and winked. She lit up in joy, and then embarrassed, she turned around and looked straight in front of her away from his view. He made a slight laugh, then closed his eyes, trying to resume his sleep. The overhead announcement was then heard that the flight should be only another thirty minutes before landing in Hawaii. They might expect a longer flight time, though, because of the bad weather situation that had just moved in over the island. Bond hoped that this sign of bad weather wasn't anything to signify something bad waited ahead for him and his family there. He silently breathed in a deep breath and returned himself to a trained guard's mental stability.

The flight touched down to an uneasy landing, a bit rough and bumpy, until all wheels were down; and the plane then coasted down the runway. The priest started talking to him in a fast tone, telling him that he had enjoyed his company and wanted to get together on the island. Bond made a queasy look, then took his hand to his throat, and shook his head from side to side; then quietly in a rough voice, he expressed a verbal apology to the priest. When they stood up and gathered their belongings before departing the plane at the terminal, the priest told him that he would say a prayer for him to get better.

Standing up before starting to depart from the plane, with bag in hand, Bond thanked the priest and felt guilty lying to a clergyman. Then he quickly explained to himself that the only thing to do was concentrate on getting back to the estate and making sure that everything was safe, including himself. He had really better watch his back here at the airport and the trip to the estate as well as what to expect on arrival there. His car, the Hummer, was waiting for him in the parking lot with a gun strapped under the driver's seat. The first thing that he would need to do would be to check the undercarriage of the vehicle to make sure there were no bombs planted there that would go off when he started the engine.

He didn't think it odd for a passerby to witness him under his car until he was actually under it, but there were no onlookers in that particular section of the airport parking lot at that time of night. He returned to stand at the side of the open front door of the Hummer after his search turned up nothing, but that made him feel despondent that he hadn't found anything. It only made him think that something was up, something more significant. He got in the Hummer and paid the attendant as he left the parking lot and watched carefully to each side as well as the front and back of his bulletproof vehicle as he drove to the estate. The drive there was quiet with relatively little traffic, which he had trouble comprehending; and instead of enjoying the peacefulness of the drive and relishing it, he feared it more because it was unusual. At the front of the gates to the estate, he stopped the Hummer and did not open the gate with the remote control placed between the visors. He checked both sides as well as the front and back of the parked Hummer; then he reached under his seat and pulled out his gun. He pushed off the safety and cocked it before even putting his hand on the door handle. In only a second, he was out from the Hummer; and he turned his view to the back of the vehicle while leaning down, suddenly apprehensive of the quiet surroundings. He made a quick sweep of the yard around where he was parked, and everything was clear. He still smelled danger though. He went back to the Hummer and pressed open the gates of the estate with the remote and let the gate open fully before driving in. After driving in past the gates, they closed automatically, and he bent forward to the side of the front of the car and then checked the rearview mirror and saw nothing but the blankness of the night sky. No stars were visible to light the sky because of the dark clouds. He parked by the side of the garage, then thought better of it, and opened the door to the garage and drove in. He did not close the door after parking inside, though. He walked out, leaving the open garage behind him.

He heard a familiar voice calling to him from inside the garage at the right side of the Hummer by the side entry door. At first, he became alarmed by hearing this sound, then retraced his steps in the direction of the voice that called out to him. He had dropped his guard but then caught himself and regained the straight, rigid stance he knew his body should convey. He was at the back of the Hummer but not yet to the side of the garage, ready to meet the person who called to him when he saw four guards carrying a lifeless body into the garage through the door that he had left open. The light in the garage went off, and he walked quickly towards the noise, then saw that the open area by the side door was vacant. He instantly turned his body to the stained wooden stairs to the side behind the inside of the door. The door at the top of the second-floor office of the garage was partly ajar.

He knew that it was safe, but he could not fight the trained feeling of surveillance and reached for his gun and held it in front of him as he turned and walked into the office. He held it with the safety on. Inside the office, his father stood to the side of a chair. He was surprised that his father was not sitting in the chair but then thought he should leave the floor open for his father to initiate conversation, especially after seeing the dead man being carted away. The coast definitely had not been clear, just what his instincts had told him.

His father waited until he had stopped his movement and stood quietly four feet from him, almost looking him in the eye. He then told Bond about the shooting earlier that evening on the estate and that the man had been identified as the last remaining Del Marco with the exception of the aged father of the clan who would be dying soon of a heart attack. Bond thought, Dying soon? His father had this whole range of schematics very well orchestrated.

Bond then told his father of the happenings in Napa that his father already knew about. He was more concerned about what happened in Washington and on the plane. He assured his father that nothing happened, then asked him about Chris and if the plan would be proceeding as scheduled.

His father then sat down as Bond leaned on the wall to the side of the chair where his father sat. His father told him of the remaining plans and what would have to be done. Very soon, there would be nothing more to fear though there would always be the normal fear in just the relevance of proceeding with their lives. The most important thing that he had to do now was keep himself hidden. At all costs, Jane was not to know that he was back on the estate. His father told him that he was going to have to fight off any inclination that he had of falling in love with her because very soon, things were going to change.

"The only thing for you to do, and I repeat the most important thing for you to do right now, is to stay out of sight and stay safe. You are my son, and I do love you. You have always been a part of this family." In stopping his speech, his father relaxed his body, falling deeper into the cushion of the chair. This message from his father hit his heart. His father, the boss, had never conveyed any emotions to him verbally before; but Bond had always known that as well as he knew the responsibilities of his job in the family. He did not reply to his father but lowered his head down, then looked very slowly back up at his father, acknowledging what he had said. He walked away from the garage and entered the house through the side door of the kitchen. He didn't worry about safety as there was a guard standing beside the door. After the shooting, the house and the estate were at a higher level of security. In the kitchen, he took a bottle of water from the refrigerator, then caught the door right before it closed and the light went out, and grabbed a bottle of beer with his other hand, then headed for his bedroom. He thought of how he had left his bags in the Hummer but didn't feel the urgent need to go back and get them out. In the heightened state of security, he knew his father had already had the car emptied and swept.

Inside his bedroom he checked, and the drapes were closed. He turned on the overhead light in the bathroom but did not go in. He closed the door halfway, then sat down on the edge of the bed.

Stay away from Jane and have no feelings for her. He twisted off the cap of the beer bottle, then put it down on the nightstand, not even taking a sip from it. He clasped his hands together and breathed in his closed hands, then turned his head from side to side, and made an indistinguishable sound. Then he reached for the beer and took a swallow, then grabbed the pillows and placed them against the headboard; and then he leaned back, relaxed his body, and enjoyed the beer while he tried to free his mind of all thoughts.

In this relaxed state with the dim lighting from the half-closed door to the bathroom, the room was peaceful. He surrounded himself with the serenity. In the quietness of the room, his gut feeling thought it felt a presence. He fought the action of opening his eyes, wanting nothing more than to just fall into the deep stupor of sleep. I'm staying somewhere else tonight, he decided. The next morning, he would have to stay hidden from Jane. He was to wait outside and be close to the water and the guard towers but still be out of view because Jane would be outside, and she was not to see him until his father told him it was okay to be seen. She was expecting Bond to come back, and there had to be a certain course of events happening in the right order for this final plan to work out.

Bond had questions to ask about every sentence that his father spoke, but he was too tired and exhausted to ask them, mostly not wanting to hear any more orders from his father that he would have to carry out. A release was what he wanted, and sleep was the only thing that he wanted more than a release. He nodded his head to his father, then left the estate in the Hummer with one of the guards driving. Bond closed his eyes, trying to block out all the things that were racing through his mind.

He managed to fall asleep during the drive to the hotel. The guard checked him in, then followed Bond up, and made a sweep through the room. Bond nodded his head to the guard, then closed the door, dropped his bag and his jacket on the floor, fell onto the bed, and was instantly asleep. The guard stayed outside the locked door of the hotel room.

In the upstairs bedroom, Jane was at the easel with the stereo playing background music. The window was open, but only enough to let in the evening breeze but still shield her from being seen by any outside intruders. She froze in fear. Something was wrong, but she did not know what. It must have taken her five minutes to unlock her body from this strange stance that her body had taken up when she froze; then she fled to the open window, closed it, then closed the drapes completely.

She retreated to the bathroom, then looked at her reflection in the large over-the-counter mirror and did not like the idea of someone looking back to her, even though the reflection looking back at her was only herself. It somehow made the situation more fearful to her at the time. She ran back into the bedroom then to the wall on the other side of the bed, took one of the pillows, and held it against her chest as though it was a shield of armor to combat the flying bullets of an attacker.

She dropped her body to the floor but did not stay all the way down. Her eyes still showed on top of the bed covers. She looked like a child retreating from fear and felt like it too. She tried to ease her racing, trembling heart, fearing that Bond had been shot again since she hadn't seen him back on the estate. In the normal pattern of the flow of things, Bond would have already been in her room after the gunshots to reassure, protect, and hold her, offering the closest thing that she could feel to love at the time, the time since she had been hurled against her will onto this island. He didn't come to her. She looked towards the door but was fearful of it and who might come barging through it, feeling that the likelihood of it being Bond was slim, if even remotely possible. The normal backtracking in her heart to the vision of Chris was gone. The only other person that she thought of now besides herself was her daughter, Lauren. She cried inside her heart, having the distinct feeling that she would never see Lauren again and never be able to tell her that she loved her. She longed for the feeling of holding her and feeling her love back.

The longer she sat in silence on the bedroom floor, the more scared she became while, at the same time, she tried to rationalize in her mind that everything was safe now. In the duration of the never-ending battle of wits, she freed the lock consuming her body and rose up off the floor. She stood in silence against the wall to the side of the bed. She circled the room with her eyes, deliberating in which direction to move and if she should move at all. Wanting nothing more than to fight the force consuming her, feeling at war with herself, she moved to the front of the bed, then turned her back, and looked to the locked door of the bedroom that went to the hallway. She started to move, then stayed in a frozen stance, listening for any sound. Not even the sound of the rain could be heard. She moved to the bathroom and splashed her face with water, dried it on a towel, then went back to the bedroom, and grabbed herself, feeling a deep chill going down her spine.

Quickly, she went to the stereo and turned it on. The tray containing the CD popped out, and she took the CD out; and instead of placing it back on the shelf to the right of the stereo, she just dropped it open on the floor and rummaged through the stack of CDs and took out the one she was looking for. She placed it inside the machine, then pressed the Play button after it had finished reading the disc. She skipped over it, playing the first song, then programmed it to play the tenth song on the CD. She knew this without even having to look at the cover for the number. The music started playing—a soft, relaxing sound. She sat on the pillow on the floor and appeared slightly more relaxed. The lyrics started with Meat Loaf singing "Heaven Can Wait." The music quieted her mood coming in through the fibers of her flesh. She was meditating to it, listening to every word, and feeling it. In the course of the next hour, she played that same song over and over. In the queer rationalization of all the things that pertained to that moment, she did not daydream to the haunting, repeating past with Chris. Chris did not even factor into her present mood. Bond consumed her mind—the fear of his loss, the remaining hope that she had that ran through her heart. Unable to even let herself cry, she sat there, locked in the state that she put herself in listening to the song and periodically looking to the locked door—looking and listening.

CHAPTER 34

The plane landed on the island of Guam. There was a bus waiting outside the airport gates that took the stranded airline passengers to a hotel—nothing fancy, but it was nice; and it served the purpose of giving the groggy, complaining people some rest before returning to the plane after the weather pattern passed and the plane could be serviced. Guam was a tropical paradise, but Chris saw only the estate in Hawaii as paradise. The similar climate and the tropical foliage there did not ease his mind for he could make no comparison by any means. Waiting in the line to check in at the hotel lobby, Chris read a pamphlet on the island's history, but he avoided reading about the military and tourist spots on the island.

Ferdinand Magellan discovered Guam in 1521. Spain made the island a possession in 1561; then the United States got it in 1898 after the Spanish-American War. Japan attacked the island on December 7, 1941, and captured it five days later. On July 21, 1944, the United States forces recaptured Guam, and the United States declared Guam a territory on August 1, 1950. Its supervision was transferred from the navy to the Department of the Interior, and the people there became U.S. citizens. In 1962, a typhoon destroyed 95 percent of Guam's buildings.

Chris was pushed to the counter, then handed a pen to sign his name, and take the key to his room. He stopped briefly holding the pen, then signed a name of no distinction, thinking that in a moment of distress it wouldn't be analyzed. It wasn't. The person behind him had already taken the pen from the counter and pushed him aside to sign his name and get his room key.

Inside the bottom-level room, he saw that the shutters were partially open, but he did nothing to close them. He went to the bathroom, dropped his bag against the door of the room, then took off his clothes, and got under the sheets, knowing full well that he'd have a wake-up call in the morning to get back on the flight. That was also one of the reasons that he didn't completely close the shutters—the light from the morning sun would awaken him. It did, and he opened his eyes thirty minutes before the phone rang. He lay awake in the bed waiting for the ring of the phone before he went to the bathroom to shower and get ready for the day. He repacked his bag and left the room, then met his fellow passengers getting on the bus to the airport and then on the plane for the island of Hawaii. He was calm through every movement he made, looking like a professional traveler. He asked no questions of his fellow passengers and offered no answers. He remained silent, not even thinking any thoughts to himself until on the plane when it was over the deep waters of the Pacific Ocean traveling east to their destination.

He left the airplane on the island of Oahu. Inside the airport, he waited for his bag at the carousel while taking everything in. He watched and searched all surrounding crevices where someone could observe him. Once holding his luggage, he went to the private plane section of the airport; and a familiar face tipped her head to him, and he then tipped his head to her in return and boarded a helicopter.

That morning at the estate, Jane woke up from her bed and look puzzled, wondering how she had gotten up from the floor and into the bed. She didn't remember doing that. Did she do it sometime during the course of the night? Maybe it was in a dream or something, and she just didn't remember doing it, or did one of the guards come in and put her on the bed? This is really starting to freak me out, she thought to herself. She got up out of the bed still dressed in the clothes she was wearing the night before, then went into the bathroom to shower and dress. She remembered that the boss had told her to wear the pink whispering-hem dress that day. She put on her makeup for the day with a shade of lipstick that would accent the pink of the dress. She feared what this day would hold in store for her. She would see somebody, but she feared who it would be or who she would be told that she wouldn't be seeing anymore fleeing from flying bullets.

Downstairs in the dining room, the table was set exquisitely—for breakfast anyway. She wondered who the other party would be that might be joining them other than the boss and herself. Closer to the table now, she saw that it was still only set for two. The newspaper was on the wooden chest behind where the boss sat, and it was folded shut but still uplifted like it had already been read. She thought he was not here though it looked like he had been there earlier. A hand rested on her shoulder from behind, and she jumped in fear, then thought this person touching her might be Bond. She smiled and filled her body with joy, then turned around in one sweeping motion.

Most surprised seeing who it was, she quickly fought away the frown she'd started and turned her face back to a quiet smile. He went to the head of the table, then sat down, and poured coffee in her cup. She verbally thanked him out loud, then wondered why the change in his usual morning behavior. This day was surely going to offer or hold something different, and she was more than curious but still fearful and remained quiet, waiting for the boss to initiate the conversation.

A servant came to the table and uncovered a silver-domed serving plate. The boss looked over the items on the plate, then nodded his head, and the servant placed the plate at the center of the table. Jane looked at the plate and was surprised in not seeing the usual fruits and breakfast pastries of some sort. That morning, the centerpiece of the table contained a hot plate of steaming eggs Florentine surrounded by fresh oranges. A plate containing two poached eggs over an English muffin with fresh cooked spinach in between and a light hollandaise sauce poured over each one of the eggs was placed in front of her. She made no derogatory comment about the breakfast and automatically looked over to the chair where Bond usually sat, listening for a dry comment from him about the present situation. In not seeing him there or even a place setting at the place where he usually sat, her eyes grew solemn, and she looked down at her plate. Slowly, she took up her knife and fork and started slicing into her breakfast. The boss made note of all of her actions but did not comment to her about this. He instead took his fork into the morning's breakfast and started eating, not opening his mouth to speak to her until his plate was empty, and he was on his second cup of coffee. He looked at her; and she noticed his stare, then placed the bite of food on her fork back down on her plate, wiped her face with the cloth napkin from her lap, and looked at him, being quiet and giving him her full attention.

"Things are looking up." He said this in a delighted tone, which caused her to raise her eyebrows at the idea of happiness overwhelming the dark clouds that surrounded them. "Jane, you will be leaving us here at the estate today."

She pulled her face up in surprise, yet she still felt angry. She had wanted out, out of there, out of the locked feeling of the estate; but right now, there were so many unanswered questions, disappearances of people—all of the people that she loved and who were a part of her life now. Then she thought that was it—her life now included these people. But what life or what identity was he going to tell her to be now? Who was she? Who had she become? Or was there perhaps someone else in between these two people who were really the same person? She took her hand up to her face, then scratched the side of her neck, and looked down to her plate then away from the table. She tried to focus on him but couldn't.

"Who? What? Yesterday you told me that the danger would soon be over. Then last night, I heard gunshots and remained shaking in my room all night." She moved her clasped hands over her mouth, then shook her head. "I don't know anymore . . . well, I never knew in the first place, or maybe I did in the first place. But what happened to that? I'm taken away from the life that I had and pushed into a new life, a new identity. If you hadn't interfered with my life, would I have ever known that I was once a different person? Well, the life that you had me changed into was good. I never asked any questions, and everything worked out. I had my daughter, and I didn't miss the man who was killed because he was not part of my new life." She instantly sat straight up in the chair, feeling fear to what she just said, blaring this out to him, the father and boss of the whole Mondello family. She looked down and away from the table to the side of the room where she had entered. There was no way that she could face him. Panicked fear went through her being. She searched in desperation at what to do to escape. Why? Why didn't he say something, anything?

He reached for a slice of fresh orange from around the plate of eggs. He ate it, then raised his napkin to the table, and placed the rind of the orange on his empty plate, then placed the napkin over the top of the plate. He got up from the chair, then pushed it back in under the table, and started to turn away. He stopped and placed his hand over the top of the chair. He looked at her, and in an even yet uplifted tone, he told her to pack her bags and get ready to leave the island.

Bond was going to be returning to the island by plane later that morning, and he wanted her to be ready for him when he got there. Happiness and love, excitement and joy filled her body all at the same time as she heard him speak these words to her. She tried hiding her uplifted joy, but it was too late. The boss had already seen this and laughed inside himself seeing this reaction from her, but he did not let on. "Go up to your room, and get ready. I'll have someone come and knock on your door when it's time."

Before she could move her head to the side to watch him leave the room, he was already gone. She then looked back down to the table, still covered with uneaten food. Was what he just told her true? Was Bond going to be returning to the estate later that morning, or was he setting her up for a fall? Bond was going to be returning to the estate, but he told her to pack her bags to leave the island. Where was he sending her? Was Bond going to be going with her? Before she let her heart feel the elated feeling of that possibility, she reminded herself of the lonely reality that surrounded her—the emptiness and fear, the feeling of desolation.

Feeling weakened, she got up from the chair, then stood behind it, holding on to it as she slid it back under the table. She left the room and went up the stairs, stopping only long enough at the base of the stairs to say hello to the silent guard watching and on duty there. Climbing the stairs, she thought it odd that he was waiting there at the base of the stairs like he was taking inventory of everyone coming and going, but she was the only other one in the house she thought as she climbed the stairs. At the top, she stopped, hoping that she was the only other one in the house, at least upstairs, right now. There was no guard to walk her up the stairs and into her room to do a sweep of the room before she entered. What was going on?

The boss was very sure of himself and his actions. He was alone. Bond was not there, and there were not any other guards there to watch for his safety. This was especially odd after the shooting the previous night. More problems to overwhelm her she, thought to herself. She felt a scary feeling—that of her body leaning backwards at the top of the flight of stairs. She caught herself from a horrific fall down the stairs and quickly ran to her room. With her hand on the doorknob, she turned it, then had second thoughts about opening the door to that room that had become hers and offered her sanctuary and safety—the safety of being alone where she could still be herself.

Then she thought, at this point, what difference did it make? The only thing to fear in death was the pain. Dragging her body back into the room, she saw that the bed was already made; the drapes were drawn open to a day that had turned sunny, and her suitcase and bag were laid out empty on top of the bed. The sun brightened her spirits. She tried not to pay attention to the fact that the suitcase was lying open on the bed and walked over to the sliding glass door. She opened it, stopping in front of it to feel the breeze against her skin. She felt no fear, then turned her attention back to what the boss had told her. Bond was coming back. Why else would he tell her to pack her suitcase? She had to be going somewhere with Bond. He had mentioned a new life . . . maybe, just maybe . . . She walked back to the bed; then disregarding the task of packing, she instead went to the covered painting by the window. Just ten minutes ago, she had felt like trashing the painting or splashing black paint over it, but now she suddenly wanted to finish it even more.

She held the paint palette and accented the wings with gold paint at the tips surrounding them. The arms were spread out freely in the motion of flight. The figurine, the woman in the painting, was in motion, now up and out of the broken shell that had kept her trapped. She now had the freedom of flight, flying away and out from the boundaries that had kept her hostage. A resurgence came over Jane, and all her fears had become freed from her body as she did the final touch-up on her painting.

Quickly, she opened all of the drawers of the dresser and took out all of her clothing and belongings, then went to the closet and emptied it as well. She felt no sorrow. She only counted the minutes until she'd be able to see Bond and kiss and hug him. In thinking this, she reminded herself that she was mad at him, then thought life was too short to hold any minute, petty grudges that were insignificant. She could picture his face and the idea of him standing next to her. She wanted him, Bond, more than anything else right now. She periodically shivered, caught up in the imagined excitement of seeing him.

The boss waited outside in front of the garage. Bond stood inside one of the open garage doors behind the black Hummer that was parked there. He swept the view of the surrounding area, then put his head down to a guard who stood to the side of the garage to the right of his father. The guard made a brief nod to him, then took a mobile transmitter from his pocket, and checked with all the guards on the perimeter of the estate about the safety of the moment. He got the signal that it was, at that moment, all safe. He then walked around the back of the car and over to the passenger door, which he opened for the young girl inside to get out. The girl was wearing black slacks that hugged her legs all the way down to her ankles. She also had a black leather vest with chains and jewelry that dangled from it. Her hair was pushed back into a ponytail, then tied with a bright-patterned scarf that matched the stretchy knit top that she wore underneath the vest. Long hoop gold earrings dangled from her ears. Her makeup was subdued with the exception of the bright pink lipstick.

Bond escorted her to his father's side, then introduced her. "Father, I would like to introduce you to Lauren, Jane's daughter." The boss tipped his head to her and held her hand up to his mouth and lightly kissed it, then gently released her hand from his grasp.

"It is a pleasure to meet you."

While chewing gum, she spoke to him. "So are we going to live here or what? You know I have to have my own room, and you can't tell me what to do. I listen to my own music, and I'll have it as loud as I want. And I don't go by that ten o'clock curfew anymore. And you know, I'll be driving soon, so one of these cars in that garage is mine?" She stopped talking and resumed chewing her gum even more loudly; then she looked at her long bright blue fingernails.

The boss stood there and took everything in that she told him but made no reaction to her words. He turned, walked a step away from her, then spoke to Bond who stood three feet back from them while she was conversing. "Bond, cage her!"

Bond snickered, then took her bags from the vehicle, and escorted her to a downstairs bedroom. He informed her that she would have to wait there until she would be told when to leave the room bond for her not to get alarmed by this. It was only for this short time that she would be told she would have to follow orders. She stood back, dropped her body, and huffed. "I know. You went over all of that in the car driving here. Do you think I'm that old and I have no memory? I mean, really."

After hearing this last comment and watching her actions, Bond couldn't wait to get back to the quietness of his bedroom with the door locked. While he stood to the side of the open bedroom door, she went into the room; then he took her bags in and asked her a question. "Are you sure that since your mother has been away that a clergyman and his wife took care of you?"

She turned to him. "Yeah, and now it is my turn to get even." Bond let loose of her bags, then left, going quickly to his room.

He opened the door to his bedroom, then stood back, and remained standing still. He looked to the open frame of the door, then looked to the room. For the first time, a feeling of emptiness pierced his soul. Not liking the feeling that he was experiencing, he closed the door to his room and went down the hallway to the front of the house and stood to the side of the living room behind the dining room and looked at the stairway and the front door. Then in a quick motion, remembering how his father told him that he had to remain hidden from view, and he knew whose view his father was referring to, he quickly retreated to his father's office. His father was there as well as another guard. He looked up showing surprise at seeing Bond, but he kind of expected that he would show up. The boss waved for the guard to leave and close the doors behind him.

Bond stood back. He knew he had his father's attention, but his father did not look at him. It made him feel rather unnerved. He knew this was his father's usual behavior, but due to the severity of the things to come . . . But that was it. Bond now wondered what was coming, and he didn't know why he didn't know the plan of things to come. Then he wondered whether he would be the successor, or most likely, would it be Chris? That was another question—where was Chris? Not hearing or seeing a reaction from his father, Bond moved forward and sat down on the leather chair in front and to the side of the desk. His father nodded his head to him, which he thought was odd because he did not want to feel like his servant. He wanted, more than anything, to feel like his son. But that was his job, and that was the family that he was in, and it was his life. He could say nothing but felt everything.

Having gotten as comfortable in the chair as he could without letting his emotions show through to his father, Bond swallowed deeply, then looked him in the eye. "Is Chris . . . is Chris coming back?" There was no response. "What finally did happen in Guam? You told me that he was there, but was he? Or is that it? Did they get him in Guam?" His father showed a firm, sorrowful, solemn expression, which surprised Bond and made him worry.

"Stay close to Jane. Wait at the beach, but stay there undercover. She cannot see you until the time is right, and I'll . . ." Bond waved his hand in the air, then nodded his head, knowing what he would say next. "Jane will be waiting in the tower." He sat back, surprised from what he just heard. Why would she be waiting in the tower? Was there further danger on the estate? But Jane's daughter was there. There were too many questions right now, and he did not want to feel under the subjection of any hidden motives. There was no rhyme nor reason to any of this that his emotions did not factor into. He got up from the chair slowly, waiting for his father to say something more to him. He made each motion take longer than necessary, wanting to hear something from his father's mouth; but the longer he took to get up and out of the chair and leave the office, the quieter his father became, not saying a thing. Bond gave up and then started to leave, but he stopped right at the door out of the office as his father spoke. "I'll tell you when it's time to take Lauren outside. She will be outside too. I want Jane to see, but—"

Bond cut off his father's speech. "But not until the time is right." His father nodded. "I'll keep hidden and protect her, but with That Girl, it won't be easy. I'll wait for your call. I will be outside on the porch downstairs by the kitchen at the end." His father said nothing as Bond left, so he knew that what he had just said was acceptable to his father.

Walking out of the office and down to the outside patio, Bond wondered if Chris was, indeed, coming back; or would he be coming back with someone else, and he himself would be leaving the island with Jane. He did like her, but Jane would be a replacement for what he had lost. It was his brother who had lost Jane and their daughter, Lauren. Closer to the end of the hallway, past the doors of the kitchen, he heard gunshots. He drew his gun from behind his belt, lifted it in front of his view, then released the safety, and cocked it. He ran swiftly and quietly down the hall and stopped at the door to Lauren's bedroom where the noise came from. He stopped, hearing screaming, then kicked the door open, and drew his gun out to all sides of the room while turning. His stature was stiff and composed as it needed to be when killing an intruder, an intruder into their lives. Lauren looked up at him, very at ease. "Ease up! It's only a rap recording on the CD boom box."

Bond dropped his stance, lowered his gun, and breathed in quietly and opened his mouth wide to yell something to her. Then he quickly closed his mouth and spoke in a normal tone. "You are the reason why I am single and will not have children." His pocket phone rang just then, and he stepped back into the hallway, leaving the door open but with one foot placed in the doorway. "Yeah, she's right here. I'll bring her out, but I don't know how I will keep her quiet and in one place." He listened to the voice on the other end of the phone. "Oh yeah, the dogs. The dogs!" He hung up the phone with a smile on his face, then had Lauren follow him to the outside area. They waited behind a tall palm behind a guard tower. Outside, Bond watched a guard take Jane to the open beach area. Then he dropped her bags on the solid sand and opened the tower door for her to go up the stairs. He saw her say something and give resistance to what she was told to do, and he was thankful that he was not the one giving those orders.

He looked for his father but did not see him. Then he looked up and saw Jane standing at the top of the guard tower looking towards the sky. Maybe she is bird-watching or something. I'm still not seeing my father anywhere out here. This worried him. He called another guard to watch Lauren, then went through the back doors of the kitchen, and walked through the house and into his father's office. He was not there. Further worried, he checked the outside garage and did not find him there either. The last place he could think of would be his bedroom. Bond made a quick surveillance of the outside grounds of the estate, then ran into the house through the front double doors. Inside, he looked for Jane, but then he remembered she was up in the guard tower already. He ran to this father's bedroom, then entered with his gun out but still on safety. His father was lying on top of the bed, curled up, and clenching his heart with his hand.

Bond yanked open the nightstand drawer and got out his father's medication. Opening the cap with his teeth, he lifted a water glass to his father's mouth, then gave him the pill to swallow. He held his father's head back and stayed with him, holding his head in silence while his feelings tore through the room. His father conveyed thankfulness in his eyes as he looked to Bond and touched the hand that supported his head. "Just give me a minute to rest, and we'll return to the beach."

Bond said nothing to what he just heard. The plane he knew was coming, but he didn't know whether it was to take him and Jane away or to bring someone else in. He now knew the answer. The passing moments that normally would have just eaten at him having to remain there in silence and not doing anything passed slowly but more easily than ever. He helped his father to the outside patio door; then a guard helped him to the beach from there. Bond went back through the kitchen and regained his stance where he had waited earlier and got a smug remark back from Lauren. He didn't say anything back to her, but she wanted to know whether he missed her while he was away. He shook his head to her and said nothing.

The helicopter was heard in the air above the estate, and then they saw it land on the water close by. Jane looked to it eagerly from the tower and fought the inclination to run down the stairs and out the door to the helicopter as she eagerly awaited seeing Bond.

The guard had the boss seated on a bamboo caned-back chair at the edge of the cement patio by the beach. Bond was watching them. The guard said something to his father, who shook his head, and the guard stood erect to the side of him. The helicopter landed on the beach just off the edge of the estate in a roped-off area. The door of the helicopter opened, and then a guard appeared in the doorway. His father waved for Bond to come forward. He ran to the outside of the tower at the back of where Jane looked down to the plane. His father motioned for him to stay there, and Bond was given a jacket matching the color of the jacket worn by the man on the helicopter who had now come out into view, except for his face, which was hidden by the guard in the doorway. The man wore a hat that covered most of his hair. Once ashore, the man from the helicopter was helped, with a guard walking on each side of him, to the bottom of the tower. His father then waved for Bond to come out into the open where Jane could see him from the tower.

She saw him, smiled at him, and started to yell his name from the top of the tower where she stood. He could see her start to climb down the tower stairs; then he waved his hand in a motion for her to stop and told her to stay there, and he would be right up. She stayed there and smiled as a gentle wind ran through her hair and blew it away from her face. At the open door to the tower, Bond hugged Chris, then stood back for him to go up the tower stairs as he remained out of view again.

Jane turned as the wind grew more forceful. Chris's body now stood close to her, and arms went around her body. Then the arms came loose from the hug and pushed the hair out of her eyes. "Chris! You're not dead. I knew it! You're here, you're here. It's you."

He smiled at her and laughed. "But I am not Bond."

"Oh, he is good, but you are so much better!" They embraced in a deep hug, then locked in a kiss. Vincent looked up to the two of them and smiled. Bond walked from his hidden place at the side of the tower and went over to his father's side. His father looked up to them, then back to Bond at his side.

"Bond, what do you think of being the head of operations?" Bond looked at him surprised and happy but expressed concern at what his father just told him. "Chris. I know you thought Chris would take over, but he is going to be leaving—leaving after he gets a brief rest here. But you will be the one in charge here."

"He'll be . . . Chris will be leaving?"

"Yes, with Jane and her daughter, their daughter. If you think that I could stand either Jane or the daughter or, for that matter, both of them here on the estate . . . I want my remaining years to be peaceful." Bond laughed as he said this, and the boss did too.

Chris and Jane released from their hug. "You have packed a suitcase. You know you are going to be going somewhere." She lifted her eyes, fearful of leaving him. He saw this and realized her fear. "Not just you. We both are going to be leaving and our daughter, Lauren, too." Jane looked him in the eye, first defensive of having to leave the island, but then she wanted more than anything to be with Chris and was agreeable to anything.

"Where are we going to go? Back to Chicago?"

"No. We're going to California. We'll be running the business there and raise Lauren. It looks like you'll need my help with her!" They laughed, then kissed.

"You know, we'll have to have a honeymoon . . . Lake Tahoe?" He replied back to her, "Honeymoon? That sounds great, but Lake Tahoe? How about Lake Como?"

She hugged him and replied back, "And leave paradise?" They locked in a hug and kiss, and Vincent and Bond as well as all the guards looked at them and the golden sun that shined down upon them.

The End